To my brothers and sisters from the Wick, who live and die by the words "I will try."

Contents

CARDINAL VIRTUES

WAR OF THE SUBMARINE: BOOK 1

R.G. ROBERTS

Originally published on Kindle Vella as season 1 of *War of the Submarine.*

Cover designed by MiblArt.

The Norwich University Cadets Creed

I believe that the cardinal virtues of the individual are courage, honesty, temperance and wisdom; and that the true measure of success is service rendered–to God, to Country, and to Mankind.

I believe that the fundamental problem of society is to maintain a free government wherein liberty may be secured through obedience to law, and that a citizen soldiery is the corner-stone upon which such a government must rest.

I believe that real education presupposes a sense of proportion in physical, mental, and moral development; and that he alone is educated who has learned the lessons of self control and open-mindedness.

I believe in Norwich, my Alma Mater, because within her halls throughout the years these tenets have found expression while men have been taught to be loyal to duly constituted authority in thought and word and deed; to view suffrage as a sacred privilege to be exercised only in accordance with the dictates of conscience; to regard public office as a public trust; and finally to fight, and if need be to die, in defense of the cherished institutions of America.

- K.R.B. Flint, Norwich University Class of 1903

Prologue: An Unjust Peace

"An unjust peace is better than an unjust war." Marcus Tullius Cicero, Roman Statesman

2 August 2037, Port Victoria, the Seychelles

No one noticed the pattern yet, but *accidents* in the Indian Ocean were becoming common for the U.S. Navy.

It started with little things: food gone rotten before its time, critical parts arriving days or weeks late, or unusually belligerent locals picking fights with sailors on liberty. Nothing capable of stopping the world's premier Navy. Just annoyances. Inconveniences.

"It's fucking sludge, sir." Chief Machinist's Mate Wendy Roce scowled, holding up the sample vial of what was supposedly maritime diesel fuel, commonly known as DFM. "Maple syrup is more viscous than this."

Lieutenant Commander Alex Coleman blinked. He was a slender man, of average height, with blue eyes and blonde hair as long as Navy regulations allowed—which wasn't long at all. He stood easily on the aft deck of the sleek black submarine nestled up against one of Port Victoria's busier piers. Chief Roce had interrupted his afternoon walk around with this news, and he frowned at the vial she held.

"Looks more like molasses to me." He shoved his hands in the pockets of his navy-issue blue coveralls. "Definitely not 'clear and bright,' that's for sure. No way is any engineer with a brain putting this in a diesel engine."

Chief Roce barked out a laugh. She was short and stout, built like a brass oak tree topped with red hair. "I'd rather drink the stuff and vomit."

Alex eyed the so-called fuel. No, that wasn't fair. He was sure there was *some* fuel in the mix, along with lord knew what. Mud? Tar? Chocolate sauce? It looked like one of the gross concoctions his daughters made when they were little.

No trained fueling team would miss this gunk.

Not by accident, anyway.

Alex glanced aft and down at the local fueling company hired by the Navy's local agent in the Seychelles. Their job was simple: top off USS *Kansas'* (SSN 810) diesel fuel tanks. *Kansas*, like every other American fast attack submarine, was nuclear powered, but she had an emergency diesel. Multiple redundancies meant emergencies were rare, but no submariner liked deploying unprepared. Any unscheduled port visit—like this one—was a great excuse to fill up.

Until things got complicated.

"You thinking what I'm thinking, XO?" Roce asked, following his gaze.

"That those guys look shady as shit?" Alex replied in an undertone. "Yeah."

The trio on the pier fidgeted, pretending to check the fuel fittings' alignment, and then one stepped away to call someone on the phone. The taller of the two—Alex didn't catch their names when they arrived an hour earlier—turned to glare at the submarine fueling crew as they milled around on deck.

"We ready?" he asked. "We fuel? À présent?"

Roce muttered obscenities. Alex raised his voice before she could get warmed up for a good old-style chief petty officer rant.

"We still need to do more testing!" he said. "Give us a minute."

"Pas de quoi. We charge by the hour." Something else in French, and they laughed.

"Cheerful bastards." Roce rolled her eyes and kicked at imaginary dirt on the hull. The sound-absorbing tiles along *Kansas'* spine didn't even scuff.

"Easy, Chief. It doesn't pay to antagonize the locals."

"You say so, sir." She gestured at the sample vial, her blue eyes dark. "But I've never seen fuel get this messed up by accident without anybody noticing, if you catch my drift."

"Accusations won't help us, either." Alex sighed, wishing today—of all days—wasn't when the captain dropped out of pocket.

But Commander Rothberg's habit of putting off dental work caught up with him less than a month after they departed Groton, Connecticut, for deployment to the Indian Ocean, and now he needed a pair of infected and broken teeth removed and implants put in. He was probably out like a light by now.

That left this problem squarely in Alex's court. As *Kansas'* executive officer, or second-in-command, everything on the boat was his problem. With the captain away, everything was also his *decision*, including bad fuel and chief petty officers convinced the locals were out to get them.

Not that Alex thought this entirely innocent, but incompetence was a lot more common than sabotage. Besides, the Seychelles was a friendly port, and they made a *ton* of money off visiting American warships, not to mention tourists.

Pity *Kansas'* crew wouldn't get much in the way of liberty today. Assuming Commander Rothberg's surgery went well, they'd be underway before dark, which wasn't nearly enough time to get properly drunk and stupid.

Not that it'll stop some of them from trying.

"What's our move, sir?" Roce asked.

"Let's start by talking to these fine gentlemen and see what they say." He forced a smile. "Should be fun."

Roce laughed. "I got your back, XO."

"Here's hoping I don't need that." Alex didn't doubt Roce could probably break one of the locals in half if it came down to a fight, but lordie, he didn't want an international incident today. Not three weeks into deployment.

Alex led the way forward and down the brow—or gangway—connecting the submarine to the pier, with Roce on his heels. Their approach seemed to unnerve the local fueling crew; the one on the phone backed up a few steps before stopping, watching them warily. The other two pasted on obviously fake smiles and approached.

"Is there a problem, Monsieur?" the tallest one asked. He wore glasses and had shifty eyes, but maybe Alex was just paranoid.

Alex forced his tone to be pleasant. "Your fuel quality seems off." He snagged the vial out of Chief Roce's hands and held it up. "I believe the technical term is 'murky.'"

"That is not our fuel," the local replied, shaking his head. "Our fuel is good."

"You're saying *we* gunked it up?" Roce stepped forward before Alex could stop her.

"Oui." The local shrugged. "Or perhaps your system needs cleaning."

"This didn't even *get* into our system, 'Monsieur,'" Roce growled. "We took this sample right off the inlet line from *your* tanks."

"No. C'est impossible." Tall local waved his hands. "This is your doing."

"*What*?" Roce lurched forward, stopped only by Alex's upraised hand—which she ran straight into. The chief backed off, muttering again.

Alex turned back to the pair of locals just in time for them to exchange a smile. His eyes narrowed. "Let's get one thing straight, all right? I don't really care *where* this bad fuel came from or how it got here. Whatever happened, it's not getting pumped on board this submarine. You got that?"

"I do not see how this is our problem." The shorter local crossed his arms.

"It's your problem because you're either going to get us good fuel, or you're going to turn around and take this sludge back to whatever pit you scraped it out of." Alex cocked his head and smiled his best smile. "Understood?"

The tall one scowled. "This is the only fuel we have. Take it or nothing."

"Then we'll just go without, and you won't get paid." Alex shrugged. "Crappy day all around, but hey, that's the breaks."

The local-on-the-phone stepped forward, and the trio bent their heads together, whispering in rapid fire French. Alex couldn't understand a word of it, but he was betting on the fact that they needed money more than *Kansas* needed fuel.

After all, *Kansas'* diesel tanks—used only for their Caterpillar model 3512B V-12 marine diesel engine and bow thruster—were about 85% full. Sure, Navy regs said that they should sit around 95% or better, but Navy regs *also* said they shouldn't use bad fuel. 85% was plenty of fuel to get them to their next port...and then some.

"This is the fuel we have. You won't find better on the island," the tall one said, sticking his chin out.

"Then we won't find fuel on the island. I'm good with that." Alex turned back to Roce. "Chief, have your boys and girls disconnect their hoses and stow all our fittings. I'll call the husbanding agent and have him reverse whatever payment's been made, since it seems these folks don't want to deal honestly with us."

"You can't do that!" the tall one said as Chief Roce grinned.

"Disconnect and stow, aye, sir." She wheeled to face her team. "You heard the XO, people. Let's get this crap off deck, pronto!"

Sailors scrambled to obey as Alex continued to watch the three locals. All glared, but none tried to stop *Kansas*' sailors from draining and disconnecting the fueling hoses, which they promptly returned to the truck on the pier. None of the locals helped, but the fittings were standard worldwide. No one needed them.

One phone call later, and the tall local had someone new to complain to when he learned he wasn't getting paid. He was still ranting when the fueling truck drove away.

Commander Camille Dubois, French Intelligence, watched from the end of the pier and shrugged. As the architect of this campaign of accidents, delays, and inconveniences—anything to make the American presence in the Indian Ocean just that much less comfortable—she accepted that not every plan would come to fruition. She was a realist.

One failure did not matter.

She would catch up to USS *Kansas* another day.

9 November 2037, Toulon, France

Admiral Jérémie Bernard's bushy eyebrows always communicated his mood. Junior officers feared them like monsters in the dark; senior officers avoided Bernard when his eyebrows started working. Today, they bounced up and down: he was planning something.

The admiral perched in his chair behind a polished wooden desk. Had Jules ever seen Bernard like this? The admiral was a nitpicker, the gorgon threatening incompetents across France's submarine force. Not that Jules made a habit of running afoul of him, but he enjoyed watching others cry when they did.

Bored, Jules' eyes flicked to the window. Bernard's corner office at the Toulon Naval Base overlooked the piers of nine sleek fast attack submarines. *Nine.* Fifteen years earlier, France had a grand total of six nuclear fast attack submarines. Today, she had over fifty, and the best belonged to Captain Jules Rochambeau.

Jules was a tall, handsome man with black hair and unsettling green eyes. He was also France's best submarine captain, and he knew it. That gave him a little latitude, even with Bernard.

"You wished to speak to me, mon Amiral?" Jules asked.

"Oui." Bernard sat back, licking his lips like a satisfied cat. "You know Commander Camille Dubois?"

"Bien sûr." Of course. Jules turned to the woman in the chair across from Bernard's desk. She was beautiful in a French way, with almond-shaped eyes and long dark, hair. She wore the same uniform as Jules and met his gaze with a slight smile.

"We have met, Admiral," she said. "Though it has been some time."

"Good." Bernard leaned forward, gesturing Jules into a seat. "What I am going to say does not leave this office. You"—he pointed a finger at Jules—"will not inform your crew. And Commander Dubois, you will cease your...clandestine operations and transfer to my staff, effective immediately."

A chill ran down his spine. This sounded more interesting than the standard spying mission he expected. Jules sat up straight. "May I ask what operations you refer to, mon Amiral?"

Camille's smile was small and secretive, enough to send a jolt straight to body parts that were not ones Jules should think of in a professional environment. "I have spent the last six months arranging *accidents* for our American friends," she replied. "Coincidences, you understand. Small things."

"To what purpose?" Jules tuned back to face Bernard.

"Underwater resource exploitation and the Race to the Ocean Floor have changed the world," Bernard replied. "Our concerns are no longer limited to those within our borders. As you know, we have partnered with India to develop bases and underwater stations throughout the Indian Ocean. This has made France rich. But there remains one obstacle to greater power."

"America." Jules sat back, rolling his eyes. "The land of interference."

Bernard nodded. "We must break their hold on the Indian Ocean. Their navy is not as powerful as it once was; they have reduced size while we built better submarines. They still believe they are the best in the world, but their government is weak."

"America will not leave short of war." Camille's eyes were hard, now. Did she also resent how often French was forced to play second fiddle to America?

Once, they were allies. In fact, a long legacy of friendship laid between America and France, but decades of being treated like children—despite France's glorious history and experience!—left their mark. And even in this new world, one where the riches of the ocean floor were open to anyone with wit and scientific knowhow, America wanted to be the world's police.

The fact that they now lacked the strength to force the world to their will seemed lost on the Americans.

"They will if public opinion *makes* them leave," Bernard replied.

"How?" Jules asked. "America has cared little for public opinion in the past."

"They will if it is backed by sufficient military force."

Jules felt his eyes narrow. "Without war?"

"Oui."

Camille shook her head. "They are too proud."

"That is why we will use their pride, Commander." Bernard smiled like a cat with its paws covered in cream. "We will also use your background in intelligence. You will lead them on a merry chase—and then Captain Rochambeau will be waiting. We will not sink them." He held up a hand when Jules' jaw dropped. "We will humiliate them, increase their feelings of isolationism, and tell them—once and for all—that the world does not want their so-called *help*."

Jules scratched his chin. "Americans have never retreated when confronted."

"They will if we make them the villain of the piece." Bernard's eyes glittered. "And then *we* will fill the power vacuum."

Jules cocked his head. Could France become a world power once more? His nation made powerful alliances in the last decade—openly with India, quietly with Russia—and was richer than in centuries. Was the risk worth the potential gain?

A literal sea of riches awaited any country strong, quick, and savvy enough to take them. This could usher in a glittering future for France...and he could be at its heart.

Slowly, Jules turned to meet Camille's dark eyes. His thoughts—and hopes—were clearly mirrored there. This opportunity could decide *their* futures as well. Breaking American influence on the world made almost anything possible.

And with France on top, how far might Jules Rochambeau go?

Ten hours later, *Barracuda* got underway under the cover of darkness. Her crew believed they were on an extended training mission; only Jules knew better.

Barracuda was the first Advanced *Requin,* built to dominate the world's oceans in a world where oceanic strength could increase a country's income tenfold. France hadn't possessed such military might since before the Second World War, but now she was a world power—assuming the rest of the world would recognize her as such.

Jules thought Napoleon would approve of *Barracuda* and her under-construction sisters. She was so silent that his country had lied to their allies about her capabilities, a precaution Jules found amusing in the beginning, but quite useful now. Even most of the French Navy remained in the dark.

He slipped underneath a French frigate, *Bretagne* on the way out of Toulon Harbor, pinging them with active sonar once *Barracuda* was well clear.

Predictably, *Bretagne* swung into a radical turn, dropping noisemakers and increasing speed. Laughing, Jules deployed his sub's communications wire and lifted the microphone.

"*Bretagne*, this is *Barracuda* Actual, over," he said as the watch standers in his control room grinned.

They were in high spirits, which was good. Jules would need their best, even if he couldn't tell them why.

Several long minutes passed before a disgruntled voice replied: "This is *Bretagne* Actual, over."

"I am sorry for any inconvenience I caused you with my impromptu exercise." Jules bit his lip to stop from laughing on the radio. "Next time, I will warn you, over."

"I would appreciate it," was the stiff answer.

"Perhaps you would care to hunt us for a bit?" Jules asked. There was no harm; he knew *Bretagne* wouldn't be able to track *Barracuda*. But the practice would be good for his crew.

Not so much for *Bretagne,* whose crew was undoubtedly disappointed when they parted ways four hours later. But *Barracuda* was ready.

Jules returned to his quarters to re-read his secret orders. Were they daunting? Perhaps. He was no stranger to ambition; Jules wished to run the French Navy one day, so he appreciated those who reached for greatness. And France would not regain her position as a world power without risk.

It would be worth it, he decided.

It would have to be.

PART 1:
COURAGE

Chapter 1

Armistice Station

20 November 2037

The only good thing about their current assignment was that *Kansas*'s crew scored some liberty at Armistice Station. Going "ashore" to an underwater station wasn't that different from being on a submarine, but after fifty-nine days underway, off the boat was off the boat.

Lieutenant Commander Alex Coleman, the executive officer of USS *Kansas*, was no stranger to that need. He was slight but not too short, with short-cropped blonde hair and laughing blue eyes. He was a swimmer, not a weightlifter, and he wore the uniform of the U.S. Navy naturally. He also really needed a beer.

Armistice Station was the biggest underwater station in the world, over a mile of stubby habitats perched like giant blue spiders above the floor of the Indian Ocean. It was one of the few stations where a submarine could dock without a TRANSPLAT, or Transportation Platform. Most stations had one or two surface TRANSPLATS, depending on size. Armistice Station had *seven*, one of which played host to USS *Kansas*, a *Virginia*-class attack submarine.

Kansas wasn't important enough to dock at one of the underwater SUBPLATS, of course. Those were full of cargo submarines—a recent phenomenon following the Rush to the Ocean Floor—or tourist boats. *So many* tourist boats.

Fifteen years earlier, the idea of a tourist submarine was alien; now, the damn things bumbled along like half-blind but friendly manatees, clogging up shallow water and complicating naval operations. The bigger ones ventured out here, pouring millions in revenue into the station.

Armistice Station was rich in resources and tourism, boasting the largest aquarium in the world, plus an underwater theater. There was even an amusement park under construction.

Hundreds of underwater attractions sucked most of Alex's sailors in like magnets. He wandered for a few hours, peeking into the hanger for Armistice Station's new sub racers before buying a present for his wife at Fangtooth's. Eventually, he settled in at a bar named Rocco's, people watching and nursing a beer.

"Drinking away the salt, XO?"

Alex looked up and grinned. "I didn't think that was possible, COB."

"Probably easier for you than me." Master Chief Chinedu Casey, *Kansas'* Chief of the Boat, gestured at the chair across from Alex. "Mind if I join you, sir?"

"Seat's free, even if the beer's overpriced."

Chuckling, Casey sat down, a bottle of Bud Light in hand. He was a broad-but-stereotypical Navy master chief, with graying brown hair and more tattoos than Alex wanted to count. The most visible one required a waiver from the Bureau of Personnel, a set of thorny roses creeping up his neck.

As COB, Casey was *Kansas'* senior enlisted man, while Alex was the boat's second-in-command. They were close to the same age—Casey beat him by three years—and two legs of *Kansas'* command "triad."

"They must've realized you were American," Casey said. "That means they charge twice as much."

"Probably." Alex laughed, leaning back in his chair. Americans weren't particularly popular in the nations bordering the Indian Ocean, but he was past caring. Fifty-nine days stuck in a metal tube with 130 of his closest friends wore on the nerves. Especially when you were the Executive Officer and the designated "bad guy."

This was his last liberty port with *Kansas*. The next time the attack submarine pulled in, Alex's relief would meet them. Then he'd be free to go home and spend time with his wife and daughters, to relax and refresh before commanding a boat of his own. His two-year tour had been long and uneventful, not counting sailors' liberty antics.

"The alternative's the boys and girls being stupid, so I guess I'm glad the drinks are twenty bucks a pop." Casey saluted Alex with his beer.

"You can say that again." Alex sighed. A long-awaited port call made the XO busy afterward; Alex bet on at least two liberty incidents dramatic enough to reach his level. Maybe more. *Kansas* was wound tight.

Casey took a swig of his beer. "Whatcha think about the terrorist threats to Armistice Station, XO? I just caught a news broadcast, and it seems like there's been a couple more."

"I think the next few weeks will be exciting." Alex bit his lip; saying more out in the open was stupid. Still, he half-hoped they could accomplish something worthwhile. *Kansas* had a great crew, but using an attack submarine as a guard dog for an underwater station was like building a steel wall around your mailbox to secure your junk mail.

Naval Intelligence was torn between believing the threats to Armistice Station and calling it one giant hoax. A year ago, a bomb scare caused a panicked evacuation of the station, only to find that the "bomb" consisted of PVC pipe and green Play-Doh. The station's administrative council refused to evacuate again without hard proof, and Alex couldn't blame them.

The last evacuation cost over a hundred million dollars. Transporting thousands of people by sea—at short notice—was almost impossible. It wasn't as though people could just walk outside.

"Ours is not to reason why, right?" Casey grinned. "Guess we should just be grateful that we get a few days off before—"

Two ringtones cut him off; Alex grimaced. Armistice Station had cell service for locally sold phones, which the Naval Detachment's commander provided to *Kansas*. But there was no way they'd both get calls from Groton, CT at the same time.

"Shit. Me and my big mouth," Casey said. Alex ignored him.

"XO."

"CDO here, sir," the voice on the other end said. "We've received FLASH traffic concerning a terrorist threat to Armistice Station."

Alex froze. So much for enjoying five days in port. "I'm on my way to the boat. You called the captain?"

"I tried, sir. He's not answering," Lieutenant Sue Grippo sounded tense. She was *Kansas'* Navigator and had the duty. She was one of the boat's three department heads immediately below Alex in the sub's hierarchy. Sue was also *Kansas'* top lieutenant, razor sharp and damned good at her job.

"I've got COB with me. I'll have him hunt the captain down." A cold feeling gnawed at Alex's gut. *Kansas'* Commanding Officer, Commander Chris Kennedy, took command just four days before they got underway. Two months of working side-by-side meant Alex *should* know Kennedy well...but there was still a gap there, something about Kennedy that said he wanted to stand on the mountaintop alone.

Perhaps he'd been too close to Kennedy's predecessor. Commander Rothberg let Alex run the show, but Kennedy gripped power like a miser. *He's new. It'll wear off.* Alex had seen it before. But what kind of CO didn't answer when the boat called?

"Yes, sir," Sue said.

Alex took a breath, his heart hammering. So far, this deployment was routine, despite mounting tensions between the United States and many nations bordering the Indian Ocean. But if this message was right...

"Start a crew recall," he ordered. Prying sailors out of dozens of bars, museums, and shops would take hours. Better to start now.

Sue acknowledged the order, and Alex hung up, glancing at Master Chief Casey.

"Looks like we got a whopper here, sir." Casey put the rest of his beer down unfinished. "Or another false alarm. Senior Chief Salli called me."

"Good, then you're up to speed." Alex glanced around, but he picked the bar furthest from their TRANSPLAT for a reason. There were no *Kansas* sailors here. "That means you get captain-finding duty while I play ringmaster back on the boat."

Casey frowned. "Captain forget his phone?"

"Or isn't answering it." Alex shrugged. He refused to speculate; his job as XO was to support the captain, no matter what. "Doesn't matter. Let's get to work."

"Aye, sir. I'll find him."

Exchanging a nod, the XO and COB headed separate directions. Alex's walk back to *Kansas* took twenty minutes; Armistice Station was long, and *Kansas* was moored against the easternmost TRANSPLAT. Running through the station—even if Alex were a runner, which he wasn't—would get him arrested by the local police. That was a SITREP—situational report—Alex just didn't want to write.

Finally, he reached the TRANSPLAT elevator, only to wait in a line while a bunch of drunks went up to the cruise ship docked across from *Kansas*. Alex spent ten minutes watching juvenile twins run rings around their father before reaching the top, cutting right to avoid the tourists and reach *Kansas'* brow.

Kansas (SSN-810) was a *Virginia*-class submarine and a 460-foot long Swiss Army knife. A nuclear-powered fast attack submarine capable of shooting enemy ships or submarines, spying, deploying SEALs or shooting Tomahawk Land Attack missiles, she commissioned just seven years earlier in 2030. She wasn't as shiny as the brand-new *Cero*-class rolling out of shipyards with indecent haste, but she was a good boat with a good crew.

Her black hull contrasted with the sleek-but-shiny yachts, container ships, and colorful cruise ships on the pier, silhouetting the boat against the setting sun. Alex ran a practiced eye over the submarine, but the lines were secure and watchstanders alert.

Sue waited on the quarterdeck, fidgeting. She was short, with black hair and dark eyes complimenting her olive skin, but her glasses only slid down her nose like that when she was reading too much. Alex hurried up the brow, pausing to salute the American flag and then the Officer of the Deck.

The boat remained quiet. Everything seemed in order, and the slight vibration under his feet confirmed that Sue ordered the engineers to take the reactor out of standby. *Time to put your big boy pants on, Alex. You're the XO, and the show's on.*

If not, walking away from a twenty-three-dollar beer was a damned waste.

"Whatcha got, Nav?"

"Sir, I couldn't say it over the phone, but the FLASH message said we have indications and warnings of a terrorist attack planned within the next twenty-four to seventy-two hours."

"Shit." That was the real deal. "How're we looking?"

"All stores loaded and we're ready to go. We just need the crew."

"And the captain," Alex sighed. The worried look on Sue's face matched the awkward tenseness pinning his shoulders back, but all he could do was shake his head.

Master Chief Casey would find Kennedy. Until then, Alex needed to dig up all the information he could about this terrorist threat.

Two hours later, the chief of the boat returned with the captain.

By then, Alex had changed into coveralls and plugged into Seventh Fleet's intelligence network, inhaling every threat assessment he could find. He met Casey and Kennedy on the quarterdeck, noting the wary way the COB watched Kennedy navigate the brow. Casey met his eyes, jerking his head towards their captain.

Fuck.

"What's going on, XO?" Kennedy asked, tripping as he stepped off the brow and brushing off a petty officer's helping hand with a grin. Kennedy rubbed a hand over his mostly bald head; he kept his hair buzzed short, probably to hide how much was lost. What was left of the hair was light brown, almost blonde, and matched his eyes.

Christ, he was drunk. Alex was no saint—he liked being drunk and stupid as much as the next sailor—but with the boat tied up to a TRANSPLAT and potential terrorist threats in the air? That was a giant fucking nope.

"FLASH traffic from Seventh Fleet." Alex tried to ignore the aroma of hard liquor wafting off his superior. *Holy shit. How can you get that drunk in four measly hours?* "A terrorist group stole a passenger submersible. Intel says they're heading towards Armistice Station."

"And we got the call." Kennedy's nod was a head bob. Then he squinted. "How long ago?"

"Two hours. Nav couldn't reach you on your cell." *Neither could I, but let's not mention that.* Alex stuffed his hands in his pockets to stop a rude gesture.

"Must've broken it. All right. How's the recall going?"

Alex's lips twitched as he fought back a smile. "You're the last one, Captain."

"Good, good." Kennedy sounded a little soberer, so Alex shoved his judgmental thoughts in a box. "What's the message say?"

"We're ordered to get underway to hunt down a waterborne terrorist threat to Armistice Station," Alex replied, jerking his boss up short.

"What? Really?" Kennedy scoffed. "Couldn't they send a surface ship for that?"

"Not when intelligence indicates the terrorists have stolen a Neyk Offshore Four submarine," a new voice interjected. Civilian submarines were all the rage; advances in technology made them cheaper than ever. Neyk Submarine, the biggest sub builder, grew into a Fortune 500 company almost overnight in 2029.

Alex turned to see a newcomer walking up the brow. He did a double take; she wasn't a member of the crew, or even American. What was a *French* commander doing here?

Kennedy gaped; Alex stepped forward, lest his less-than-sober commanding officer make an ass out of all of them. "How can I help you, Commander...?"

"Camille Dubois." Her smile was nice enough to make half the crew drool, including their CO. Kennedy's look was a little *too* appraising, and Alex tried not to grimace. She continued: "I apologize for appearing with little warning. I believe an email from Seventh Fleet announcing my presence should arrive...shortly."

"Alex Coleman, XO." He waved her past the Officer of the Deck and shook her hand; Alex saw Sue searching message traffic on a tablet out of the corner of his eye, her glasses still trying to pop off the end of her nose. "Welcome aboard. May I introduce Commander Chris Kennedy, our captain?"

"It is a pleasure, Monsieur le Capitaine." She shook Kennedy's hand with a smile that said she knew exactly what she was doing, and Alex wanted to kick his boss.

Kennedy grinned. "The pleasure's mine."

Does he have to be such a cheerful drunk? Alex cleared his throat. "Not to be a Debbie downer—"

"Debbie downer?" Dubois cocked her head.

"Sorry, just a phrase." Alex's face heated. "Anyway, what I was trying to ask is why you're here."

"Ah. Of course." Dubois shrugged gracefully. "My government and yours thought it wise to send an expert on the current threat. I am here to brief your crew and to accompany *Kansas* on the hunt for the terrorists."

"I...see." Alex glanced at Sue, who nodded. So, Dubois belonged here. Fantabulous.

Alex supposed he should be thankful for any help, but why did this short-notice mission grow weirder by the moment? Still, he had a job to do, so he directed Sue to escort Dubois below, and started work to get *Kansas* underway. Kennedy didn't do much other than stare at Dubois' retreating rear end, a lazy smile on his face while he leaned on the sail.

"Let's get you a shower, sir," Master Chief Casey said before Alex could do something he'd regret. Sure, Kennedy was single—and Alex had no business caring about who he ogled—but drooling on your counterpart from another Navy was a few degrees south of impolite.

Alex threw a thank-you glance Casey's way as the COB ushered the captain down the ladder. Hitting the TRANSPLAT because Kennedy was too drunk to drive a car, let alone a submarine, would put a cherry on top of an already crappy day.

Four hours later, Alex gathered *Kansas'* key players in the wardroom for an intelligence briefing. The wardroom was *Kansas'* officers mess, library, living room, and basic home away from home. It was a tiny space, with one table and just ten seats, paneled in fake wood and blue vinyl. All fifteen of *Kansas'* officers could squeeze in if five plastered themselves to the walls, but several officers were always on watch when underway. A flatscreen television perched on the aft wall, or bulkhead, in Navy parlance, surrounded by pictures and mementos of *Kansas'* port visits. That screen made the wardroom the best place for classified briefings like this one.

Kennedy, fresh off a nap, shower, and coffee, looked more like his normal self at the head of the table, which meant he was almost as smart as he was arrogant. Casey looked tired, and Sue frazzled. Alex, sitting opposite Kennedy, felt like he'd been kicked in the midsection by a mule; Seventh Fleet's intelligence estimates looked *bad*, and there was nothing about this situation that sat well in his stomach. There were too many questions.

Lieutenant Lee Kang, *Kansas'* weapons officer, sat next to Sue. Their engineer was on watch—someone always had to be—but Alex invited a handful of chief petty officers and division officers to round the group out.

Lieutenant (Junior Grade) Chris King, their assistant navigator, was sandwiched between Senior Chief Sanelma Salli, their senior sonar operator, and Lieutenant (j.g.) Bianca Souza, the assistant weapons officer. Three other chiefs rounded out the party; Alex figured they could brief the rest of officers, later. For now, he needed their best team in the loop.

And now it was time for his favorite activity in the entire fucking world: public speaking. At least he knew these people, except Dubois. He served with most of them for two years, and Alex had their respect. Kennedy was the only *Kansas* wildcard. He was a go-getter, motivated to be the absolute best, even if he was a hard drinker and a flirt. That bothered no one in the Navy. They were *sailors.* A few warts were expected.

Besides, with the U.S. Navy's rapid expansion over the last six years, not even the most prudish admiral minded if the captain chased a skirt or two, provided said skirts were into being chased. Oh, joy; Kennedy started tapping his foot. Time to get on with it.

Alex cleared his throat. "As you all know, our liberty was cut short by an emergency. Intelligence received credible indications and warnings of a pending terrorist attack against Armistice Station.

Then, several submarines disappeared from a civilian boatyard in Port Louis this morning."

Maybe that explained the French interest. Port Louis, Mauritius, kept strong ties to its former colonizers. He continued: "A terrorist group has claimed responsibility. Furthermore, they've announced their intentions to target an underwater station in the Indian Ocean."

Dubois stood. "Charte de la Liberté des Océans—or the Ocean Freedom Charter, in English—has proven bothersome in this part of the world. They advocate for a repeal of the Underwater Treaty of 2035 and argue that no underwater settlement should be subject to international law. They are believers in...how do you say? Anarchy."

"Why would they target Armistice Station?" Lee Kang asked. "It's the biggest *independent* underwater habitat in the world by a factor of three."

"More like five," Sue muttered.

Lee waved a hand. "But why go after a station that no country can claim? That makes no sense."

"Because that's where the money is." Kennedy rolled his eyes. "Armistice Station is *rich*. Famous people come here. Governments drool at the thought of their revenue. Terrorists want attention."

"Oui." Dubois smiled. "Charte de la Liberté des Océans is a new terrorist group, but they have significant funding. We are uncertain who is providing the money, but the threat is real. And as your captain said, Armistice Station is the most tempting target in the vicinity."

Alex chewed his lip. He couldn't argue that Armistice Station was a likely target; it was also only 550 nautical miles away from Port Louis. One other point left him curious, however. "When you arrived, you said they stole a Neyk Offshore Four," he said. "None of the intelligence we received indicates what kind of submarine the terrorists are using. There were multiple types in that boatyard, including three versions built by Migaloo, two Tritons, and A Nomad 2000. Why a Neyk Offshore Four, especially if it's not the military model?"

"XO's right." Kennedy frowned. "The late model Migaloos are much faster than anything Neyk builds. Some of them are even faster than we are."

Alex saw a few sets of eyes go wide. *Kansas* was a Block V *Virginia*-class submarine, one of the last in her class. She was a lean and fast attack submarine, capable of a submerged speed of forty-two knots. Alex knew of few submarines that could match her, and only the new *Cero*-class was faster. *Unless rumors about the new Russian and French subs are true.* Not his problem.

"DRM has a...source within the CLO." Dubois grimaced, referring to the French Directorate of Military Intelligence. "I am not at liberty to say more, but we are confident that the terrorists are using the Neyk Offshore Four."

"All right." Kennedy sat back, his eyes on Dubois. "Carry on."

"Our sources indicate that the CLO wishes to ram their submarine—which will be full of explosives—into the center of Armistice Station. They hope that secondary explosions from the battery plant will destroy the rest of the station, and our engineers believe this likely to work.

"Intelligence shows that the CLO took the submarine to an undisclosed location to load the explosives. We are uncertain if they are using TATP or PETN, but either way, the results could be catastrophic."

Alex grimaced. His undergrad was in civil engineering, but he liked chemistry. Either Triacetone Triperoxide or Pentaerythritol Tetranitrate would do the job. Both were more powerful than TNT and could break an irreparable hole in *any* underwater station. Hell, either would bust *Kansas* wide open if they were stupid enough to be in the explosions' path. Why was none of this in the intelligence information provided by Seventh Fleet?

Still, he listened to the rest, despite the unease building in his gut. Dubois seemed to know her business. Who was he to argue?

When she finished, Alex rose. "Our mission is simple: locate and intercept any suspicious submarines in the vicinity of Armistice Station. We are authorized to use whatever force necessary to stop a terrorist attack on the station, up to and including deadly force." Saying those words sent a chill down Alex's spine. "*Illinois* is on her way to assist us—as is a surface action group consisting of one cruiser and two destroyers—but no one else will arrive for three days. The maximum speed of *any* of the civilian submarines is sixty knots, which means the terrorists could be within range of Armistice Station now. Seventh Fleet is coordinating with the locals to make sure we're appraised of expected arrivals. Anyone else will be considered suspicious."

Kennedy's eyebrows went up. "I'm sure we can trust French intelligence. We'll investigate every contact but our focus will be searching for a Neyk Offshore Four."

Alex blinked. "Of course, Captain."

"Anything else?" Kennedy looked around the room, but the rest of the assembled officers and chiefs looked as surprised as Alex. Years wore the old NATO bonds threadbare; everyone knew that the French worked with the Indians to claim as much territory on the bottom of the Indian Ocean as possible. Yes, the U.S. and France had been friends for many years...but you had to live in a cave to avoid the inflammatory political rhetoric flying around these days.

No one asked questions.

Chapter 2

Fumbling in the Dark

Sue took the watch in the attack center, known as "the conn," to start the hunt. The cramped space was on *Kansas'* second deck, directly under her sail. Lined with wall to wall computer screens and other equipment, control felt cramped with more than dozen people inside.

Facing the bow, Alex ran his eyes over the various watch stations. Sonar, Navigation, and the Piloting stations were to his left. Fire Control, Electronic Warfare, and Special Ops—not currently manned—were to the right, with chart stations and additional command and control consoles floating in the middle of the space like sharp-edged electronic islands.

"Investigate any submarine large enough to carry a significant cargo of explosives." Kennedy crossed his arms, scowling.

"Significant, sir?" Sue asked.

Kennedy's frown grew; Alex could see a storm brewing. Had the coffee stopped working already? Kennedy's expression screamed hangover headache, so Alex intervened. "Anything displacing over fifteen tons," he said. "Smaller boats will splat against Armistice Station like bugs on a windshield."

That made Sue smile. "Aye, sir."

Most civilian subs were smaller than fifteen tons; even with the explosion of underwater technology, builders didn't have the money to construct bigger submarines—or the buyers to sell them to.

In contrast, *Kansas* and her sisters displaced ten *thousand* tons. But they were built to military standards and full of stores, torpedoes, and a nuclear reactor. Not to mention a crew of 135. The Neyk Offshore submarines displaced between 100 and 300 tons; the Neyk Offshore Four was the newest of the bunch and clocked in at 199.

"XO, a moment?" Kennedy asked, gesturing for Alex to follow him aft.

Alex shot Sue a reassuring smile before tagging along; within a few minutes, they were in Kennedy's stateroom behind a closed door.

The captain's cabin was the biggest on board, which didn't say much. The single bed folded up into a couch, and there was a tiny table with two chairs next to Kennedy's desk. Like everyone else, he stored his uniforms and other personal gears in standup lockers, though his—like Alex's—had the dignity of being decorated by fake wood. Everyone else got bare metal.

"I appreciate your effort to anticipate any threat, but we need to stay focused here." Kennedy dropped onto the couch like a moody teenager. "Intelligence tells us it's a Neyk Offshore, so that's what we'll concentrate on."

"Sir, Seventh Fleet still hasn't confirmed that. I shot the staff intelligence officer an email, but they—"

Kennedy cut him off with a raised hand. "They wouldn't have sent Commander Dubois with us if they didn't trust her intel."

Alex took a deep breath. "I'm not sure that's a safe assumption to make."

"XO, this could *make* us. Both of our careers. But we have to be decisive." Kennedy squirmed into a sitting position and kicked his feet up on the nearby chair. He leaned forward. "We can't let these terrorists slip through our fingers. That would ruin us."

That would ruin you, Alex didn't say. He'd probably survive. "Not to mention killing thousands. Or worse."

"Of course. We need to save them." Kennedy waved a hand. It wobbled. "That's obvious. It's our duty."

"Agreed. I just don't want our watchstanders looking so hard for Neyks that they let someone else get by." Alex wished his gut would stop heaving. He hesitated. "Intel's been wrong before."

"Good point." Kennedy grinned. "Well, either way, it'll be a fruitless search for the first few hours. I'll catch some shut-eye now while you monitor things. Don't wake me up unless we find the Neyk."

"Aye, sir."

Alex checked a sigh. He could reason with Kennedy when he was sober.

Unfortunately, sobriety did nothing for Kennedy's perspective. He slept for almost twelve hours while Alex drank too much coffee and tried not to micromanage anyone. By the time their captain showed his face in the wardroom, Alex's head was pounding. Not trusting himself to be polite, he headed over to the sonar corner instead of eating lunch, his stomach a rolling mess of coffee and grease from breakfast.

Kansas got underway just before dinner. By the time the intelligence briefings finished, and they settled into a patrol pattern—no easy feat, protecting a three-hundred-and-sixty-degree bubble around a mile long station—it was past 2200 hours.

Kennedy went down just before midnight and slept until 1100, leaving his XO to mind the store. Alex knew that one of them needed to be awake during a hunt like this, but he never expected his captain to be so inconsiderate that he forced Alex to stay awake for over twenty-four hours.

Alex had done stupider things, but that wasn't the point.

"You look beat, XO." Senior Chief Salli smiled wryly.

"You look like the truck that ran over me hit you, too, Senior." Alex forced a chuckle and ignored the urge to get an eighth—or was it seventh?—cup of coffee. More caffeine meant he wouldn't sleep this side of Christmas. He was on the drunk side of sleeplessness already.

Salli shrugged. "You know how it is, sir."

"Don't wear yourself out, all right? We're going to need your ears, not to mention your experience with the UUVs."

Sanelma Salli was a Navy veteran, with twenty-plus years in uniform. She was an expert on every sonar system the Navy possessed, including the new Underwater Unmanned Vehicles *Kansas* and the other Block Vs carried. UUVs, pronounced "U-Vees," had decent sonar capability, but most COs hated using them since they were a copper-plated *noisy* bitch to launch and recover.

"Speaking of which, sir, UUV One is cranky. I haven't reported it to the OOD yet because it's just a twitch in the controls, but it's something we've got to keep an eye on."

Alex nodded and started to open his mouth.

"You deployed the UUVs?" Kennedy asked from behind him, making Alex spin around.

"Swimming three of them out was the only way we could cover so much real estate," Alex replied.

Kennedy pursed his lips. "I see."

Kansas only had five UUVs—and the things wandered off and sank if not carefully watched—but Alex felt using three was a risk worth taking. "I split the area around Armistice Station into four sectors," he said. "We have the western sector, which is the closest approach from Port Louis, and the UUVs—"

"I can see that XO, thank you." The words might have been polite. They weren't.

Was Alex taking this too personally? Maybe he was just tired.

"Now that you're up, I'm going to catch a bit of sleep, Captain. I'm beat," he said after a moment of tense silence.

"Go ahead. Hopefully I'll have more luck than you did."

Alex didn't have the energy to respond to that little barb.

Six hours later and feeling vaguely human, Alex hopped in the shower. The captain and XO's cabins shared a small but private bathroom, or head, in Navy parlance. It was the best perk attached to his job. Submarines were chronically short on space, and Alex treasured privacy.

Most attack submarines weren't built with enough racks for their entire crew, let alone space for luxuries. The ten most junior sailors even lived in the torpedo room, which meant they pulled all their personal gear—and their bunks—out of the way if enemy action threatened. But being XO meant his own stateroom, and sometimes, a little bit of quiet. Alex loved his job, but sometimes, having a place to himself was nice.

It also helped him stay sane. Still, a month from now *Kansas* would be in Alex's personal rearview mirror. His promotion to full Commander was already approved and he'd put the rank on tomorrow. One more shore tour and then command of his own boat, something he dreamed of since—

"You in there, Alex?" Kennedy's voice interrupted his thirty seconds of hot water, and Alex turned it off.

"Yes, sir. I'll be out in a sec." Grabbing his towel, Alex escaped back to his own stateroom. Rank hath its privileges; the captain got the head when he needed it.

"Come by when you're done," Kennedy's voice floated after, so Alex did just that, throwing his coveralls on and heading out through the hallway.

Once outside his door, he almost ran over Lieutenant Grippo. She flinched, and Alex paused. "Everything okay, Sue?"

"Why wouldn't it be, sir?" Her smile was strained.

"You tell me, Nav."

Another twitch; this one was mostly a shrug. "We've found nothing. Captain's a bit...testy."

Joy. There went the hope of twelve hours of sleep turning Kennedy reasonable. "Dare I ask?"

Sue shrugged. "Weps has the watch, but the captain had me relieve him so he could do a torpedo room inspection. Three of the new kids didn't stow their gear so well, and the captain didn't like it."

"You mean he ripped their heads off." Alex wouldn't have said that if Kennedy's door was open, but Kennedy never left his door open.

"Pretty much, sir. Laid into Weps pretty good, too."

"I'll talk to him." Alex managed not to sigh.

Talking the captain out of a temper was part of the XO's job. Kennedy had been in this business too long to get pissed about petty things like new sailors not securing their personal items for sea. Worst case, if *Kansas* went to battle stations torpedo, someone would throw their stuff out of the way. Why was he sweating the small shit like this?

Sue slumped in relief. "Thanks."

Alex smiled. "Get some sleep, Sue. You look like you need it."

"Can't, sir. I go back on watch in two hours, and I've got spot checks to do."

"Your spot checks can wait. Catch a nap." No way did Alex want their battle stations Officer of the Deck wrung out. There was no knowing when or if they'd run into trouble, Sue needed to be sharp when they did.

"Aye, sir." Bobbing her head, Sue headed aft towards her own stateroom, squeezing past a sailor in the one-person wide passageway.

Time to face the ogre. Alex knocked on Kennedy's door.

"Come in!"

Alex stepped in and closed the door. Kennedy was at his desk again, but Commander Dubois sat at the small table, smirking.

"Something new come up, Captain?" Alex fought not to let his eyes flick back to Dubois.

"Oui," Dubois shook herself. "Yes. One of our Anti-Submarine aircraft picked up faint traces of a Neyk Offshore Four moving south from the vicinity of Diego Garcia."

"Diego Garcia?" Alex frowned, shoving his hands into his pockets when no one told him to sit in the empty chair. "No terrorist in their right mind would get near a British-American naval station."

Diego Garcia used to be the U.S. Navy's backwater, full of heavy lift ships crewed by civilians and not much else. Now a destroyer squadron was based there, and rumor said a few submarines would call Diego Garcia home soon. Hell, there was talk of home porting attack subs in Australia. With underwater stations growing like mushrooms under the Indian Ocean, the U.S. Navy needed all the nearby bases it could get.

"Of course not." Dubois' eyes narrowed. "But inexperienced submariners might think being closer to land is safest."

Alex chewed his lip for a moment. "Okay, I can buy that. Mostly. But why would they be way up there if they're coming from Port Louis?"

"Maybe they onloaded their explosives further away than we thought." Kennedy didn't sound concerned, but Alex's internal alarms blared.

None of this made sense.

"Diego Garcia is twice as far from Port Louis as Armistice Station," he said. "The Maldives—and India—are further still. Why go there when you have the entire coast of Africa and all its outlying islands to choose from?"

"Who knows the mind of a terrorist?" Dubois shrugged. "Perhaps they were able to bribe someone in Diego Garcia. It is not just an *American* base, after all. The British are always...unpredictable."

"Why they're there doesn't matter." Kennedy waved off Alex's argument. "If an aircraft caught a whiff of them, we need to move in that direction. The further out from Armistice Station we catch them, the better."

"They detected a Neyk Offshore Four, but is there any indication this is the *right* submarine? Neyk's press releases say they've sold a hundred of them." Alex asked.

Kennedy glared.

"Most of them are in the Mediterranean and other inland seas," Dubois replied, folding her hands. "DRM is certain that this is the correct submarine. They traced it to Port Louis."

"How?" Alex asked, and then realized how rude the question sounded. "Sorry. But most people don't understand that identifying a specific submarine isn't easy unless you already have its sonar signature on file. I thought no one tracked the sub leaving Port Louis?"

If they had, this would be a lot easier.

"I *am* a submariner, Commander," Dubois snapped. "I understand the difficulty."

"Right. My apologies." Alex gulped. Why was Kennedy's smile so smug? Did he enjoy seeing his XO shove his foot down his throat?

"No apology necessary. We are all, as you Americans say, 'on the same team.'" Dubois smiled again, far too pleasantly. Alex forced himself to nod.

"Then back to my point: how do we know this is the right boat?"

"Intelligence has confirmed it. Unfortunately, I cannot provide anything more than that. I am sorry," she said.

"And we'll accept the assessment of French intelligence," Kennedy cut in, shooting Alex a look of death. "Seventh Fleet said to cooperate, and we will."

Alex got the hint. "I'll talk to Nav and get a navigation plan drawn up to head north."

"Good." Kennedy sat up straight, his eyes still locked on Alex. "I'm not letting anything get in the way of saving people, XO, you got that?"

"Yes, sir."

You think I want *Armistice Station to get blown up?* he almost asked. But he had work to do. Pissing his captain off further would only get in the way.

One 600 nautical mile, sixteen-hour, sprint later, *Kansas* arrived in the vicinity of where the Neyk could be if she drove at her best economical speed towards Armistice Station. Two hours after their arrival, they detected nothing except sea life and a few merchant ships pounding by on the surface. A pacing and frustrated Kennedy told Alex to take the boat to periscope depth to download the mail, but even that evolution turned boring in a hurry. Now they were back on station, running lines from east to west and hoping to get lucky.

Meanwhile, Alex retreated to his stateroom to check his own email. But the response from the staff intelligence officer left him queasy.

XO,

I'm not sure where the French are getting the information they've provided. None of our sources confirm that the suspect Neyk is anywhere near Diego Garcia. In fact, we have no sources providing information on this matter. In the absence of other intelligence, Seventh Fleet advises you to work with the French and accept their input with caution.

The email went on in bureaucratic ass-covering-ease. No one wanted to tell *Kansas* to shoot at the sub Dubois claimed was the terrorists' vessel, but no staff officer with half a brain would tell them *not* to, either. No one wanted to be wrong. Not with thousands of lives in the balance. Rubbing hands over his face, Alex contemplated emailing his wife. She was busy, and he didn't want to bother her with the ugly details, Nancy knew all about staff officers being indecisive assclowns who left the decisions—and their consequences—up to the idiots on the pointy end.

His phone rang. "XO."

"Sir, it's COB. You might want to come up to control," Master Chief Casey said. There was yelling in the background.

Dogshit on a shingle. Today gets better and better.

"I'll be right there."

A fast walk took Alex to control within thirty seconds. Unfortunately, by the time he ducked through the open hatch, Kennedy was on a roll, and Sue was his target.

"I told you to sprint and *drift!*" Kennedy flung his hands up, almost smacking a battle lantern. "Your nav plan was supposed to let us hear the Neyk, not let them walk right by!"

"Sir, the speed Commander Dubois recommended we use for the Neyk wasn't their best—"

"Enough! There's no need to make things worse by insulting our allies. Do I have to think of *everything* here?" Kennedy gestured at the navigation plot. "Now we have *no* idea where the terrorists are. Doesn't it feel good to have made a difference?"

Sue went bright red; Alex stepped forward, arranging his features to be as neutral as possible.

"What happened, Captain?" he asked.

Kennedy spun to face him. "The nav plan *you* approved made us lose the Neyk. French intelligence indicates they're two hundred miles past us!"

"Then I guess we have to chase them. We can still catch up," Alex glanced at the plot and did some quick math. "Even if they're moving at thirty-one knots, we have an eleven-knot speed advantage. We'll beat them to Armistice Station by a few hours...assuming that French

Intelligence was right about when they were in the vicinity of Diego Garcia."

"It is correct." Dubois sniffed. When had she arrived? Great, now their passenger had a ringside seat to the family squabbles.

"Then we'll be fine, provided we head for Armistice Station at flank speed now," Alex said, hiding his frustration in a balled fist.

Kennedy glared. "I want to see the Nav plan within ten minutes."

"You'll have it, sir."

Alex didn't watch Kennedy storm out with Dubois on his heels. Instead, he headed over to where Sue stood by the periscope display, still red faced and furious.

"*He* approved that nav plan, too," she hissed, glaring at the hatch Kennedy exited through. "Based on that French commander's recommendation, who said the terrorist 'wouldn't dare' go faster than twenty knots."

"I know, Sue." Alex patted her shoulder.

"How can you just let him throw shit like that at you, XO? Commander Rothberg—"

"This isn't the place or the time," he said gently. "We've got a nav plan to build and terrorists to stop, okay?"

"Yes, sir." Sue crossed her arms and sighed. "We're going to have to sprint like hell to beat them there."

"I know." That meant *Kansas* had no chance of detecting the Neyk along the way, even with modern sonar. Alex grinned. "Unless some miracle happens, and you pick the same course they did."

Sue laughed. "If that happens, I'm insisting we surface so I can get lotto tickets."

"I'll buy them for you."

Thirteen hours later, *Kansas* returned to the vicinity of Armistice Station. They'd now wasted more than a day rushing back and forth with nothing to show for it. Even worse, instead of resting the crew during the transit, Kennedy insisted on running drill after drill.

Alex, whose responsibility it was to make *Kansas* ready for any hypothetical combat situation, tried not to chafe at the repetitiveness. Yes, the last time an American submarine fired a torpedo in anger was in World War II, but there was no reason to exhaust people in the name of "readiness." Six drills later—each an hour long—the crew was ready to drop.

Meanwhile, Dubois poured over intelligence, scheduling four separate meetings—two during Alex's planned sleep periods—to go over the profile of the Neyk Four and the terrorists' probable courses. Kennedy hung on every word, quizzing watchstanders mercilessly.

"We need to find them soon," he said to Alex two hours after they returned to Armistice Station. The watch team was busy identifying and tracking the many submarines around the station, but Kennedy pulled Alex out of control to talk. The gleam in his eye made Alex's stomach roll; so did the way Kennedy bounced on his toes. "*Illinois* and the SAG will be here in eighteen hours."

"Having help will be great." Alex felt like someone had poured a gallon of salt in his eyes. Even coffee couldn't cure the pounding in his skull. "One of the UUVs crapped out and sank. We're down to two on station unless you want to launch another."

"Of course, I do! You're not understanding my point, Alex. We need to find them *before* anyone else gets here." Kennedy leaned forward. "I'm—*we're*—not going to waste this opportunity to shine."

Alex took a breath. "We'll all do our best, sir, but I'm more concerned about keeping the station safe than finding glory."

"There's nothing wrong with wanting both."

"I didn't say there was." Alex fidgeted. Not getting defensive was hard when Kennedy looked like Alex was trying to steal all his Christmas presents.

"I know you're not terribly ambitious and that you abhor attention"—Kennedy spoke as if this was a crime—"but the way forward in the Navy today is to make a difference. I *intend* to wear stars before too many years pass, and this is my one chance to get noticed." He waved his command-at-sea ring in Alex's face. "You'll never have one of these if you keep *this* up."

Alex grimaced. Kennedy was right; you only had one shot at command of a submarine. If Kennedy got promoted, his next command would be a squadron or a submarine tender, neither glamorous. An attack sub was his best opportunity to make a name for himself.

He was wrong, however, about Alex's lack of ambition. No, Alex didn't want to be an admiral—he didn't know why any sane person dreamed of playing bureaucratic politics with a side of nerve-wracking public speaking—but he wanted command.

All he had to do was get through the next month, and then he'd be on track for a boat of his own. But he wouldn't buy one of those shiny gold braggart rings. The command-at-sea pin on the uniform would be more than enough for him. If the Navy wanted him to have some shiny ring to show off, they'd issue him one.

"I hope that frown on your face is due to your own lack of ambition rather than your thoughts on my future career." Kennedy's words made Alex jump.

"Something like that, sir." Alex thought fast. "I was just thinking of crew rest. Everyone is exhausted—"

"And it'll all pay off when we find the terrorists. There will be glory enough to go around when we send them to the bottom."

A chill raced down Alex's spine. He wasn't immune to the lure of being the boat to stop the CLO. He just didn't want a tired officer of the deck driving their submarine into a seamount *before* they could find the enemy—or, worse yet, shooting the wrong submarine. "I suppose there will," he said, and took his leave.

Kennedy was too excited to be talked into common sense, so Alex wouldn't try. He'd go around the glory hound, instead.

Chapter 3

More Good News

Three hours later, with every sub within a twenty nautical mile bubble identified, Alex felt secure enough to hit his rack. Kennedy was awake, so Alex figured he could get a solid four hours of sleep. He needed more, but at least four hours would put him on the sober side of lack-of-sleep-drunk.

Four hours took him to 0500 local, too, which translated to nine in the morning in Japan, the location of Seventh Fleet's base. Sure enough, after waking up and taking a shower to wash away the fatigue, another email from fleet intelligence awaited him.

> *French intelligence remains the only source we have on the ground,* the staff intelligence officer replied. *Or the only one we think we have, anyway. We have no indication of where the CLO bought or onloaded explosives. However, there is a persistent rumor that they're also trafficking people from India.*

> *A British airborne anti-submarine asset detected a Neyk Offshore Four conducting a personnel transfer with a ferry south of the Maldives. They onloaded nine Indian nationals and no luggage. No traces of explosives. The aircraft could not track the Neyk after it submerged due to heavy traffic near Alderman's Outpost, but it looks like this might be your target.*

The Neyk pulled into Alderman's and purchased enough food to last a fifteen-person complement about two weeks. Alderman's security scans picked up nothing to note.

Alex sighed. Alderman's Outpost was a joint Australian-Maldives mining and oil drilling station not far from India's southernmost tip. A lot of submarines and surface ships transited that area; the Maldives were a short hop away, as well as two other major stations.

Tracking one small submarine with so many contacts cluttering the picture was challenging for any aircraft, particularly when they couldn't lay down sonobuoys without attracting attention. But why would the terrorists go up there? No way could they onload explosives at the station. Alderman's security was legendary.

Unless they hadn't onloaded explosives at all—

His phone rang, and Alex jumped. "XO."

"COB here, sir. We need you in control again." Casey sounded worried, but this time there was no yelling in the background—just the buzz of focused voices.

But a master chief with over twenty years in the Navy didn't call the XO when he wanted someone to hold his hand, so Alex forwarded the email to Kennedy and rose. "I'll be there in a sec."

"Thanks." *Click.*

Leaving the phone off the hook, Alex hurried to control.

Whatever disaster he'd expected wasn't there; instead, Kennedy stood in the sonar corner looking over Senior Chief Salli's shoulder.

"I'm dead sure it's a Neyk Three, Captain," Salli said as Alex walked in. "They've got a compressor on the sixty-two hertz line that was pulled out for the Four because it—"

"Neyk Three, Four, whatever. It's close enough," Kennedy cut her off. "Intelligence could be wrong." The captain spun around. "Officer of the Deck, query the Neyk again."

Sue nodded despite the worry in her eyes. "Aye, Captain." She lifted the microphone: "Unidentified submarine six miles east of Armistice Station in position 22°49'30" S 68°46'19" E, this is U.S. Navy submarine. Request you identify yourself and state your intentions immediately, over."

"Add that they risk being fired upon if they don't answer," Kennedy ordered.

Biting her lip, Sue glanced at Alex for confirmation. *This is such a bad idea.* But he had no business countermanding the captain, so he nodded. Sue repeated her previous transmission, adding:

"If you do not identify yourself, you will be declared hostile and fired upon, over."

The temperature in control seemed to drop ten degrees. Only Dubois and Kennedy exchanged excited glances. Was this for real? Dubois insisted it was a Neyk Four!

"Morning, XO!" Kennedy beamed when he spotted Alex, crackling with enthusiasm. "Glad to see you've joined us."

"Good morning, Captain." Alex ignored the subtle barb and headed over to join Master Chief Casey, who stood by the weapons corner, glowering at a wall of displays and control dials, arms crossed and eyes narrowed. Alex leaned in to speak to Casey in an undertone: "What's up?"

"The captain's all over this Neyk Three," Casey whispered. "The computer says it's a Three, and its tonals say it's a Three, but he doesn't want to believe that. Either that, or the intelligence he was so hot on five minutes ago is wrong."

"You're worried."

Casey barked out a humorless laugh. "Shit, sir, I'm all for shooting bad guys, but I'd rather not shoot the wrong ones."

"Same." Chewing his lower lip, Alex glanced at Sue. Underwater communications were hit and miss; underwater telephones—called Gertrudes by the U.S. Navy—had advanced significantly in the last ten years, but a sub still had to be listening.

International communications frequencies for surface ships and aircraft got hashed out decades ago, but the various submarines of the world still wouldn't agree how to talk to each other. "Don't a few local navies around here have the military variant of the Neyk Three?"

"Yep. Four or five of 'em." Casey jerked his head towards their CO. "Try telling him that."

"I take it you did." Alex knew Casey's original rate was sonar operator, and he figured the master chief had been good.

"Twice." Casey crossed his arms. "Not likely they're going to answer if they are. *We* wouldn't answer them, neither."

It went without saying that a lot of people in this part of the world didn't want to talk to "interfering" Americans. American credibility was in the crapper these days, and it didn't help that those smaller nations were now rich enough that they didn't need American protection.

"Give me that." Kennedy snatched the microphone from Sue; she flinched and stumbled back a step. He struck a pose, his words short and clipped: "Unidentified submarine six miles east of Armistice Station, identify yourself *immediately* or be fired upon."

Alex's jaw dropped. "Captain—"

"Whatever it is, it can wait, XO."

Several seconds passed in silence; Alex's stomach churned. Meanwhile, Kennedy turned to the weapons corner, shoulders back and eyes bright. "Weps, warm up—"

Crackle. The speaker to Kennedy's right sputtered to life. "...station calling"—*buzz*—"this is Indonesian Navy submarine *Chang Bogo*," an accented voice said. "Say again your last, over."

"Shit." Kennedy dropped the mic like it was radioactive.

Sue had the guts to pick up the microphone and reply: "*Chango Bogo*, this is U.S. Navy submarine Eight-One-Zero. We just wanted to confirm your identity, over."

"This is *Chango Bogo,* roger, out." The transmission ended with a *click*; signing off like that was rude, but no local Navy would call an American submarine out. Even when they were being assholes.

"Look at us making friends with the locals," Alex muttered, feeling cold.

Casey snorted. "It's a fine Navy tradition, sir."

"Find me that Neyk Four," Kennedy snapped at Sue. Her face was red with embarrassment, but the captain either didn't care or didn't notice.

"OOD, aye."

Kennedy stormed out with Dubois on his heels. Alex wandered over to where Senior Chief Salli and Sue huddled together over the sonar consoles.

"You *told* him that it was a military Neyk Three," Sue hissed. "Why the fuck won't he—"

"Morning, Nav," Alex interrupted.

Sue turned, her posture still rigid. "Morning, sir." She hesitated. "Did you...?"

"I saw and heard," Alex said. "But this isn't the time or place to bitch about it." He couldn't very well add that he knew the captain was over-eager and aggressive. Kennedy was the captain, and his officers and chiefs knew better than to criticize him in public.

"Yes, sir. Sorry." Sue flushed again.

Alex smiled crookedly. "No need to apologize. Let's just find the terrorists and let the rest take care of itself, all right?"

"I can do that, sir." She sighed. "I just...we're just a little on edge."

"I know. It's okay. We all fuck up sometimes. Remember mine with the tug?"

"Yeah." She finally smiled. "I thought Commander Rothberg was going to rip your head off for that."

"Me, too." Patting her on the shoulder, Alex gestured for Master Chief Casey to follow and headed out of the space in Kennedy's wake.

"You going to mention to the captain that he should have pinned O-5 on you yesterday?" Casey asked after they were out of control.

Alex's heart skipped. "He's been a bit busy." *Busy almost shooting other navy's submarines.* Damn, what would've happened if *Chang Bogo* hadn't answered? And why didn't Kennedy seem worried about that?

"Yeah, but making full-on commander is a big fucking deal. I know admin put it on his calendar." Casey frowned. "I made sure of it."

"I think we're all distracted by these terrorists, Master Chief." Alex wished Casey would stop. Sure, getting promoted was nice, but the ceremony was just a formality. The promotion already went through. He'd get paid, regardless.

Casey shot him a look. "You sound pretty fucking unexcited for someone about to put on full commander."

"I'm not big on attention." Alex shrugged. And he still felt like vomiting.

"Sir, I figured that out twenty minutes after you reported on board." Casey grinned. "Still doesn't mean you shouldn't get recognized, *or* that the captain should've forgotten."

"We've got bigger fish to fry." Alex hoped his tone would end that conversation, but Casey rolled his eyes. "Speaking of which, let's go talk to the boss about the current mess."

"You ain't getting out of it that easy, but I'll shut up for now," Casey replied, squeezing past a pair of sailors working on a T valve.

Alex forced a smile but said nothing. The walk to Kennedy's stateroom was short, and they went the rest of the way in silence. Unlike previous classes of American submarines, the attack center was on the same deck as the officers' staterooms.

As always, Kennedy's door was closed. He knocked.

"Enter!" Kennedy shouted.

Alex walked in, Master Chief Casey on his heels. Casey closed the door, muttering something, and Alex knew why. Kennedy sat with Dubois at the table. *Again?* Alex didn't think there was anything untold happening between the pair—Kennedy was too ambitious to be that stupid—but it was still weird. Both looked up.

"You have a minute, sir?" Alex asked. "I got an email back from Seventh Fleet Intel. A British plane tracked a Neyk Four doing a personnel transfer with a ferry near Alderman's Outpost. They think it might be our guy."

"Oh?" Kennedy perked up. "Where's Alderman's, again?"

"West of the Maldives," Alex replied.

"So much for doubt concerning why the Neyk would be so far north." Kennedy smirked.

Alex tried not to grimace. "Sir, the aircraft observed a pax transfer, no luggage. The manifest the ferry submitted indicated all the passengers were Indian. Fourteen people. And no explosives."

Kennedy waved a hand. "They might have onloaded the explosives earlier."

"Or not at all," Alex said. "They *did* pull into Alderman's, and there's no way Alderman's bomb sniffers would've missed explosives."

"No. C'est impossible." Dubois shook her head. "This may be a second Neyk sent as a decoy. Or they disguised the explosives."

"Ma'am, if they can do that, why the hell use a submarine?" Alex rolled his eyes. "Anyone with technology to mask explosives can ship straight them into Armistice Station in a cardboard box."

"XO's got a point, sir," Casey said.

Kennedy scowled; Dubois glared.

"I'm not convinced our target has no explosives, XO." Kennedy shook his head. "The idea of anyone blowing up Armistice Station is horrific, but there are some sick bastards in the world. We'll proceed as intelligence dictates."

French intelligence, Alex couldn't say. Not with Dubois there. He needed to get Kennedy alone, but Dubois stuck to him like a limpet.

What the hell was her game, anyway?

Hours ticked by. *Kansas* investigated and queried seven more contacts, none a Neyk Four. Worse, another one of their UUVs sank, shorting out when halfway through its battery power. It was an unpredictable mechanical short, perfectly explainable and unlikely to get anyone fired. But who wanted to explain to taxpayers why six million bucks of their money now lived on the bottom of the Indian Ocean? Kennedy sure didn't, judging from the way he yelled at Alex for delivering the good news.

With seven hours left before the SAG, or Surface Action Group, arrived, Kennedy was on edge. He prowled in and out of control, distracting watchstanders and spinning Sue up every time she twitched the wrong direction. Kennedy's new favorite sport was tormenting the navigator.

"Mind if I steal you for a sec, sir?" Alex asked from the entrance to control. As far as anyone could tell, Dubois was asleep. Alex wished Kennedy would do the same, but the captain was too keyed up.

"You find out anything useful, XO?"

"I got another intel report from Seventh Fleet."

"Come on." Was that a scowl? He was all about French intel, but American intelligence reports made him frown. Alex couldn't figure the guy out.

A moment later, they reached Kennedy's stateroom and shut the door. Part of Alex wanted to check the closet for Dubois; she'd been anchored to Kennedy's side since getting underway. But that would be impolite.

"Seventh Fleet intel still isn't sure about explosives or the CLO's intent." Alex handed over a hardcopy of the email.

Kennedy read it and rolled his eyes. "Deadly force is still authorized if they won't communicate their intentions."

"If," Alex stressed. "That says we need to talk to these guys."

"We'll see."

Alex took a deep breath. "Sir, I'm not sure what the French angle is here."

"Huh?" Kennedy looked up from the message.

"Commander Dubois seems...stuck on shooting these guys." Butterflies danced in Alex's stomach. "Her enthusiasm worries me."

"That's my concern." Kennedy speared him with a glare. "Commander Dubois is a naval officer doing her duty. Nothing more."

"From where I'm sitting, it seems like she's trying to get us to do her dirty work," Alex replied.

"That's enough, XO. You're not privy to the conversations she and I have had concerning this situation. She has my full confidence."

Alex checked a sigh. "Yes, sir."

"That'll be all." Kennedy's tone left no room for argument, so Alex left the stateroom, heading back to control.

He might not be able to stop this clusterfuck, but at least he could mitigate the damage.

Chapter 4

Career Suicide

Two hours of paperwork later, sonar detected the Neyk Four. As fate would have it, Sue was on watch again, finally calm without the captain poking at her every five minutes. Kennedy made a show of *getting proper rest* and pranced off to his rack an hour earlier, decreasing the tension level in control by a factor of at least four.

Alex, doomed to wakefulness while the captain napped, camped out in a corner with a stack of enlisted performance evaluations and let everyone ignore him. Lest another false alarm spin things up, he told Sue to delay waking the captain until they had a positive identification, buying *Kansas* another twenty minutes of blessed calm.

"OOD, tonals and blade rate match a Neyk Four," the sonar watch reported. "Range thirty thousand yards, bearing zero-zero-four and moving from right to left."

"Very well." Sue twisted to look at Alex.

"I'll call the captain," he said. No reason to give Kennedy a reason to pick on Sue again. "You close the Neyk."

She smiled faintly. "Aye, sir."

Alex grabbed the phone, waiting six rings for Kennedy to pick up.

"Captain," the groggy voice said.

"Sir, it's the XO. We've found the Neyk Four."

"Don't do anything until I get there!" *Click.*

Alex hung up the phone, a heavy feeling curling in his stomach. Everyone was too quiet; side conversations about sports and trivia ceased. French and American intelligence contradicted one another, but no one said *not* to shoot. Armistice Station was too rich, too big. No government wanted to risk twenty thousand lives.

The problem with that math was that the Neyk had people on board, too. When did they become unimportant?

Alex tried to swallow the dryness in his throat. It didn't work.

"What do we have?" Kennedy asked before he even had a foot through the hatch. He slammed it shut behind himself, the sound ringing in the too-quiet space.

Alex's eyes widened; he never heard Sue's report. Kennedy walked in carrying the firing key. Firing keys—officially a Fire Interdict Switch, or a FIS—were a new addition to American submarines. Combat systems became more integrated and automated in the last decade, leading to the installation of a master firing key.

A submarine might keep the local firing keys in the torpedo room, but even with those inserted, *Kansas* couldn't shoot a torpedo or missile without the master key.

This was peacetime. The key lived in Kennedy's stateroom safe, the combination to which only Kennedy and Alex knew.

Kennedy strode over to the weapons corner and inserted the firing key, turning it until it *clicked*. "Firing key is green!" He turned it until the key clicked. "Set battle stations, torpedo."

Shit. This was real.

Five minutes later, with every watertight hatch shut, *Kansas'* crew was ready for combat. No American submarine had fired a torpedo in anger since World War II—would they be the first? Nerves left Alex light-headed. This was *Kansas'* chance, but what if they were *wrong*?

Kennedy didn't seem concerned. The captain stood in the center of control like some conquering hero, hands on his hips and back straight. Alex shoved his hands in his pockets and walked over to the sonar corner.

"What's the Neyk doing?" he asked.

"Stumbling around like a one-legged donkey in the dark." Senior Chief Salli shook her head. "I can almost hear these cats without the amplifiers, sir."

"Weird." Alex chewed his lip. "I think—"

"Firing point procedures, tubes one and two," Kennedy ordered.

Nodding to Senior Chief Salli, Alex crossed to the weapons corner. As XO, verifying every firing solution was his job. Alex didn't have to agree with Kennedy to do his job. Besides, generating firing solutions early was excellent practice. *Kansas'* weapons team was top-notch, and their solution was ready in just a few minutes. Alex went over the numbers twice before nodding at the weapons officer, Lieutenant Lee Kang.

"Solution set," Lee reported.

"Solution checked," Alex said.

Kennedy grinned. "Very well."

Dubois, standing behind Kennedy, smiled. Was that victory in her eyes? *Not yet.* Alex glanced down at the plot. The range was down to twenty-four thousand yards now that *Kansas* turned on an intercept course.

The Mark 48 CBASS torpedo had a maximum effective range of twenty-one nautical miles at fifty-five knots. *Kansas* carried sixteen warshots and ten dummy torpedoes used for exercises. Standard practice was to shoot torpedoes in pairs. They were well within range, but shooting from further out made for inaccuracy. How long would Kennedy wait? And why jump straight to torpedoes?

Alex walked over to stand next to his boss, trying to ignore Dubois' glare. "You want to try contacting them, sir?"

"They won't answer, but go ahead." Kennedy shrugged.

"Aye, sir." Great. Kennedy wanted to put the guy with a fear of public speaking on the underwater telephone. No way was that an accident.

Taking a deep breath, Alex lifted the Gertrude handset. He swallowed a few times before words came, but he couldn't chicken out now. Not with *Kansas* closing the Neyk Four at a mile every two minutes. *Intercept in twenty-four minutes, but we're not trying to ram her. When will he shoot?* Everything Alex read on Neyks said their underwater communications suite left a lot to be desired. Clearing his throat, Alex depressed the talk button.

"Unidentified Neyk Four submarine northwest of Armistice Station, this is U.S. Navy submarine, over."

"Terrorists ain't gonna say jack," someone muttered. Alex twisted to give FT1 Roberson a stern look, and Roberson's eyes snapped back to her console.

The silence was ominous, however.

"Unidentified Neyk Four submarine northwest of Armistice Station, this is U.S. Navy submarine, over," Alex repeated. It would be so much easier if he could just use *Kansas'* name. But security precautions said no.

Still nothing.

"Range?" Kennedy demanded.

"Twenty thousand and closing, sir," Salli replied.

"Make tubes one and two ready in all respects, including opening the outer doors," Kennedy said. "All stop. Initiate hover."

"All stop, aye. Initiate hover, aye," Master Chief Casey replied. He glanced Alex's way as *Kansas* glided to a standstill, and Alex could see worry in the COB's brown eyes.

Control suddenly felt ice cold.

Another attempt to communicate with the Neyk Four only produced static. Taking a deep breath, Alex turned to Kennedy. "Captain, I recommend we close range to ten thousand yards. He might not be able to hear us."

Gertrude use was notoriously spotty among civilian submariners. Hell, half their underwater radios didn't even work. There was no way to know if the Neyk was even listening.

"If you think I'm getting any closer to an underwater bomb, you're crazy." Kennedy's grin softened the reply, and a few people laughed, but Alex knew a rebuke when he heard one.

"Sir, we don't know that he's a bomb," he said. "Intelligence reports contradict—"

"Not now, XO."

Alex's mouth snapped shut. Pressing would only piss Kennedy off. Kennedy was the type of CO who always had to be right. *Damn the torpedoes, full speed ahead?* Alex scowled. *Even Farragut would hate this idiot.*

He shouldn't call his CO that, not even in the privacy of his own mind. Alex couldn't make himself care. He twisted to look at the tracking party. "What's our range to Armistice Station?"

"Eighteen thousand yards, sir," Roberson replied.

"Thank you." Alex nodded.

Eighteen thousand yards was nine nautical miles. The French thought the Neyk was packed with TATP or PETN, neither of which had an underwater blast radius of half that. The Neyk needed to ram the station to do real damage. There were a dozen ways to stop that from happening, including placing *Kansas* right in the Neyk's path.

Yeah, suicide wasn't Alex's go-to choice, but neither was murdering civilians by accident. Kennedy already proved himself willing to shoot the wrong submarine just ten hours earlier. What if he was wrong again?

The U.S. had enough enemies in this part of the world. How bad would it get if they shot up a boat full of Indians? Things between India and the U.S. were already a mess. The Indians had threatened to eject the U.S. ambassador after detecting USS *Jimmy Carter* leaving their waters four months earlier. The Navy claimed it was a navigation error, but everyone with internet access knew *Jimmy Carter* was a spy submarine.

"We should not wait," Dubois said from Kennedy's left.

"Max underwater range for the amount of TATP or PETN they could carry is about five thousand yards," Alex snapped. "That means we still have time. Is there a reason you don't want us to make sure these *are* homicidal terrorists before shooting, Commander?"

"I do not like your tone." Dubious sneered.

"And I don't like your willingness to murder civilians." Alex crossed his arms. "Looks like we're even."

Casey gasped; several mouths dropped open. Alex was beyond caring. Kennedy wasn't stupid, but Dubois spent the last few days egging on his dreams of glory. Kennedy wanted to be *noticed*. Killing terrorists was the quickest way to the top when war wasn't going to happen.

"That's enough, XO!" Kennedy lunged between them. "Your objections have been noted. Can you do your job, or do I need to relieve you?"

That stung. Alex almost dared Kennedy to relieve him—until inspiration struck. *I can do one better.* He took a deep breath.

"I can do my job, sir," Alex replied, feeling strangely calm. "Though I could use a minute, if you don't mind."

Kennedy smiled, all teeth. "Go ahead."

"Thanks." Alex looked his CO right in the eye, but the glee in Kennedy's gaze no longer made him feel sick. Just angry. Turning, he headed towards the hatch, not looking at anyone.

"French intelligence is certain there are no civilians on board," Dubois said. "If they refuse to answer your hails, Captain, they cannot mean well."

Time to say goodbye to my career. No one noticed how his path out of the space took him right by the panel containing the firing key. A quick flick of fingers turned the key to the off position, and Alex slipped it into his pocket.

He didn't stick around to listen to Kennedy's reply. Alex just closed the hatch and headed down the ladder to his stateroom, ducking into the head to splash water on his face. Kennedy would notice what he'd done before long. So, he needed to hide the firing key, preferably somewhere he could reach it in a hurry in case he was wrong.

Shit, what if he was?

This gamble didn't just put his career on the line; it risked thousands of lives. Quick math told Alex that he couldn't do something like lock the firing key in his own stateroom safe. That was too far from control. Giving it to someone else to hold was out of the question, too. No way was he forcing someone to choose between loyalty to the XO and the CO. Uneasy instinct told Alex he'd win a popularity contest, but he refused to draw someone else into his little mutiny.

Fuck that noise. It's only mutiny if I'm wrong. Alex's stomach rolled. Why the hell wouldn't Kennedy listen? Instead, Dubois ran him in merry little circles, leading him to ignore every bit of intelligence provided by his own government. This was insane.

Alex glanced at himself in the mirror and wished he hadn't. His blue eyes were bloodshot and anyone who knew him could tell something was wrong. But it wasn't like anyone would assume the stupid firing key grew legs and walked out on its own. They'd know it was him. Even if Alex was right, there'd be hell to pay.

He was okay with that if it meant saving lives.

Squaring his shoulders, Alex ducked back into his stateroom, grabbing a piece of duct tape. Balling up the key and its chain, Alex stuck it to the piece of tape and walked back out of his stateroom. Forward forty feet, he paused outside the hatch leading to control. Quickly, Alex stuck the tape to the smooth underside of a power panel. No one would look there, but he could grab it if everything went straight to hell.

Opening the hatch to control, he almost collided with Master Chief Casey. Worry lined Casey's face, his brows pulled down over his eyes like angry hoods. "Startin' to worry about you, sir," Casey whispered.

"I just needed a minute." Alex contemplated bringing Casey into his little one-man conspiracy, but he didn't want to sink the COB, too. "What's changed?"

"Captain made a half-hearted attempt to hail them again, but nothin' answered 'cept shrimp fucking." Casey growled under his breath. "Poor fuckers are still coming in at six knots. My dead grandma would drive a submarine faster."

"XO, I'm glad you're back." Kennedy turned to Alex wearing a smile that didn't reach his eyes. "Now, if you wouldn't mind taking your station with the firing party, we can get on with this."

Yeah, that too-polite tone was the sound of Kennedy composing Alex's end of tour fitness report in his head. Alex pretended not to notice while Dubois gloated. "Yes, sir."

Not that they'd fire a damned thing without the key in. Alex headed over to stand next to *Kansas'* weapons officer, watching Kennedy out of the corner of his eye.

The bastard was excited. Eager, like trying not to bounce on the balls of his feet while his eyes took in every person in the space. Kennedy ignored Alex, however. Was his conscience acting up? Maybe Alex could work on that. Dubois was a mysterious piece of work with goals he couldn't understand, but Kennedy was a fundamentally decent person.

Shit. Master Chief Casey noticed the lack of firing key. His station was closest to the panel, and Casey's head snapped around to look at Alex, his eyes wide.

Casey was a *Kansas* old-timer. He'd been on board a year longer than Alex and in the Navy for twenty-six years. He was smart, good at his job, and more loyal to the Navy than any single officer. Like all Chiefs of the Boat, he was a consummate professional who viewed saving officers from themselves as his duty.

Alex held his breath, waiting for Casey to draw Kennedy's attention to the missing key.

Slowly, Casey nodded. Then he turned back to watching the helmsman.

Relief almost swept Alex's legs out from under him. He leaned on the nearest bulkhead, chest tight. Damn. Every minute ticking by brought the Neyk Four another 200 yards closer to *Kansas*. Every minute was a chance they might hear a hail.

"Range?" Kennedy demanded, reading Alex's mind.

"Sixteen thousand yards, sir," Salli replied.

"Very well." Kennedy's lips pressed into a thin smile; Alex knew he was fighting a grin.

"Should we try talking to them again, sir?" Alex asked. "The last thing we need is an international incident caused by bad intel."

There. If he could paint Kennedy as the victim of mistaken intelligence instead of—

"I have already told you that our sources are certain." Dubois rolled her eyes. "I understand that you have not seen the raw data, Commander Coleman, but I have shown them to your captain, and he agrees."

Son of a bitch. Dubois backed Kennedy into a corner. *She's too clever by half.* Alex knew when he was outclassed. He just wished he knew *why*. What the hell was Dubois' goal? Why would she want them to shoot a submarine full of Indian civilians? France and India were in bed together, had been for years. They even shared military technology. Hell, India bought French torpedoes and diesel submarines in droves!

"I think if this cat wanted to talk, he would've done it already," Kennedy replied after an ominous silence. "Verify your solutions are up to date, Weps."

"Firing solutions set and ready, Captain."

Kansas was not alone tracking the Neyk. Unbeknownst to the American submarine, a second nuclear attack submarine hovered directly beneath her, silent and armed. This submarine also had two Mark 48 CBASS torpedoes loaded in tubes one and two. Her other four torpedo tubes, however, contained F21 Artemis torpedoes manufactured at the Naval Group headquarters in Paris, France.

France did not use CBASS torpedoes, but Lockheed Martin gifted a quartet of them to the French Navy years earlier, hoping France's growing submarine fleet needed more torpedoes than Naval Group could provide. However, Lockheed Martin underestimated French pride. Yes, their Navy tested and shot two of the four torpedoes. No, they would not buy more of them.

They then listed the other two as disassembled and discarded, saving them for a very special moment.

Captain Jules Rochambeau was one of the few aware that moment had arrived. Tensions in the Indian Ocean were high; French and Indian interests head-butted with Australia at every turn. America, typically, bumbled into the middle of that mess without understanding or caring for local politics. They sided with Australia without considering India's logical hegemony over the region or legitimate French interests. Most people forgot that France never relinquished her Indian Ocean colonies. French nationals lived in those waters, unlike Americans.

Thus, Rochambeau's *Barracuda* deployed on special orders from Admiral Bernard. Rochambeau knew only the broad strokes of his country's plans—no mere submariner was well-placed enough to know them all—but he knew that France needed resources. Competition among European nations bordering the Mediterranean Sea was fierce, and no one wanted oil wells peppering their own coasts.

The Indian Ocean, however, was vast and full of oil, precious metals, and more. France needed those resources. India was willing to share, particularly in return for French-built submarines and weapons.

Barracuda was an advanced *Requin*-class submarine, commissioned just a year ago in 2036. She was, in her captain's unbiased opinion, the quietest submarine in the world. He'd certainly maneuvered her underneath the Americans without *Kansas* noticing.

So much for the vaunted American submariners' skill! They still thought they were the best in the world, were still blissfully unaware that other nations equaled and then surpassed their technology.

Now was not the time to disabuse them of that notion, however. Now was time to watch and listen, to wait and see if *Kansas* would sink the Neyk Four. Rochambeau bared his teeth in a hungry smile. If Camille did her duty and *Kansas* fired, *Barracuda* would vanish as if she had never been present.

If *Kansas* did not fire...

Rochambeau's smile grew.

Chapter 5

False Flag

Kennedy put his hands on his hips like some storybook hero. Was he posing for the VDR? Someone should remind this overexcited windbag that photo opportunities came *after* the messy stuff.

"Tubes one and two...*fire!*" Kennedy ordered.

Lee slapped the firing buttons for both tubes. Everyone held their breaths; *Kansas* was about to become the first American sub to fire torpedoes at a civilian target in over eighty years.

Alex shoved his hands in his pockets.

Nothing happened.

"Captain, I think we have some sort of malfunction here," Lee said.

"What?" Kennedy whirled, eyes wide. His hands flew off his hips, flapping uselessly. The right one caught on the periscope display camera, and Kennedy's jaw dropped.

So much for posterity. Alex felt a little sick despite his thoughts. He'd just disobeyed an order—or close enough, even if no one ordered him *not* to steal the firing key—in a world where orders *must* be obeyed. Sure, the Geneva Conventions said that following orders was no excuse, but Kennedy's orders hadn't been illegal or immoral. Just *wrong*.

How the hell could doing the right thing feel so wrong?

"The firing key is fucking gone!" FT1 Roberson said. Everyone turned to face her.

Everyone except Alex, whose eyes remained on Kennedy.

"*What*?" Kennedy yelped, color draining from his face.

"It's not there, Captain," Roberson repeated.

"I can fucking see that!" Kennedy surged forward, looking at the deck under where the key should be. Several people joined his search. Sue took two steps forward and stopped, seeming lost as her watch team fell apart, looking under consoles, behind monitors, and under peoples' feet.

Alex felt like an island of calm amidst the insanity. It wasn't *quite* chaos, but no one paid attention to their duties. He hadn't expected the missing key to be so distracting. Even the sonar team started crawling under their consoles, headsets off.

"Senior." Alex caught Senior Chief Salli by the arm. "You're our eyes and ears. Let others look."

She blushed. "Sorry, sir."

Alex just gestured her back to her console and then noticed Master Chief Casey's eyes on him. After a moment, Casey wandered over to his side.

"You're fucking crazy, sir," Casey whispered.

Alex's stomach did a backflip. "Tell me about it."

Casey just grimaced. "I think this might—"

The Gertrude speaker to Alex's right crackled. "US Navy submarine, this is"—*crackle*—"Neyk Four submar...can you...over?"

Spinning, Alex grabbed the handset so quickly he almost tripped over his own feet. "This is US Navy submarine, say again, over."

More static greeted him.

"Give me that!" Kennedy yanked the handset out of Alex's hands. "Unidentified submarine, this is U.S. Navy submarine. Identify yourself *immediately*, over."

"...Neyk..." A chirp and then more crackling. "...pass—over."

"What is this bullshit?" Kennedy glanced wildly around the space. "And where the hell is my firing key?"

Fuck. Alex tried not to look guilty, but this mystery didn't need Sherlock Holmes. He was the only one who left the space since *Kansas* manned battle stations, and Kennedy was no idiot. Self-centered and aggressive, yeah. Not stupid.

Kennedy zeroed in on Alex, his eyes bulging. "*You* did this!"

"We should focus on getting comms with the Neyk, Captain," Alex replied, ignoring the way his heart thundered into his throat. "It sounds like they have passengers on—"

Hands hit his chest; Alex stumbled back into a weapons panel, barely catching himself before falling. Eyes wide, he stared at Kennedy, unable to believe that his CO had laid hands on him. Physical violence wasn't—

"Fuck comms!" Kennedy lunged forward until they were almost nose to nose. "Give me the goddamned firing key!"

Throat tight, Alex straightened and looked his captain in the eye. "We need to establish their intentions *before* shooting."

"Fuck their intentions. I just gave you an order."

Yep, there went his career. But doing the right thing was worth more than that, right? Alex opened his mouth, only for Salli to cut him off:

"Launch transients! Two torpedoes in the water, close aboard!" the sonar chief said. "Son of a bitch, they're close! Too close for a bearing!"

"Shit!" Shoving past Kennedy, Alex bolted for the hatch. Flinging it open, he grabbed the firing key from where it was taped under the power panel. Alex tore the tape off and let it flutter to the floor, lunging back into control. "Weps!"

He tossed the key; Lee caught it, inserting the key in one smooth motion. "Key is green!"

"You son of a bitch." Kennedy crossed the space to lean into Alex's face again. "I'll *finish* you for this. Your career is *over!*"

No shit, Sherlock. Alex twisted away from his CO, looking over to sonar. "Senior, tell me who the hell fired!"

"I can't hear anyone, sir." Salli shook her head. "But the torpedoes came from *close*."

"How close?" Alex asked.

"Like right the fuck on top of us." Salli grimaced. "They're outbound, though. Otherwise, we'd be dead."

"Did we fire?" Kennedy demanded as Alex dodged around him. "Weps, contact the torpedo room!"

"Sir, the tubes aren't in local control." Lee's face was stark white. "We physically *can't* have fired, Captain."

Alex reached sonar and looked at the array of monitors. The traces on screen showed only one contact, and that correlated to the Neyk Four. "Oh, fuck," he whispered.

"What now?" Kennedy looked like he wanted to murder Alex.

"Those torps are inbound the Neyk Four." Alex felt cold.

Almost on cue, the Gertrude speaker crackled. "U.S. Navy submar...fire on us?" *Buzz.* "...would you? We have passengers and are..." The transmission vanished in a sea of static.

Alex grabbed the handset without thinking. "Neyk Four, this is U.S. Navy submarine. We have not—I say again *have not*—fired on you." He glanced at the plot and did some quick math. Those torpedoes were closing on the Neyk Four awfully fast. "Recommend you turn to course two-seven-zero and come up to your top speed. Surface as quickly as you can, over."

"It won't help." FT1 Roberson met his eyes, but now Roberson looked horrified instead of cocky.

"They've still got to try."

Wild ideas raced through Alex's mind. Could *Kansas* race forward and drop noisemakers? Could she somehow distract the torpedoes away from the civilians?

"What's the torpedoes' speed?" he asked.

Salli turned to look at him, her eyes wide. "Fifty-five knots," she whispered. "All tonals match a Mark 48."

Alex's jaw dropped.

Kennedy lurched forward. "That's not possible."

"I can only tell you what I hear, sir." Salli looked back at her screens. "Computer concurs. Impact in two minutes."

The Neyk was running, for all the good it would do them. Running at thirty-five knots might buy them a little time, but no civilian submarine ever made could survive the explosive force of two warheads like the Mark 48 carried. 650 pounds of high explosive—times two!—would kill a nuclear submarine made of military grade steel. The Neyk would crack open like an egg.

Alex wanted to vomit.

Time seemed to slow. *Kansas*' control room went eerily quiet, the drama of the lost firing key forgotten. Even Kennedy was silent, watching the display with wide eyes. Eventually, Salli and her sonar team removed their headsets. This close, *Kansas'* sailors could hear the explosion through the hull. Using amplifiers might rupture eardrums.

Alex took refuge in minutiae; contemplating the fate of the civilians on board the Neyk burned too much. His stomach rolled. A Neyk wasn't a warship, wasn't made of high-end steel or compartmentalized. She had the bare minimum of compartments to meet international safety standards for a civilian submarine. Sailors on a sunken warship might escape. These civilians had no chance. They were all going to die.

Were they terrorists? Did it matter?

The torpedoes reached the wildly maneuvering Neyk. The shockwave hit *Kansas* seconds later. They weren't close enough for it to hurt, but the sub still trembled as the *boom-boom-boom* rolled through the hull. No one spoke.

Minutes ticked by. Alex swallowed, licked his lips. "We should check for survivors."

Kennedy snorted. "There won't be any."

"We still should," Alex replied. "The International Law of the Sea says—"

"The U.S. never signed that treaty," Kennedy snapped. "But fine. We'll humor your goddamned bleeding heart and go look for dead terrorists."

Except a boat with a bomb—like the supposed terrorists had—would've made a much bigger explosion.

Alex kept his mouth shut and went to work.

An hour later, *Kansas'* newly deployed UUV approached the wreckage while civilian ships and submarines from ten different nations closed to help. News helicopters buzzed over the surface, leaving Alex glad they could hide under the waves—at least no one could actually *see* them down here.

Kansas moved within five thousand yards of the downed Neyk and sent the UUV ahead, swimming it out while the attack sub initiated a hover. Three civilian subs were closer, but most of the locals kept their distance, waiting for news of survivors.

No submariner in their right mind thought there would be. Not when two torpedoes slammed into a civilian submarine.

Kennedy holed up in his stateroom again while Alex watched the UUV's camera view over Salli's shoulder, heart heavy. However, Commander Dubois remained in control, her sharp eyes watching everyone. Something about her quiet demeanor gave Alex the willies. Was she *happy*? He burned to kick her out of control, but Kennedy still thought she was on their side.

We went after the sub she sent us after, and then some mystery submarine shot it. With American built torpedoes. The heavy feeling in Alex's gut wouldn't go away. Something was very wrong here.

"Sonar never picked up secondary explosions, sir," Sue whispered, her eyes also flicking to Dubois.

"I know." Alex swallowed. Neither mentioned how that decreased the odds that the Neyk was full of explosives. *Any* explosives would've disintegrated the Neyk when a Mark 48 hit. Yet as the UUV swam forward, there was enough of the civilian sub left to recognize.

Sue's shoulders hunched. "Feels like we got the wrong boat, XO."

"You didn't shoot it, Sue. *None* of us did." Alex glanced around, saw the guilt etched in every face. "Those weren't our torpedoes, folks. Place the blame where it belongs—not on yourselves."

Crackle. A voice warbled out from the Gertrude. "American submarine, how dare you pretend you didn't kill those people? You—"

"Turn that shit off," Alex ordered.

Grimacing, Sue turned the volume down until *Sea Adventurer* finished ranting. That made four civilian submarines screaming obscenities at *Kansas,* and counting. The station hadn't weighed in yet, but it was only a matter of time.

Alex returned his attention to the monitor as the UUV got in close. The Neyk was in four main pieces of twisted, warped, and shattered metal. Its command compartment was relatively intact, if one discounted the way the rear bulkhead was ripped off and lay forty feet away from the front end. Squinting, Alex could make out the foggy outline of seats...one of which still had a body strapped to it.

To his left, someone retched.

"Who the *fuck* did this?" Sue kicked an angle iron. "There's no one else here that has Mark 48s!"

"I hear you." Alex's mind raced through that paradox. Only a handful of countries used the Mark 48 torpedo. Last he checked, none of the submarines around Armistice Station were Brazilian, Australian, Canadian, Dutch, or Taiwanese. Hell, all those nations were American allies. They wouldn't sneak up and kill a civilian submarine without communicating first.

Would they?

The world was changing, and Alex couldn't keep up.

"We need to call this in," he muttered.

Sue grimaced. "The captain said to keep comms secure until after we determined what happened."

"Not much of a fucking question about that." Alex gestured at the monitor. Chief Salli moved the UUV away from the busted command compartment, moving it towards what looked like the small submarine's cargo area. If there were explosives, they would be—

The Gertrude crackled, fuzz filling control.

"Probably just another civilian calling to yell at us." Sue sighed.

"US Navy submarine, this is French Navy submarine *Barracuda,* over," an accented voice said.

Alex's head snapped up just in time to watch an *un*surprised expression of satisfaction cross Camille Dubois' face. *What the...?*

Sue stared back at him with wide eyes. "*Barracuda's* a *Requin*-class fast attack. Practically brand new," she said. "Where the hell did they come from?"

"Senior, you have a position on *Barracuda*?" Alex asked.

Senior Chief Salli consulted with her sonar operators before shaking her head. "Nada, sir. Wherever they are, they're damned quiet. Keep them talking and I can figure it."

"Call the captain and let him know we have...another French friend in the vicinity," Alex said to Sue, trying not to look at Commander Dubois. No way was this a coincidence. No fucking way.

"Aye, sir." Sue looked unhappy, and no wonder. Kennedy would yell at his favorite punching bag. But she followed the order, anyway.

Meanwhile, Alex reached for the Gertrude handset, only for *Barracuda* to speak first.

"US Navy submarine, this is French Navy submarine *Barracuda.* Answer immediately or be subject to enforcement action, over."

"What the hell?" Alex twisted to look at Dubois. "I thought we were allies?"

Dubois smiled thinly. "Destruction of a civilian submarine is not something one tolerates, even from...allies."

"*What?*" Alex's jaw dropped. *Kansas* hadn't gotten the chance to fire. He made sure of that!

Dubois knew it, too. But she only shrugged. "I recommend you answer." Her smile was thin, but her eyes bright. "*Barracuda* does not sound willing to wait."

Glaring, Alex lifted the phone. Butterflies danced around his windpipe, but he pushed them aside. *Jesus, I hope Kennedy hurries his ass up here. He might hate me but this is way above my paygrade.* He took a deep breath.

"*Barracuda,* this is US Navy submarine, go ahead, over," he said.

Interesting that the French sub used their name on an open communications circuit. NATO ships and submarines didn't usually do that.

Alex stole another glance at the wreckage, his throat tight.

"U.S. Navy submarine, recover your unmanned vehicle and stand clear of the wreck." The French voice on the other end dripped with scorn. "Stay outside two miles or be subject to enforcement measures."

"Who the fuck does he think he is?" Kennedy stormed into control,

"Someone who just saw a lot of civilians killed." Alex swallowed. How did this look from the French perspective? Never mind Dubois.

Barracuda just watched two American-made torpedoes come from the direction of an American submarine. The conclusion was easy, if wrong.

"You're out of line, XO," Kennedy snapped. "You and I both know we didn't fire." He sneered. "We *couldn't*, thanks to you. And don't think I've forgotten that."

"Sir, if you'd rather be the guilty party in this little fiasco, have at." Alex rolled his eyes.

Kennedy glared. "Give me the handset."

Alex managed not to say something cutting. Barely. So, he forked over the handset without a word, meeting Master Chief Casey's eyes again. It was nice not to be the only one thinking this situation was going to pot in a hurry.

"*Barracuda*, this is US Navy submarine eight-one-zero," Kennedy said. "I do not recognize your authority."

Shit. Good thing *Kansas* remained at battle stations. Goading another attack sub like that was a good way to get their asses shot off.

"Eight-one-zero, this is *Barracuda*. You have fired upon and sank a civilian submarine. My government demands an immediate and impartial investigation," the Frenchman replied. "One *not* including America. Over."

"We didn't fire at anyone!" Kennedy's face went red, and his knuckles white on the handset. He turned his glare on Alex.

Gee, aren't you glad we didn't *shoot*? Alex couldn't say that. *Pity*. Instead, he turned to Dubois. "Can you contact them and tell them we didn't shoot?"

He heard what she said earlier. But he wanted to make her say it again.

Dubois obliged with a shrug. "I cannot verify that. I was not at your weapons panel."

"You saw the key wasn't there!" Kennedy's features went from bright red to ashen white. "You *heard* every word we said!"

"You may have said one thing and done another." Dubois didn't even blink. "It would not be the first time America was so clever."

The Gertrude crackled again. "Eight-one-zero, this is *Barracuda* Actual. You have two minutes to get clear before I fire upon *you*, over."

Kennedy sputtered, his eyes darting between Dubois and the handset. "You—you—how fucking *dare* you?"

"I am sorry that I cannot provide assistance, Captain," she replied.

"Come to zero-zero-zero and up to fifteen knots," Alex ordered Sue as Kennedy continued his stare off with Dubois. That course was a standard NATO safety course. Assuming *Barracuda* cared, they'd recognize it and not shoot.

"You want to leave the UUV out, XO?" Salli asked.

Kennedy threw the handset down. "The US Navy doesn't obey other country's demands! What the fuck do you think you're doing?"

"Do you want to shoot at him, sir?" Alex wanted to smack him. "Because that's our other option. And I don't know about you, but I'd rather not start World War III today."

"They wouldn't—"

"Contact on *Barracuda*, bearing two-four-four, range twelve thousand yards," Salli cut in. "She's opening her outer doors."

"She's *what?*" Kennedy went white.

"At least four outer doors open, Captain. Maybe more," Salli replied.

"*Requins* have six tubes," Alex said. "That leaves two in reserve if she wants to smack us with four torps. And her torpedo range is better than ours."

"I *know* that, XO." Kennedy started pacing again.

But Kennedy didn't counter Alex's orders as Sue brought *Kansas* around and increased speed, the UUV trailing in their wake. No, the United States didn't enjoy listening to other countries, but this was the only way to keep this from turning into an underwater shootout. *Kansas*' VDR would prove she hadn't fired. So would every other automated log. Alex couldn't blame the French for assuming it was them. Not if *Barracuda* had the same intelligence Dubois presented.

Wait a minute. *Barracuda* should have wanted to shoot based on that intel, too. What the hell was going on?

"They won't shoot," Kennedy said to no one in particular.

"We can't take that chance," Alex replied. No one else looked at Kennedy, not when he wanted to yell and play the blame game. But it was Alex's job. "France is allied with India and Russia. *They* have ties with China. If we torque this off, we could wind up in a war with all of them."

"No one's that stupid."

Alex rolled his eyes. "No one thought that in the days before World War I, either. But this web of alliances looks kinda familiar."

Even a goddamned engineer could spot the historical parallels. Colonizing the ocean floor brought a *lot* of nations into conflict with one another. Or it could. So far, everyone had acted like adults.

Knowing world history, that wouldn't last long.

"I wouldn't have taken you for a coward, Alex," Kennedy said.

Alex blinked. "What?"

"Not firing. Running away. Disobeying orders." Kennedy's smile turned smug. "I suppose conflict brings out the worst in everyone."

Alex gaped. He stopped this asshole from firing on civilians. Yeah, he knew Kennedy wouldn't thank him, but did Kennedy have to be such a prick about it?

So much for getting his own command. He kissed goodbye to his career hiding that firing key.

Chapter 6

False Friend

Two weeks later, an Indian research ship—fortuitously in the area for an undisclosed scientific expedition—recovered enough of the Neyk Four to confirm the impact of Mark 48 torpedoes. *American* torpedoes, built and sold by an American corporation. By the time *Kansas* pulled into Diego Garcia, it was all over the news. Alex locked down email on and off the boat after a few crew members reported getting emails from reporters and others begged for time to call their families.

Dubois, satisfied as a spider in the middle of her web, apologized prettily to Kennedy and promised to help with the investigation. *Of course,* she understood his position, and while she couldn't verify that they hadn't shot, she could certainly repeat what she saw.

Her nice smiles turned Kennedy's ire back on Alex, but he didn't want to deal with the crew's sudden maelstrom of doubt and fear, so he dumped that on Alex and hid in his stateroom. Meanwhile half the world shouted for American heads on a platter—preferably heads off *Kansas*—and the other half claimed conspiracy.

Kansas spent three hours after the incident at periscope depth, explaining the situation to the newly-promoted Rear Admiral Hamilton. Hamilton was the acting commodore of Submarine Squadron Eight; Captain Grossman, their *original* squadron CO, was due at court martial next week for taking bribes from contractors.

So, Hamilton was in charge, despite a lofty rank which said she should be concerned with bigger things. Unfortunately, they were now a bigger thing, and *Kansas* was ordered to Diego Garcia at best speed.

They arrived late at night, with guards posted on the pier to keep reporters out and the crew in. For the first time in his career, Alex's own navy made it dangerous to leave the boat.

Admiral Winifred Hamilton arrived at dawn. Her investigation—complete with seven aides and three legal officers—was a whirlwind of efficiency that left Alex breathless.

Kennedy and Alex both wrote statements swearing *Kansas* never fired a torpedo. Weps inventoried torpedoes in front of the Admiral to prove they still had every weapon they left homeport with. Master Chief Casey, Sue Grippo, and everyone else on watch in control wrote nearly identical statements, but the French thorn in their side disappeared without corroborating their case.

The U.S. Navy had no right to hold a foreign national, after all, and no one told the guards on the pier not to let a French commander through. Two hours after Dubois' departure, Admiral Hamilton tried to download *Kansas*' deck log and VDR...only to find both corrupted beyond repair.

Eight hours later, French news sources showed interviews with one Commander Camille Dubois, claiming the hotheaded Americans shot and killed civilians as she smiled that same smile.

Two hours later, the Neyk's manifest and passengers—vegetables and civilians to the last atom—were released. The stolen submarines, of which their victim was not one, were recovered by the Indian Navy the next day, sans explosives. The terrorists apprehended would face trial in late 2038, having never come within torpedo range of USS *Kansas.*

A flying boot broke the mirror in Kennedy's stateroom. Long-distance drones overflew *Kansas* when reporters were barred from the island (easy to do, with the atoll wholly owned by Britain and leased by the U.S. Navy). Navy helicopters threatened to shoot the drones down, and then the Navy got sued when two drones plastered themselves into an SH-60R.

The Navy's on-the-record statement that *Kansas* had not fired fell on deaf ears. By the time the torpedo inventory was complete, the story was written and minds made up. Politicians got involved. Reparations were demanded. India threatened to throw American ambassadors out, and U.S. Navy ships and submarines were barred from Armistice Station for two months.

No one knew who shot the Neyk. America's reputation, never the best in that part of the world, plummeted. Even her allies walked a careful line between disbelief and condemnation. A careful 'no comment' was the best the Australians could muster, stuck as they were sharing the Indian Ocean with the most offended country.

The Brits looked side-eyed at everyone and ran a scheduled training exercise with the French. The Russians laughed behind their hands and sold India four more *Akula*-class attack submarines. Professional navies didn't kill civilians. And when they did, everyone expected their governments to own up.

At least the ongoing discussion over who *else* might have shot took the spotlight off why *Kansas* didn't shoot. Stuck in between a furious captain and a confused-but-restless crew, Alex started to think his career might survive this inferno.

He was wrong.

Kennedy's ambition to *matter* during his command tour remained. He couldn't shoot terrorists, but he *could* get Admiral Hamilton's attention. Otherwise, he might wither and die in obscurity, and heaven forbid *that* happen. For that, he needed a convenient scapegoat, a way to make himself look better than the rest of the fuckups on *Kansas*. So, he filed charges against Alex the day before Alex transferred.

Noncompliance with procedural rules.

Conduct unbecoming an officer and gentleman.

Failure to obey order or regulation.

Misbehavior before the enemy.

Hamilton threw the last charge out, since the entire point of this disaster was that the Neyk Four was never anyone's *enemy*. But she convened Admiral's Mast for the rest the next day, after a quick consultation with one of the many legal officers still at her disposal.

Alex barely got two hours' notice, learning just as he left *Kansas* for the last time. At least his bags were packed and off the boat. He had a room over at the Bachelor's Officers' Quarters until his flight out, and he already turned over his duties to his relief. Somewhere, there was a voice telling him to be grateful for small favors.

He ignored it and headed over to Hamilton's office, located in a small green building buried between shipping containers. His dress blues were packed already; if she didn't like hammering Alex while he wore khakis, that was her problem.

Once there, an aide pointed him to a waiting area full of furniture that went out of style with the Cold War. Alex cooled his heels there for a half hour past the time his orders told him to arrive, watching Kennedy and a few others prance into the office proper. Kennedy's smirk could have poisoned toxic gas.

"It's horseshit that the captain never did the paperwork for you to put on commander, sir," Master Chief Casey said as he elbowed past Hamilton's yeoman.

Alex sighed. "I'll put it on at my next command. I'll still get paid on time."

"Still horseshit." Casey shook his head.

"What are you doing here, Master Chief?" Alex asked.

"Came to testify on your behalf." Casey's face closed off. "Someone ought to."

A lump wedged itself in Alex's throat. "Thank you." He swallowed. "But I don't want you getting tarred by this mess."

"That's my choice, sir."

Sue said the same thing when Alex told her not to come, back on the boat.

"And it's my Mast," Alex replied. "Brought on by my choices."

"You did the right thing and the captain wants to shit on you for it." Casey snorted. "If not for you, we wouldn't be scrambling to prove we *hadn't* shot civilians. We'd be dealing with the fact that we *had*."

"I know," Alex whispered. He clung to that knowledge, but guilt weighed him down. Not for having disobeyed orders, but for distracting the crew at a crucial moment. Would they have detected the mystery shooter if the drama between Alex and Kennedy hadn't been so overwhelming? Could they have stopped the other submarine in time? Would they know who shot, and why?

Or would Kennedy have just shot the Neyk, sinking his career instead of Alex's?

"Then shut your pie hole and let me speak on your behalf, sir. Even Admirals listen to Master Chiefs."

"And even Master Chiefs get screwed." Alex turned to look Casey in the eye. "The fallout will be brutal. The Navy's looking for a punching bag, and I've been elected. There's no reason for you to go down with me."

Casey laughed. "I ain't planning on going down, XO."

"I stopped being your XO when Lieutenant Commander Hunt took over this morning." Alex tried to glare; it was hard.

"Oops."

Alex took a deep breath. "I'm grateful that you want to help. Really, I am. But you can't. I made my choices and I'll take my medicine. I knew what I was getting into."

A long moment of silence stretched between them. "You sure, sir?"

"Positive."

Glowering, Casey nodded, clapped Alex on the shoulder, and left. Alex managed not to sigh in relief. Worst case, he could ride out the next few years as a lieutenant commander. Admiral Hamilton couldn't kick him out of the Navy at Admiral's Mast, although she could keep him from promoting to commander. That would be a blow—Alex's career had been stellar until this train wreck, and he'd worked his ass off to get where he was—but he could survive it. He had four and a half years left to go until he could retire at twenty.

Finally, the yeoman ducked into the office. A few minutes later, she returned, stony-faced. "The Admiral will see you now."

Wave goodbye to your career, asshole, no one said. No one needed to.

Alex followed the yeoman in, back straight. Hamilton, Kennedy, and a pair of staff officers waited for him. Hamilton was a tall woman, with brown hair not yet gone to gray, glasses, and a stern expression.

Her staffers were both dark-haired and good-looking, alike enough to look like sister and brother. Kennedy wore an ill-concealed smirk. Admiral Hamilton glared at Alex like he reeked of trash. There were no other witnesses from *Kansas*, but he hadn't expected any.

A strange feeling bubbled up as Alex listened to the charges.

"On twenty-three November 2037 on board USS *Kansas*, Lieutenant Commander Alex Coleman removed and hid the firing key. This defiance of procedure resulted in chaos in the attack center during a critical moment. When ordered to hand over the firing key, Lieutenant Commander Coleman refused to do so. His reckless actions hazarded the submarine and could have resulted in the death of one hundred and thirty American sailors," Hamilton said.

Kennedy wrote that. No way was the admiral that overblown.

"Do you have anything to say for yourself?" Admiral Hamilton asked.

He could stay silent and accept what happened, but God only knew how much of the story Kennedy had shared. With their VDR erased, no one would see the way Kennedy had shoved him. Still, words echoed in his mind: *Fuck their intentions. I just gave you an order.*

Kennedy wanted to shoot a submarine full of innocent refugees trying to escape religious persecution. The international investigation's findings didn't bear much resemblance to the intelligence *Kansas* received from the French, but it jived all too well with what Seventh Fleet provided while they hunted the Neyk.

Fuck their intentions. I just gave you an order.

Alex swallowed. "Ma'am, I do not deny my actions. I did remove the firing key, and I did not give it back to Commander Kennedy when he demanded it." Saying that Kennedy had shoved him wouldn't help his case, so Alex skipped over it. "However, we were already in communications with the Neyk and they were far enough from Armistice Station that they were not a danger. I felt our duty was to establish their intentions before shooting."

"You don't need to say that your actions are the reason *Kansas* did not shoot." Admiral Hamilton's sigh was sharpened by her glare. "If not for that, the United States would now be defending our destruction of a civilian submarine instead of proving we did not fire those torpedoes."

Kennedy's jaw dropped; Alex felt a surge of vindication.

"*However*, in light of available intelligence, Commander Kennedy's actions were not entirely wrong," she continued. "You, as the Executive Officer, were responsible for reasoning with your CO or carrying out his orders. You did neither."

Alex's heart sank. *Don't be surprised.* He braced himself.

"I find you guilty of Article 98, Noncompliance with procedural rules, and Article 92, Failure to obey order or regulation." Hamilton looked him right in the eye. "I find there is insufficient evidence to support Article 133, Conduct unbecoming an officer and gentleman. I understand you have been selected for promotion to Commander?"

Alex swallowed. "Yes, ma'am."

"I will not remove your selection. However, I will remove you from the list of prospective commanding officers of submarines. You may promote on time, but you will never command a submarine."

Alex's heart plummeted. That was better than he expected. But then why did it burn so much?

"Commander Coleman, your actions may have saved the U.S. Navy a great deal of grief," Hamilton continued. "Perhaps there will come a time when we need someone like you in command of a submarine, but your inability to follow orders is a danger to a peacetime Navy. Such conduct as you displayed cannot be rewarded and will not be ignored. I wish you luck in your future endeavors, but they will not be in the submarine force.

"Dismissed."

Heart heavy, Alex saluted, did an about face, and departed. He should be relieved; he'd finish his career as a commander, which meant a difference in eventual retirement pay of over $600 a month. No one at his next command would know about his shame. But

Admiral Hamilton's mercy killed his life-long dream of commanding a submarine.

Alex had wanted nothing else after touring *Texas* as a kid, back when the boat was a barebones hull sitting in an interior dry dock in Groton, Connecticut. His late father worked at Electric Boat as a welder, and he'd brought Alex and his brother out to see a few submarines. *Texas* had been first. Seeing her drove Alex to earn an NROTC scholarship, to become the first member of his family to graduate college, to have a stellar career where he'd been recommended for his own command.

Now Admiral Hamilton drop kicked him out of submarines. She could do it, too. Everyone knew Hamilton was on the fast track. Rumors said she'd be the first female Chief of Naval Operations. She was already the first female submariner to wear stars, respected by everyone for her ruthless competence. She had the power to make sure he never walked on board a submarine for anything more than a guided tour.

So, that was that. His career would survive, but the best parts of it were dead.

Chapter 7

Interlude

THE KANSAS INCIDENT

Mark Easley, Washington Post

DEC 29th—One month after the sinking of a civilian Neyk Four submarine near Armistice Station, the facts remain murky. The U.S. Navy would have us believe that some unknown rogue element sank that sub—killing all fifteen souls on board—using American torpedoes. On the surface, the U.S. Navy has no reason to sink a civilian submarine. The Navy is even known for canning captains under the ever-popular excuse of a "loss of confidence." Translation: the Navy is happy to blame the captain.

Yet in this case, where blaming *Kansas*' captain would surely save the Navy face, they have not. They refuse to release the sub's video logs. They refuse to allow outside observers—even those from the United Nations!—to interview the crew. What is the Navy hiding? *Kansas* was sent underway immediately after the Navy's internal investigation, and hasn't been heard from since, buried far from the eyes of the world as if we'd forget.

Thirty-six days after the murder of fifteen civilians, it no longer matters. American interests suffer around the world, with the dollar falling and international investors in American-owned underwater stations pulling out. Several underwater habitats, including Agalega Farmstead (near Mauritius) and Rochon Resort (Tromelin) have suffered hostile takeovers in which American investors were ousted by their French, Russian, and Indian counterparts. Tourists with American passports are now barred from Rochon Resort—just like Armistice Station.

The '*Kansas* Incident' continues to spark protests against heavy-handed American diplomacy and lack of accountability worldwide. Thus far, the White House refuses to comment. But with American credibility on the ropes in the eastern hemisphere, this is a troublesome trend.

14 February 2038

There were protestors on the pier.

The Seychelles were the crème de la crème of liberty ports on a Western Pacific deployment. Tropical islands with beautiful beaches and multiple casinos were paradise after being stuck on a nuclear submarine for sixty-four days straight.

Master Chief Chinedu Casey already had a hotel room with a view booked, one right on the water where he could wade out his fucking door into nirvana. Hell, the *smell* of the island had him all hot and bothered—he was ready to get off this goddamned boat. *Kansas* wasn't what she used to be.

But they'd barely got the lines across before the locals showed up, angry and shouting out beyond the Entry Control Point. Subs didn't often get to pull into the Seychelles, so at first, Casey thought they were just there to stare. No such luck.

"You see those signs?" Casey snorted. "'Americans go home.' 'Americans aren't wanted.' 'Americans' *fucking* 'kill civilians.'"

Kansas' new XO, Lieutenant Commander Alison Hunt, grimaced. She was a little woman, competent and sharp-witted. "You don't know they mean us, COB."

"Ain't no coincidence, ma'am." He glared at a pair of protestors waving a yellow sign, one he hadn't wanted to read: *Kansas Killers.*

"They'll get bored and go home."

"And until they do, we can't put down liberty call." Casey wanted to throw things. "Gonna go over like a lead balloon. Long underways ain't nothing. Crew needs a break from the tension."

"I know." Hunt tucked a strand of blonde hair behind one ear when it escaped from her bun. "Can't be helped."

"They're still fucking there, aren't they?"

The new voice made Casey turn to look at Commander Chris Kennedy as his captain came up the ladder from below, scowling. "Ungrateful shits."

Hunt gulped. "Captain, we all know that—"

"You don't know jack." Kennedy gestured rudely at the crowd. "You weren't here. That pisspot coward, Alex Coleman, was in your job, and if not for him, everything would've been fine."

Translation: if not for him, we would *have killed the civilians everyone thinks we did,* Casey didn't say, resisting the urge to hit something. Maybe he should've said something at Commander Coleman's Admiral's Mast; he might've pissed off the admiral and been kicked off this miserable shitcan of a submarine.

But someone had to take care of his boys and girls, so god damnit, Casey would. "You want me to talk to the Chief of the Guard, sir? The Seychelles police might be able to chase these guys off."

"Fat chance. Half of them probably are the local police, rounded out with some curious fingerfucking tourists."

Casey's jaw hurt. "The tourists worry me more. They don't have jobs to go to."

"Fuck them. Fuck—" The sharp ringing of a cell phone cut in; Kennedy snarled another curse and then thumbed it on. "Commander Kennedy speaking."

Two seconds into the call, Kennedy's brow furrowed, creating that little line in the middle of his forehead that screamed temper tantrum. Casey'd worked for this CO for four months now. Kennedy was smart—maybe too smart. Problem was the man didn't want to contain his emotions. A five-year-old would've pouted less.

"Yes, ma'am." Kennedy's voice was flat, but his lips curled into a silent snarl. "I understand." A long silence. "We can be underway within two hours, Admiral."

Kennedy almost threw the phone in lieu of hanging it up; Casey shifted right, in case he needed to dodge. Lieutenant Commander Hunt, less accustomed to riding the boss' emotional roller coaster, asked:

"Underway, Captain? We just pulled in."

"That was Admiral Hamilton." Kennedy spat, missing the water. The glob hit the hull, oozing slowly downwards as Casey scowled. "Some numbnuts pencil pushing weenie decided to cancel our port visit because the locals are *offended*. Cowards."

Hunt's jaw dropped. "And they couldn't can-ex things *before* we went to the trouble of mooring a sub here?"

Bang! Casey's eyes snapped to the crowd as bright light flashed just on this side of the fence. "Would you look at that? Some enterprising soul figured out bottle rockets. Hell of a way to make us feel welcome."

"Go home Americans, go home!" Someone in the crowd started it up like a goddamned football chant.

"They're good at that," Hunt muttered.

Kennedy just glared at the crowd and swore.

Kansas got underway two hours and thirty-nine minutes after mooring at Port Victoria, Seychelles, running away with her metaphorical tail between her legs. U.S. diplomats tried to spin the exit into respecting their international partners' wishes.

Some believed them.

Other nations watched...and waited.

U.N. HUMAN RIGHTS COUNCIL CONDEMNS NEYK SINKING

Erin Steeple, New York Times

FEB 19th—the November 2037 "*Kansas* Incident" sparked four separate international investigations, but the latest one has the biggest sting. This morning, upon formal completion of the joint French and Indian investigation, the United Nations Human Rights Council formally condemned the United States for the sinking of a civilian-crewed Neyk Four submarine in the Indian Ocean, just miles away from underwater powerhouse Armistice Station.

This investigation cites the use of American torpedoes to sink the submarine as the deciding factor. No other ships or submarines within one hundred miles of Armistice Station were armed with the U.S. Navy's Mark 48 CBASS torpedo. The torpedoes were also fired from the same bearing as USS *Kansas*, the nuclear fast attack submarine sent specifically out to find said Neyk. The U.N. Human Rights Council correctly notes that no other ship or submarine *could* have fired upon the Neyk from that position.

India has demanded reparations be paid to the families of the civilians on board the submarine, nine of which were Indian nationals. The crew consisted of natives of Sri Lanka (two), and Malaysia (four). Both

> nations have added their votes to such a proposal, which France has taken to the U.N. Security Council.

> Needless to say, the United States has vetoed the Security Council from discussing the matter. However, America's influence with the Human Rights Council never recovered from its low point in the 2020s. The Human Rights Council plans to publish a manifesto condemning the "cold-blooded and mercenary actions of the crew and commanders of USS *Kansas*" by the end of the week.

22 March 2038

"It's a good thing we're here, because *Jimmy Carter* is too old for this shit." Lieutenant (junior grade) Maggie Bennet grinned and brushed wayward black curls away from her face as she checked the depth on the chart.

Two hundred feet under the keel. *Not bad.*

USS *Parche* (SSN 845) crept along at barely one knot, just a smidgen faster than the current near the bottom of the South China Sea. She was invisible, probably the quietest attack submarine ever built by the United States Navy.

And there was stiff competition.

"Even a deaf sonarman's figured that one out." Her department head and *Parche's* weapons officer, Lieutenant Angela Purnell, leaned casually against *Parche*'s periscope stand. "She got spotted back in November. Indians had her all dialed in."

"Everyone knew what she was. No one knows about us."

Maggie felt the familiar thrill roll down her spine. USS *Parche* was the Navy's newest spy submarine, with dozens of listening systems hidden inside a standard-looking *Cero*-class hull. Her antennas even appeared the same as those of her sisters, at least at a distance. But they were far more sensitive.

A run-of-the-mill *Cero*-class sub was designed with spying as a primary mission, but *Parche* dialed that up several notches. She could tap underwater communications cables, launch and recover drones for audio/visual eavesdropping, and had special thrusters to allow her to hover in shallower water than the larger—and obsolete—*Jimmy Carter* could ever dream of.

Three months into her first deployment, *Parche* already gathered critical data on French-Indian manufacturing agreements, along with some Russian language transmissions they'd yet to translate.

Maggie didn't speak Russian, though she was tempted to learn. Right after she transferred to Intelligence.

Maggie's division officer tour on *Parche* taught her that submarines, as exciting and as interesting as they could be, were not her place. She enjoyed driving a sleek attack submarine and indulged in infrequent dreams about what commanding one might be like, but what she *really* burned to do was intelligence work.

Unfortunately, today Maggie was a submariner and *Parche* had a dedicated intelligence detachment made up of actual intelligence officers and specialists. Some days she got to watch; others, she got to play. Working side-by-side with them made Maggie realize what she wanted to do with her career.

"Head in the clouds again?" Lieutenant Purnell asked, smiling.

"Just thinking, ma'am." Maggie kept one eye on the depth gauge while *Parche* lurked in the middle of the South China Sea. "We started deployment eavesdropping off Mumbai, and now we're watching the biggest Chinese fleet deployment since...ever? Makes you feel like a ping pong ball."

"Ours is not to reason why." Purnell shrugged. "But if it annoys you so much, feel free to step outside and tell the Taiwanese to stop trying to silently takeover underwater stations out here."

Parche's current station was a mere twelve nautical miles away from Feng Station, the so-called jewel of the Formosa Strait. One of the newest—but biggest—underwater habitats in the area, Feng Station was the fourth largest oil producer in the world. Technically, the station was independently owned, but with 47% Chinese investors and 42% Taiwanese, it bore watching.

Not that *Parche* would do anything if the Taiwanese-North Korean coalition tried to snag this station like it did two others. Short of being shot at herself, *Parche* would merely listen.

"Technically, they bought out investors in the other two and then kicked the Chinese out as majority owners."

Purnell snorted. "Tell that to the Chinese."

Needless to say, the Chinese objected to what the government of Taiwan—which China still called an illegitimate rebellion—dismissed as legal business shenanigans. China saw nefarious intentions everywhere...and Maggie wasn't sure they were wrong. Decades of living with the threat of Chinese invasion made Taiwan a bit touchy.

"I think that's their answer." Maggie pointed at the plot, where two Chinese aircraft carriers were surrounded by no fewer than thirty escort ships. Thirty-three, at Maggie's last count.

"They say it's an exercise."

"Ma'am, if you believe that, I've got an underwater gold mine I'd like to sell you. In the arctic." Maggie snickered.

"Hey, you never know what they might find there. You remember when they found oil off the coast of Connecticut? That—"

"Conn, Sonar, rocket ignition, multiple rocket engine ignitions!" the voice of Chief Wong, *Parche's* senior sonar tech, blared out of the speaker between the two officers. "Someone's shooting missiles!"

"*What?*" Purnell wheeled around, her dark eyes wide.

Maggie's heart hammered into her throat so quickly that she stopped breathing.

"Chinese breaking radio silence," the intelligence watch reported, scribbling translations frantically. "Target is Zuoying Naval Yard."

"Make sure you're recording this," Purnell snapped. She turned to Maggie. "Wake up the captain. I think she might want to know that we're smack in the middle of what's looking a lot like World War Three."

Maggie was wrong about war.

For the moment.

PART 2: HONESTY

Chapter 8

On The Brink

6 April 2038, Armistice Station

Two lonely plastic-wrapped crates stood separate from the hundred-plus pallets unloaded from M/V *Calliope*, tucked off to the side as if forgotten. The two crates' shipping labels were orange instead of blue, and they lacked a triangle-shaped stamp, unlike the bulk of *Calliope's* loadout.

The nine-hundred-foot-long container ship moored port side to on pier four, berth 1, of Armistice Station's TRANSPLAT (Transportation Platform) Seven. The four piers stuck out like spindles from the round TRANSPLAT, which sported a helicopter landing pad, a small communications shack, and a double-sided elevator bank. Buoys marked the approaches to the platform, and seven identical TRANSPLATs lay in the distance, most visible on a clear day. Armistice Station was the only underwater habitat in the world with over four such platforms, and hers covered almost two square nautical miles, three times that of her counterparts.

Armistice Station billed itself a beacon of free enterprise and human ingenuity. You could buy and sell anything on Armistice Station, gamble, seek companionship, see the latest shows, or even ride an underwater roller coaster. Forgiving station regulations made it a waypoint for an enormous amount of freight and passenger traffic, too. Occupying prime real estate in the middle of the Indian Ocean meant Armistice Station's GSP, or Gross Station Product, was higher than that of many small nations.

"You missed these two." Damien Richelieu, a tall, swarthy man dressed in black, pointed at the two orange-labeled crates.

"Sir?" *Calliope's* logistics officer fidgeted.

"They're not on my manifest."

The logistics officer's eyes went wide. He was taller than Damien, but Damien looked like he owned a private gym or two. The logistics officer gulped. "Those are a...private delivery, Mr. Richelieu."

"Are they." Storm clouds gathered in Damien's gray eyes, making the officer stumble a step backwards. "WAAS"—he pronounced it *ways*—"paid for your cargo."

"Not...all of it?"

Damien glowered. The officer crept back another step, and Francis Bradshaw sighed from his spot near the head of the pier. Time to save the poor fool. *Story of my life.*

Not that he'd have it any other way. Francis Bradshaw liked to think of himself as an entrepreneur, albeit on a limited scale. He was unremarkable looking: skinny, shorter than average, and with dark hair and freckles he wished he'd grow out of since they made him look about twelve. Unfortunately, by age twenty-six, they were there to stay.

"They're my shipment, sorry." He breezed forward, one hand held out in welcome. "I didn't realize WAAS had stuff on *Calliope*."

"It's damn hard for any company to miss WAAS." Damien crossed his arms, ignoring Bradshaw's hand.

He felt his smile go wooden. WAAS, or the Worldwide Acquisition And Services group, was a relative newcomer to international commerce, founded in 2034 by a group of people whose underwater get-rich-quick schemes worked out far too well. New or not, WAAS was a powerhouse. Its cargos only amounted to five percent shipped on the high seas, but the company owned *sixty* percent of the cargo travelling to and from underwater stations. Not to mention the seventeen—or was it eighteen?—minor underwater stations WAAS owned outright. Armistice Station was too big for WAAS to spread its influence *too* far...but they still owned a significant piece of the pie.

The Rush to the Ocean Floor opened up undersea commerce in a big way—to realtors, miners, shipping companies, undersea farming, and even your average mom-and-pop business with a bit of extra cash. Advances in technology meant farming, mining, and even *living* underwater was cheaper and easier than ever, and the late 2020s saw a boom in ocean floor business. Armistice Station was the biggest undersea station in the world, but there were hundreds more. All with their own unique flavor.

"I'm not a company." Bradshaw held his hands up, trying to look innocent. "Just a guy who ships stuff in for friends."

"Friends?" Damien made the word sound so dirty.

"Yeah." Bradshaw shrugged. He didn't need to explain himself to this guy, but he *did* need to end this conversation in a hurry and get back to work. Thank goodness he left his stupid uniform behind! "I don't buy anything of your caliber. Mostly cheap stuff. Not the cool imports."

Everyone knew that WAAS sold the stuff you couldn't get elsewhere. Stuff that wasn't *legal* in most countries, particularly the States. Extra-risque porn, vape pods of questionable legality, recreational substances...underwater stations in international waters had few restrictions, and WAAS was the biggest seller. It was one reason tourists flocked to Armistice Station—that, and the lure of the world's biggest underwater habitat, casino, amusement park, and undersea mining area all rolled into one spider-like blob on the ocean floor. Problem was, Bradshaw sold the same stuff—to a much more limited audience.

"Right," Damien drawled. Then he turned back to the orange-labeled crates. "Shouldn't be a problem to open them up, then, right?"

"What?" Bradshaw caught his breath. "I mean—yeah, we could, but it'd be a copper-plated bitch to repack, and I've got to get back to work."

Technically, he was already late. But *Calliope's* crew sucked at keeping to schedules. *I should've asked for leave today*. Too late for that thought. Unless he could text Lieutenant Lin and ask for some special liberty...?

"Ask me if I care." Damien's smile was wolfish and sent a chill down Bradshaw's spine.

"Isn't a little guy like me beneath your notice?" Bradshaw tried not to squirm. Showing the local WAAS bully that those crates were full of restricted adult videos and Cherry-*plus* vape pods wasn't smart.

If anyone from back home asked Bradshaw what that *plus* was, he'd play dumb. Damien would know, however. WAAS sold the same products at twice the price he hawked them for.

"Of course not." Damien loomed forward; the logistics officer fled. "Nothing's beneath WAAS's notice." He smiled coldly, walking over to Bradshaw's precious crates. "Including import fees."

"I paid those already." Bradshaw tried not to swallow. Importing goods onto Armistice Station cost a decent chunk of change—more than he wanted to pay, but smuggling was the one thing frowned upon in this place.

"Yeah?" Damien tore the orange labels right off. "Prove it."

"You can't do that!"

"Do what?" Damien shot him a grin and then turned to shout at two of the station's receiving agents. "Hey, boys, we've got a smuggler here!"

"What? No!" Bradshaw turned to the station employees, one of which he knew well. Evette Thayer had been on Armistice Station two years longer than Bradshaw, and they played in the same poker league. "Evette, dude, you know I'm not—"

"You got your manifests, Frannie?" she asked, peering at the crates. Damien didn't even bother to hide the orange labels crumbled up in his left hand.

"*He* took them." Bradshaw hated that stupid nickname. An idiot in their poker league stuck *Frannie* on him a year ago, and it stuck like a bad smell.

Evette glanced at Damien, who smirked.

"I don't see nothin'." She shrugged. "You know that means we've got to impound your shipment and take you in."

"I know that means WAAS pays you off, yeah." Sighing, Bradshaw threw one last look at the crates. He might get them back if he paid the fines fast enough, but the station probably'd auction them off to the highest bidder. Which would be WAAS. As usual.

"C'mon," Evette said. "Don't make this harder than it has to be. I don't want to cuff you or anything."

He groaned. "Fine, let's just get it over with."

Evette led the way off the platform. Bradshaw managed not to look back at Damien Richelieu's gloating face, but he *did* hear the crates pried open.

Shit, how was he going to explain this to the dozen people he promised Cherry-*plus* to?

The television in USS *Fletcher's* wardroom showed the Armed Forces News Network, which usually featured silly feel-good pieces about life in the Navy. The fluff felt a little more alien these days, what with tensions rising in the Indian Ocean *and* the South China Sea, but that only meant AFN doubled down on the specials about uniform changes or haircut regulations.

But a satellite uplink to local news channels was hard to get when your ship pounded across the ocean at twenty-five knots, covering 600 nautical miles every day, and AFN was always available. AFN also poached news from a variety of sources, which those who endured the optimistic crap could catch up on world news.

This snippet sounded like it was borrowed from the BBC. The anchor was better dressed—and better spoken—than her American counterparts.

"Today, the United States vetoed a resolution from the rest of the United Nations Security Council. The proposed resolution was backed by all member states of the Security Council, including three of the other four permanent members: China, France, and Russia. The UK abstained from the vote.

"The proposed resolution condemned the United States for meddling in the growing Chinese Civil War with surprisingly strong language. As most viewers know, tensions between the two Chinas escalated two weeks ago, when the People's Republic of China claimed that Taiwan provided assistance to North Korean forces in capturing two underwater stations claimed by China. Taiwan's vehement denial of the charges ended in the Battle of the Formosa Strait, where an attempted amphibious attack on Taiwan ended in a bloody stalemate.

"The United States immediately moved to aid Taiwan, leading to the current standoff in the Security Council. This seems to be yet another flashpoint in an already-troubled region. Skirmishes in the Indian Ocean and South China Sea continue, with loss of life and property damage mounting—

"Captain?"

Commander Nancy Coleman, commanding officer of USS *Fletcher*, looked away from the television on *Fletcher's* starboard wall. She was a good-looking woman with long brown hair and sharp green eyes. Nancy was the kind of captain who radiated strength; she was a steady and practical sort, with a strong sense of fairness her crew loved. She was alone in the wardroom until her operations officer, Lieutenant Viola Hawkins, walked in. Viola was a short woman, built like a barrel and twice as tough. Nancy could almost look her in the eye while seated.

"What is it, Viola?"

"There's been a skirmish near Diego Garcia." Viola chewed her lip. "The Indian Navy fired on *Sam Nunn* and *Spruance*."

"What?" Nancy came out of her chair so fast she almost fell down, dropping the romance novel she was reading between news segments.

"Both took damage. *Spruance* has a fire amidships, but it's under control. *Sam Nuun* damaged an Indian destroyer before everyone withdrew." Hand shaking, Viola extended the classified message tablet.

Nancy took the tablet automatically. Her hands felt cold. *Spruance* and *Sam Nuun* were *Arleigh Burke*-class destroyers. They were five hundred feet of pure warfighting power, equipped with a high-powered phased array radar, ninety-six vertical launch cells for missiles, torpedoes, and a five-inch gun.

Arleigh Burkes were the Swiss Army knives of the U.S. Navy, capable of shooting down ballistic missiles, sending Tomahawks ashore, defending an aircraft carrier, or even duking it out with other surface ships or submarines. But they'd never fired a shot in anger at another warship. Until now.

The message didn't say much, other than reiterating India's demand that the United States and United Kingdom evacuate the base at Diego Garcia. India was the region's biggest supporter of independence for the Chagos Archipelago, but the U.K. thus far refused to leave.

"Shit," she whispered. "This is not what we need right now."

"No kidding, ma'am." Viola grimaced. "We're rushing to defend Taiwan, and now we're shooting at the Indians?"

"We better hope that blows over." *The Navy isn't what it used to be*, Nancy didn't add. The U.S. Navy was still big and mean—but they weren't alone. Exploiting undersea resources meant nations like India, France, and Russia had a lot more money to burn...and they spent it on ships and submarines. Newer ones. She shook her head. "No one wants a war."

Even if we aren't the meanest kids on the block these days.

Viola fidgeted. "You sure that applies to China, Captain?"

"China v. Taiwan's been brewing for decades." Nancy shrugged to cover her racing heart.

Ten years ago, it looked like China and Taiwan might come to a peaceful agreement. But revenue from ocean floor mining gave Taiwan the money to stand up to their larger neighbor, and suddenly, the game changed. The Indian Ocean and South China Sea were rich in both tapped and untapped resources...and thus, particularly volatile. Everyone in the Navy knew war would come. It was only a matter of time.

"Yeah, and we're stuck in the middle," Viola replied.

Nancy grimaced but didn't comment. Her opinion didn't matter. What mattered was that the U.S. Navy would stand shoulder-to-shoulder with their Taiwanese brethren, just as they had for decades. Even if it meant threatening the Indians along the way.

There were times Nancy hated this job.

"Any new orders from *Enterprise?*" she asked.

Fletcher was running point for the *Enterprise* Strike Group. The carrier and her other escorts—two other destroyers and a cruiser—steamed ten miles behind *Fletcher*. Rumor said the *Tripoli* Expeditionary Strike Group would join them soon, but *Tripoli* and her escorts were down near Australia and would need more time to arrive. Meanwhile, *Enterprise* turned and burned to meet up with the USS *Gerald R. Ford* Strike Group, based in Japan and a lot closer to the South China Sea than the Northern Arabian Gulf deployment Nancy's crew departed on two months earlier.

"Just to watch for submarines. Admiral McNally's flown a dozen messages asking for an attack sub to join up with us, but so far, no dice."

"Crap time for *Missouri* to bend a screw, yeah."

Some people said *Missouri's* captain exaggerated the damage to get away from Admiral McNally's micromanaging. Rear Admiral Jeff McNally was a submariner, not a surface warfare officer. He didn't know jack about deploying destroyers, and it showed. His chief of staff, the number two guy at the Strike Group, was also a submariner...but at least he knew what he didn't know. And at least the pair generally concentrated on making *Missouri* miserable, not *Fletcher.*

So far. Nancy suppressed a grimace, glaring at the blue wardroom tabletop. Not having a sub along opened the strike group up to the threat of enemy submarines, and no surface officer in their right mind liked that, even in pseudo peacetime. She knew more about submarine operations than most of her brethren—it came from being married to a submariner—and not having *Missouri* along made her uneasy.

Worse yet, *Fletcher* wasn't an *Arleigh Burke*-class destroyer; she was the fourteenth ship of the newer *O'Bannon*-class. But in this case, newer didn't mean better.

Designed to be built quicker than their older counterparts, *Fletcher* and her sisters lacked a towed sonar array. Their onboard sonar worked well enough at short range—and low speeds—but racing along like this left *Fletcher* deaf. Only a submariner would stick *Fletcher* on point and keep both *Arleigh Burkes* in close.

"I'll be in CIC if you need me, ma'am," Viola said.

Nancy looked up. "Twitchy, are we?"

"A little."

Me, too, a captain couldn't say. Not one who'd been in command for only four months. Nancy had to look calm and confident. Appearing that way while making sense out of an idiot admiral's orders was hard, but this wasn't Nancy's first time working for a moron. Surface Warfare Officers were experts at getting the job done with too few resources. She'd manage.

Bradshaw's in the slammer again.

The text gleamed on his screen, cheerfully unaware of the trouble it caused, already awaiting him when Alex got back from the pool. He groaned, not even bothering to muffle the sound. No one here knew him; he was just one more guy in a locker room that held a hundred on a slow day. No need for the image of the perfect naval officer here. Besides, Alex felt like he ran his command by cell phone, even underwater.

Command. *Yeah.* It even came with the fancy title of *Officer-In-Charge, Naval Detachment Armistice Station.* But this was the only command he'd ever get, thanks to Chris Kennedy. In charge of a team of five officers in a sea of thousands of civilians, stuck on a station that had a hate-on for the U.S. Navy in particular. Joy.

It's too easy to do the right thing, Staff Sergeant Walters said back at the Wick when Alex was young and impressionable. But no one talked about the consequences, did they? Alex shook himself and closed his gym locker. Bitterness was pointless. So, he sighed, tied his shoes, and picked up his phone. He hit the dial button as he rose from the locker room bench and waited for the person on the other end to pick up. "What'd Bradshaw do now?"

"Sounds like smuggling. Again," Lieutenant Commander Stephanie Gomez replied. Alex could almost hear her rolling her eyes. Steph was the second-ranking member at his tiny command, billeted as the detachment's operations officer, but also dual hatted as Alex's unofficial XO.

"Fucking fantabulous. Where's Jesse?" Alex headed out of Sea Quest Fitness's locker room. This was what he got for going for a swim during lunch.

"On the phone trying to unfuck the stores loadout for *Medgar Evers*."

"I thought they underway an hour ago?"

Alex exited the fitness center, entering a domed walkway that wouldn't seem out of place in some stateside mall. Its name was Newell Tube, and only the blue tint of the lighting hinted that they were underwater. Dodging a pair of tourists, Alex hung a right and headed towards the nearest "outertube" joiner, or station. Tubes were the stations' walkways, all named for famous ocean explorers, lined with shops, entertainment venues, and airlocks.

The outertubes, however, were *outside* the station. Their cars travelled on a track sheltered by a flexible housing that looked like a playground tunnel. Those tunnels looped around the station, forming a multi-lined underwater high-speed rail.

The line at the Newell station was fifty deep; Alex grimaced and bypassed it. Walking back towards the station's center would take forever, particularly at the height of tourist season. Back when he was a tourist, he hadn't known ways around the crowds, but after months on the station, Alex knew every shortcut.

"They got delayed when some French frigate poached their vegetable loadout," Steph said.

"Today's a great day, huh?" Alex asked. "Jesse looks like he's going to be done anytime soon?"

"Not unless he bribes the station manager." Steph's snort was audible. "And we all know how much Madame Ledoux loves the U.S. Navy."

"Hey, at least she likes you more than she does me." Alex slipped between two street vendors, one hawking earrings and the other stuffed animals. He was half-tempted to pick up one of those overpriced and glittery dolphins, but his daughters were too old.

"Jesse's the only one she likes, sir."

"True." Alex headed up Picard Tube, resolutely not wondering if his supply officer *had* bribed the station manager. They probably had the budget for it, but the U.S. government got weird about things like that.

Lieutenant Jesse Lin was a perpetual smiler good at making friends, so he probably hadn't bribed anyone, not that it would be a surprise in this place. Jesse was also Logistics Specialist Second

Class Bradshaw's direct superior, making him the doubly logical choice for this job.

Alas, Jesse was unavailable.

"I'll go fetch our miscreant child," Alex said, slipping into line for the outertube at Picard. Most of that tube was under construction, and so the wait was much shorter. Hopefully, that wasn't because the last car just departed, but that would be his luck, wouldn't it?

The outertubes didn't have a set schedule, but one showed up every ten minutes. Outertube joiners peppered the edges of the gigantic underwater station, and their cars followed multiple and confusing tracks. Locals mastered those within a few months; tourists never did.

Steph chuckled. "Good luck, boss."

"Thanks. I think." Alex hung up and resisted the urge to slump into a nearby wall.

Being the boss wasn't all perks. Armistice Station was a nice place to visit—doubly so with the amusement park open—but it was a crummy place to live. Particularly with his wife at sea and his teenage daughters back home in Connecticut. Shore duty was meant to be a chance to spend time with your family, to recharge.

So much for that.

Alex *could've* resigned his commission when he was drop-kicked out of the submarine community. But he took his medicine, and here he was.

Squaring his shoulders, Alex stepped into the outertube car. This was his job, and he would do it—

His phone rang again, making him jump. "What's up, Steph?" It wasn't like her to call back so quickly. Steph generally preferred to text.

"Message traffic just came in concerning the IO Peace and Cooperation Summit. It's back on again, starting in three days. Also thought you might want to know that they swapped out Admiral Wongchai for Admiral Hamilton as senior navy rep."

"Say *what*?"

Chapter 9

Change of Plans

The outertube ride to the brig was long enough for Alex to finish his call and start stewing. The Indian Ocean Peace and Cooperation Summit—known to the media as the Great Summit—had been cancelled twice in the last two weeks, the last time "for good." But now it was back on, due to start in *three goddamn days*, all with his favorite admiral playing a major part.

He was so screwed.

First, however, he had a job to do. Getting into the brig required a special code, but one of the few useful perks of Alex's job was that he got administration codes for most parts of the station. There weren't guards like you'd see at a jail, just three layers of security systems that all required that same code. Once through the main doors, Alex faced the front desk, where two uniformed security specialists sat.

Evette Thayer was the senior of the pair this shift, which meant Alex didn't have to deal with the Station Manager. *Small blessings.* Evette sat at the security desk near the station's small brig, playing with her phone. She was older than Alex, with dark skin and eyes, and liked to vape a pipe of something that smelled like peaches. Most importantly, Evette was tolerant of miscreants like Bradshaw and one of the nicest people on the station.

Which meant she didn't hate the *entire* U.S. Navy for killing fifteen people next door to this station five months ago. Telling anyone on Armistice Station that some mystery submarine shot two American torpedoes was a waste of time; Alex learned to live with the barbs.

"Hey, Evette." He shoved his hands in his pockets. "What's the damage this time?"

"Smuggling fine. Third offense, so it's six hundred bucks," Evette replied and then arched an eyebrow. "Beats killing people."

Alex sighed. "Can you release him to me? I'll make sure he pays."

"Normally, no, but since we all know you navy types can't leave, sure." She smiled. "Sides, it's not Frannie's fault he got mixed up with WAAS."

"WAAS? Really?" Alex tried to steer clear of how station politics and money braided together into a great big ball of riches. He was here to look out for U.S. Navy interests—and because it was the *last* place he wanted to be, so naturally the first place Admiral Hamilton decided to send him.

"Yup." Evette puffed her vape pipe.

"I suppose I shouldn't be surprised." Sighing, Alex signed the release form, glancing around the little brig. It was probably the ugliest place on the station, all solid bars and drab grays, but even the waiting area had viewscreens to the outside sea. Both waiting benches were padded plastic and more comfortable than they looked. Settling in to wait for Bradshaw to saunter out of the cell, Alex crossed his ankles and pretended not to notice how every security worker *other* than Evette ignored him.

"Hey, sir." Bradshaw grinned. "Fancy meeting you here."

"Yeah, fancy that for the fifth time." Alex rose, shaking his head. The other two charges were drunk and disorderly—which, in fairness to Bradshaw, was more like disorderly at a poker game. The young petty officer didn't drink much, but he did love to gamble.

Bradshaw's grin faded. "I'll pay them before the end of the day. Promise."

"Yeah, you'd better, or I'm on the hook for it. And no fucking way am I explaining your bullshit to my wife."

"Could be fun?"

Alex snorted. "Not as much as you think. "She's a SWO. Good with missiles and guns. And you have to salute her, too."

"Okay, I'll pass." Bradshaw smirked. "Sir."

"You know, one of these days, you're going to cause enough trouble to make me do something about it," Alex said.

"C'mon, you know I'm worth my weight in gold. No one's as good at Armistice Station bullshit as I am." Bradshaw held the door open, and they walked through it together, heading for the nearest outertube.

"Which is the reason I haven't kicked your ass out of the Navy yet."

Bradshaw snickered like he knew the threat was hollow. And it was.

The Navy kept an office on Armistice Station mainly to provide a local contact for ships passing through. By all rights, Alex's job should've been a supply officer's post—he mostly made sure ships and subs got the food and stores they ordered, and that sailors didn't trouble the locals. And then dealt with the inevitable fallout drunk or high sailors caused at local business while visiting ships and subs dealt with their troublesome children. Unfortunately, pissing off Admiral Hamilton had its perks, including being stationed three hundred feet underwater and nine thousand miles from home.

He'd been drop-kicked out of the submarine community. Four months into the new job, it still stung.

"You need me to do anything for the summit, sir, or should I shimmy back to my habitat and put a uniform on?" Bradshaw asked as they boarded the outertube car.

Alex cocked his head. "How'd you know it was back on?"

"Little birdy told me." Bradshaw shrugged. "It's back on for Saturday, right? With Rear Admiral Hamilton and whatshisname, the politician, coming."

"In four days." Keeping a professional face on was hard, and Alex gave up after a brief effort. How the fuck did he go from being on track to command a fast attack submarine to dealing out ice cream and playing junior concierge?

If he never saw Admiral Hamilton again, it'd be too soon. Armistice Station wasn't big enough to hide from her. He was the senior representative of the U.S. government, which meant the summit was his problem. *Why the fuck couldn't they appoint an ambassador to this place? It's practically an independent nation. I am not qualified for this bullshit.* He shook himself.

"Get changed and head to the office," Alex said. "I've got to go talk to Madame Ledoux about security arrangements."

Bradshaw didn't need to be told twice before vanishing. Alex, however, headed to the Naval Detachment office, first. He was so glad to be rid of that mess when it was cancelled. First, India refused to attend. Then France took issue with the security arrangements. The United States stood on ceremony and refused to send a delegation of less than fifteen. Australia wasn't invited initially and was mortally offended, while China refused to be in the same room as Taiwan. Then the French killed the whole thing a second time by bringing up the *Kansas* Incident and torquing the U.S. President off. Now it looked like everyone *except* the belligerents would attend—but, wait. That wasn't true. India and the U.S. shot at one another just that morning.

This was going to go over as well as shit on a shingle.

Barracuda departed Saint-Denis, Réunion, in the dead of night. Saint-Denis was the capital of the French overseas region in the Indian Ocean, a hub that grew more important with each passing day. The meat of France's undersea empire was based in the Mediterranean, but her Indian Ocean holdings were nothing to laugh at. While other European powers decolonized in the mid-twentieth century, France quietly held onto multiple islands off Africa's east coast, and from those islands spawned dozens of undersea stations. Technological developments allowing for easy and safe ocean floor exploitation made all those stations rich. Now, French naval and commercial power reached a higher peak than the days of Napoleon.

That point of national pride did nothing to improve Jules Rochambeau's mood.

"This is foolishness," he said to his new first officer, Commander Camille Dubois. Camille simply smiled.

"Think of your reputation should you be able to pull it off."

"Mais, non. Flattery will get you nowhere." Jules sat back in his chair with a huff. "I am a submarine commander, not an infantryman."

"Infantrymen would poke holes in precious bulkheads, mon Capitaine." Her smile turned thin. "Surely they do not expect you to run around shooting like some action hero."

Jules shook his head. "Of course not. Admiral Bernard is not an idiot." Then he glared. "Which is what you want me to admit."

"Oui." She did not bother trying to look innocent. "Do you disagree with the objective?"

"No." He sighed. "I am not certain how I feel about supporting China in their civil war—their territorial ambitions will turn outwards once they defeat Taiwan—but if hegemony is our goal, it must start with Armistice Station."

"And it would not hurt to return to the site of your greatest victory, no?" Her eyes gleamed.

"That was not a victory." Jules scowled. He cared little for the civilians killed in the Neyk Four; collateral damage was inescapable, even in a shadow war. He followed orders, which was enough for his conscience. What he disliked was the secrecy of it all. Jules wanted to defeat his nations' enemies *openly*. And he wanted credit for it.

"Humiliating our American 'friends' is always a victory. I found my own part in it quite sweet."

Jules found Camille a cold fish. He respected her—otherwise, he would not have accepted her as his second-in-command—but his blood ran hotter. Camille was competent but tricky, as dangerous as a domesticated panther. *Perhaps that is good. I might bed her if she frightened me less. Or if I thought she wouldn't betray me if it suited her.* That thought made him smile.

"Alas, we have our orders." He shrugged. "I will follow them, even if I would prefer to visit a different type of humiliation upon the Americans." A wolfish grin. "Such as in the Strait of Malacca."

"Our Indian friends would not take kindly to that," she said. "It might also lead to war."

"No one wants war." Jules waved a hand. "Not a real one. We simply want the Americans to stop meddling in our hemisphere. Once they see that they are no longer the world's superpower, they will retreat."

"If the chaos I witnessed on *Kansas* is any indication, they will not do it well." Camille seemed pleased by this.

Another shrug. "Quel dommage." Such a pity.

Two hours later—after a long time in an uncomfortable waiting area and more fretting than he liked to admit—Alex reached the Station Administrator. Aida Ledoux's job was like being an unelected mayor on steroids. Armistice Station was in international waters and independent, governed only by station regulations and international law. Three thousand people lived and worked on the station, with as many as six times that in transient visitors on any given day. Madame. Ledoux was a busy woman, and Alex rarely saw her unless an American sailor did something stupid.

He never enjoyed their conversations.

"Commander Coleman, I cannot give your people further access to the security systems," she said, not rising from the chair behind her desk. Her office windows went from floor to ceiling, and although their thickness distorted the seascape slightly, the view remained breathtaking. "If I give it to you, there are six *other* countries that will demand the same. We don't have the bandwidth."

Alex pasted on a smile to cover his stomach heaving. "I'm sure that—wait a minute, six *more* countries? Last I knew, only five countries were invited."

Math, Alex was good at. By his count, the U.S., Britain, Australia, India, and France made five. Who were the other two? Had China and Taiwan decided to talk instead of duking it out? *That'll make for ten thousand people dead for no good reason after the Battle of the Formosa Strait, but stranger things have happened.*

"Russia and Japan also have confirmed delegations on the way." Ledoux's too-sweet smile set Alex's teeth on edge. She was a head shorter than him, but three times louder. And meaner. Alex supposed she needed to be to run this place.

He wished she'd offer him a seat, but she never did. Alex could conceal his nerves better when sitting.

Sometimes, he wondered if what happened on *Kansas* cracked his self-confidence. His inability to save the civilians on the Neyk Four still ate at him, even more than his decision not to tell Admiral Hamilton about Kennedy shoving him.

Yet complaining about a little push seemed self-serving. Maybe it could've taken Kennedy down with him, but what was the point? Alex was okay with sacrificing his career to save civilians, but throwing it away for nothing burned.

He still wanted to prove who shot that *Neyk*, but only conspiracy theorists believed it was the French submarine *Barracuda.*

"Right. Thanks." He swallowed the urge to swear. Even more fun. At least the Japanese were still friends. Their navy was pretty good, too. "Can you at least provide an electronically shielded meeting space for our team?"

"I'm afraid they'll have to rent something from one of the hotels. We can't show preference to one delegation over another," she replied.

"Every hotel conference room is booked," Alex said. "It's spring. Every high-end corporation with a couple million bucks to rub together has conferences here."

"I'm sorry, but that is not my problem." Ledoux didn't even try the fake smile again, though she didn't *quite* roll her eyes. "I *trust* you won't do something violent to clear space."

Alex flinched. Ledoux never missed a chance to poke at him for the *Kansas* Incident. She was half-French and one hundred percent convinced that Americans sank the Neyk Four. No amount of explaining could change her mind; Alex stopped trying months ago.

"Sorry, but that's not my style." *If it was, we* would *have sunk that fucking Neyk*, he didn't add.

"Biên sur." She sneered. "So you say."

Two of Ledoux's assistants joined her in glaring from outside the open door. Talk about a no-win situation. Any good tactician knew when to withdraw; Alex was outnumbered and the least popular person in the room.

"Thanks for the help." Turning on his heel, Alex walked out of her office, collecting Steph on his way.

His blonde-haired operations officer was in the waiting area, talking to one of Ledoux's security technicians. Lieutenant Commander Stephanie Gomez was one of the most competent officers he ever had the pleasure to work with. Steph was tall—two inches taller than Alex—tough, and tenacious. She was a good old girl, complete with a southern accent and a love of guns. Alex, born and bred in Connecticut, was her opposite. They clashed over sports, culture, and food—and were friends for life.

"I managed to snag two rooms at the Reunion Hilton for the delegates to sleep in," she said as they walked out. "The security guys *claim* they'll take care of everything, but this thing is less organized than a mud diving contest, sir."

"Tell me about it."

During his two-hour wait, Alex gathered as much data on the new-old summit as he could. Admiral Hamilton and Under Secretary of State Martin Fowler—and their aides—would arrive Friday, one day before the summit began. Getting to an underwater station in the middle of the Indian Ocean was difficult by air—Hamilton and Fowler would have to get on a ship or sub that could use one of the TRANSPLATS.

Helicopters didn't have the legs to get to Armistice Station from Mauritius, the closest land mass. Odds were, they'd join a warship coming out of Diego Garcia...assuming tensions lessened.

Alex forced himself to stop gritting his teeth. That wasn't his problem. His job was to manage an admiral and a politician coming to make peace. *And hotel rooms, meeting spaces, security...the general care and feeding of important people.* This was not why he joined the Navy.

"We'll have to let them camp in our office between sessions." Alex scowled. A small, three desk office space was *exactly* what he wanted to share with Admiral Hamilton. Maybe he could just disappear.

"At least no one can eavesdrop on them electronically?" Steph tried to smile.

"Horseshit." Alex snorted. "Even the *shielded* places leak information like a sieve."

Steph's eyes focused on a family passing to their right, dressed in bright colors and covered in souvenirs from Cousteau's Underwater Adventure Park. "I...might have fixed that a while ago, sir."

Alex stopped cold. "Might." He studied his principal subordinate, who now watched another family, this one speaking rapid French. "Explain."

"I'm kind of good with computers, sir. And I got annoyed when another teenager hacked us. Not that we've got anything important to hide, but still. The kid messed up Suppo's stores lists for *Jason Dunham* before I caught him."

"Is you saying you're 'kind of' good with computers akin to LS2 Bradshaw saying he's 'barely' involved with smuggling?" Alex asked.

She flushed. "It's not really smuggling if there's no laws against anything?"

"Steph, please fucking tell me you're not involved in Bradshaw's little commercial empire." Alex wanted to shake her. Steph was sharp and dedicated, a hell of an officer. She'd have made a good submariner, which was the highest compliment Alex could give to a surface officer. And he never thought her dishonest.

"Not involved, sir. I just wrote him a couple of security programs."

"Is that what skimmers get up to for fun?" Alex asked.

Bradshaw came up in the surface world, too, stationed on ships, not submarines. Alex ignored Bradshaw's wheelings and dealings because the kid was brilliant at his job. But he thought better of Steph.

She shrugged. "This place loses its appeal after the first month, sir."

"Don't I know it." Alex gave her a hard look. "All right. I'll put you in charge of security for our team, but if LS2 does anything stupid—"

"He won't, sir. He's smarter than he lets on."

Alex eyed her. "Suppo says he's disgruntled and getting out of the Navy." Lieutenant Jesse Lin should have been the easiest of his small crew for Alex to identify with. Jesse spent his time split between surface ships and submarines and was an affable, smiling sort of fellow.

"No offense, but Jesse's a brick." Stephanie's grin was quick. "A nice brick, but he's not the most observant cat. He still hasn't cottoned on to ninety percent of Bradshaw's schemes."

Not laughing was hard. "Insulting your fellows is unbecoming of an officer and a lady, you know."

"I'm a SWO, sir. We eat our young."

Alex just shook his head.

Chapter 10

Playing Chess Blindfolded

9 April 2038

"I'll send another message to SURPAC, sir," Captain John Dalton promised as he hung up the phone.

USS *Enterprise's* flag bridge buzzed with activity, but no one approached John as he scowled. Being Rear Admiral McNally's Chief of Staff was exciting—not to mention career-enhancing—when the admiral cooperated. With the strike group's deputy commander home on leave for the birth of his third child, John was the second most powerful man in the *Enterprise* Strike Group, a status he normally reveled in.

Not right now. Admiral McNally was *still* wrapped up in *Missouri's* absence. Yeah, not having a fast attack sub along for the ride created problems. John was a submariner himself, not long removed from command of his own fast attack boat.

But it wasn't the end of the world. The kerfuffle at Diego Garcia was almost nine hundred nautical miles south of their intended track. Damaged Indian ships wouldn't come north to contest *Enterprise's* transit through the SOM, and intelligence said the remaining Indian fleet retreated to port after the scuffle.

Admiral McNally might harp on the danger of a submarine sneaking up to intercept the strike group, but John didn't think that likely. If the Indians had a sub along, the two American destroyers wouldn't have escaped that little battle. India didn't have the most advanced submarines in the world, but they bought a *lot* of them over the last decade, both from Russia and France. Sure, they could wait in the approaches to the SOM, but John doubted it.

No sane Navy wanted to pick a fight inside the SOM, or Strait of Malacca. Combined with the Strait of Singapore, it was one of the Earth's busiest waterways. A quarter of the world's commerce passed through the SOM, over 50,000 ships per year. That came out to an average of almost 400 civilian ships *per day.*

The *Enterprise* Strike Group was peanuts in comparison. A battle in the SOM would kill too many innocents. Even advanced torpedoes missed, sometimes, and missiles...well, missiles liked to shoot the shiniest radar contact they saw when their seekers went live. No one wanted to shoot up civilians by accident.

"One last thing, John," a voice said from behind him.

John rose and turned away from the computer, belated calls of "Admiral's on the bridge!" ringing out from a watchstander behind him. Admiral McNally loved sneaking onto the flag bridge with no one noticing him. Damn him.

"Sir?" he asked. John wasn't frightened of admirals, but military courtesy was military courtesy.

He was the son of an admiral and a general, fully aware of his own competence and firm in the belief that if he did his job well, he should never fear his boss. John might not be the most photogenic guy—good sub food left him with a belly he couldn't shake and hatred for running meant he never tried very hard—but McNally treated you well if you knew your stuff. John did.

"Contact Seventh Fleet, too. Maybe they have someone lurking in the SOM," McNally said.

John shook his head. "I already asked. They said no assets available."

"No assets available." McNally scowled, his voice rising to mock the answer. "Do those idiots *not* realize that destroyers got *shot at* this morning?"

"I doubt they missed it, sir," John said as gently as he could. Diego Garcia belonged to Seventh Fleet, which meant that the Admirals outranking McNally judged McNally's arguments insufficient. McNally knew that, of course. He just didn't like it.

The closer they got to China, the more the admiral's fretting increased. Two weeks ago, McNally would've taken *Missouri's* bent screw philosophically. This was the fifth time he'd brought it up today, and lunch was just over.

"They have *no* idea what we're facing out here." McNally started pacing; staffers buried themselves in their consoles, pretending they couldn't see the boss freaking out. "We're four days out from the SOM. We'll be in *combat* fifty-seven hours after that. And they can't be arsed to give us a fucking submarine? We might as well go dancing naked on the flight deck for all the cover the Navy's giving us!"

"Seventh Fleet says there's two boats coming down with the *Ford* Strike Group."

McNally huffed. "At least that's something. Can't one of them join us sooner?"

"Not without getting past the entire Chinese Navy," John said.

Satellite imagery made the South China Sea look like a parking lot. Every ship the PLAN owned was underway, along with the entire *Republic* of China Navy belonging to Taiwan. Only one major battle happened so far, but the dozen minor skirmishes bothered John. The news claimed both sides were backing off while negotiators went to work, with India acting as an intermediary between the two countries.

John thought the truth was simpler: Taiwan proved her mettle in the Battle of the Formosa Strait, and China wanted to take a moment to reassess. China expected a quick, bloody invasion, and instead got knocked on their collective communist asses. But people and resources were cheap for the world's largest Army and Navy. Everyone knew China would win Round Two.

Which was why *Enterprise* and her cohorts rushed eastwards while *Ford* burned south from Japan. The U.S. and Taiwan were old friends, and no one doubted America would stand by Taiwan. The only question was if they'd have to fight their way through the South China Sea to get there.

"Any submariner worth their salt can sneak past those idiots," McNally said.

John grimaced. "They're good at ASW, sir."

"We're better." McNally's eyes narrowed. "You telling me you couldn't have crept *Cero* under that armada?"

"Probably. But it'd be ugly if they spotted us. Particularly if the politicians still hadn't sorted out our ROE." Peacetime Rules of Engagement were different from wartime rules. Less than three days away from intervening in a shooting war, Washington still dithered over whether China was an enemy or not.

"They're hoping our presence stops the shooting." McNally rolled his eyes. "It probably will. Even China doesn't want to piss us off."

John swallowed. "China's Navy is twice our size these days,"

McNally waved a hand. "Quality trumps quantity, every time. The Chinese are a brown water Navy. They're not in our league. No one is."

John sighed. McNally, now staring at the floor-to-ceiling tactical display, didn't notice. McNally was old school. He grew up in the days where the U.S. Navy was the biggest, baddest player in the world. Commanding the *Enterprise* Strike Group was his first time back at sea since commanding a submarine tender eight years earlier. John, freshly promoted to captain and not long out of command of his own submarine, knew the world changed a lot in that time.

China wasn't the only Navy to worry about. India's buildup was terrifying in scope. France's presence in the Indian Ocean increased ever since the *Kansas* Incident, too. Even Russia—once a paper tiger and now the Bear once more—deployed down here. And no one liked the U.S., except Taiwan and Australia.

Even Taiwan thought *Kansas* sank that Neyk Four. They just couldn't say it without losing American support. John knew better, but how the hell did you prove that to your allies?

"Of course, sir." John wished McNally would leave so he could get back to planning an adequate defense in case someone *did* shoot.

"Take a walk with me, John," the admiral replied. "Captain Edwards invited me to Pri-Fly for flight ops. Learning about carrier operations won't hurt your career at all."

"Lead on, Admiral."

John could carve out contingency planning time later. McNally was right—if John wanted command of his own strike group someday, he needed to start learning now.

Her stateroom on USNS *Amelia Earhart* was bigger than the entire wardroom on the submarine Freddie Hamilton once commanded. A T-AKE, or dry cargo ship, like *Earhart* had three different VIP suites, and as a two star admiral, Winfred Hamilton rated the best.

Unfortunately, even a submariner could only hole up in a stateroom for so long, so she settled into the common area with a book after breakfast. Seeing the sky while underway was a novelty, but part of Freddie longed for the peculiar smell of dirty socks and fried eggs of her last command.

"There you are," her traveling companion said, crossing the room to loom over Freddie on the couch. Martin Fowler sneered. "I thought you'd be on the bridge."

"*Earhart's* crew doesn't need me to micromanage them." Freddie made herself smile. Civilian merchant mariners crewed T-AKEs, with a small navy detail for security. These people knew their business far better than Freddie ever could. She knew seven ways to *sink* a cargo ship, but operating one was not her forte. And who would want to? These things were dreadfully slow.

"*Someone* ought to. They're sloppy," he said.

Martin Fowler was the Under Secretary of State for Arms Control and International Security Affairs, and he fancied himself an expert on the military. Three days in his company proved otherwise, but Freddie was too polite to say so. He was a tall man, with red hair slicked sideways and wore suits more expensive than Freddie's car. They were usually blue, which brought peacocks to mind instead of the patriotic image Fowler probably aimed for.

"They're civilians." She focused on her book, lest she roll her eyes.

"They're still *Navy* civilians. Given the tension in this part of the world, you'd think they'd be on their toes."

"Aren't we here to calm things down?" Freddie slid a bookmark into her novel, looking up as calmly as she could. She couldn't concentrate with this egomaniac around. Hadn't anyone ever taught him that towering over people like this was massively rude?

Fowler huffed. "That's the easy part."

"I'm glad you're confident. Care to make the same wager on the China conflict?" Freddie didn't want to call that a war, not yet.

"SECSTATE is trying to convince the president to let them duke it out without our help." He shrugged. "Interfering will ruin our trade relationship with China."

"If we don't, Taiwan gets curb stomped," Freddie said. Taiwan might have the upper hand now, but in the long run, China's sheer numbers would win.

"Not our problem."

"It is if we don't want World War III to break out!"

"Nobody wants a war," Fowler said. "We're way past that. The U.N. will sort things out between the two Chinas and that will be that."

"Yeah, that's why the president sent *two* carrier strike groups out to help Taiwan." Freddie would give her left leg to be in Jeff McNally's shoes, but he was years her senior. Her next job—if she did this one well—might be command of a carrier strike group. But her second star was too new.

"They'll be recalled." Fowler waved a hand. "It's just a show of force."

"I hope you know something I don't know, Mr. Secretary, because what I read in message traffic sounds a lot less reassuring."

"You military types *always* see war where diplomacy will win," he scoffed. "The Navy's the worst of the bunch, too. How many years have you spent harping on other countries' naval buildups and saying we need to do the same? You *want* a fight."

Freddie blinked. "I wouldn't say—"

"Not that you'd ever get one," Fowler said. "No one in their right minds would put a woman in command where a war might start."

"*Excuse* me?" Freddie's jaw dropped. Was this stuck-up, political creature really going *there*?

"It's nothing personal. It's all political." Fowler laughed, finally backing off a few steps. "Heaven knows, I don't have a problem with women in uniform, but the optics would be terrible if something went wrong."

"The...optics." Freddie ground each word out, her chest tight. She'd been in uniform for over twenty years. The sub community was one of the last corners of the Navy to let women in, but Freddie had been the first woman to command a fast attack submarine.

She'd been the first woman to command a submarine squadron, too, but she'd opened the doors for others! Nineteen women were in submarine command today, with countless others in the pipeline. Women peppered the Navy's hierarchy, too, with thirty-three percent of admirals lacking certain private parts and proud of it.

"Can you imagine how people would freak out if we had a woman in command of one of those strike groups?" Fowler sounded like a two-year-old.

Women in command weren't new in the Navy, but Freddie was used to idiots like this. She smiled her sweetest smile. "I imagine it's hard for some men to deal with."

"It's the *politics*. Men get stupid when women are in danger." He sniffed like she didn't understand his point.

Freddie wanted to decorate the carpet with his face, but admirals didn't get to do the fun stuff. "The ones I've worked with seemed more concerned with my abilities than my lack of gonads, but I suppose the Navy is simpler than politics."

"It is. You leave the heavy lifting in these discussions to me, and we'll be just fine." His smile was patronizing, and he probably thought it kind.

"Of course," Freddie said. "I'm here to advise you, after all."

She could see why the Chief of Naval Operations pulled out of this gig and left Freddie, one of his assistants, holding the bag. Two days on the same ship as Martin Fowler would make Admiral Chan commit murder. Being on the same underwater station as him would send CNO nuclear. Besides, China and Taiwan were the big fish to fry. Compared to that brewing war, a small shooting incident with India was nothing.

Hopefully, Freddie could talk to her opposite number in the Indian Navy and work something out that stopped the shooting before things got worse. If not...she'd help this idiot convince everyone else.

Somehow.

Chapter 11

Disparities

Alex brought his team together for one last planning session on the morning of 9 April, mostly to combat his own jitters. The last three days of scrambling to organize the American end of what the media called The Great Summit left him jumpy and winded.

Maybe the politicians back home didn't want to ruffle feathers, because they opted not to send dozens of government lackeys to Armistice Station. Help would've been nice, though. Alex was no diplomat and didn't care to learn politics.

CNN played on the TV in the corner; Alex snuck a glance at it as his people dropped into chairs. Step was the only one in the office when he arrived, elbows deep in some program or another. He'd learned not to ask.

"India has demanded reparations from the United States for damage to INS Trikand, *the frigate that engaged two American destroyers along with the Indian destroyers INS* Chennai *and* Kochi," a reporter said on the television. A busy military base showed in the background—was that Diego Garcia?

"In a surprising turn of events, India has demanded full sovereignty over the entire Chagos Archipelago, not just Diego Garcia. This stunning demand turns attention away from the brewing war between China and Taiwan, turning the spotlight onto the Great Summit, set to begin tomorrow on Armistice Station."

"At least we don't have to worry about drones here," Steph said around the pen in her mouth.

"Yeah, it's the one law this place actually has." Bradshaw scowled. He was perched on a stool next to Steph's desk, watching her go through the security settings for their small office. A stool that *mag-*

ically appeared two days earlier and bore a striking resemblance to those in a bar three tubes north, right down to the logo of a cat riding a horse.

"You and laws really don't get along, do you, LS2?" Alex asked.

"Depends on how you define 'getting along,' sir." Bradshaw looked up at him and grinned. "We spend a lot of time together, me and laws."

In the midst of sipping coffee, Alex spat it right back in the cup. "Jesus, Bradshaw. What the hell did I do to get sentenced to commanding you?"

"You know you love me, boss. Just like I love this place."

"I thought you hated it here?" Lieutenant Jesse Lin, Alex's supply officer, asked, his nose crinkling.

"Love, hate, it's all the same, Suppo." Bradshaw laughed; Alex rolled his eyes.

"All right, children, let's stay focused," he said. "Suppo, do we have tablets and phones for everyone?"

"I got phones for everyone, but only tablets for Admiral Hamilton, Secretary Fowler, and their aides. Lotus was sold out," Jesse said, referring to the biggest electronics store on the station.

Armistice Station had station-wide cell phone and internet connectivity, but only if your device was compatible with their particular network. Most American-sold phones and tablets didn't work on the station, and God forbid an admiral or a politician live without a phone.

"Good enough," Alex said. He was sure Admiral Hamilton would find fault, but Lotus wouldn't get a new shipment until next week. Hopefully, the summit would be over by then. "Ops?"

Steph didn't look up from her screen. "Two different hackers tried to set up eavesdropping programs inside our security system. I rerouted them to listen in on Pancho's."

Bradshaw snickered. Pancho's was one of Armistice Station's biggest strip clubs, featuring a large menu of "escort" services. Its back rooms were legendary; almost everything short of assault and murder was legal on the station.

Alex shook his head. "Pretty sure I don't want to be a fly on that wall."

"That's what they get for trying to eavesdrop, sir." Steph's grin made her dark eyes dance.

"I really can't control you people, can I?" he asked, laughing.

"No, sir," Steph and Bradshaw answered together. Jesse looked mildly horrified.

"Sir, I'm not—"

"Don't worry about it, Suppo." Alex waved a hand. "Okay, back to business. Ops has the electronic end covered. The security detail will be a mite peeved that Suppo couldn't get them tablets, but they'll live. Where's GM1 Olson?"

"Trying to talk her boyfriend at the Hilton into another room or two," Steph replied, chewing on a pen.

"Isn't that my pen, Ops?" Bradshaw asked.

"You want it back?"

"Ew."

Steph giggled. "This from the guy who burned his asshole trying to light a fart on fire."

Jesus, Alex thought that was only a rumor. But he didn't have time for stupid sailor games. "I thought Olson was dating a guy at Cousteau's?"

"That was last week." Stephanie shrugged. "Now it's the gym guy at the Hilton. He thinks he can get her an extra room or two for the security detail to base out of."

"Right." He only had a crew of four, but they sure were colorful. Gunner's Mate First Class Amy Olson fit that description perfectly: short, smart, and a spitfire. "Let me know if she has any luck."

"Mm-hm." Stephanie's attention returned to the screen.

"What else can I do?" Jesse asked.

Alex turned to face his always earnest supply officer. *Heaven help me, he* is *a brick*. Alex sighed. "Admiral Hamilton and Secretary Fowler will arrive on USNS *Amelia Earhart*. Make sure the cargo ship gets everything they need—and try to get them a better TRANSPLAT than Platform Seven, will you?"

"Platforms one through six are booked solid, but I'll see what I can do, sir," Jesse replied.

Bradshaw's head popped up. "A guy in planning owes me money. I can help, Suppo."

Jesse flushed. "I wouldn't want..."

"Go for it," Alex cut in. The last thing he wanted was to listen to Admiral Hamilton berate him for parking *Earhart* out in the boonies.

Each of Armistice Station's eight TRANSPLATS—including the one completed last month—had pier space for twenty-four medium sized ships like *Earhart*. Larger ships, like cruise liners, took up multiple berths and smaller ones could squeeze several in per slip.

Platform One was the most desirable, being dead center on the original part of the station. Higher numbers crawled outwards from there. Platforms Seven and Eight were way out at the end of the station—though geography and construction rates actually left Platform Eight closer to the center than Seven—and required a long walk or an outertube ride to get to the exciting stuff.

Cruise ships claimed the closer platforms, with billionaire's yachts tucked in between. Oil tankers, commercial fishing boats, and cargo ships dominated the next closest; Armistice Station exported oil, manganese, and 1,500 tons of fish per day.

Armistice Station was an international powerhouse: rich, diverse, and growing like mold. Hell, three additional habitats started construction in March. Combined, they'd add almost another square *mile* to Armistice Station's footprint. One was another underwater oil rig, but the other two contained an underwater water park and a casino. *This place is like Vegas on crack.* Not that Alex ever went to Vegas. Maybe he'd invite his wife out the next time Nancy had leave. He'd already thrown away his career—what was a few thousand bucks?

"All right," he said after a moment. "We've got three hours to get the rest straightened out, so stay on your toes and try not to piss anyone off. Steph, you'll be with me to meet our guests. Jesse, head over to the Hilton after you and Bradshaw hit up planning. Try to catch Olson and see if her newest boyfriend worked some magic."

"Yes, sir," they all said.

While his team worked, Alex headed up station to check on preparations for the summit itself. Technically, that wasn't his job, but the butterflies dancing in his stomach said he had to do *something*. He hated shit like this.

Media started coming in yesterday, and his own personal boogeyman—woman?—arrived in three hours. Hamilton drop kicked him out of the sub force. No doubt she was responsible for sending him to this dead end. It wasn't like you could bury someone much deeper than 300 feet underwater.

Exiting the Elkman tube, Alex hung a right and joined the flow in the Cook tube, the station's main drag. He passed two outertube joiners along the way, but avoided the crowds waiting for Armistice Station's underwater train.

Bluejacket's Conference Center was at the north intersection of Cook and Ballard. Cook ran in a circle and Ballard shot off it like an extra limb, going the deepest of all Armistice Station's levels. It was more of a building than a proper tube, with six stories, the bottom of which sat on the ocean floor. Only Ballard touched the bottom; every other tube perched on spindly legs like a misshapen spider.

Bluejacket's occupied the three lower levels of Ballard, a sprawling set of conference rooms and fancy restaurants built to cater to executives and the ultra-rich. The place was booked solid through 2041, and Alex had no idea how the Great Summit acquired space on short notice. *Probably bribery, who am I kidding?*

Heading down a wide staircase that looked like it belonged on *Titanic*, Alex noticed security teams sweeping all six floors. One of the few perks of being the naval detachment's OIC meant that Alex's security clearance allowed him access to almost any part of the station, and the guards waved him past. Within five minutes, he entered the Challenger Room, blinking in the sudden bright light.

A long wooden table was the centerpiece of the Challenger Room. Why the hell would someone haul that polished monstrosity down to the bottom of the Indian Ocean? Using a constructed composite would've been easier, but some brainchild probably thought wood looked more dignified. *Guess they weren't going for cheap*, he thought, looking at the paneled walls and decorative light fixtures. The room even smelled like wood, though slightly artificial—Alex bet they used an air freshener for that.

"What are *you* doing here, Commander Coleman?" Aida Ledoux spun to face him, hands on her hips and eyes narrowed.

Alex blinked. "I came to see how preparations were—"

"That's not your business." Ledoux came three strides closer, almost right into his face.

"Excuse me?" Alex burned to step back but stopped himself.

"I need you to leave."

"What?"

"Immédiatement." She slashed a hand in the direction of the door as Alex blinked in confusion.

"Ms. Ledoux, as the senior American representative here on the station"—God, Alex wished he was anything but—"I'm responsible for ensuring our team is prepared. That includes putting eyes on the meeting space."

"Well, you have seen it." She crossed her arms. "Now get out. We are in a hurry and do not have time for you."

Alex glanced around the room. Nothing seemed out of place. There wasn't missing paint on the walls or any other emergent problem; why was Ledoux so adamant?

On the other hand, he was merely a guest in her playground. Her not-so-politely worded demand bore the force of law on Armistice Station. Alex smiled tightly.

"Glad to help." He gave her a curt nod and departed, heading back up the stairs. On the way up, he almost bumped into a group of French sailors speaking rapidly among themselves.

Skittering out of the way, Alex watched the group disappear into the Challenger Room. No one yelled at them.

Interesting.

Chapter 12

Boogeymen

The boss was nervous, and that wasn't his style.

Steph Gomez had worked for some real characters in her career so far. Her first CO was a screamer, fit to blister bulkheads with insults and swear words. He'd been a hell of a ship driver, though, able to make USS *Liberty* spin circles on the head of a pin. She learned a lot there, though not about leadership.

Her second ship was better, though Steph was billeted as an engineer there, not her forte. But Surface Warfare Officers were jacks of all trades, masters of none, so she did her time in a ship's dark underbelly like everyone else. Being a department head was different. There, she got to choose her job, and she was the Operations Officer, first on a destroyer, and later a cruiser. Both of those COs were sane human beings and good leaders. Captain Rosario on *Belleau Wood* was the best she worked for until she met Commander Coleman.

He wasn't the kind of boss you wanted to go to war with, but hey, they weren't at war. Unlike Alex, Steph volunteered to come to Armistice Station. She wasn't married and juggling the schedules of every navy ship that wanted to come to the world's largest underwater station was career enhancing. Challenging, too. *Admirals* knew her name, and Steph liked that. She'd been in just under ten years, and she wanted to make the Navy a career.

That was why she volunteered to go up to Platform Three to meet Rear Admiral Hamilton. Sure, Hamilton was a submariner, but she was also a woman. Female admirals were still rare, and Steph wouldn't pass up the opportunity to impress one.

Besides, seeing the sun was nice. Wandering up to the TRANSPLATs to sunbathe was discouraged, but Steph was a Louisiana girl used to long, bright days.

With twenty ships or subs tied up to each, the platforms were always busy. Cranes, conveyor belts, and passengers vied for space. Usually, the passengers lost. Armistice Station's ready lifeboat got a lot of use; there were at least two man overboards every day. Today's was a sixteen-year-old who tried to take a picture standing on a bollard, only to slip and fall right into the Indian Ocean. His phone, presumably, was still on the bottom, and good riddance to that.

None of this explained why Alex was fretting. He wasn't a fretter. Sure, he didn't like public speaking—which was fine with Steph, since she was always happy to step up—but he was a pretty cool cucumber. He didn't sweat the stupid stuff, unlike most everyone else.

Even Captain Rosario got wrapped around some pretty silly problems back on *Belleau Wood*. The liberty incidents they dealt with daily on Armistice Station would've given her apoplexy. Commander Coleman just took it in stride, usually with a smile and a joke to loosen things up.

But there was a frown on his face as they watched Armistice Station's boatswain's mates swing a brow over to USNS *Amelia Earhart*. The forty-thousand-ton cargo ship dwarfed the sleek black super yacht astern of her, but was a gray blob next to the giant white cruise liner across the pier. Admiral Hamilton and Secretary Fowler were nowhere in sight, but that wasn't surprising. Junior officers waited on their seniors, not the other way around.

"You okay, sir?" she asked, watching his hands go into his pockets and come out again. They were in uniform, something they only did when Navy ships visited. The locals didn't like it the rest of the time, not after the *Kansas* Incident.

Alex shrugged. "Yeah."

"Not to be rude, but you're a shit liar." Steph grinned. "Didn't we both have to memorize some honor code or another about that? At some little military school in Vermont?"

"That was a long time ago." But he laughed, which Steph counted as a victory.

"I guess it's easier to remember when you're not old." Not that she was much younger than Alex; Steph graduated college in 2031, just six years after her current boss.

Both commissioned at Norwich University, the nation's oldest private military college. Predominantly an army school—with a large smattering of marines—Norwich didn't graduate many naval officers. Steph only served with three others so far in her career, one a classmate also on her first ship. Norwich grads were predictable in their unpredictability, known for thinking outside the box. Working for one was nice.

"Easy now. You're not far off that terrible fate, yourself," he said.

"At least my chosen profession lets me see the sun." She gestured at the sky. "Current billet aside. I hear spending years underwater makes you age faster."

Alex surprised her with a scowl. "Not a problem I've got these days. Current billet notwithstanding."

"I don't follow."

"Let's just say I'm not here because of my popularity in the sub community," he replied. "Or with Admiral Hamilton."

Steph opened her mouth to ask more, but a ringing bell over *Earhart's* 1MC, or general announcing system, cut her off:

Ding ding, ding ding, ding ding. Then a voice announced: *"Rear Admiral, upper half, departing."*

Steph's eyes tracked up the brow as Admiral Hamilton walked down, trailed by a lieutenant commander—probably her aide—and two guys in fancy suits. One of those had to be the Under Secretary of State, but Steph had no idea which. Winfred Hamilton was a few inches taller than Steph, and her brown hair either hadn't gone gray or was dyed. She wore a frown before she got even halfway down the brow, and when her eyes landed on Alex, they narrowed.

Steph and Alex both saluted; Admiral Hamilton returned it.

Hamilton frowned.

"Commander Coleman. I hadn't expected to see you here," she said.

"Admiral." His face closed off, the easy smile gone. "Welcome to Armistice Station. Allow me to introduce Lieutenant Commander Stephanie Gomez, my operations officer."

"It's a pleasure, Commander." Hamilton offered Steph her hand, a courtesy she didn't extend to Alex. What the hell kind of bad blood was there between these two? But Steph shook the hand; she wasn't an idiot. And she was so not getting in the middle of a mess Alex clearly wanted her outside of.

"Nice to meet you, ma'am," she replied.

"This is Lieutenant Commander Maria Vasquez, my aide," Hamilton continued, gesturing at the short, impeccably groomed woman by her side. Vasquez's smile seemed genuine, however. "Under Secretary of State for Arms Control and International Security Affairs, Sampson Fowler, and his assistant, Mr. James Gage."

More handshakes were exchanged. Fowler looked down his nose at all four naval officers; Gage looked around with wide eyes. No one bothered to introduce the security officers trailing the quartet. Both looked bored.

"Are we going to stand here all day, or is there somewhere better to go?" Fowler sniffed the air, glaring back at *Earhart*.

Steph didn't miss the slight scowl on Hamilton's face as Alex replied: "There are rooms reserved for you at the Reunion Hilton. Unfortunately, due to the short notice, you'll have to share with your aides."

"That's unacceptable." Fowler scowled. "I'm the Under Secretary of State for Arms Control and International Security Affairs!"

"The hotel is booked." Alex shrugged. "It's the height of vacation season."

Fowler crossed his arms. "I don't care. There must be something you can do. Or *someone* more senior can."

"I'm afraid I'm the senior American representative—"

"Let's not ask for the impossible, Mr. Secretary," Hamilton said. Was it Steph's imagination, or did she straight up ignore Alex? "I'm sure Commander Coleman did everything he could."

Alex colored slightly at her arch tone, and Steph couldn't help swallowing. *This is going to be an interesting week.*

"Then let's proceed with this train wreck." Fowler rolled his eyes. "At least we're here early enough to start informal conversations. I trust you've at least reserved *some* sort of conference room."

Steph cringed, and then watched Hamilton's eyes zero in on that.

"You're welcome to use the conference area in our offices," Alex said, his face twitching. "It's electronically shielded against eavesdropping."

"At least that's something." Fowler rubbed the back of his hand over his mouth like he was chasing away a horrid smell. Could politicians pout? Steph wanted to say something, but along that road was career suicide. So, she kept her mouth shut.

So did Alex.

Nancy hated video calls. She had a thousand better things to do, like promoting STG2 Arnold or figuring out which shipboard prankster stole the medical dummy this time.

Fletcher's satellite bandwidth left a lot to be desired, too. Getting up in video with the flagship meant disconnecting every *other* internet hub on the ship that wasn't classified, which led to disgruntled sailors and a bad connection. The Navy's classified video messaging software looked like a rip-off of the long-dead Skype program, too, only less reliable.

Unfortunately, Admiral McNally loved his *face-to-face* chats, so here Nancy was, sitting at the wardroom table with her XO, Lieutenant Commander Ying Mai. Ying was a *Fletcher* old-timer, on board ten months longer than Nancy. She was the XO for Nancy's predecessor, too, and was originally his relief. Alas, Commander Murray decided to diddle a second class petty officer, so Nancy got *Fletcher* and Ying's move upstairs was delayed. As far as Nancy knew, Murray worked for some defense contractor these days, counting beans and bullets. She didn't pity him.

Sighing, Nancy played with her class ring and tried to conceal her boredom. She hated sitting still, hated the idea of the staff job awaiting her after this one. Command was the pinnacle of a naval officer's career—everything after this was downhill.

Unless she could get a cruiser. *That* would be worth it, but with Nancy's luck, she'd end up sitting in a building "commanding" a destroyer squadron. She loved the Navy, but the Navy wasn't always good at loving her back. The work-life balance sucked, and being married to a submariner meant it was a miracle they'd managed to have two kids when they were young and dumb.

"Captain Rosario, what are the results of your liberty incidents in Rhodes?" McNally asked from the screen.

Nancy stifled a groan. Was he *still* on about that? Yeah, some sailors were stupid, but sailors were *always* drunken fools, and at least the Greeks understood—

"Four sailors went to Captain's Mast, sir," Captain Julia Rosario of USS *Belleau Wood*, replied. *Belleau Wood* was a cruiser, and thus the second most important ship in the strike group, behind the carrier. Her captain was widely respected and *had* to hate this conversation, but Rosario's calm expression never twitched.

"And?" McNally demanded.

Did Nancy see the admiral's chief of staff cringe in the background? Probably. He didn't have much patience for this crap, either, though she expected him to hide it better. *He* liked that staff bullshit.

Rosario blinked. "Three were found guilty and fined a half month's pay for two months. The other was busted down a rank, which I suspended due to extenuating circumstances."

"What *kind* of extenuating circumstances?" McNally's eyes narrowed like Rosario was the one who'd lit off a restaurant's fire extinguisher and sent two shipmates to the hospital.

Nancy checked to make sure her microphone was muted before glancing at Ying. "Does he have to do this? Being treated like a miscreant child who can't manage my own warship is grating."

"Admirals are admirals, ma'am." Ying shrugged, then grimaced. "Heads up, our turn on the grill is incoming."

Straightening, Nancy un-muted the call. McNally's eyes zeroed in like the lasers General Dynamics promised they'd install on her ship but never managed.

"Commander Coleman, what happened with your sailors who broke curfew?" McNally asked.

"All are on Liberty Risk, sir," Nancy said. Captain Dalton's friendly email warned her not to ignore her own problem children, even if they'd only been five minutes late.

Who could guess their bus would get in an accident? Nancy was generally more hard ass than hand holder, but she would've let the sailors go with a warning. But not with Micromanager McNally in command of the strike group.

"Good news," McNally said. "Now, Captain Dalton will brief our updated transit plan. COS?"

Dalton clicked a few buttons, and a PowerPoint slide replaced the images of Nancy's fellow captains. Nancy suppressed a smile. People who said the Navy ran on PowerPoint weren't wrong. Missiles they could do without, but Microsoft Office? Not a prayer. The slide showed the approaches to the Strait of Malacca, along with the strike group's intended course.

"We'll reach the Strait of Malacca in just under two days. Our transit speed will be twenty-five knots," Dalton said. "*Belleau Wood* will have two helicopters up, one ahead of the formation, and one astern. *Fletcher* will be the ready deck for the forward helicopter, with *John Finn* the same at the tail end. *Kidd* will have one helo at alert 5, ready to launch at the first sight of trouble. All three helos will be outfitted with the standard snooping package and armed for a surface engagement."

Nancy pushed the talk button as the slide vanished. "Will there be an alert ASW helicopter?"

Dalton twitched; McNally answered: "Your helo should be outfitted and in the hanger, Commander. We can't afford to anger the locals by using an anti-submarine helo during transit."

"Of course not, sir," Nancy replied. "But if you swapped the ready deck to the carrier, we could have my helo on deck, and—"

"Absolutely not. That helo will range in front of the formation, and I want the closest deck ready. *Fletcher* will remain our forward eyes and ears for sub threats."

"We may not be the best for that job." Nancy pressed on when she saw McNally's heavy eyebrows wiggle. "Our organic sonar capabilities degrade significantly at high speed."

McNally glowered. "Don't you have dampers for that?"

"Not very good ones." Nancy grimaced. "The newest version of the program—"

"I'm sure you'll manage, Commander. My experience with the next gen dampers says they outperform manufacturing specifications. And I like *Fletcher's* speed up front."

Nancy felt her shoulders tense. "Yes, sir."

She ignored the rest of the discussion. Captain Rosario voiced concern about refueling the helicopters since international law only permitted "transit passage" and the run through the SOM was 550 nautical miles.

Captain Edwards from *Enterprise* wanted more fresh fruit and vegetables, and the two *Arleigh Burke* COs worried about gas. The older destroyers were gas guzzlers compared to Nancy's *O'Bannon*-class; that was one thing the Navy did right when they built the newer ships.

Anti-submarine warfare capability *wasn't* something the Navy did well with *Fletcher* and her sisters, however. Nancy didn't mind danger, and if they faced a surface threat, she'd gladly take on two of any other nation's destroyers and call the odds even. But McNally expected *Fletcher* to detect subs with only her under-the-bow sonar dome.

Despite what McNally said—and whatever different brand dampers subs had, because Nancy knew the damned things weren't the same—the odds of that happening at twenty-five knots were about twenty percent.

That left a lot of undetected submarines.

"Looks like we're first into the meat grinder," Ying said after they disconnected.

"Hopefully, he'll change formation before we get to the South China Sea." Nancy sat back and sighed. "I think Captain Dalton caught on, at least. He's the guy that ran the *Saratoga* strike group ragged a few years ago. He knows how much our sonar suffers at speed."

"He is? I had a friend on *Hoel*. They said *Cero* was practically impossible to hear."

"Yeah, he's pretty good." Nancy didn't like playing on friendships in the professional sphere, but she knew John Dalton pretty well. Not as well as her husband did—John and Alex combined were trouble waiting to happen—but well enough that *she* suggested John as their older daughter's godfather.

It didn't hurt that John was also married to Nancy's college roommate. Janet Dalton had good taste.

Ying scratched her chin. "At least Chinese attack subs are loud?"

"The nucs are, anyway." Nancy shook her head. "The odds of anyone shooting at us out here are low, despite what happened near Diego Garcia. We won't have that going for us once we get closer to China."

"Not unless the politicians talk *really* fast, yeah."

"You ever known that to work?" Nancy rolled her eyes, waving off Ying's answer.

They both knew war was coming. It was inevitable, so long as China wanted to reclaim Taiwan. The U.S. Navy spent *years* planning for this.

China continued clinging to a strange marriage of communism and capitalism, all the while insisting Taiwan's government and people were rebels. Taiwan, on the other hand, claimed to be the legitimate government of China.

That uneasy state persisted for decades, but internal conflict in China was on the rise. Several splinter groups within China—most of them in Hong Kong—demanded democratic representation and more freedoms...which Nancy knew would lead to war.

Autocracies worked like that. China needed an external enemy, and Taiwan was the nearest target.

Unfortunately for China, Taiwan had a big, mean friend. And the United States meant to stand with their friend, even if it meant getting in a shooting war with the People's Republic of China.

"That was a lot less fun than I hoped," Steph said as they walked away from the Hilton.

"Tell me about it." Alex tried not to groan. He was supposed to be professional, and Steph worked for him. But getting rid of Admiral Hamilton and Secretary Fowler was the highlight of his day, and damn it all, he trusted her.

"And we get to do it all over again tomorrow!" Her smile was bright and fake.

"Just be grateful they'll be stuck in meetings we don't have to go to," he replied.

"Small favors, right, boss?"

"Very small." Alex didn't like feeling tiny. Every time Admiral Hamilton looked his way, it was clear she wanted to squash him like a bug.

"So, what's up between you and Admiral Hamilton, sir? You never did say." Steph asked as they hung a right and entered the Bass Tube.

Lotus and Pancho's were to their right, the latter with a sign out saying they were at capacity, already. Speedsub Racers took up a hundred feet of the Bass' left side, with a line fifty deep. This consisted of colorfully dressed college students with daddy's money to spend; renting a fast, colorful, two passenger mini-submarine cost about a thousand bucks an hour. Speedsub Racers had twenty of the things, when they all worked, and rumors said the owners planned to open another site next time the station expanded.

Staring at that line wouldn't get him out of answering, would it? Alex sighed.

"I was XO on *Kansas* six months ago."

Stephanie stopped to gape. "For the *Kansas* Incident?"

"That's the one."

"Shit." She glanced at Pancho's and then back to Alex again. "You guys didn't...?"

"Fuck no we didn't." No need to tell her about how he'd doomed his career. Alex *still* didn't regret that. To hell with Chris Kennedy and his glory hunting. "But we don't know who did."

Alex swallowed. Admiral Hamilton might have cleared *Kansas* of wrongdoing, but no one believed that. The French-led international investigation concluded that *Kansas* was the only sub on the bearing the torpedoes came from, yet even the French admitted *Kansas* had a full torpedo room when the U.S. Navy begrudgingly allowed inspectors on board. In the end, the international community didn't officially blame *Kansas*, but the lack of exoneration shouted what they thought was the truth.

"Why the hell would they send you *here*?" Steph asked. "Were they *trying* to cause an international incident?"

Another voice answered before Alex could speak. "That is a terribly good question," Camille Dubois said.

Alex spun. Dubois wore her dress uniform, as did the man to her right. He was a captain and just as annoyingly photogenic as Dubois. His hair and eyes were dark, his bearing proud to the point of arrogance. Both watched Alex and Stephanie with predatory glares that reminded him of Admiral Hamilton, just worse.

"What the hell are you doing here?" Alex snapped.

"Armistice Station is an independent station, no?" Dubois smiled the same smug smile she wore when *Kansas'* logs proved mysteriously erased. "We are here for—how do you say?—liberty."

He'd never wanted to hit a woman so much.

"I hope you enjoy it," Alex said through gritted teeth.

"I shall enjoy it *far* more now that I know you are here." She said something in French to her companion, who laughed. The only word Alex caught was *Kansas*, but that was enough.

"Telling stories again, Commander?" he asked, pasting on his own false smile.

She laughed. "Why would I need to do that?"

Steph looked between the two like she was watching a cage match, her eyes wide and uncertain. "I think we should get out of here, boss," she whispered.

"You Americans are terribly inhospitable," the French captain said, his eyes gleaming. "A Frenchman would invite you for a drink and become friends."

Alex bit back a snarl. "I think it's a bit late for that."

"Capitaine Jules Rochambeau of *Barracuda*." Rochambeau held out a hand.

"Commander Alex Coleman." Alex shook his hand, because what the hell else was he supposed to do? The alternative was causing an international incident.

Shit, he wanted to. He *recognized* that voice, the cold one that miraculously showed up after the Neyk sunk, pinning all the blame on *Kansas*. Rochambeau didn't look like a murderer, but what else did you call someone who sank a sub full of civilians?

That idea no longer felt like a conspiracy theory.

"Oui." Rochambeau smiled. "Camille has told me *much* about you. I must admit that I admire your...tenacity."

"Do you." Alex felt cold. Had Dubois told this man what happened? Why would the French want to shoot a civilian submarine, anyway? Nothing made sense.

"Very much." The bastard sounded sincere.

Fury wanted to make Alex's hands shake. "Excuse us. Some of us have work to do."

"Biên sur." Rochambeau nodded. "It was a pleasure."

"Yeah." Alex gestured to Steph and they headed further down Bass as Dubois and Rochambeau ducked past the capacity sign and into Pancho's.

"What the hell was that about?" Steph hissed after twenty feet. "Sir."

"Fuck if I know." Butterflies reared up into Alex's throat. Meeting Dubois was a coincidence. Nasty, sure, but nothing important.

Steph frowned. "How do you know a French commander?"

"She was a liaison on *Kansas* when the Neyk went down." *She's a lying piece of shit, but I still don't know why.*

"Is she the one who said we did it?"

"Yep. And *Barracuda* was the French sub that showed up right when everything went to shit, too."

Alex glanced over his shoulder to glare at Pancho's, but the pair was long gone. *Good fucking riddance.* But why were French officers here on liberty during the summit? Particularly *these* French officers. Something was happening *way* above his paygrade, and Alex really didn't like mysteries. He needed more coffee to deal with this shit.

Chapter 13

Happenstance

10 April 2038

Five minutes after Nancy walked into *Fletcher's* anchor windlass, looking for contraband, mis-stored cleaning chemicals, and a pallet of sodas that mysteriously disappeared during *Fletcher's* last underway replenishment, she found the missing medical dummy.

"Really, gents?" She twisted to look at Lieutenant (junior grade) Karam and the three boatswains' mates by his side. Karam was *Fletcher's* First Lieutenant, in charge of deck division, the most rough and tumble sailors in the Navy.

Senior Chief Albertson grinned sheepishly. "If I said it's part of an ongoing prank war, would you be willing to let it go, Captain?"

"Do I *want* to know who you're pranking?"

"Not you?"

Nancy shook her head, biting her lip to resist a laugh. "That's ominous." She glanced at Karam. "You in on this, Ali?"

Karam flushed. "I plead the fifth, ma'am."

Nancy's radio crackled before she could answer. "Captain, Officer of the Deck, we're being queried by the Indian Navy."

"I'll be right there," she replied, twisting to look back at Karam and his sailors. "We'll postpone this spot check for now. I'm sure you don't mind, do you, Boats?"

Senior Chief Albertson chuckled. "No, ma'am. We'll be ready whenever you are."

"I don't doubt it." Nancy smiled. They both knew anchor windlass was one of the destroyer's trouble spots, but Albertson's boys and girls had it spotless today.

No way was the missing pallet of soda hiding in there, either. Nancy's thieves must have found new homes for their misbegotten gains.

She'd find them eventually. Just not today.

"All our problems come on Tuesdays, Captain." Albertson grinned.

Nancy laughed before heading for the nearest ladder, sprinting up six decks to the bridge.

Her smile vanished as she entered *Fletcher's* pilothouse. Normally one of her favorite places, today the air crackled with tension. The bridge was on the destroyer's top level, with windows on three sides. A modern warship's nerve center was in their CIC, or Combat Information Center, but all ships were driven from the bridge. Nancy strode in the aft door, slamming the lever down and dogging it shut.

Navigation radar consoles were to her left and electronic charts to her right. The helm was straight ahead, a young sailor gripping the wheel with white knuckles. The Quartermaster of the Watch whispered with his Boatswains' Mate counterpart, while the Officer of the Deck and Conning Officer—both junior lieutenants—stood near the centerline.

"Captain's on the Bridge!" Boatswain's Mate Third Class Holloway noticed her first.

"Carry on," Nancy said. "What's going on, OOD?"

Lieutenant (junior grade) Marci Matthews turned to her. "Ma'am, we've been queried by the Indian Navy. I gave them the normal spiel about operating in international waters in accordance with international law, but they got testy."

"Define 'testy.'"

"They're demanding we provide our ultimate destination." Marci grimaced.

Nancy frowned. That was abnormal, not to mention rude. Tensions between American warships and their former friends and allies were still high; France blaming the U.S. for the *Kansas* Incident made them few friends in the Indian Ocean, particularly with nations who lost people on board the Neyk submarine. But the Indian Navy was a professional organization. They knew how this game worked.

A professional organization we exchanged missiles *with four days ago*. Crap. *Fletcher* was the on duty query ship, still leading the strike group by five miles, but it was time to kick this one upstairs. Nancy cleared her throat. "All right, let's—"

An accented voice interrupted her, hissing out of the nearby bridge-to-bridge radio. "American warship, this is Indian Naval Ship *Porbandar*. Identify yourself, your destination, and state your intentions. If you do not respond immediately, you will be subject to enforcement actions, over."

"You want to take that, ma'am?" Marci asked, her eyes wide.

"Sure. Hand it over." Nancy took a deep breath.

Subject to enforcement actions was Navyspeak for *I can force you to do what I want.* Nancy used such words on her last ship when sent to hunt down resurgent Somali pirates. But no one said things like that to the U.S. Navy.

"*Porbandar*, this is U.S. Navy Warship One-Five-Five," she said. "I am operating in international waters in accordance with international law. My course is one-two-seven and my speed twenty-five knots. Request you stay clear, over."

"*Fletcher*, this is *Porbandar*," the other voice replied, making Nancy's eyes narrow. "State your intentions and destination immediately, over."

Marci hissed; Nancy shrugged as nonchalantly as she could. "He can read *Jane's*," she said. "No big deal."

Except U.S. Navy warships didn't identify themselves by name on open radio channels, and the Indians knew that. *Porbandar's* rudeness was no accident.

"*Porbandar* is a *Visakhapatnam*-class DDG." Marci thumbed through their own copy of *Jane's Fighting Ships*. "Thirty-two VLS cells for Barak 8 surface-to-air missiles and sixteen cells for BrahMos anti-ship missiles. One 127-millimeter Oto Melara gun and four CIWS mounts. Carries two Sea King helicopters and has four torpedo tubes."

"Thanks, Marci." Nancy's heart pounded.

The two destroyers damaged near Diego Garcia faced a *Visakhapatnam*-class guided missile destroyer and hadn't done too well. But both those destroyers were *Burkes*, and only carried eight Harpoon missiles between them. *Fletcher* had sixteen, and hers were Harpoon Block IIs, the newer version that could be fired from their vertical launch system instead of canisters strapped on as an afterthought.

Fletcher might not be great against submarines, but she could take an Indian destroyer. Maybe even two.

But she couldn't shoot first. Their standing Rules of Engagement said that *Fletcher* could only fire if fired upon. Nancy glanced at the radar. *Porbandar* was fifteen miles away, an eyeblink for a BrahMos missile. Those things were the fastest cruise missiles in the world and could get up to Mach 7, or over 4,500 knots. *Fletcher's* Harpoons were a lot slower.

"Call CIC and have them get on chat to the strike group. Let them know our Indian friends are being pushy," she said to Marci before lifting the bridge-to-bridge handset again. "*Porbandar,* this is *Fletcher* Actual. My intentions are peaceful. I am in transit to the Strait of Malacca, over."

De-escalation was in order. Admiral McNally might not like her forking over information, but Admiral McNally wasn't here, and their destination was obvious to anyone with half a brain. Did submariners even know how to talk on bridge-to-bridge?

"*Fletcher* Actual, this is *Porbander*," the snooty voice sounded a little less angry. Was that good? "We will remain outside ten nautical miles of your vessel. Recommend you do likewise, over."

"This is *Fletcher* Actual. Roger, thank you, out." Nancy hung up the handset, mind whirling.

"You think they'll keep that promise, ma'am?" Marci swallowed.

"We'll find out. I'll be down in Combat."

This was a development Nancy needed to call in herself. Admiral McNally might obsess over the submarine threat, but a surface engagement would ruin his day, too.

Besides, *Enterprise* was well within BrahMos range.

Thank God Alex didn't work at the Hilton. Judging from the way Fowler bitched about everything in their office—from the temperature of the coffee to the color of their lights—he was hell on hotel staff.

Then again, they were trained to deal with difficult customers. Alex was trained for submarine warfare. Not that he'd ever get a chance to do that. *Don't be an ass. You made your choices.* He'd do the same thing all over again, assuming he had to. But it still burned.

"I need a liaison. Someone who knows how this place works," Fowler said, sitting in Alex's chair with his arms crossed.

Alex was surprised he didn't have his feet up. *Someone should tell him he's wrinkling his expensive suit, or does he just make his aide iron it?* One thing that Armistice Station didn't do well was dry cleaning; most of the substances used in the process were toxic in one way or another, and no station manager with a brain wanted to dispose of more hazardous waste than they had to.

"We've already briefed your security teams with a complete layout of the station," Alex replied, resisting the urge to shove his hands in his pockets. There was no need to mention how that layout included places on the station not fit for public viewing; Ledoux didn't need to know how Steph hacked into their systems a long time ago. "Lieutenant Commander Gomez will escort you to Bluejacket's each day—"

"To what?" Fowler asked, then busied himself brushing nonexistent lint off his shoulders.

Someone didn't read the briefing packet. Alex forced a smile. "Bluejacket's is the name of the conference center where the summit will be held."

"Of course." Fowler glared.

Alex tried not to flinch, but it was hard when Admiral Hamilton's eyes followed him. Maybe Alex should've told her the truth. But with Kennedy gunning for him, who'd believe the XO?

"I noticed that Bluejacket's only has one entrance," Hamilton said. "Is that going to be a problem?"

"According to Madame Ledoux—she's the station administrator—that will make security checks easier," Alex replied.

"We have to go through *security*?" Fowler rolled his eyes. "How typical of the military."

"Armistice Station got four terrorist threats in the last three months," Alex replied. "They take security seriously here." *As should* any *place hosting so many nations,* he didn't add.

Fowler sniffed. "I suppose they'll want to do something barbaric like pat us down."

"They have body scanners for that, Mr. Secretary."

Fowler's smile was poisonous. "You didn't reply to my request for a liaison." He twisted in his chair, eyeing Jesse. "What's your name?"

"Me?" Jesse's eyes widened. "Lieutenant Lin, sir."

"You'll suffice."

"Mr. Secretary, I'm not—" Jesse blinked. "I mean, Steph will be your escort, and I'm sure she's more qualified."

"I'd be happy to be your liaison, sir," Steph said. "I'm our Anti-Terrorism Officer in addition to being the Operations Officer, and I'm familiar with the station's security plans."

Fowler's eyes narrowed. "That won't be necessary. I'm sure you're busy."

"Actually, Jesse's busier than I am. He's working with *Amelia Earhart* to..." Steph trailed off when Fowler shook his head.

"Thank you for your opinion, Lieutenant Commander," he said.

Admiral Hamilton's eyes narrowed. "Mr. Secretary, is there a reason why you want a *supply* officer instead of someone trained to assist you?" she asked. "Or is this another case of your 'optics'?"

"Who I want as my liaison isn't your business, Admiral."

"No, but it is my profession." Hamilton was the only one in the room unaffected by Fowler's deepening glare. She folded her hands. "You may not be aware that supply officers are restricted line officers, which means—"

"I know what it means! I've studied your precious military, thank you very much! I am *aware* of how this works," Fowler rose, looming over everyone. "Lieutenant Lin is far more respectful, and I will have him as my liaison."

"Respectful?" Hamilton echoed as Steph flushed red.

Had Steph somehow pissed Fowler off? Alex frowned. She hadn't gone near the politician on her own, had she?

"My decision is final." Fowler sneered. "And as the chief of this mission, I'll hear nothing else about it from you, Admiral. Your narrow military perspective is not required."

Hamilton's return glare could melt HY-80 steel. Alex wanted to enjoy the encounter; watching someone take Freddie Hamilton down a peg was nice. Except Fowler reminded Alex of the petty tyrant Kennedy was when things didn't go his way. Wasn't that a happy thought? Feeling grudging respect for Hamilton annoyed him—which in turn made Alex feel small and petty.

"Lieutenant Lin will be happy to assist you, Mr. Secretary," Alex said before anyone could explode. How was he the peacekeeper here? Someone had to say something, though. He swallowed back nerves. "Commander Gomez will continue to work background security for the summit."

Steph shot him a look he couldn't read, and Hamilton seemed dissatisfied. But what the hell was he supposed to do when an Under Secretary of State waltzed in making ridiculous demands? Jesse could do the job, sure. His talents laid elsewhere, but he wasn't incompetent. Bradford called Jesse as blunt as a post and twice as thick, but maybe Fowler would like that. This political shit was for the birds. He was so over his head.

Thankfully, Fowler left—with Jesse in tow—a few minutes later, grumbling something about shopping for his wife before the summit started in the afternoon. Jesse dragged his feet and shot pleading glances Steph's way, but she just shrugged. Alex gestured her over after Hamilton and her aide left.

"I'm sorry about that," he said. "I don't think..."

"That he likes women in uniform? Yeah. You can say that, sir." Steph glared at the door Fowler swanned out. "He might as well be wearing it in neon lights on his ass."

"Yeah. That." Shit, this kind of misogynistic asshole wasn't supposed to be allowed out in public, and the government definitely wasn't supposed to employ them.

"I'll survive, sir." Stephanie sighed. "He's not the first twatwaffle I've encountered, and he's only here for a few weeks."

"Less, if they fuck this up." Alex sighed, glancing around the conference room. The Armistice Station grapevine said the other delegations arrived last night and early this morning. China *almost* sent a team before bowing out at the last minute, which simplified things mightily. They were still pissed off about the American strike group headed towards their front yard, though that was a problem for the United Nations.

They were in emergency council, according to the news. A message from USS *Fletcher* said that the Indian Navy was feeling frisky, and Alex wondered how that would play out during the summit. Not that he'd be around to see. He wasn't important enough to sit through the meetings, a minor fact that made Alex feel warm and fuzzy. Who wanted to listen to politicians argue all day?

"You know, boss, it's funny you say that," Bradshaw said from the doorway.

Alex turned. "Where the hell did you wander off to? I thought Suppo asked you to make sure there were breakfast munchies out for this meeting."

"I forgot?"

"Forgot so much that Ops had to buy donuts from that scam down on Earle, yeah. Good job," Alex replied.

"Sorry 'bout that, Ops." Bradshaw tried a winning smile on Steph, who ignored it.

"Sure you are," she said.

"Olson and I got distracted by some French marines," Bradshaw replied, gesturing at the petty officer to his right. "She wanted to flirt with them."

"As if." Olson snorted.

Gunner's Mate First Class Amy Olson was sharp where Bradshaw was sneaky. She was the picture of the straight-and-narrow sailor, high speed and dedicated. She made every rank on the first try and aced every test. Unlike Alex, she volunteered to come to Armistice Station, and she liked it here, which made her a weird friend for Bradshaw to make, but the two argued like siblings.

"French marines?" Alex blinked. Armistice Station was a long way from France. Who wanted to bring marines all the way down here?

"Do French subs carry marines?" Steph said at the same time.

"Not if they're as small as ours," Olson replied, tucking a strand of curly red hair behind her left ear. "And not this many. There were a god-awful lot of them."

"A lot as in how many?" Alex asked.

"Couple dozen?" Bradshaw chewed his lip—oh, great, he was chewing tobacco. Again. Alex wished that gross stuff would just die, but for the damned surface navy clung to it. Bradshaw swirled his dip around before adding: "Maybe more."

"I counted fifty-three." Olson shot Bradshaw a triumphant look, reminding Alex of his younger daughter lording knowledge over her older sister.

Alex's frowned. "Fifty-three marines sure enough don't fit in a fast attack submarine."

"You're sure those Frenchies were on a fast attack?" Stephanie asked.

"Yeah." Alex swallowed back memories. "*Barracuda* is one of the new *Requins*. On par with our *Ceroes*, maybe better. So, assuming those marines didn't come in with *Barracuda*, where *did* they come from?"

His people exchanged glances. "I can pull up manifests for other visiting ships?" Steph said. "They won't say they're carrying French marines, but maybe there's another French ship here for liberty."

"I think we'd of noticed," Bradshaw said.

Olson snorted. "Only if they wanted stuff from your not-quite-illegal friends."

"Hey, it makes for a good information network." Bradshaw gestured around. "And it gets me out of our palatial office and away from your snooty self. Three wins, if you ask me."

"Bite me." Olson smiled sweetly.

"Any time, Guns."

"Enough." Alex sighed. "Get out there and see what you can find out. *Both* of you."

"Aye, sir," both enlisted sailors replied. They continued squabbling as they left the office, and Alex watched them go with exasperated fondness. Both predated his tour on Armistice Station, and the longest he'd seen them go without an argument was about an hour.

"You think the number of Frenchies is important, boss?" Steph asked after they left.

"Might be. Might be nothing." Alex shoved his hands in his pockets, studying the polished floor. Armistice Station's janitorial staff was as efficient as everything else in this place. Alex's people didn't even need to take their trash to the incinerator.

Steph chewed on another pen. "Don't they usually ask us for help with getting stores since they don't have a team here?"

"Yeah, they do." Alex rubbed his chin; he hurried through shaving that morning, and it showed. "They must've hired a local husbanding agent."

"Pity we can't wander up and ask those French sub guys we ran into yesterday," she said.

"If you're implying that them being here *plus* a boatload of marines is weird, your point is taken." Alex frowned. "Something's up."

"You think we should tell the Admiral, sir?"

"Maybe later." Alex wanted more information. Hamilton wouldn't take guesses well. She didn't *like* people working outside regulations, and Alex preferred to avoid another tongue-lashing.

She'd already ruined his career. He'd keep his dignity, thanks.

Dismissing one's summit partner like a small child was frowned upon. Not that Freddie Hamilton knew much about children, but she suspected most four-year-olds were more mature than Under Secretary Martin Fowler. Certainly more knowledgeable than the peacock. Listening to Fowler carry on about the growing tension in the Indian Ocean gave her a headache.

"They'll stop shooting. No one wants to take on the U.S. Navy," he said over lunch.

Freddie wished the bastard hadn't somehow reserved a table at The Blue Mod. Freddie had never been to Armistice Station before, but even she knew The Blue Mod was one of the top ten restaurants in the world. The waitlist was *weeks* long—some said months—and the food annoyingly good.

The décor was underwater mountains and the plates were edged in silver; this place knew it was amazing. Fowler's table for four included Freddie and both their aides. Luckily, Mr. Gage and Lieutenant Commander Maria Vasquez got along better than the admiral and the secretary, generally steering the conversation away from touchy topics.

Fowler sent poor Lieutenant Lin off to find some present for his wife rather than inviting him to lunch, a task the lieutenant accepted with surprising aplomb. Freddie supposed it wasn't *too* much of an abuse of power, and besides, she felt sorry for Lin, who clearly wanted to give Fowler a wide berth.

"I'm glad you're confident in our abilities, Mr. Secretary, but I'm not sure the Indians share your awe," she said, putting her fork down. "They wouldn't have shot at us otherwise."

Fowler waved a hand. "It's posturing. Their team wants something—probably Diego Garcia. We'll give them less than they ask for, of course."

"Shooting missiles isn't *posturing*." Freddie's eyes narrowed. "Nineteen American sailors are dead and another forty are injured. Two destroyers will need a shipyard to fix them. If that's not an act of war, I don't know what is."

"Only if diplomacy breaks down," he said. "We'll fix that here. Don't worry your little head, Admiral."

Freddie hadn't burned so much to smack sense into a man since her first department head told her she'd never qualify as a submariner because she had boobs. But she wasn't a hotheaded junior lieutenant these days, so she held her tongue. "Correct me if I'm wrong, but arrogance rarely makes international friends."

"Well, if anyone's to blame for the current situation, it's the Navy."

"Excuse me?"

"The *Kansas* Incident started this mess." Fowler smirked. "Weren't you responsible for that investigation?"

"I was."

"Well, the Indians and their allies—France and Russia, among others, in case I have to remind you—are still unhappy. I expect it to come up this afternoon when we argue about the shooting at Diego Garcia. Nearly as many people died on that Neyk your Navy claims it didn't sink."

"*Kansas* didn't sink the Neyk," Freddie snapped before she could stop herself.

"So you say. But we all know how the military loves its secrets, don't we?" Fowler *hmm*ed under his breath, giving her a knowing look as he sipped some frou-frou hot tea. "The international investigation disagrees."

"The international investigation determined—just as I did—that *Kansas*' torpedo room was just as full after the shooting as it was before it." Freddie sucked in a deep breath. "*Kansas* didn't fire those torpedoes."

She wasn't sure if *Kansas* would have. Chris Kennedy checked every box in his career thus far; he wasn't an idiot, and she didn't think he wanted to shoot civilians. His former XO, on the other hand, was the kind of unpredictable individual Freddie hated. *And now I'm saddled with him here*. Heaven help them all if Coleman disobeyed orders he didn't like and endangered this entire summit.

Fowler laughed. "And I'm sure the Navy's never snuck torpedoes into a submarine."

"Do you have any idea how big a Mark 48 CBASS torpedo is? They're nineteen feet long. Hard to sneak around," Freddie said.

"They also weigh about thirty-five hundred pounds, Mr. Secretary," Maria added, her dark eyes unreadable. "Torpedoes aren't something you can tuck in the back of a truck and hand to a sub. You need a crane."

"As fascinating as your torpedo trivia is, I'm only telling you what our...friends in this region are saying," Fowler replied. "The truth doesn't matter. We have to deal with the politics of the situation—or *I* do. It'll be better if you keep your mouths shut."

"I'll do my job, Mr. Secretary." Freddie couldn't handle this conversation any longer; she'd skip dessert. "Speaking of which, will you excuse us? Maria and I have some background information on local navies to cover."

"Enjoy."

Fowler waved them off, and Maria put her tea down to follow Freddie. They walked out into Armistice Station's busy Cook tube, conspicuous in their uniforms against a civilian crowd. A few people paused to glare, but Freddie ignored that. She couldn't waste energy on angry civilians.

"He's a piece of work, ma'am," Maria said after the door to The Blue Mod closed.

"The glories of government service." Freddie chuckled. "Ours is not to reason why, right?"

"You say so, Admiral."

Freddie chuckled. Maria was her second aide since putting on stars, and by far the best. An admiral's aide was responsible for the care and feeding of their admiral and a myriad of other odd jobs.

Maria could rattle off information like an encyclopedia, talk a hotel into changing their room to somewhere away from the spring break crowd, and select a great wine to go with dinner. She was also good at smoothing over rough edges left behind by Freddie's whirlwind of efficiency, and, overall, made her admiral appear friendlier than she was.

Oh, Freddie was no rebel. She walked a careful line in her career, from commissioning in 2009 to being the first female submariner to put on admirals' stars. She graduated from the Naval Academy before the Navy grew comfortable with women in submarines, but Freddie never put a foot wrong.

She was the first of her class to earn her submarine warfare pin, the top of her class at sub school, and the first woman to command a fast attack submarine. Most submariners commanded one submarine, if they were lucky. Freddie earned her second, commanding a ballistic missile submarine instead of a tender as a captain.

That boomer, USS *Columbia*, taught Freddie patience. She needed it today.

"Let's get to work. The Indian team has a few naval officers along for the ride. Maybe we can talk sense with them."

Maria fidgeted. "They sent an admiral and no politicians. Not exactly what you do if you want to make a difference."

"Well, unless you want to be like our narrow-minded political friend," Freddie started, "we'd better—"

"Excuse me, Admiral," another voice interrupted.

Freddie turned to find Stephanie Gomez approaching. "Commander?"

"I'm sorry for interrupting, ma'am, but I thought you might want to know that a French frigate arrived early this morning, *Bretagne*."

"Thank you," Freddie said. "Do you expect them to impact the summit?"

"We're not sure, ma'am." Stephanie sighed. "There's also a French attack submarine named *Barracuda*. And...at least fifty French marines wandering around the station."

"Is that normal?" Maria asked.

Stephanie shook her head. "No. French traffic here increased in the last few months, but never two warships at once."

"Someone wants to flex their muscles." Freddie chewed on the news for a moment. She remembered *Barracuda*. More importantly, she remembered the coincidence that put one of France's newest attack subs *right* on Armistice Station's doorstep while a French intelligence officer pressed *Kansas* to shoot a civilian submarine.

No one could prove anything, but Winfred Hamilton wasn't born an idiot.

"France owns three major stations in this area, with a stake in three others," Maria, ever the encyclopedia, said. "Rumor says they're building two more between Reunion and Port Louis."

"It's not a rumor," Steph said. "Both contracting companies are basing out of here to build them. The companies building them are Indian."

Freddie cocked her head. "Have you reported this?"

Stephanie flushed. "I...we thought it was common knowledge, ma'am. It's no secret on the station. Work started five months ago."

"Hm." Freddie wouldn't yell at the messenger. She couldn't even yell at Coleman, no matter how much she wanted to. The sub community's least favorite son arrived on Armistice Station four months ago, though whichever brainchild thought to send him here was beyond her. She shook herself. "Thank you, Commander. I appreciate the update."

"Glad to help, ma'am."

Gomez vanished back into the crowd, leaving Freddie and Maria alone.

"You think the French are up to something, ma'am?" Maria asked.

"I think we're in a corner of the world where we have zilch for influence and no one likes us." Freddie scowled. "Whatever friends we had abandoned us when that Neyk went down."

"We still don't know who did that, do we?"

"I doubt we ever will."

Chapter 14

Complications

"COS, the CO of *Fletcher's* on the POTS line for you," the staff officer of the watch said to John.

"*Fletcher?* Why?" John stood and walked over to the outside phone line on *Enterprise's* flag bridge. Technology was better on surface ships; his sub had three lines for the entire boat, and they only worked when *Cero* was shallow enough to communicate with the outside world. And that was better than the boats John grew up on, which needed to be at periscope depth to talk to anyone, assuming you wanted to betray your position to the enemy.

Being able to call home from deployment was a novelty, and his wife appreciated it. Janet was ex-Air Force and a veteran of John's four submarine deployments, so he didn't *have* to call her. John just liked to.

"Commander Coleman didn't say, sir," the watch officer replied, vacating the seat.

"Guess I'll find out." John smiled and plopped into the still-warm chair. *Some stuff is the same everywhere.* Even on an aircraft carrier, space was at a premium. Every seat had its purpose. He lifted the phone and pressed the *talk* button. "Captain Dalton here, what can I do for you?"

Calling himself a captain was still a thrill. John hadn't expected to make the rank early, but he sure hadn't said no. But he was still a *junior* captain, all things considered. Now that John was the second-in-command of the entire *Enterprise* Strike Group, it was a delicate balance. Both the captains of *Enterprise* and *Belleau Wood* were senior to him, but he was the admiral's right hand.

One of the less appetizing perks of the job came when destroyer drivers called John with their woes.

Because no way was this a social call. Nancy wasn't the type to use an official line for that, not when tensions were high. Or ever, probably.

"I'm sorry to bother you, sir, but I wanted to discuss the Admiral's call," Nancy Coleman said from the other end, her voice level and professional. The call quality was good on the carrier; sub lines always featured a side order of clicking and buzzing.

"Is there a problem, Nancy?" he asked.

"I'm still concerned about *Fletcher* being on point," she replied. "Our ASW capabilities are...less than I'd like."

John frowned. Nancy brought the topic up on the last captain's call, but most commanders wouldn't kick their worries upstairs a *second* time, particularly after the admiral shut her down. He racked his brain for information about *Fletcher* and came up blank. "I admit I don't know much about the *O'Bannon*-class. Tell me what your concerns are."

"I don't have a tail," Nancy replied, referring to her towed sonar array. "And the dampers connected to my sonar dome have been CASREP'd for months. There's something wrong with the program no contractor can fix. And even before that, they were nothing to write home about."

John blinked. "Don't all destroyers have a towed array?"

"The early *O'Bannons* don't. We're scheduled to have one back fitted when we go into the yards next year."

"I see." John didn't know much about surface ships, but he knew sonar. Sonar was a submarine's only eyes. A towed sonar array and a sonar dome both listened passively, but the towed array's distance from a sub's—or ship's—own noise increased its efficacy tenfold. Without a towed array, *Fletcher's* motion through the water made passive sonar almost useless...especially if her dampers weren't working.

"John, I'll fight air battles or any two surface ships you point me at, but we can't hear jack at this speed," Nancy said. "I recommend putting *John Finn* or *Kidd* out front. Tuck us in close to the carrier for air defense and stick one of the destroyers with a tail out front."

"I'll talk to the admiral, Nancy," John replied, and then hesitated. He wouldn't say this to someone else, but... "I can't promise he'll listen, though."

John knew his admiral could be prickly. He wouldn't like a mere commander questioning his formation choices, which meant John had to bring this up carefully.

Hell, given the choice, *John* would stick the cruiser out front. Nancy and *Fletcher* handled the last incident with the Indians well, but a more senior captain, like Rosario on *Belleau Wood*, was better suited to deal with those shenanigans. McNally was less likely to shit on Rosario, too.

Maybe that tact would work. *Fletcher* was almost as good at air defense as *Belleau Wood*, and cruisers had towed arrays. They were also bigger and scarier, which might give the Indians pause.

Not that the Indians wanted to shoot. No one wanted a war.

"Madame Ledoux, it is a pleasure," Captain Jules Rochambeau said in French. Camille stood a half step behind him and shook Aida Ledoux's hand after Jules released it.

"The honor is mine, Monsieur le Capitaine." Ledoux's smile looked strained. "Is your presence here a sign that your government is prepared to act?"

"*Our* government, Madame." Jules gave her a sweeping bow. "All is arranged. I am in command of the expedition."

"That is excellent news. Will you wait for the summit to end?"

"As soon as your inconvenient guests depart." A thrill ran through him, leaving Jules feeling warm despite the relatively cool air of the station. He found Armistice Station's ventilation system impressive; it was more efficient than *Barracuda's*. However, the temperature in Ledoux's office was a touch lower than necessary. It suited the woman, he decided with a smile. Perhaps she did that on purpose. "As soon as your inconvenient guests depart."

"What if an agreement is reached?" she asked.

Jules laughed. "The Americans will not bend enough. They do not recognize that their influence in this part of the world is waning while France's grows. They will not give the Indians what they want. But, after the *Kansas* Incident, our desire to appease the United States has vanished."

"I will be glad to be rid of them." Ledoux's eyes gleamed. "Even their small naval detachment is onerous."

"Oui."

Jules did not care if the American naval detachment strayed into the crossfire. Yes, his meeting with Commander Alexander Coleman was carefully orchestrated. Camille told him much of *Kansas'* irritating former executive officer, but Jules found him disappointing. Coleman was perhaps clever, but he lacked the intestinal fortitude to fight. Perhaps he left it on *Kansas*. Camille certainly found him more impressive than she had Commander Kennedy, drooling fool that he was. Kennedy followed Camille like a dog after a bitch in heat. Coleman was apparently more immune to her wiles, yet he had still failed to beat her.

There was a lesson in that. Jules resolved not to trust his second-in-command too closely, at least not yet.

Master Chief Chinedu Casey started counting the days until his transfer the day the Neyk Four sank. He wanted to be Chief of the Boat for an attack submarine since he joined the navy twenty-four years earlier, but the last six months were the worst of his career. Even putting aside the fucking "*Kansas* Incident"—calling it that earned anyone in his vicinity an obscenity-laden rant—Commander Chris Kennedy just wasn't the type of captain a COB wanted to work for.

"You look like you need a drink, COB," Lieutenant Sue Grippo said. She stood in the doorway to the tiny cubbyhole Casey called his office, a space just big enough for half a desk and two uncomfortable metal chairs. Her smile looked pasted on, exhausted and brittle.

"Five or six would be better, Nav." He gestured her in. "Pull up a chair."

Officers didn't come to the COB for counseling the way enlisted sailors did; they outranked him, even the new kids straight out of sub school. But department heads were usually smart enough to ask for advice. Sue was a frequent visitor.

"Do I look that bad?" she asked.

"You look like you just went a few rounds with the captain and lost, if you don't mind me saying, ma'am."

"It only took one for him to knock me out flat." Sue sighed. "He doesn't like our new orders."

"Fuck, Nav, I don't, either." Casey snorted. "I was looking forward to some nice R&R in Perth before heading home. The way our 'six' month deployment became eight and is fixin' to become ten wears everyone down."

"I know."

Kansas got turned around the moment the Indians picked a fight over Diego Garcia. Then they got to turn circles in the water for a week before the powers that be decided to send them north. Worst part was, they'd been a day out of Perth, and *Kansas'* sailors could pretty much taste the beer and good food waiting for them in Australia. A short meeting with a submarine tender left the boat supplied enough for another month, but that wasn't the same as a liberty port.

"He still all riled up about it?" Casey asked.

"'Riled' is too mild a word, Master Chief. I think the XO's hiding in her stateroom." Sue slumped in her chair. "Captain ripped me a new one about not knowing where to meet up with the *Enterprise* Strike Group and didn't care that their ops officer hasn't gotten back to me yet."

"He's a charmer these days, that's for sure." Casey regretted the words the moment they were out of his mouth. A good COB didn't trash talk officers, especially their captain. He grimaced. "Forget I said that, Nav."

"I heard nothing." Sue's smile grew warmer. "We're all tired."

"Here's hoping we can catch *Enterprise,* watch her underside for a bit, and then go home." Not that Casey believed that would happen. Trouble brewed in the South China Sea, and guess where *Kansas* was headed? Not in the direction of home, that's where.

"If we're lucky." Sue shook her head. "Everyone's on edge, Master Chief. Worse than before."

Worse than what happened with Commander Coleman, she didn't have to say. Casey knew. Casey still kicked himself over not standing up for Coleman at the old XO's mast; everyone knew who'd been right in that situation, and the captain shoved the blame off on Coleman, anyway. That kind of thing sat badly with a crew, particularly after a captain dared lay his hands on any one of them.

"It's our job to—" The sharp ringing of his phone cut in, and Casey grabbed it. "COB."

"Jin, it's Sanelma," Senior Chief Sanelma Salli said over shouting in the background. "Get your ass to the mess decks. Engineering and Navigation are squaring off, and it's gotten ugly."

"Fuck. Anyone throw a punch?"

"Not yet."

"Be right there." This was not what they needed. Casey slammed the phone down and turned to Sue. "Up your ass and fly, Nav. Looks like your boys and girls decided to settle some philosophical differences with the Engineering department."

"Shoot me now."

Sue led the way to the mess decks, about fifty feet forward of Casey's hidey hole. The passageways between the two were strangely empty, eerily so. Dinner was over and the watch just changed, which should've left plenty of sailors wandering about.

Instead, what looked like half of *Kansas'* crew of 135 tried to cram into the mess decks, squeezed in between tables and spilling out into the passageway. Both doors were open but clogged with sailors gaping at the ongoing shouting match.

"—and keep your hands off my man, you whore!" Electronics Technician Third Class Gladys Mills pointed an accusing finger at Machinist's Mate First Class Mary Gorska.

"Ain't my fault he realized you ETs fry your brains." Gorska smirked. "You got a husband back home, girlie. Back off."

"You've got to be shitting me," Sue muttered. "They're fighting over deployment girlfriends and boyfriends?"

"Ain't gonna stop there, Nav." Casey wished it weren't a fucking prophecy.

"They've been at it since dinner." Senior Chief Salli slipped between two sailors to join them in the passageway. "One of my boys came and got me a few minutes ago."

"I don't care who's fucking who," another electronics tech said. "I want to know when the fuck A Gang is going to fix the hot water in our goddamned showers."

Gorska rounded on him. "I keep telling you we're waiting on parts. The tender didn't have the fucking valve, and I can't just shit one out, Torres."

"Then take the part out of the hot water heater in your head and put it in ours, jackass."

"Fuck you." Gorska crossed her arms. "I ain't making every girl on this boat take cold showers because you dickweeds tweaked the heater controls until they burned out the relief valve."

"Fucking engineers making fucking excuses." Torres made a show of rolling his eyes as the other navigation department sailors around him nodded. "Always the same."

"Come say that to my face, sweetie pie." Gorska lurched towards Torres, her eyes wild.

"All right, that's enough." Casey shoved through the door, elbowing two sailors out of the way. "Calm the fuck down before someone gets hurt."

"Dunno, COB, I kinda like the idea of hurting this idiot." Gorska grinned. Several engineers whooped.

"You hear that, COB? She's threatening me!"

"Simmer the fuck down before I break both your faces," Casey growled. "I don't give a good goddamn who started this little chat. It stops now. You're all on the same fucking team, and you'll fucking act like it."

Glowers greeted his words, but no one argued. It was nice to be COB. However, an explosion like this didn't just creep up on a crew, and Casey knew he needed to address the root cause, lest things grow beyond shouting.

"I know. We've been extended again, and no one wants to spend another two months away from home. Lord knows, my old lady's gonna kill my ass when she sees me again. But this is what we all signed up for. In case you've forgotten, nineteen of your brothers and sisters were killed four days ago. Any of you idiots want to sit out a shooting war when your navy's going into harm's way?"

"Ain't no one going to start a war, Master Chief," Mills said. "No one wants to take us on."

"You gonna bet on that?" Casey planted his fists on his hips. "You want to take your cookies and go home 'cause you're so sure no one's gonna take a pot shot at the U.S. Navy?"

Mills looked away.

Casey snorted. "It's all well and good to be proud, people, but ain't no one on this boat getting overconfident. Not on my watch. We're here to do a job. Fucking do it."

It wasn't the most inspirational speech, but Casey wasn't paid to orate. At least mentioning the Diego Garcia incident reminded everyone they weren't just tearing holes in the ocean for fun. It wouldn't restore morale—nothing short of a good liberty port and a deployment end date would do that—but it might take the pot off the burner for a bit.

Alex hoped the summit's official start would decrease his anxiety, but three hours in, no joy. Admiral Hamilton wasn't going to jump out of the shadows, but he couldn't shake the jitters.

"I've got a confession to make, boss," Steph said, walking into the office.

Alex smiled wanly, looking up from his tablet. "I might be Catholic, but I'm no priest."

"Not that kind." She shrugged. "I told Admiral Hamilton about the French marines. And about *Bretagne* showing up out of the blue."

"You did." Alex's chest went tight. "You didn't think about clearing this with me, first?"

"I did." She bit her lip. "I was afraid you'd tell me not to."

Alex wanted to shout, but he had enough of leaders who did that. "I might've." He swallowed. "But you did the right thing. What'd she say?"

"She asked if it was normal. I told her it wasn't."

"I take it Olson's bevy of friends hasn't turned up any information about that, either."

Alex hated that this job turned him into a backwards marriage of supply officer, intelligence gatherer, and administrative clerk. He wasn't trained for any of this, but his instincts said something was off. Why *were* there so many French marines and sailors here? What did they want? For the second time in five months, he was at the center of a situation that made no sense...and so was Camille Dubois.

And *Barracuda*.

"Nada," Steph said. "Everything's quiet. Except for about five hundred French sailors and marines wandering around. They're everywhere now that *Bretagne* put down liberty call."

"That's not abnormal."

She snorted. "The hairs on the back of your neck are standing up, too, aren't they?"

"Yeah." Alex stood up and shoved his hands in his pockets. "My drill sergeant used to say 'you've got instincts for a reason. Use 'em.' They still say that when you got to the Wick?"

"Loud and proud, sir." Steph grimaced.

The Wick was an old nickname for their shared alma mater. They exchanged a loaded look. Norwich graduated unconventional leaders, something Alex had always been proud of—until his independent streak cost him his career while failing to save even a single life.

Hell, what did he have to lose? Investigating beat sitting on his ass. "Keep your ear to the ground," he said. "And see if Bradshaw hears anything during his shady wheeling and dealing."

"You got it, sir. I'll hit Jesse up, too. Sometimes he picks weird shit up."

There were probably five excellent reasons for the sudden uptick in French military visitors, all of them innocent. But that niggling feeling in the back of Alex's mind just wouldn't go away.

Vice Admiral Aadil Khare, Indian Navy, wore a smile that didn't reach his eyes. "The last exchange between our navies was professional and polite," he said.

"I'm glad to hear that, sir," Freddie said, standing near the ornate table in Bluejacket's. "I believe everyone regrets the engagement near Diego Garcia."

Calling it a battle would imply war. Freddie was no politician, but even she knew that. Just like mentioning that the Indians fired first would win her no friends. They were here to stop a war, not start one.

If only she could be sure Khare wanted the same thing.

"Of course, we do," he replied. "As you know, sometimes the best rules of engagement can be misinterpreted by eager officers."

"Are you saying that's what happened?" She cocked her head. *Out of all the* many *ways the U.S. Navy's fucked up in the last half century, shooting at another nation's Navy isn't on the list.* No way did she believe some Indian destroyer drivers decided today was the day to lob full salvos of BrahMos anti-ship missiles at American warships. They were lucky only nineteen died.

"I have not interviewed the captain in question myself, understand, so I can only speculate," Khare said.

"Understandably." Freddie wanted to roll her eyes.

"I believe that if your nation heeds our legitimate territorial concerns, this can end without further bloodshed."

Freddie managed not to grimace. Indian diplomats parroted that line all morning in various tones: regretful, aggressive, sorrowful, and now, blandly hopeful. They wanted Diego Garcia. The Brits almost walked out of the room when the Indians used that as an opening position, but Freddie enjoyed Fowler's expression. He looked like he sucked on a spiky lemon. She knew it was coming. Navies didn't shoot by accident, and BrahMos missiles were expensive.

"Doesn't the Republic of Mauritius have a better claim?" Freddie asked.

She knew Diego Garcia's history. Diego Garcia was the only inhabited island of the Chagos Archipelago, part of the British Indian

Ocean Territory, or BIOT. The Brits still claimed it—and the U.S. kept a base there—both in defiance of a 2019 United Nations' resolution ordering the British to decolonize the island. Diego Garcia was the choicest piece of strategic real estate in the Indian Ocean. Was India willing to go to war for it?

"Have you not heard?" Khare smiled. "Mauritius joined with us to form l'Union pour la Liberté et la Prospérité de l'Océan Indien."

His French made Freddie blink. "The what? And who is *us*?"

"The Union for the Freedom and Prosperity of the Indian Ocean," Khare replied. "India has allied with France, Russia, Burma, Thailand, Malaysia, and—of course—the Republic of Mauritius to preserve our nations' rights and liberties against any who would threaten them."

Freddie stared, feeling cold. Would a senior Indian admiral lie? Glancing left, she saw Fowler standing next to a French diplomat, white-faced and wide-eyed. *They waited until they could drop this on us*, she realized. The score of smaller nations almost didn't matter. India, France, and Russia were in bed *together*?

A look right revealed Brits looking queasy in their dignified way. The Japanese hadn't shown up, but the Aussies seemed downright offended. Both were talking to three Russian representatives who smirked openly. Small wonder why; they had good relations with the Indians before the *Kansas* Incident. The Neyk's sinking splintered nations in the region. Few took America's side, but Australia had, and now they were locked out of this so-called union.

"This is not how alliances are announced, *sir*." Fowler glowered at the French ambassador. He claimed to be the count of something or another.

"I assure you that our ambassador to your country has notified your government," the Frenchman replied.

"Be it as it may, there are international norms for these things!"

"So you say, Monsieur." The French ambassador offered a mocking half bow before walking away.

By the time Freddie turned back to her companion, she realized Khare had also abandoned her. That left her with nothing to do except gravitate towards her least favorite person in the room.

"I think we've been played, Mr. Secretary," she whispered.

Fowler turned his glare on her. "Tell me something I don't know."

"Why don't we skip that, and you tell me what this means?"

"I don't know." He scowled, wiping hands against his perfect silk trousers. "Not yet. Maybe nothing. They might be trying to intimidate us into leaving Diego Garcia. If SecState can't get us out of the fight in Taiwan..."

"We can't fight on both fronts, and they know it." Freddie wanted to swear. Once, the U.S. Navy prepared to fight two major wars plus a regional conflict on the side. Now they were lucky if they could manage one fight, particularly against a Navy as big as China's. Never mind the naval buildups France, India, and Russia executed over the last decade.

"That's *your* problem," Fowler spat.

Freddie stopped herself from mentioning how he called himself a naval expert just a few days ago. "It will be if they start shooting."

"They won't." Fowler shook his head and then shook it again. "No one wants a war."

"Then why'd they shoot in the first place?" she asked.

Fowler had no answer.

Chapter 15

Contraband

11 April 2038

"You've got to come pick the shit up. No way am I gonna deliver it." Bradshaw crossed his arms. "Do I look stupid?"

"C'mon, man, it's a CIVMAR ship. Nobody's going to care," Gunner's Mate Second Class Joe Hines replied. "And we're getting underway tomorrow."

"Fuck no. I love my dip, but the Navy's outlawed the stuff, and it's illegal in most states." He wagged a finger in Hines' face. "I'll sell it to you, but I'm not stupid enough to get caught with it. You got to come grab it this afternoon." Bradshaw knew that ships with combined civilian and navy crews frequently ignored naval regulations they didn't like, but he wasn't about to get arrested because Hines felt lazy.

Particularly not with how *weird* things were on the station right now. Bradshaw loved Armistice Station's peculiar cross of lawlessness and innovation, but his usual contacts were quieter than normal, and people seemed to be holding their breath. Particularly non-Americans.

"Come on. I could just go buy it from somewhere on the station if I wanted to do *work*." Hines crossed his arms, blue eyes narrowed.

Bradshaw laughed. "Yeah, sure. That's why you asked me in the first place. You don't want to get caught, and keeping it inside the family gives you protection."

Hines glared, but gave in, just like Bradshaw knew he would. The Navy forbade smoking on ships years ago, but chewing tobacco lasted longer. Even once banned, officers and chiefs mostly turned a blind eye, until the whole goddamn world decided tobacco was evil. Now, dip was hard to buy outside places like Armistice Station, whose management didn't give a flip for what the FDA said about it.

You could buy almost anything on Armistice Station, and Bradshaw's racket selling it to passing Americans was profitable. Sometimes other nations, too, which was what made him head to the shiny frigate across the pier from *Earhart*.

Bretagne made *Earhart* look like a fat, old lady. Even if *Earhart* wasn't a lumpy and slow cargo ship, she entered service in 2008. The American ship was thirty years old, and it showed. Her crew took good care of her—Bradshaw couldn't spot chipping paint or a ton of running rust—but her fueling rigs were a decade out of date and even her lifeboats looked ancient.

The French frigate, on the other hand, was sleek and nasty. She was eleven years younger than *Earhart* and looked like she'd just left the shipyard. Everything gleamed, from the 76-millimeter OTO Melara gun up forward to the flight deck back aft. *Bretagne* was a variant of the FREMM multipurpose frigate, one of the most common classes in Europe. They were tricky customers, faster and better armed than American frigates.

Right now, *Bretagne* was knee-deep in a stores onload. It was the second day of the summit, and the French finally figured out what they needed to buy from the locals. It looked like eggs, fresh fruit, and some frozen meat. Nothing fun like energy drinks or ice cream. *Perfect timing.*

"You got anyone who speaks English around?" he asked the nearest sailor with enough rank to matter. But not too much. He didn't want the French equivalent of a chief chasing him off.

She was cute, short, and glared like he killed her grandmother. "Why?"

"My name's Francis Bradshaw," he said, glad he'd changed out of his uniform. "I'm a purveyor of hard-to-find items. If you have anyone on board who has certain...needs, I can meet them."

Her eyes narrowed. "We don't want your kind here."

"Whoa, not that kind of needs." Bradshaw held his hands up. Damn language differences! "I'm not a pimp. I meant *things*, not people. Like tobacco. Or goldfish. Or whatever it is that's hard to get at home." He smiled. "Almost everything's legal here, and I can help you find it."

Even drugs, he didn't say. Bradshaw didn't like dealing in the hard stuff, but if she asked, he'd point her at someone who did. Drugs were the one thing he was sure would get him kicked out of the Navy and ruin his sweet gig. Even Commander Coleman couldn't ignore drugs.

"I don't care what you're selling," she said. "Get lost."

"Hey, I'm just trying to be friendly."

"You don't want to be friends here." She turned towards him, her expression guarded but less hostile. "You understand?"

"No...?"

The French sailor looked left and right before focusing on him again. "This station is going to be a bad place to be American. Leave with your ship."

Bradshaw blinked, confused until he realized she must have seen him coming off *Earhart.* "Uh, it's not my ship, and—"

"Then go anyway. You'll want to." She bit her lip as someone called to her in French. "I can't say more. I have to go."

"Wait!" Bradshaw tried to say, but she hurried away without looking back, grabbing a flat of eggs on her way. "What the hell?" he muttered.

No one answered, but several other French sailors shot death glares his way. How the hell did he piss them off?

His phone chirped as Alex walked past Green Skies, Armistice Station's premier dive shop. *Need more information on French military on station—WAH,* the text read. A moment passed before Alex remembered they'd preprogrammed his number into the phones bought for Admiral Hamilton and Secretary Fowler. *WAH* stood for Winifred Alice Hamilton. Jesus, his least favorite admiral was texting him.

Rgr, he texted back.

"GM1, did you find anything else about the French?" he turned to ask Amy Olson. Olson accompanied Alex when he paid a visit to *Earhart*'s civilian master. Captain Soboda was uneasy, too, and not because he had to share a pier with a French frigate. But no one knew what to do about the odd sense of impending doom, so Alex headed back towards his office with Olson in tow.

There was a weird feeling in the air, like hundreds of people holding their breath. Even the tourists seemed to notice; they seemed to be spending money like there was no tomorrow. Alex's stomach churned. Or was that just his imagination because Freddie fucking

Hamilton was less than a mile away at any given time and she *again* held his career in her hands? *Four more years until I can retire*. He never expected to look forward to that date.

Did his anxiety make him a coward? Alex never questioned his own bravery until Kennedy did, but now he wondered. Maybe he left his nerve back on *Kansas*. Wasn't that a happy thought? Maybe he needed to retire, do something bland like teach high school students to march in circles in NJROTC.

"A, uh, friend of mine says a bunch of them came in on motor vessel *Empire Conveyor*. She's French-flagged, but her last stop was in Mauritius," Olson replied. "The IMO database says that *Empire Conveyor* has room for about a hundred and fifty passengers in addition to cargo."

"That's a lot of marines." Alex fished a hard candy out of his pocket and popped it in his mouth. Chewing something always helped him think. "Assuming they're full."

"Could've brought tourists, too." Olson glanced up from her phone. "Bradshaw's going to try to get their manifest when he hawks his current scam to them."

"Your newest boyfriend couldn't help with that?" Alex asked.

"Nope." Her smile turned a touch contrite. "Sir."

"Pity." Alex couldn't—and didn't want to—track Olson's romantic entanglements. He rubbed his temples to try to banish the sudden ache. Hamilton would text again. Probably soon. The thought made his chest tight.

Think, asshole. Alex let out a breath. That tense anticipation wasn't a product of his imagination. Were there more French speakers around than usual? Armistice Station was the proverbial mixing bowl, with residents from all corners of the world. Most spoke English—it was the top maritime language—but other languages rarely stood out. He opened his mouth to ask Olson what she thought when her hand slapped down on his arm.

"Come on." Olson pulled Alex towards Lotus' store front. The display was full of televisions and tablets—every one of which was on the same channel.

"...the BBC has received multiple reports of a series of explosions ripping across mainland China. At last count, fifteen—no, now seventeen—government buildings have been bombed," a short anchor wearing glasses said. The background was full of drone-recorded video of burning buildings and people in the streets.

"The government of Beijing places the blame squarely on terrorists, although no group has thus far taken credit," the anchor continued. "The death toll is rising rapidly, with at least three hundred reported dead and twice that many injured. This dramatic use of violence comes just as the Chinese Navy is said to be readying for a second amphibious assault on Taiwan, after the first assault was shockingly repulsed by Taiwanese forces just days ago. Sources within the Chinese government claim that the military blames party politicians for reducing the size of the first assault wave. The second assault is said to be much larger, but whether it will be launched after so much destruction is yet to be seen."

Alex's jaw dropped, and he blinked several times. He knew the *Enterprise* Strike Group was only two days away from the Strait of Malacca. A day and a half from there and they'd be in Taiwan's front yard, ready to help the longtime American allies. But this changed *everything.*

Would China keep fighting, or might they make peace? And if so, would the Indians and their allies back off? No one wanted to tangle with the American gorilla alone. Hope stirred in his chest.

His phone chirped again. *Get message traffic concerning Chinese terrorist attacks from AME*, Hamilton ordered via text. *Need to know what this changes.*

Will do, Alex typed back. His hands were clammy, and his heart racing. His office lacked a secure computer, so they couldn't receive classified message traffic, but *Earhart* could. Where was Steph? Alex shot her a message: *Meet me on AME. Need to check traffic.*

On my way, she replied, and he tucked his phone back in his pocket to look back at the televisions. They still showed scenes of burned out buildings and ambulances carrying wounded away. Most of the hits seemed to be in Beijing, and—

"Commander, something's weird here," Bradshaw hissed in his ear, making Alex jump.

"Jesus, Bradshaw! Where the fuck did you come from?"

Several people shushed them and glared, so Alex led his miscreant petty officer to the other side of the tube, leaving Olson watching T.V. Bradshaw grinned, but then the expression vanished.

"Something's wonky with *Bretagne*." Bradshaw chewed his lip. "I went to—well, you don't want to know—and I talked to this cute little French petty officer. But what she said wasn't so cute. She said this station was going to be a bad place to be an American, and I should leave."

"What?"

"She wouldn't say more, but I got this trying-to-help-but-shouldn't-be vibe from her." Bradshaw shrugged. "Like I said. Wonky."

"You sure she didn't just want to chase your ass off?" Olson asked, approaching to elbow Bradshaw.

"Nah, I know what that looks like. Happens all the time."

Alex looked between his two sailors, and then glanced back at the televisions. Logic told him the two events couldn't be related, but what if they were? *Grand conspiracy theories only happen in movies.* He shook his head. Even if the explosions were the work of a nation state instead of terrorists, France and their allies wouldn't want China knocked out of the fight. They needed the broiling Chinese war to distract the United States. Otherwise, they'd never get what they wanted without a war.

But no one wanted war, so none of this made any sense.

Chapter 16

Countdown

"Do you think these events change anything, Admiral?" Ambassador Meghana Batra asked after they were secluded in a private conference room within the Ballard complex.

Admiral Khare hesitated, thinking through the day's sessions. The diplomats talked in predictable circles, going back and forth over the ownership of Diego Garcia. The British—greedy colonists, all of them—were irate, and the Americans were hardly better. Despite learning about India's new alliance, the United States acted as if no one would ever dare flout their authority.

Somehow, he suspected they had yet to do the math. The American navy was outnumbered by the Union for the Freedom and Prosperity of the Indian Ocean, or ULP, by almost three-to-one. Khare knew the numbers by heart. Successive American politicians' desire to spend military funding on domestic projects downsized the U.S. Navy in the early 2020s, and they'd been slow to drive investment on the ocean floor. The fools let private corporations take the risks underseas—and reap the benefits. Thus, while billions in revenue flowed into India, France, and Russia's government coffers, America lagged behind.

"No, I do not," he said. "China is vast. Even this amount of damage is something they can absorb. Particularly if the culprit turns out to be Taiwan, vice domestic terrorists."

"Do you think it will?" Batra arched one sculpted eyebrow.

Meghana Batra was a small woman, dressed in traditional Indian garb, but she radiated competence and charisma. Unlike the second-rate politicians other nations sent to the Great Summit, India sent one of her finest. Batra's star was rising, and Khare was content to work with her. Being in favor would not hurt his future career prospects one bit. Khare aimed to be the youngest Chief of the Naval Staff in Indian history. He had six years left to accomplish that goal.

Breaking some American heads along the way would merely make things sweeter.

"It would be...foolish of them," he replied. Not to mention strategically ineffective. Taiwan was the underdog in their battle with China. That engendered a great deal of sympathy from the international community, more than China wanted to admit. Taiwan would not jeopardize that by targeting civilians.

"Foolishness rarely stops people, in my experience." Batra frowned. "Do you think we should ease our position regarding Diego Garcia?"

"No. Not for a moment." He flashed a smile. "If we continue pressing, and American finds itself at war with China—which they will, should they persist in supporting Taiwan—something will have to give so that they do not *also* end up at war with us. It will be Diego Garcia."

"And if the British make a fight of it?"

Khare laughed. "We could destroy the better part of their navy in an afternoon, Madame Ambassador."

"Please do not exaggerate. I am not unschooled in military realities."

"With our allies' help, I am not exaggerating," he replied. "I have a healthy respect for the Royal Navy. They have set the standard by which all professional navies must measure themselves for centuries, but they are not the force they once were. The Australians worry me more."

"How so?" she asked. "It is my understanding that the Royal Navy still outnumbers the Royal Australian Navy."

"Australia is much closer. I would prefer to invite them into our alliance, although I understand the political reasons why we will not." Khare grimaced. "Still, if we could pry them out from between Britain and America's skirts, we could encircle the Indian Ocean with friends."

Batra shook her head. "They rebuffed our every attempt. Say what you will, but the Australians are loyal to their former overlords."

"Pity."

"So, your advice is to continue demanding sovereignty of Diego Garcia?" she asked.

"Yes, Madame Ambassador. Faced with the might of China, America will need friends—or at least neutral parties—at her back. They cannot fight us and China at the same time."

Batra nodded.

"That fucking Indian destroyer is shadowing us." Captain Ernest Edwards glared at John like it was his fault before shrugging. "I don't like being in BrahMos range like this."

"If what I read on those things is right, you'd have to be outside three *hundred* nautical miles for that." John snorted. "We're inside BrahMos range for half the Indian Navy."

"Point." Edwards sat back in the CO's chair on *Enterprise's* bridge, scowling at the horizon. John stood beside him, marveling at how nice it would be to have a command chair to fight from. Attack subs didn't have space for luxuries; some of the older ones had tiny fold down chairs for the captain, but someone forgot to install that in the *Cero*-class. "I'd settle for him being out of radar range."

"He is being a little rude for a surface ship, isn't he?" John asked. "I keep forgetting you guys assume everyone can see each other up here."

"It's easier from the air." Edwards barked out a laugh. "You sub types just like to hide."

"Don't throw stones. You sound like you'd like hiding about now."

"Stealth's a great gig if you can pull it off, but my fat lady here has one hell of a radar cross-section," Edwards said. "You can't miss us."

"Yeah, you're loud, too." John grinned, but his smile faded when one of his staffers approached with a message tablet. "What's up?"

"Flash traffic, sir," the young lieutenant said. "Nineteen government buildings got exploded in China. PACOM says get to Taiwan ASAP."

"Explosions *where*?" Edwards demanded, only for one of his own officers to hand the same message over.

John scanned it, trying to think through the repercussions as quickly as he could. *Nothing good. Nothing at all.* "The admiral see this?" he asked.

"Not yet, sir. He's napping."

"Wake him up," John ordered. McNally was easy going about most things, but he'd go ape if someone sat on this. John handed the tablet back and watched the lieutenant scurry off before looking back to Edwards. "Change formation base speed to thirty knots." He hesitated. "The destroyers can manage that, right?"

"Yeah. *Belleau Wood* can't get much better, though." Edwards twisted in his chair. "Officer of the Deck, pass immediate execute, change formation speed to thirty knots."

"Officer of the Deck, aye!"

"The cruiser's the slowest ship out here," Edwards said in an undertone, one non-surface officer speaking to another. Like all nuclear carrier captains, Edwards was an aviator. In his case, a F/A-18 pilot who transitioned to F-35s later, along with two tours as a test pilot. Like John, he spent decades learning one profession before branching out to include surface warfare.

"You're all crazy slow, as far as I'm concerned," John replied. "Except maybe the carrier."

They exchanged grins. *Enterprise* could outrun her escorts by at least ten knots; John hadn't asked how fast she was and was sure it was classified. Hopefully, he wouldn't need to find out. But John's old command, *Cero*, was faster still. America's newest attack submarines clocked in at over fifty-seven knots in sea trials, five better than the builder's best estimate. Not that John ever took *Cero* up that fast, even for fun. Speed meant noise, and noise was death.

Except out here where people could *see* you. Then being quiet did no good.

John remained on the bridge as *Enterprise* and her escorts came up in speed, missing the way *Cero* vibrated under his feet. You could barely feel a thing on *Enterprise*, even when the seas were rough. John should be grateful; like many submariners, he got seasick on the surface. But not on a carrier. Carriers were so damned big.

"Admiral's on the bridge!" a sailor called several minutes later. John turned to greet his boss.

"You came up in speed?" McNally asked.

"Yes, sir. Thirty knots is the best the cruiser can do."

"Very well." McNally frowned. "Do we need to update our transit plan?"

"I'll re-do the time distance for the increase in speed, but it shouldn't change much," John said. Then he remembered his promise to Nancy Coleman. "Except...this might be the time to look at the formation itself. *Fletcher* is way out there by herself, and without a tail, she's never going to pick up enemy submarines."

McNally shook his head. "*Kansas* should meet us on the other side of the SOM. She can lead the formation from there on out. You think that'll make Coleman shut up?"

"Uh, probably." John tried not to grimace. "She's got legit concerns, sir."

"They won't matter once we have *Kansas*." McNally waved off John's frown. "I'm not worried about subs in the SOM. Who wants to drive through there without surfacing, anyway? That's a great way to get run over."

"Yeah, it's happened before," John said. The Navy didn't like to advertise it, but American submarines transiting close—but not on—the surface had indeed been run over. Sometimes, and even more embarrassingly, by other U.S. Navy ships.

Still, he didn't understand McNally's new casual attitude. Four days ago, he was on fire over not having an attack sub. Now he didn't think *Fletcher* would run into enemy subs while on point? Usually, John had a good read on his boss. This gave him whiplash.

"All right, let's get down to the flag bridge and look at what's going on in China and what that means to us," McNally said before John could ask.

"Lead on, sir."

Rummaging through message traffic gave Alex jack shit and nothing. Admiral Hamilton didn't like that—he could feel her glower through the text—but no one had any idea what China would do. Hell, the news gave him more information than classified sources did, which left him watching television in the office and eating candy out of the bowl on the table.

The death toll in China was up to nine hundred, thanks to an apartment building that collapsed after the explosions. Every news channel played images of the carnage on repeat, speculating about who did it while China girded for war.

"Have you found *any* useful information, Commander?" a voice demanded from behind him.

Alex jumped to his feet, his heart jackrabbiting in his chest. "Admiral."

She waved off his formality, glowering. "Has the intelligence community pulled their heads out and analyzed this mess yet?"

"No, ma'am." Alex swallowed, glad she didn't seem to blame him. *Don't get cocky, idiot. She still hates you.* "Captain Soboda promised to let me know if anything...insightful comes in."

"Very well." She sighed.

They watched the news for several long minutes, until Alex could take the silence no more. As an introvert, Alex was usually happy to keep his mouth shut, but sharing a room with Admiral Hamilton gave him the willies. Screwing up his courage, he asked: "How'd the summit go, ma'am?"

Brown eyes flicked over to glare at him. "It ended early on account of events," she snarled. "And before that, it was one circle after another. This new 'Union for the Freedom and Prosperity of the Indian Ocean' is marking time until we find out if we're shooting at China or not."

"Have the Indians mentioned reparations for those who died on *Sam Nunn* and *Spruance*?"

"Fat chance. They implied the encounter was our fault, even though logs from both destroyers prove otherwise." Hamilton's frown promised a storm.

"What are they playing at?" Alex didn't like politics, and he couldn't understand why someone would want to lie for a living.

"They're *politicians*, Commander," another voice interjected.

Alex and Hamilton both turned as Under Secretary Fowler pranced into the room, looking as puffed up as ever. He wore a new suit, this one lighter blue than the last. The second security officer entered the office on his heels, and then stopped just inside the doorway to join his fellow. Neither said anything, but both relaxed.

This had to be a pretty cake detail for security pukes. Armistice Station's crime rate was low; the punishment for any infraction was a steep fine or exile from the station. The rare heinous criminal was sent to their home country, giftwrapped for trial.

"Mr. Secretary." Hamilton didn't *quite* scowl.

Fowler gave Alex a patronizing smile. "I imagine they don't teach you much about politics at the Naval Academy."

"I didn't attend the Academy, sir." Alex didn't add that he had a degree in National Security and Strategic Studies from the Naval War College, which contained a hefty dose of international relations. He suspected Fowler wouldn't care.

"Oh, well. Of course." Fowler waved a hand, his disdain ratcheting up a notch. "At any rate, our Indian friends—or, should I say the entire 'Freedom Union'—have established a firm position. But it won't last. They'll give in time, particularly once things calm down between China and Taiwan."

"That doesn't look calm." Alex gestured at the television.

"That's what I've been telling him," Hamilton muttered.

"It's a speed bump. SecState will be there tomorrow, and we'll work something out," Fowler replied, crossing to Alex's chair and sitting in it without asking. "China's first assault was ruinously expensive for both them *and* Taiwan. It isn't sensible to continue the fight. It will cost both sides too much."

"Wars aren't usually waged in the name of common sense, Mr. Secretary." Hamilton's tired look said they'd had this argument before. No way was Alex touching it with a ten foot pole.

"I have heard and noted your opinions, Admiral," Fowler snapped.

"Don't misunderstand me, Mr. Secretary," the admiral said. "I hope you are right. But I fear your assessment is overconfident."

"I am a student of history." Fowler puffed up again. "I know how this works."

Yeah, that sounded like a recipe for disaster. Alex scowled. Who left this guy in charge of America's future, anyway?

The next day started like any other at Shanghai Naval Station: foggy, and with an exhausted fervor borne of a country ready to go to war. Almost five thousand miles from Armistice Station, Shanghai was the largest port in the world and the People's Liberation Army Navy's largest base. The first fleet to attempt an invasion of Taiwan departed from there, and the second would get underway in four hours. The base crawled with personnel, loading stores and weapons onto ships.

Shortly after 0900, local time, a squadron of Harbin Z-19 helicopter gunships lifted off. No one blinked; they were too busy to pay attention to a mere dozen helicopters taking off.

Ten minutes passed before air controllers realized these aircraft were not on their flight plan. By then, the Z-19s—each carrying eight HJ-8S air-to-surface missiles—turned away from the northern airfields and south towards the piers. The Z-19s and their weapons were designed decades earlier, but the HJ-8*S* "Hongjian" missile still had a good warhead. One designed to target surface ships and submarines.

These twelve helicopters carried 96 missiles between them. There were forty-nine warships in port. Twenty were amphibious ships full of People's Liberation Army (PLA) infantry ready for the invasion. Thirteen destroyers, nine frigates, and seven diesel submarines waited with them. The replenishment ships, nuclear submarines, and two aircraft carriers normally stationed in Shanghai were already underway, but the fleet slumbering pier side remained powerful.

All guarded for an attack coming from the southeast; Taiwan was the current enemy. America was expected soon. No one expected an attack from inland, not from People's Liberation Army Navy helicopters carrying PLAN weapons.

The Z-19s split apart, one helicopter transitioning to hover at the head of every pier. By then, watching sailors' curiosity turned to horror as Hongjian missile boosters ignited and fire filled the morning sky.

With an approximate speed of 220 meters per second, there was no time to hide. A few close-in weapons mounts swiveled to meet the threat, but none had time to fire. Another salvo of missiles followed the first, and then another, and another. Within ten seconds, forty-nine warships were aflame.

Turning, the helicopters vanished into the fog.

Chapter 17

Through a Narrow Lens

12 April 2038

They said God protected fools and mariners. Master Chief Chinedu Casey sure as hell hoped that was true, because his captain needed protection on both fronts.

"Why the *hell* didn't you tell me about that fight on the mess decks?" Kennedy tried to pace in his small cabin, but there wasn't enough room. Casey perched against the table to squeeze out of the way, but it still nearly earned him an elbow to the gut.

"Captain, it wasn't a fight. The boys and girls are just on edge. Give 'em a job to do, and they'll be okay," he replied. There was no use saying that he knew Kennedy would overreact. Kennedy was the type who vacillated between wanting to be the *cool* captain beloved by the crew and a harsh disciplinarian.

"That's not your call to make, COB."

"Beggin' your pardon, sir, but I'm the Chief of the Boat. Enlisted morale is my job. Nobody threw anything worse than a few nasty words. They'll get over it."

Casey wanted to ask who played rat and went to the captain, but Kennedy wouldn't tell him. The CO, XO, and COB were *supposed* to be a team, but working with Kennedy was like swimming upstream. Sometimes it was possible, but it was always exhausting. Their XO of four months, Lieutenant Commander Allison Hunt, was a good sort, but she had Kennedy's number, too. No one survived arguments with the captain. It was better not to start one.

Kennedy's glare wanted to melt steel. "I prefer to know what's happening on *my* boat."

"I'll be sure to tell you next time, Captain." *Long after the fact.* Casey took a breath. "Anything else bothering you? You seem on edge."

Enlisted sailors weren't supposed to ask their captains that question, but Master Chiefs were an exception. Casey's primary duties revolved around the enlisted crew, but only an idiot COB thought he didn't need to watch the care and feeding of the officers, too. And this CO needed special stroking.

Kennedy sat up in his chair, his blue eyes intense. "We've been directed to meet the *Enterprise* Strike Group as they exit the SOM," he said. "We'll have to go through the Sunda Strait."

"Surfaced? That's not real stealthy."

"Of course not! We're almost at war."

Casey frowned. "That's going to be a bitch and a half, sir. There's a lot of traffic in there, and the average depth is what, sixty-something feet?"

"Close enough." Kennedy shrugged. "We'll make it work and surface when we have to. The strike group doesn't have a sub escort, so I want to transit as fast as possible. Twenty-plus knots. Better, when there's enough water under the keel."

"Twenty-plus?" Casey's jaw dropped. The Sunda Strait was a 15-mile-wide waterway between Sumatra and Java. The strait was very deep to the west, the direction *Kansas* would enter from, but sloped upwards as you moved closer to the islands. *Kansas'* navigational draft was thirty-four feet, and her sail was taller than that. They usually wanted at least two hundred feet under the keel before they submerged. Staying at periscope depth in sixty feet of water was *technically* possible, but only if you were an idiot. *Kansas* was sure as shit not going to be the next U.S. sub to run into an underwater mountain.

Even worse, twenty knots was faster than a lot of the merchant traffic. *Kansas* would have to *dodge* some of those ships to avoid running right up their asses. Or she might get run over by some speed demon.

There were no good options here, just shitty and shitactular.

"You heard me, COB." Kennedy scowled. "I'm not letting *another* opportunity pass us by. The crew deserves to be remembered for more than just that mess at Armistice Station."

"Yeah, I can agree with that." Casey didn't say that *Kennedy* wanted the limelight. They crossed that bridge four months ago.

"Then let's get to work!" Kennedy's glare transformed into a grin as he bounced out the door, heading for control.

Casey followed, hoping like hell this *opportunity* didn't lead to another disaster.

The third day of the summit started with a strange feeling in the room. Fowler stole the opportunity to embark on a long speech about old alliances and overcoming prejudice; Freddie tried not to cringe when the French representative laughed.

Interestingly, Madame Devereux had a new companion with her today, a French submarine captain. He was good looking in a Mediterranean way, with a tanned complexion and darker hair and eyes. He looked bored, even more so than Freddie, and his laughing eyes met hers as Fowler pontificated, as if inviting her to share some joke she was sure came at America's expense.

Freddie's eyes narrowed. She glared until he shrugged and looked away, saying something to Madame Devereux in an undertone.

"Monsieur, every point you have made ignores the Chagos Archipelago's legitimate desire for freedom," Devereux said when Fowler finished.

Fowler flushed. "The original inhabitants of the Chagos Archipelago no longer exist, Madame. Their descendants abrogated their claim when they departed the islands."

Freddie winced. Leave it to Fowler to be stupid enough to bring that up. He ridiculed the simple military mindset, but he really was a believer in might making right, wasn't he?

"Departed by *force*, sir," Admiral Khare jumped in.

"We cannot and should not attempt to fix the sins of our forefathers." Fowler sniffed. "In fact—"

"Allow me to continue, please," the British representative cut in. Freddie wanted to hug him. "After all, the *British* Indian Ocean Territory remains an integral part of the United Kingdom."

Fowler reddened. Freddie sat back to listen as the argument circled back to the same point for the fourteenth time. Why did the French and the Indians look pleased to cover the same territory? At this rate, they'd get—

A hand landed on her arm, and Freddie turned to look at a white-faced Lieutenant Jesse Lin. Fowler's escort didn't attend sessions, and the theoretically private meetings weren't to be interrupted. Yet the room was suddenly full of twitchy aides.

"Admiral, Mr. Secretary, we've just received reports of an attack on Shanghai Naval Base," Jesse whispered. "Forty-nine warships are damaged or sunk."

"What?" Freddie felt cold. She couldn't believe her ears.

"Yes, ma'am." Jesse shrugged.

"Who attacked them?" Fowler demanded.

"No one knows yet, sir. Taiwan says it's not them."

"Of course, it's them!" Fowler's voice carried, and heads turned. "What kind of idiot are you?"

Jesse flushed. Freddie stood. "Ladies and Gentlemen, I'm sure we've all received the same news. May I suggest another recess?"

"A splendid idea, Admiral," Khare said, nodding before withdrawing to a side room.

The American delegation didn't *have* a conference room in the Ballard complex, which left them trudging back to the Naval Detachment's offices through Armistice Station's public transport. Freddie nudged Jesse into the front of their group, aware of Fowler glaring at the lieutenant's back.

"Don't ever do that again," Fowler snapped.

Freddie blinked. "Do what?"

"Speak for our delegation. That is *my* job." Could a four-year-old pout more than Fowler? Freddie didn't have kids and wasn't sure.

She shrugged, blood boiling. Having an ego was mandatory at their level, but only fools let it get in the way of doing their duty. "You seemed occupied with berating Lieutenant Lin."

"I am not—"

"I think we should continue this discussion in private, don't you, Mr. Secretary?" Freddie said. "There are ears everywhere."

"We're being followed by three Frenchmen," Maria cut in when Fowler made to respond.

Freddie wished she didn't find the way his mouth flopped shut so damned satisfying. Not having a proper intelligence officer along was an oversight Freddie wished they could correct. Since they couldn't, she used Maria to watch the eavesdroppers.

"Oh," Fowler was blessedly quiet for the rest of the walk.

Three hours later, Alex would've given his left arm to get the admiral and the politician out of his office. Even worse, Fowler appropriated his candy bowl, so Alex couldn't even grab some starburst to make himself feel better.

The news provided a non-stop barrage of non-answers, which made everyone in the room cranky. Everyone except Steph, who typed away at her laptop at the conference table, ignoring everyone else.

Alex poured himself a third cup of coffee, filling up the Darth Vader mug his first chief gave him on his division officer tour. One of his favorite things about Armistice Station was its four exotic coffee shops, all from different countries. Today's blend was from the New Girkaru estate in Kenya, and it was one of Alex's favorites so far. Too bad Fowler and Admiral Hamilton drank most of it with lunch. It was too expensive to buy much more.

"Hey, boss, I've got something," Steph said without looking up.

Fowler glared, but Alex crossed the room to look over her shoulder, sipping his coffee. "What's up?"

"Someone's claiming responsibility for the attack. They call themselves the 'Democratic Republic of China' and say that units of the Chinese Army and Navy have defected to them."

"Say *again*?" Hamilton slammed her coffee cup into the table, spilling its contents. They dribbled into a steaming puddle on the floor next to her foot.

No one moved to clean it up.

"They've uploaded multiple statements online and are offering to hold a press conference in two hours. That's going to be *all* the fu—um, all *over* the news." Steph's eyes flew across the screen. "They're claiming to be the legitimate government of China, *allied* to Taiwan."

"Sweet Jesus." A chill ripped down Alex's spine. He was no historian, but every naval officer knew the history between China and Taiwan. After the communists' victory in the Chinese Civil War, the remnants of the democratic government fled to Taiwan. Even today, Taiwan called itself the Republic of China.

The *People's* Republic of China claimed to own Taiwan and spent eighty-plus years threatening violent reunification. Now, with war on, a *third* Chinese government cropped up?

"You can say that again." Hamilton swallowed.

"I need to call for instructions," Fowler said.

"You can use the secure phone at my desk, Mr. Secretary," Alex said, gesturing. Fowler half-stumbled there.

Would this mean a three-way shooting war? No. *Allied with Taiwan*. Alex finally remembered to sip his coffee, his mind working. Meanwhile, Steph pulled up a video of some Chinese naval officer or another. Alex couldn't remember all their rank insignia, but she looked like an admiral.

The Democratic Republic of China seeks to represent all of China, the subtitles read as the Chinese admiral spoke. *We cannot allow these heinous attacks on our brothers and sisters on the island of Taiwan to continue. We will therefore overthrow the tyrannical government of the communist party and reunite China once and for all.*

"This could mean another civil war," Hamilton whispered, walking on wooden legs to stand next to Alex.

"Two at the same time?" Alex asked.

"Shit."

"Outgoing calls aren't working," Fowler snapped, storm clouds coloring his expression again.

"Really?" Alex turned.

"Try it for yourself if you don't believe me." Fowler scowled. "Lieutenant Lin, escort me up to *Earhart*. I'll use their communications."

Jesse gulped, freezing with a sandwich halfway between his plate and mouth. "*Earhart* got underway yesterday, sir. She's not due back until the end of the summit on the eighteenth."

"Whose brilliant idea was that?" Fowler flopped into a chair at the table, huffing.

"Staying moored here is expensive?" Jesse sounded like he wanted to sink into the floor. Alex knew how he felt.

"Fine." Fowler turned to glare at Steph. "Show me that."

Sighing, she slid her laptop across the table to the politician. Meanwhile, Alex dropped back into his own chair, lifting the phone. It wasn't actually a landline; all of Armistice Station's communications lines snaked up from the station along the TRANSPLAT struts to antennas on the first four platforms. This one was as secure as any uncontrolled data line on a civilian station could be, with software that scrambled and unscrambled conversations at either end. Theoretically, anyone tapping into the line would hear only gibberish.

There was no dial tone. Alex hung up the phone and tried again. Still nothing. Frowning, he pulled his cell out. It had no service, either.

"There's no service anywhere," he said.

"Same here," Jesse said from the desk he shared with Bradshaw.

Steph glanced at her phone. "Yeah. Nothing."

"Is this *normal*, Commander?" Hamilton asked.

"No, ma'am." Alex fought the urge to fidget. "We've never had service problems here."

"They brag about that," Steph added. "Insufferably."

Alex's lips twitched into a smile, but Hamilton's frown made it vanish. "Is this a case of everyone and their mother trying to call out at the same time, or are we looking at a denial-of-service attack?" the admiral asked.

"Um." Alex blinked.

"Why would someone attack here and leave the internet up?" Steph shook her head. "I can video call and send email." She twisted to look at Fowler. "Do you have Skype at the State Department, Mr. Secretary? I can get you through that way."

If she couldn't, Steph would just hack her way in, but there was no reason to say that. Hackers made admirals nervous, and Hamilton hated him enough, already.

Another two hours passed before Fowler reached anyone for updated instructions. During that time, the United Nations Security Council met, voting to condemn the so-called Democratic Republic of China and calling for peace. Taiwanese representatives—not technically members of the U.N. but allowed to be present—confirmed the existence of this unified Chinese government.

The U.S. vetoed the resolution accusing the new DROC of war crimes, on the grounds of lack of information on the actual attack.

Predictably, the State Department had eyes only for China and didn't care what happened out at the less-Great-than-ever Summit. Fowler scowled up a storm as he was told to wait and yelled at some poor assistant. Alex watched with growing horror.

Was this how World War III started?

Nah.

"We should wait," Admiral Khare said as soon as he walked into Armistice Station's governing complex.

This room, called "Central," was the command center, the heart of the station. Monitors lined the walls, showing environmental statuses, ships and submarines docked, the number of resident personnel, and more. One could shut down almost any system in the station from here—even the safety protocols. Yet it was the one room on the station without that faint blue tint to the lighting; Central was stark white, as bright as day. Captain Jules Rochambeau appreciated Central's functionality without liking the environment; he preferred soft yellow light, or even red lights, when faced with banks of computers.

Jules shrugged. "To what end, Monsieur l'Amiral? Our governments are in agreement. There is no reason to delay."

Khare scowled. "The new developments in China are disturbing. If the United States does *not* intervene..."

"They will," Jules said. "And if they do not, they will not have the strength to interfere. And even if they do...our actions will be nonviolent."

"Simply forceful?" Khare laughed without humor.

"Oui."

"I envy your confidence." Khare looked annoyed, but what did Jules care?

Their plan was solid, if not a match to his original brief. Reduce American influence without bloodshed. The Americans would argue, but they would have no choice. They were too invested in Taiwan to let China take over—and China had too big of a military for this single attack to handicap their navy. Jules did not *like* the task he was given, but he would see it through. In the end, his nation would benefit.

Both their nations would, assuming the Indians didn't get cold feet. The Russian representative absented herself from such discussions, but Jules knew that the Red Bear itched to regain its old prominence. Russia would not object, even if they would not actively participate. Yet.

"It is not confidence," he replied. "It is acceptance of reality. In order for our nations to act freely in this area of the world, we must reduce American influence. Their continued interference harms all of our interests."

"Hm." Khare eyed him. "Was the *Kansas* Incident scripted to accomplish that same end, Captain?"

Jules met his gaze. "I know not of what you speak."

"Of course, you do not." Khare chuckled. "Because you and your submarine just 'happened' to be present when the Americans faced off with that Neyk Four."

"Armistice Station has always been a friend to France," Jules replied.

"Yes, and your new executive officer was not the liaison whom America has blamed for the 'misunderstanding.'" Khare rolled his eyes. "Do not take me for an idiot, Captain. My country is aware of what your nation has done to manipulate events."

Jules smiled and spread his hands. "Well, I suppose one ought not be shy, then."

"Indeed." Khare made a face.

"Does your country not approve?" Jules asked innocently.

Khare huffed. "Our approval does not matter. We are already involved."

"Then I am afraid that I am not worried about your tender feelings, Admiral." Jules smiled, showing teeth. "Our nations have agreed that this is my operation, non?"

"Yes." The word was a hiss.

"Then allow me to show you that France will follow through on our obligations. We will back your play for the Chagos Archipelago. You will support us here."

"Of course, I will." Khare's expression was no happier, but at least his voice was firm. "I understand my duty, *Captain*."

"Très bien." Jules turned to the third person in the room, who had watched their conversation in silence. "Madame Ledoux, can you confirm that the Russian delegation has departed?"

"Oui. Their ship left one hour ago."

"Excellent. Then, would you be so kind as to cut off all communications except bridge-to-bridge radio?"

"I would be delighted." Ledoux smiled, probably thinking of her growing bank account.

Not that Jules minded. Making one wealthy woman richer served France's purposes. They would make the money back within a year. Besides, it would not come out of the Navy's budget, so what did he care? He nodded his thanks. "Merci."

"Pas de quoi," she replied, and walked over to the nearest keyboard. Four keystrokes later, she nodded. "Fini."

Jules turned back to Khare. "Now we begin."

Chapter 18

Calm Before the Storm

Dinner was pizza delivery, which Admiral Hamilton seemed to find a novel concept on an underwater station. Steph was used to it, though she certainly didn't mind when the detachment's budget stretched to buying food.

Pizza Hut tasted great here; it didn't have the different spices the pizza chain used in other countries and tasted just like it did back home. However, pizza didn't help her mood when Fowler appropriated Steph's laptop to keep in touch with the state department. She had a tablet, sure, but tablets weren't the best for typing.

"You been with the admiral long?" she asked Maria Vasquez. Maria was a submariner, but they were the same rank, and she seemed cool. She had to be on the fast track, too, to be Freddie Hamilton's aide.

"About a year." Maria shrugged. "She's a good boss."

"She's sitting right here, Maria." Hamilton didn't look up from a book on her own tablet, but Steph thought she saw a smile.

Maria grinned. "That's why I'm saying nice things, ma'am. I save the terrible stuff for behind your back."

Hamilton snorted out a laugh. "Very well."

Yeah, she had to be a good admiral to work for if she had a sense of humor. In Steph's experience, they usually didn't, so that said something about Hamilton.

"Any of you fine ladies and gentlemen want a beer?" Bradshaw stuck his head in the conference room to ask. "Suppo and I are headed to the store."

Fowler scowled. "Aren't you supposed to stay sober while on duty, Sailor?"

"With all due respect, Mr. Secretary, I live here," Bradshaw said. "It's after working hours."

"I thought better of you." Fowler directed this at Jesse, who stood behind Bradshaw like he was on the wrong end of the firing line.

"Sir, I, uh..." Jesse gulped. "We could stay, I suppose."

Bradshaw glared at his boss. "I'll take Olson, sir. We'll be sure to get you something soft and bubbly instead of beer."

Bradshaw grabbed Olson by the arm, dragging her out the double doors of the outer office before anyone could object. Fowler watched them like they were lepers.

"Is this the kind of organization you run, Commander Coleman?" he demanded.

And *that* made Admiral Hamilton frown. Did Fowler have to find fault with *everything?* Steph bit her tongue, watching her boss look up from his computer. Alex had retreated to his desk when Admiral Hamilton stuck around, but it didn't offer much privacy. The individual desks were just cubicles.

"Sir, my sailors are adults." Alex's voice was deceptively calm, but Steph saw the way his eyes narrowed. "And I'm not their mother. I don't monitor what they do off duty, provided it brings no discredit down upon them or the Navy."

"Hm." Fowler glanced at Hamilton for backup, but she focused on her book again. *No love lost there*, Steph thought. "That sounds like a terrible way to represent the United States of America."

"If you wanted better, you should've sent an ambassador," Alex retorted. "Sir."

Fowler went purple. "You—you—"

"That's enough, Commander." An edge entered Hamilton's voice, and her brown eyes were cold.

"Yes, ma'am." Alex looked down again, deflating.

Man, Steph *burned* to know what history lay between those two. But she couldn't ask.

"Mr. Secretary, can I get you anything?" Mr. Gage interjected, clearly used to calming his boss down. "Or, if you like, I can ship the gift you purchased for your wife."

"I'd be happy to help," Jesse said.

"That's a lovely idea. Thank you for being useful, James." Fowler favored his aide with a smile, but no aide who liked his boss would jet out of the office as fast as Gage did.

Unfortunately, that left Steph and Maria alone with her boss, the admiral, and a cranky politician. Who continued to monopolize Steph's computer.

That didn't stop her from poking around the internet to find more information on the mess in China. Typing without a keyboard was annoying, but Steph's search terms finally led her to a Chinese-language website that her browser dutifully translated.

"Hey, check this out," she said. "I found a Taiwanese news website that just announced that the Taiwanese government *confirms* their alliance with the Democratic Republic of China. They've vowed to bring down the communist party and reunite China under the flag of democracy."

"You hear that from State yet, Mr. Secretary?" Hamilton asked.

"No." Fowler scowled yet again, poking listlessly at Steph's defenseless touchscreen.

If he breaks that, I'm going to get the Navy to buy me a new Alienware. Trying to ignore the byplay, Steph clicked another link. "They've...holy shit, entire *ships* are defecting to the DROC. There's reports of a pro-democracy mutiny on *Liaoning.*"

"Are you kidding?" Maria's jaw dropped. "That's...that's civil war!"

"Show me." Hamilton rose and crossed to her in three long strides; Steph handed over the tablet and watched the color drain out of the admiral's face.

Steph knew how she felt. The American-Taiwanese alliance went back decades; trouble in China and Taiwan meant trouble for the U.S. Conventional wisdom said that Taiwan couldn't win a war without American help—but if they had allies in mainland China... *This could change the world.*

"Is anyone going to tell me what the hell *Liaoning* is?" Fowler asked.

Hamilton waved a dismissive hand. "Chinese aircraft carrier." She swallowed. "Fuck. Hong Kong declared independence. And now the links don't work. You think the website's blocked?"

"It shouldn't be. Let me see." Steph grabbed the tablet. But Hamilton was right. Clicking on anything just got her an error message. "Weird."

"Entire internet's down," Alex said from his desk.

"No way." Steph clicked to the Armistice Station homepage.

Nothing.

Then the overhead loudspeaker crackled. *"Ladies and gentlemen, we apologize for the inconvenience, but we have a station-wide loss of internet connectivity. Our teams are working diligently to restore internet as soon as possible."*

The message repeated in six languages.

Steph chewed her lip, getting up and walking over to where Alex stared at his screen. "This seem as weird to you as it does to me, boss?"

"Nah, a loss of cell and wired phones four hours ago coupled with a station-wide internet outage is normal." Alex snorted. "Happens every day."

"Yeah." She perched on his desk. "You want me to call Central and see what I can find out?"

Alex smiled ruefully. "With what phone?"

"Shit." Steph felt like an idiot and snuck a glance at Hamilton to see if she'd heard the gaffe. "Should I head down?"

"Not a bad idea. Go ahead."

Unfortunately, Steph's great idea was shared by about a thousand other people, all of whom crammed the tubes near Central. She barely got within sight of the control center before Aida Ledoux turned everyone away, apologizing for the inconvenience and promising to have internet *and* phones back up as quickly as possible.

Steph scowled. If she wanted fluff, she'd read a romance novel.

Master Chief Casey was in control when the message came in. As fate would have it, Lieutenant Grippo had the deck, just as she always did when shit went down. Casey felt sorry for the Navigator on most days; she was competent and smart, but telling the captain that was a fool's errand. Kennedy started hating Sue way back during the goddamned *Kansas* Incident. Now, Kennedy picked on everything from the clothes she wore on liberty to the words she used in reports.

"Check this out, COB," Sue said, handing the message tablet over.

R 121500Z APR 38

FM COMSUBPAC//

TO USS KANSAS SSN 810

INFO COMSUBRON 29

BT

SECRET/NOFORN

SUBJ/REDIRECT TO ARMISTICE STATION//

RMKS/1. ARMISTICE STATION LOST ALL VOICE COMMUNICATIONS AT 120935Z APR 38. INTERNET AND VOIP COMMUNICATION LOST WITH ARMISTICE STATION AT 121205z APR 38.

2. CIVILIAN INTEREST IS HIGH. MULTIPLE NEWS OUTLETS REPORTING LOSS OF COMMUNICATIONS.

3. USNS AMELIA EARHART (T-AKE-6) HAS ATTEMPTED MULTIPLE COMMUNICATIONS WITH STATION AND HAS BEEN WARNED OFF APPROACHING DUE TO UNFORESEEN MECHANICAL AND ELECTRICAL DIFFICULTIES.

4. THERE ARE AN ESTIMATED ONE THOUSAND AMERICAN CIVILIANS ON BOARD ARMISTICE STATION.

5. EFFECTIVE IMMEDIATELY, KAN IS DETACHED FROM ENT CSG. KAN WILL PROCEED TO ARMISTICE STATION AT BEST SPEED AND ESTABLISH COMMUNICATIONS.

6. ONCE ON STATION, REPORT TO COMSUBPAC.//

"Fuck me sideways with a rubber mallet." Casey read the message again, just to be sure. "Captain's going to be pissed."

"Because we're going back to Armistice Station?" Sue asked.

Casey barked out a laugh. "Because no one's shooting there." *Fucking glory hound.*

"They might if they see us," Sue said, looking at the deck.

"Eh, they don't hate us that much." Casey hoped they didn't, anyway. *Kansas* didn't fucking shoot that Neyk, but he knew what most of the world thought.

"You don't get online much, do you, Master Chief?" Sue's laugh was bitter. "I made the mistake of looking up the '*Kansas* Incident' on Twitter."

"Twitter's a fucking cesspit. Always has been." Casey shrugged. "'Sides, that's not the point. Point is the captain's gonna go apeshit once he sees we're going back there instead of where the water's hot."

"You want to be the bearer of bad news, or is it my turn?" she asked.

"I thought I'd take it to the XO and let her have her time in the fire." Casey grinned without humor. "She and I can double team him. Not your job to take another bullet."

Lieutenant Commander Hunt wasn't grateful when Casey dropped that turd in her lap—you didn't have to be on *Kansas* for long before you realized that the captain was willing to twist the boat into a fucking pretzel to get noticed—but she took it in stride. After all, half the XO's job was to make the captain look good. Kennedy just took more effort than average.

Ten minutes later, the pair stood outside Kennedy's stateroom, waiting for the captain to get off the shitter. Another fifteen minutes passed before he opened the door. "We're still ten hours out from the Sunda Strait. What's Nav fucked up this time?"

"Nothing to do with the navigator, sir," Casey said when Hunt blinked. The XO clearly thought she could redeem Sue in Kennedy's eyes; Casey knew nothing short of a transfer could fix that. Unfortunately, Sue would leave first, which meant Kennedy had a chance to deep-six her career.

Alas, there were some things even Master Chiefs couldn't fix. Casey needed to focus on the present.

Kennedy glowered. "Then what the hell are you beating down my door for?"

"We got a new set of operational orders, Captain," Hunt said. She was a tall woman who Kennedy hated looking up at, with bright red hair and freckles. Her glasses made her look like some sort of ultra-athletic nerd, which meant she fit right in with submariners. Casey liked her. She was good at her job and didn't hold stupid grudges, unlike present company. "Straight from SUBPAC."

"Give me that." Kennedy snatched the message tablet out of Hunt's hands, making her blink and gaze at him like he was a misbehaving child. Kennedy didn't notice; he just read the message and started swearing. "You've got to be fucking shitting me! Couldn't they find someone else to go back to that godforsaken place?"

"Guess not, sir." Casey wouldn't gloat, no matter how much he wanted to. Yeah, he was about as excited to go to Armistice Station as he had been for his last prostate exam, but anything that directed Kennedy's ire away from the crew was good. "You want I should tell the Navigator to plot a new course?"

"The XO can do that," Kennedy snapped.

"Aye, sir," Hunt said, taking the tablet. "I'll get right on it."

Hunt departed without a further word, leaving Casey with a still-fuming CO. He'd have to thank the XO for that later. Fortunately, it was just a bunch of swearing and posturing. Nothing he hadn't seen before.

Nothing he wouldn't see again, either.

Captain Jules Rochambeau watched his marines form up wearing a faint smile. Commanding marines was not his forte, but how quickly they followed orders was certainly gratifying.

"All your officers have their assignments, Commandant Moreau?" he asked.

"Oui, mon Capitane." The young officer beamed. "We are ready to do our duty."

"Make it quick and quiet, mon ami." Jules was warmed by Moreau's enthusiasm for what he felt was an annoying and slightly dirty task, but they did say marines were simple sorts.

Moreau frowned. "Should France's glory not be spoken of proudly, Capitane? We will finally take steps to regain our proper place in the world, and—"

"Once it is done, oui. Until then, silence and secrecy are our friends, non?"

"Bien sûr." The young marine's head bobbed. Something in his eager expression made Jules twitch.

He pushed his worries aside. "France will regain her rightful place, Commandant. But we will do so gently and graciously, so that none can say we did so without honor." Jules waited for another nod. "Now, deploy your marines and find your targets. Quickly."

PART 3: TEMPERANCE

Chapter 19

First Moves

Entering the mouth of the Strait of Malacca, *Fletcher* steamed two miles ahead of the *Enterprise* Strike Group. *Belleau Wood*, the cruiser, was ahead of the carrier by two thousand yards, with *John Finn* and then *Kidd* bringing up the rear.

Their formation speed settled out at thirty-one knots, the top speed every ship could steam. Wincing, Nancy imagined *Belleau Wood* straining at the seams; the early *Bull Run*-class cruisers just weren't as fast as General Dynamics planned. The later ships could make the promised thirty-five knots, but *Belleau Wood* was second in her class. Without ripping out both her shafts and main reduction gears, there was no way to speed her up.

Nancy sat back in her chair on the bridge and watched the sun set, the faint whine of happy gas turbine engines drifting in through the open bridge wing door to her right. Her watch team—plussed up for the eighteen-hour transit through the Strait of Malacca—watched the horizon and their radars for contacts.

Tactically, a nighttime transit was the child of a great idea and a nightmare. Daytime transits minimized contact misidentification, but darkness remained the best way to sneak up on someone, particularly when there were a lot of ships around.

The Chinese knew they were coming—the Communist regime tended to execute governmental idiots—but Nancy would consider it a victory if they got to the South China Sea faster than China expected. She just wasn't sure what would happen when they arrived.

The phone to her right rang; Nancy snatched it without letting her eyes leave the horizon. "Captain."

"Ma'am, it's the XO," Ying Mai said. "New just broke. Hong Kong's declared independence."

"Is that confirmed?" Nancy asked.

"Third fleet battle watch reported it," Ying replied. The XO was in the Combat Information Center while Nancy stayed on the bridge; they'd swap in a few hours so each could keep an eye on the big picture. "Intelligence seems torn. There's also reports of the Chinese Army firing on protestors in Beijing."

"Great. Just great." Nancy looked over her shoulder as the Officer of the Deck talked to another ship on the bridge-to-bridge radio. Lieutenant (junior grade) Marci Matthews was on watch, and she didn't need a lot of supervision. Her exchange with the other ship was professional and short.

"Yeah. China's going to pieces."

Nancy propped her feet up on the window ledge in front of her. "Okay," she said. "This doesn't change our mission. Let's get through the SOM. Admiral McNally can deal with the rest."

"Let the admiral deal with it, aye." Ying's smile was audible. "Better him than me."

"Me, too," Nancy breathed, and then hung up the phone. International relations were something she studied in college, not her job in the real world. Her job was to put warheads on foreheads—if her nation called upon her to do so.

Nancy wasn't sure if she wanted to stay in the Navy past twenty years—just four more—or if she wanted to do something else when she grew up. Command had always been her goal, but seeing the Navy shit on her husband for doing the right thing soured her a bit on this business.

"Combat, Bridge, any submerged contacts?" Marci asked through the tactical intercom.

Nancy didn't bother to turn her head as the Tactical Action Officer replied: "Nothing we can hear through our own noise, Bridge."

Nancy suppressed a smile. Her Combat Systems Officer was on watch, and CSO got a mite testy when asked silly questions. Yet again, Nancy wished for a towed sonar array, but short of Santa Claus showing up with a sleigh full of hydrophones, she was out of luck.

"Captain, *Porbandar* has closed to within five miles of the formation. They're paralleling our course," Marci said.

Nancy sat up straight. "They have?"

"Yes, ma'am. We've got a good visual now. Track 5079 on your display."

Frowning, Nancy glanced at the repeater over her chair. *Porbandar* was the Indian destroyer that agreed to remain ten miles away from them just a day and a half earlier. "What the hell are they playing at?"

Marci winced. "No idea, ma'am."

"That was rhetorical." Nancy softened the words with a smile before picking up the phone to call her XO again.

Ying answered on the second ring. "Combat, XO."

"XO, our Indian friend is back again. Wake up the cryppies and see if they can figure out who *Porbandar's* talking to."

"You got it."

"Thanks, Ying." Nancy hung up again and returned to staring at the horizon.

She didn't need this right now. The *Enterprise* Strike Group was en route towards a shooting match with the Chinese. Did the Indians want a seat at the table...or just to watch?

"*Kansas* got redeployed to Armistice Station to investigate their sudden silence," Captain Tanya Tenaglia said, dropping into a seat on *Tripoli's* flag bridge.

Tanya was the deputy commander of Expeditionary Strike Group 15, a surface warfare officer with twenty-four years' experience, almost all of it in amphibious warships, ships designed to carry and deploy marines. Unlike her boss, she was right at home on USS *Tripoli* (LHA 7). The red haired, dark-eyed woman fit in on the helicopter carrier's flag bridge like an alligator did water. She was even short enough that she didn't duck going through watertight doors.

If Tanya found it galling to work for a submariner who found that same bridge at least three times too large for comfort, she didn't let that show.

Rear Admiral (Lower Half) Marco Rodriquez barked out a laugh, scratching at the five o'clock shadow he always seemed to sprout. He was a Hispanic man of medium height, with hair as long as Navy regulations let him keep it, and dark eyes that gave incompetent subordinates nightmares. "I bet they fucking loved that."

"I expect *Enterprise* will cry for a fast attack soon." Tanya folded her hands and ignored his swearing. "Do we offer up *Lionfish*?"

"Hell, no," Marco said. "First, I'm an asshole who likes to keep my toys. Second, it wouldn't do them any good. If I read that Link display right, *Enterprise's* strike group will be in the SOM within the hour. *Lionfish* couldn't get there soon enough to matter a good goddamn."

"You're reading the display correctly, sir." Tanya grinned. "Apparently, even submariners can be taught."

"Hey, even I fucking know that the new boats have Link 18. Look, *Lionfish* is up with us, like a competent submariner damned well should be." Marco pointed at the icon representing the attack submarine attached to his command.

An expeditionary strike group was a lot less impressive than a *carrier* strike group; Marco commanded a helicopter carrier and an amphibious transport docking ship. A dock landing ship (LSD) rounded out his quartet of marine-carrying amphibious ships, but he left that behind when ordered to sprint north. LSDs were just too slow. Marco did have two destroyers along as escort, plus a lone *Cero*-class submarine, *Lionfish*. Sexy or not, the *Tripoli* group was his, and scheduled exercises with the Australian Navy put them in the southern Indian Ocean when the call came to head to Taiwan.

Timing, Marco knew, was everything in this business.

Marco Rodriquez knew he was rough around the edges. He swore too much, drank to excess, and was a submariner whose knowledge of Marines consisted of avoiding them in bars. He still wasn't sure how he ended up an admiral at all, unless it was because he was just that competent. It certainly wasn't because he was great at making friends.

He liked to pretend he was slower than he was, too. Marco's hard exterior hid a *studier*, one who'd never admit how much he loved nuclear power school. For example, he knew that Satellite Link 18 was the child of the Navy's older Link systems and Cooperative Engagement Capability. It allowed ships—and submarines!—to trade track data in real time.

The Navy could cover the globe in Link coverage if they wanted to, but ships in the Indian Ocean didn't need to be distracted by what some idiot destroyer driver got up to in the Atlantic. Ships and subs could even shoot off another unit's track, which was something Marco still found amazing. He grew up in a world where submarines had to hear something to kill it. Now, they could hide and let a surface ship or aircraft do the dirty work.

"How much longer until we hit the Sunda Strait?" he asked.

"Eleven hours." Tanya frowned. "*Enterprise* will blow past us a couple hours later, and then we'll follow them around."

Marco glowered. "But not catch them."

"No, sir. Amphibs are just too slow."

"How do you skimmers fucking live?" Marco made a show of yawning. "I feel like I'm out for a Sunday afternoon crawl."

Tanya laughed. "We entertain ourselves by confuddling submariners."

"That much is working. This is a damned slow way to go to war."

"Presumed war," she said. "China might be too busy fighting itself to fight us."

"Do you really think our luck's that good, Tanya?" Marco rolled his eyes. "Nothing's that goddamned easy. And the Chinese are sure as fuck going to take *someone* down with them."

"Your optimism astounds me, sir."

"Damn straight it does." Marco heaved himself out of his chair. "All right. I'm going to go catch some shut eye. Make sure the battle watch doesn't do anything fucktarded while I get my beauty rest."

Tanya laughed and opened the watertight hatch for him. "No fucktardedness, aye, sir. Though I do think that's your *beast* rest, isn't it?"

"Careful, missy, or I'll get you and your fucking dog, too." Marco paused in the hatch to mock glower. "And don't you start on mixed metaphors. I'm an admiral and I get to say whatever stupid things I want."

"Admiral, can you even *find* your stateroom without my help? It's a big ship."

"Oh, fuck off." Grinning, Marco headed down the passageway, hung a left, and then realized that flag country was to the left and down a deck. Damnit these stupid surface ships.

Three hours into the SOM, just after one A.M. local time—courtesy of a time zone change that brought them deeper into the wee hours of the morning—Nancy swapped places with her XO. Comfortable in her seat in *Fletcher's* Combat Information Center, she reviewed enlisted evaluations and kept an ear open for trouble.

The Tactical Action Officer, Lieutenant Commander Davud Attar, sat to her left, monitoring every ship sailing within thirty-two nautical miles of the strike group.

At the north end—the wide end of the cone—the SOM was spacious. But then the strait necked down to less than one and a half nautical miles. That sounded like a lot of space until you realized that over three *hundred* ships transited through that choke point daily. That equaled thirteen ships entering the SOM per hour.

Some were huge oilers and container ships that made Nancy's destroyer look like a bathtub toy. Others were commercial fishing boats, private yachts, and the ever-present dhows, used for fishing, tourism, and anything imaginable.

Together, those ships all crammed into a 550 nautical mile long superhighway. Transiting at night didn't lessen the traffic, either. The SOM was the nautical equivalent of jumping on Interstate 95. Everyone drove fast, no one signaled, and you just hoped ships would stay in their imaginary lane.

"Captain, SSES just called. Satellite imagery captured an Indian Surface Action Group underway from Brunei. Intel says they had a port visit there," Lieutenant Commander Attar said.

Nancy looked up. "I thought that port visit lasted until the fifteenth?"

"Apparently, they left early and got underway sixteen hours ago."

"Weird." Nancy glanced at the large screen tactical displays in front of the command consoles in CIC. One was zoomed in to 32 nautical miles, but the other was at 128. The Indians could travel a long way in sixteen hours—about 320 nautical miles if they averaged twenty knots—but *Fletcher* couldn't see them unless someone else had a radar track. "What's our range to Brunei?"

Attar clicked a few buttons. "About eleven hundred nautical miles."

Nancy felt some of the tension in her shoulders ease. "Say they're transiting at twenty knots, that gives us closure of fifty-one knots. Easy math says about twenty-one hours from their underway until we meet them."

"So, five hours from now."

"Sounds about right. Send it to *Enterprise*."

Nancy studied the tactical display for a long moment. Traffic was heavy but predictable, and the XO was on the bridge to babysit the watch team if needed. She turned back to the evaluations. She only had two Master Chiefs on board, but they were both superstars. Their evaluations were due at the end of the month, and Nancy liked to get things done early.

Armistice Station was four hours ahead of Greenwich Mean Time, which meant the decision makers back home were supposed to be awake. Alex had no idea if the Navy noticed—or cared—when Armistice Station dropped off the map, but he figured the State Department might take note that they were short one annoying, know-it-all diplomat. Had they tried to reach out? There was no knowing.

The hours of silence were unnerving. The station was too quiet; normally, Armistice Station's nightlife rivaled any major city. Tonight, tourists returned to their hotels early and the clubs were empty. Alex had never seen the tubes so barren at twenty-three hundred. Even the outertubes weren't full of drunks.

The number three outertube—this one decorated with pictures of whales—slid to a stop, and Alex waited for the chime before leaving his seat. Slinging his bag over his shoulder, he stepped out into the Newell tube and hung a left. He passed Rocco's—trying not to think about his last days on *Kansas*—and headed up a set of stairs into Sea Quest Fitness.

The fitness club was quiet, too, with just one person behind the desk. She took a cursory look at Alex's membership card before returning to some game on her phone. Tucking the card away, Alex headed into the locker room, bypassing the area full of treadmills, free weights, and other exercise machines. The outer wall was fully glass, offering a view into 300-foot-deep water no other station could match.

Back when he first arrived on the station, Alex was mesmerized. Powerful outside lights let patrons see fish, small subs, and sea life gently waving in the current. For a submariner, a window into the ocean was the height of luxury, and Alex loved it.

But the next view was better. Changing into his bathing suit, Alex shoved his bag and clothes into his locker and hurried to the pool. The world's news media laughed when Armistice Station installed an Olympic-sized pool underwater, but that pool was a thing of beauty. And its bottom was glass, perfectly clear.

Swimming there felt like you were skimming near the bottom of the ocean, just with no need for a tank or fins. The Sea Quest pool was Alex's favorite place on Armistice Station, and he swam at least once a day.

Alex was a qualified diver. His first submarine, USS *Virginia*, couldn't get enough enlisted sailors through the submarine SCUBA course, so Alex volunteered. He even kept up his qualifications across three submarines and two shore duty stations, despite no requirement to do so. He *liked* to swim, and diving was fun, particularly here at Armistice Station, where there were three different dive boats and two dive operations out on the platforms.

But there was something special about being so close to the ocean without having to wear a mask.

The pool was almost empty, an unexpected perk of babysitting an admiral and a politician. For a moment, Alex almost forgave the Navy for dropping this summit right in his lap, Admiral Hamilton and all. Diving into the water for the first time in three days—for the first time since Hamilton's arrival—felt almost sinful.

Swimming was simple. No one could bother him; he didn't feel overcrowded by people—the worst part about living on this station—and Alex just concentrated on the water. One stroke, then another.

Forty-five minutes later, Alex could almost forget he had to face Admiral Hamilton in the morning. Pleasantly tired, he climbed out of the pool. Maybe now he could sleep.

After a shower and a change of clothes, Alex exited the fitness center, his backpack slung over one shoulder. He passed the outer-tube station and paused before deciding to walk the long way back to his quarters in Habitat Two, off Earle Tube. Might as well take advantage of the quiet.

He passed a few people, mostly couples heading back from late dinners. Seeing them made acidic bitterness rise; here he was, on shore duty, the time the Navy said he was supposed to "recharge." But his family was thousands of miles away in Groton, Connecticut. Talking to them on the phone daily, even by video, wasn't the same. He hadn't seen Nancy, Bobbie, or Emily in four months. Bobbie—Roberta, named for her grandmother—was starting to look at colleges, and he couldn't be there.

Worse yet, neither could Nancy. She was on deployment, rushing from the Med to the South China Sea. Leave it to his wife to be where things were hottest, just when Alex was caught on the ass end of nowhere.

Blaming Admiral Hamilton for that wasn't really fair, either. Honesty compeled Alex to admit this little gift could be traced right to Chris Kennedy's door. *Kennedy would like this damned place,* he thought. *Hell, he got drunk as a skunk the three hours he was here. He'd fit right in.* Except tonight. It was still too quiet. Alex turned out of the Newell tube and into Mattera—

And almost ran right into a French marine.

"Excusez-moi," the marine said as they both jumped aside.

"My fault." Alex reseated his bag on his shoulder.

The marine hurried off. Why was a French marine wandering around so late, particularly in uniform? Sailors wanted to shed their uniforms before going on liberty; surely, French marines were the same. Alex barely started puzzling over that before he heard more voices speaking in French.

Coming around a bend, he spotted another group of marines, this one outside the Armistice Excelsior. Alex cocked his head. The Excelsior was the nicest hotel on the station and one of the most expensive in the world. Rooms there cost almost as much as Alex made *monthly*, and the Navy took good care of its commanders. Even the disgraced ones.

He couldn't understand a word they said, but the crowd *next* to the marines seemed much less...French. Two gentlemen around his own age stood at the edge of the crowd, muttering to one another. Both looked tired and disgruntled. One wore old-fashioned checkered pajamas—no surer sign that he had money—and the other looked like he dressed in the dark, in sweatpants and a blazer. The others in the crowd were equally disjointed; they wore a hodgepodge of clothing and a few seemed to have forgotten their shoes.

Alex inched closer, sticking to the shadows. Once in earshot, he caught snippets of conversation.

"...going to sue the hotel if this takes much longer," the pajama-clad man said.

"Really, they should *compensate* us for this," a blonde woman said to a brunette. The blonde wore an elegant blue evening gown; her companion wore a bright green robe and slippers.

The brunette yawned. "I just want to go back to bed."

"...still don't understand why they'd drag us out here in the middle of the night," another woman said. She sounded British to Alex. Or was she Australian? Her husband was definitely Australian.

"Rank insanity," he replied in a thick accent, rubbing a bald spot on his head.

"Is this going to take much longer?" the sweatpants and blazer-wearing man stepped out of the crowd to ask.

"Just a few more minutes, Monsieur," one of the marines replied.

Another marine—this one looked like an officer—said something to two of her men, who hurried inside the hotel. There were still over a dozen marines watching over a crowd of three times their size...all of whom were native English speakers, Alex realized. He heard a few British and Australian accents, but most seemed American.

Alex glanced at his phone. It was just past midnight. Was there a problem at the Excelsior?

The officer stepped forward. She reminded Alex of Camille Dubois, nowhere near as stunning, but with the same haughty confidence. "Messieurs et Mesdames, if you will come this way, we will escort you to your transportation," she said. "Please follow Lieutenant Caron."

"Transportation?" Pajama man asked. "To where?"

"Off the station, of course," the officer replied. "International agreements have been reached, requiring all American and British nationals to depart Armistice Station *immédiatement*."

"*What*?" several people spoke at once.

"I am *not* leaving without my belongings!"

"We're Australian, mate," the bald Aussie said. "Does that mean we can go back to bed?"

"No, you must leave as well." The officer's glare swept over the crowd, and as she gestured, multiple marines stepped forward.

Holy shit, they were armed. With pistols only, but what the fuck were *armed* French marines doing on an independent station? Something weird prickled up Alex's spine.

The crowd hissed, drawing back. Alex did the same, heart pounding. He knew of no international agreements that required Americans and their closest allies to leave Armistice Station. The station was well into international waters and governed by local laws—what few there were. Someone would have gotten word to Alex about this. Wouldn't they?

Suddenly, the lack of cell service and internet seemed a lot less innocent.

Heart pounding, Alex tuned out the crowd's continued arguments. Sleepy civilians would give in and obey armed marines; he couldn't help them. Instead, he retraced his steps silently, barely daring to breathe. Finally, he made it back to the Newell tube. There was no one else in sight, so he hurried back to the outertube joiner.

Thank God the outertubes ran on autopilot. One arrived within two nerve-racking minutes, and Alex jumped in without looking at its destination. Once the door slid shut, he pulled his phone out of his pocket and dialed Steph. Local calls still worked; only off-station calls were disabled.

Yeah. Not an accident.

Three rings later, Steph picked up. "Yes, sir?"

"Sorry to wake you, Steph, but some weird ass shit is going on," Alex said. "French marines are pulling Americans, Brits, and Aussies out of the Excelsior and telling them they have to leave the station."

"What?" Covers rustled as she sat up. "That's...*what*?"

"Hell if I know. They're claiming there's some international agreement." Alex watched the sail by as the outertube reached thirty knots, sailing around the edges of Armistice Station. "Something's fishy as fuck here."

"I hear you there," Steph said. Something clanked in the background. "I'll be ready to roll in a sec. What do you want me to do?"

Alex hesitated. What could he *do*? He had too little information and so many questions. Was this happening station wide? Were the French acting alone? Could this just be one obnoxious, overreaching officer?

No way.

"Meet me at the Hilton. Grab Secretary Fowler and his aide; I'll get the admiral," he said. "Call Jesse and have him wake up Olson and Bradshaw, then go grab the security details. Tell them to meet us at the office."

"Aye. I'm on it." Steph hung up, leaving Alex alone with his thoughts in the outertube.

What the hell were the French playing at? None of this made sense. No one had legal authority to push anyone out of Armistice Station; even Ledoux had to jump through several, well-documented, legal hoops to expel someone without clear misconduct committed. France's armed forces had zero authority here.

He was missing something, but what?

Chapter 20

Mistaken Identity

13 April 2038

John's eyes burned with fatigue. He tried to nap earlier and failed, catching only an hour or so before the sun went down. Sleeping on a submarine was never hard, no matter the time; John was out like the proverbial baby and could sleep through anything short of Armageddon or a phone call. Here on the carrier, however, John couldn't catch a wink when it was light out. Or when the carrier conducted flight ops. *Daylight and aircraft. Two things that* really *make me feel at home.*

Who the hell wanted a bed where jet engines roared at odd hours, anyway? This surface stuff was for the birds. Returning to the flag bridge didn't make him less tired, but at least being useful was an option.

"COS, we just got a message from Seventh Fleet. A Chinese helo buzzed *Jeremiah Denton* and *Michael Monsoor*," the battle watch captain reported from her station to his right. "*Monsoor* illuminated the helo and warned it off, but it shot a pair of C-802s. *Denton* shot the missiles down and they splashed the helo. No American casualties. Both ships are undamaged. *Ford* CSG is now in the East China Sea"

"God." John rubbed his eyes. Both *Denton* and *Monsoor* were part of the *Ford* Strike Group. "Any change to ROE?"

"No, sir. Rules of Engagement remain unchanged. Weapons tight, warning yellow."

"Aye." John grimaced. "Forward the message to the boss, please."

He tuned out Lieutenant Andrea Rubino's call to Admiral McNally. McNally would be cranky; it was just past four in the morning local time, and chiefs of staff existed so admirals could sleep. But news of a China helo taking potshots at American warships couldn't wait for morning.

Minutes ticked by like hours while John doodled the math on his console. Once the *Ford* and *Enterprise* strike groups joined up—plus the amphibious strike group under Admiral Rodriquez—they'd have two carriers, three cruisers, nine destroyers, a helicopter carrier, and an amphib whose purpose John couldn't remember. And three attack submarines. The combined force was bigger than anything America fielded since the Cold War, but compared to China's order of battle, it was miniscule.

Someone back in Washington thought their little show of power would deter the Chinese, but what if it wasn't enough? John swallowed.

"*Belleau Wood* reports a narrowband contact on her tail," Rubino said.

John straightened so fast his back cracked. "Submerged?"

"Sounds like. Bearing either one-two-five or three-zero-five. They're requesting to maneuver to prosecute."

John checked a sigh. He failed to convince McNally to swap *Fletcher* out for one of the other destroyers, but at least *Enterprise* dropped back to 2,000 yards behind *Belleau Wood* so that the cruiser could stream her own tail. Now that effort bore fruit.

Unfortunately, even the most advanced passive sonar arrays had difficulty determining what direction a sound came from. That was why submarines had multiple arrays programed to work in concert.

Unfortunately, a surface ship just had their sonar dome and (usually) a towed array, which was just a string of hydrophones travelling underwater on a very long wire. At over thirty knots, the sonar dome's passive sonar was more useless than John expected. It couldn't filter out enough of the ship's own noise, which was why surface ship drivers liked streaming their tails.

But the tail still got two bearings for every sound, the real bearing and its inverse, exactly 180 degrees out from the contact's location. The usual way to overcome that was maneuvering...which was just a *bit* difficult in a strait growing narrower by the mile. The *Enterprise* Strike Group entered the SOM's traffic separation scheme five minutes earlier. They were in the inbound traffic lane, and just like driving a car, you couldn't start swerving all over the place.

"Tell them negative. We're in the VTSS," John ordered.

"BWC, aye," Rubino replied.

John turned to his plot, looking at the lines of bearing *Belleau Wood* transmitted into Link. The strike group's course was one-one-zero, which meant the contact was either off their starboard bow or their port quarter. *A sub astern isn't nearly as dangerous as one ahead.* John fiddled with a grease pencil. Most subs in this part of the world were diesel-electric. Those boats were damnably quiet, but they weren't as fast as their nuclear counterparts.

John wished using active sonar wasn't considered so rude by other navies. "You'd better call the admiral again," he told Rubino.

John tuned the phone conversation out, instead donning a headset to listen into the command-and-control net. Most of the chatter was about navigation, something surface ships discussed endlessly. A few minutes passed.

"Echo Bravo, this is *Belleau Wood*," the cruiser said. "Submerged contact matches tonals from a *Kilo*-class diesel submarine, over."

"This is Echo Bravo, roger, out." Rubino turned to John with wide eyes.

"Relax," John said. "Fourteen different countries are still operating *Kilos*. Russia sold them to anyone with money back in the day."

"You mean like the Germans do today?" Rubino laughed, but her eyes were a touch too wide.

"Yep. The French, too. But *Kilos* are older and louder. Even a surface ship can track them." John grinned.

Rubino shook her head. "You sub guys are all the same, aren't you?"

"Well, you skimmers certainly seem to think so." John might've said more if not for Admiral McNally's arrival on the flag bridge. Instead, he rose and briefed his boss on the situation. "Sir, *Belleau Wood* has a passive contact, probable *Kilo*-class."

McNally frowned. "Who around here still has *Kilos*?"

"India, Myanmar, Vietnam, and Indonesia," John replied. "India's got four left; the rest are all decommissioned or sold to other navies."

Today, most of the Indian Navy's submarines were French-built *Scorpenes*. Some were diesel electric and the later models were AIP, or air-independent propulsion. All were quieter than *Kilos* bought from Russia in the early 1990s. Those boats were antiques. Were they even seaworthy?

Even an antique could shoot a modern torpedo.

"China has them, too," McNally said. "Send one of the helos to investigate."

John felt his heart skip a beat. "You think they'd send a boat all the way—"

"More likely than an Indian one creeping around out here. Theirs are ancient deathtraps." McNally shook his head. "Send the helo."

"Aye, sir." John nodded to Rubino, who frowned.

"Admiral, sending a helo violates transit passage. They have to continue in one direction—"

"And we're five inches from war with China. Send the damned helo," McNally snapped. "If someone complains, it's on my head."

A few moments later *Belleau Wood's* helicopter, callsign Striker 964, turned to investigate. John cleared his throat.

"Sir, do you want to launch the ASW alert helo?" he asked. "*Belleau Wood's* helos are configured for SUW. They don't have dipping sonar."

McNally nodded. "Do it."

"*Fletcher*, this is Echo Bravo," Rubino said over the command circuit. "Report time to launch ASW helo, over."

"Echo Bravo, *Fletcher*, thirty mikes." Nancy Coleman's irritation came clearly over the radio—and no wonder, since she voiced concerns on this same topic days ago. "Rolling helo out of the hanger in five, over."

"Echo Bravo, roger, out."

John returned to his seat and watched the icon representing Stricker 964 zoom forward of the formation, buzzing past *Fletcher* to look for an enemy submarine. It was probably nothing. The sonar contact might even be a whale. Stranger things happened.

"Echo Bravo, this is *Belleau Wood*, Striker 964 reports periscope gone sinker, over."

"Shit!" McNally threw himself into his command chair. "*Belleau Wood*, this is Echo Bravo Actual. Have Striker 964 remain on station. Break, *Fletcher*, go active, over."

Both ships acknowledged the commands; John's heart crept up into his throat and made a nest there. Nothing was more dangerous than a sub you *knew* was there but couldn't see. Most subs came to periscope depth before shooting; only idiots wanted to torpedo the wrong ship. But were they a target, or was the *Kilo* just snorkeling?

Or maybe just trying to get away from pesky American ships?

"Echo Bravo, this is *Belleau Wood*. New contact, track 4015. Probable *Kilo*-class submarine bearing one-three-seven from *Enterprise* at nine thousand yards," the cruiser reported. It sounded like Captain Rosario. "Sending Striker 964 FLIR video to *Enterprise*, over."

"Send the strike group to battle stations," McNally ordered as video flickered up on the port viewscreen. It was black and white, from the helicopter's Forward Looking InfraRed camera, and showed a dark shadow right underneath the surface. "And someone wake up Captain Edwards and get aircraft in the air!"

Staff members scurried to do his bidding. Within a minute, *Enterprise's* general alarm began donging. A voice from the bridge rang out over the 1MC:

"General Quarters, General Quarters, all hands man your battle stations. Set material condition zebra throughout the ship. General Quarters." The words repeated, and then the alarm donged again.

John turned to his admiral. "Sir, we might want to hold off on launching aircraft. I think the winds are—"

McNally held up a hand, and John sighed. *Enterprise* needed wind over her deck to launch. Speed through the water created some wind, except the weather today meant the wind came from the south. To launch aircraft, *Enterprise* would have to either sprint ahead and leave her escorts behind or turn around. Two options: bad and worse.

Twenty-eight minutes until *Fletcher* could launch an anti-submarine warfare configured helicopter. They'd have to roll the bird out of the hanger, unfold the wings, and fuel it. Twenty-eight minutes was a lifetime against a submarine. *Enterprise* didn't even have sonar, so she relied upon *Belleau Wood's* sensors to hold the track.

"Sir, I recommend coming left to open the range to the submarine," Rubino said.

"And present our broadsides to a Chinese torpedo?" McNally reared back as if slapped. "Do I look crazy?"

Everyone on the flag bridge stared. John scratched his ear.

"Sir, we don't know the *Kilo* is Chinese," he said.

"Shut up, John." McNally's eyes never left the screen, but John still flinched. McNally wasn't stupid. But there was little color in the admiral's face, and his knuckles were white where they gripped the cord between his headset and the console.

Minutes crept by.

"Echo Bravo, this is *Fletcher*," Nancy's voice blared out of the command circuit. "My SSES reports chatter on military frequencies—break, active sonar bearing one-five-niner, I say again, *Fletcher* has been pinged by active sonar, identified as Shark Gill, over!"

Shark Gill was the NATO name for the Rubikon MGK-400 sonar system, which was only on the original-build *Kilo* submarines. The later ones had different sonar systems. John knew submarine capabilities and limitations better than he knew the stats for his favorite baseball team.

"How many of China's *Kilos* are the first build?" McNally demanded.

"Two, sir," John replied before anyone else could. "India's are all—"

"*Belleau Wood*, Echo Bravo Actual, kill track 2015 with ASROC, over," McNally ordered.

John froze. "Admiral, India's *Kilos* all have that radar, too. We can't shoot without knowing whose boat this is!"

"India wouldn't ping a destroyer with active sonar unless they intended to shoot, and I am *damned well* not going to be the first American admiral to lose a ship in combat since World War II!" McNally's face was bright red and his words a bellow as he turned back to the command circuit. "*Belleau Wood*, Echo Bravo Actual, did you copy my last?"

"*Belleau Wood*, roger. Spinning up Basset." Captain Rosario's voice was clipped and tight.

"You don't want to be the first person to fire, either," John leaned forward to whisper.

How long did an ASROC need to fire? John's usual experience came on the receiving end, not the launching one.

RUM-139 Anti-Submarine Rocket launched torpedoes were an American surface ship's quickest way to kill a submarine at long range. Launched by a missile out of a cruiser or destroyer's vertical launch system, the torpedo was delivered by parachutes into the water, at which point its onboard engines kicked on and it homed in on the submarine. John knew how to dodge them, but not how long a cruiser needed to fire one.

"Your objection is noted, Captain." McNally glared. John met his eyes, praying the admiral would realize what he was about to do.

Every officer in the U.S. Navy always knew they wouldn't take the first shot in a war. They'd get shot at, take their lumps, and then turn the aggressor into a parking lot. That tradition went back to World War I.

"Echo Bravo, *Belleau Wood*, Basset away, track 4015."

It was too late.

Alex got lucky; the outertube dropped him off near the end of Bass, only twenty feet away from the Fisher tube. There to the Hilton was a quick two-minute walk. Thankfully, there were no marines out front; Fisher was quiet, save for a group of teens playing with their phones down near Grey's Dive Shop. Pushing the doors open, Alex went for the stairs instead of the elevator, taking them two at a time until he reached the third floor.

Room 318 was Admiral Hamilton's. Steeling himself, Alex rapped on the door with his knuckles. He counted to five, and then knocked again.

An eternity seemed to pass before Freddie Hamilton threw the door open, her hair askew and wearing an old Naval Academy t-shirt. "Commander Coleman, I *hope* this is good."

Damn. He'd hoped for Maria Vasquez.

Alex swallowed. "Ma'am, can I come in? It's important."

Hamilton glowered but stepped aside to let him pass. Maria was awake, too, sitting up in bed and blinking sleepily. *Fuck. What if this is nothing?*

French marines don't round up Americans for nothing, jackass.

Alex waited for the door to shut before clearing his throat. "I just passed a bunch of French marines hauling American, British, and Australian civilians out of the Armistice Excelsior. They were told they'd be transported off the station immediately."

"Say again?" Hamilton stared at him like he'd grown two heads.

Maybe he had.

"The marines cited some sort of international agreement, but unless the world's changed one hell of a lot while we've been out of comms, that sounds like bullshit to me," Alex replied. "I don't know what the hell's going on, but we need to get you and Secretary Fowler away from a hotel until we find more out."

He wished *Amelia Earhart* was still at the station, but they departed two days earlier. Hell, if *Earhart* hadn't left, communicating with the outside world would be easy.

"Where to, Commander?" Hamilton matched actions to words, throwing on clothes while Alex hurriedly turned his back. Maria did the same. Both women were submariners, too, and modesty took a back seat when trouble started.

"I've got a bridge-to-bridge radio in the office, and the rest of my folks will meet us there. Commander Gomez should be waking up the Secretary right now," Alex replied. "Once we're there, we can go topside and try to raise *Earhart.*"

Hamilton nodded. "She might not be in radio range, but it's worth a try. Let's do it."

Alex's phone rang. "Coleman."

"Sir, it's Steph. Secretary Fowler and Mr. Gage want to know what the hell is going on." There were voices in the background, mostly Fowler, who whined more than Alex's teenaged daughters.

"Tell them we're on the way to the office and I'll explain there."

"Aye, sir." Steph hung up, cutting off whatever complaint Fowler started to voice.

Hamilton bared her teeth in a humorless smile. "He's a dick, isn't he?"

Alex surprised himself by laughing. "Ma'am, I don't think I've got a high enough paygrade to criticize politicians."

"Mine isn't either," she replied, hefting a bag. "Let's go."

Parachutes flared, and a Mark 54 lightweight hybrid torpedo dropped into the water. Despite his misgivings, John watched the helicopter FLIR video in fascination. How many times had he wondered what an ASROC-launched torpedo looked like going into the water? Now he knew.

The torpedo's engine kicked on, sending it after the *Kilo* at over forty knots. Compared to a nuclear submarine's top speed, forty knots was nothing, but a diesel like the *Kilo* couldn't make much past twenty. Less on battery. The torpedo didn't have far to go, either; it landed barely eight hundred yards short of the *Kilo*. The *Kilo* traveled two hundred yards in the time it took the Mark 54's motor to start, but once the torpedo started pinging, it was over.

A forty knot torpedo could cover those thousand yards in less than a minute.

"All units, this is *Belleau Wood.* Torpedo in the water! Enemy torpedo in the water bearing one-five-five!"

Ten terror-filled seconds passed before *Enterprise* heeled hard left, the great carrier vibrating as her helmsman slammed the throttles to flank speed. Capable of almost fifty knots, *Enterprise* still couldn't outrun the Chinese Yu-6 torpedo, which ran at 65-plus. Worse yet, the Yu-6, like the American torpedo it was based on, was wake-homing. It would run up a ship's wake until it exploded under their stern. The torpedo's high explosive sodium hydride warhead was built to crack submarine hulls. A warship's keel would last about 0.2 seconds.

But what ship was it aimed at?

John's chest felt tight. McNally was pale and sweating, staring at the console like he couldn't see it. They were passengers, now; it was up to Captain Edwards and the other COs to execute their torpedo evasion maneuvers. John could see the carrier's escorts doing just that on the plot. The formation wheeled left, ships snaking through the water and dropping noisemakers to confuse the wake-homing torpedo.

A flare on the video screen made John turn just in time to see an underwater explosion centered on the FLIR video. The water jumped up as if a giant balloon was under the surface, cascading back down to form a convex hole of suction until the waves returned to normal.

"Echo Bravo, *Belleau Wood*, Striker 964 reports good hit." It wasn't Captain Rosario this time; she was busy fighting to keep her cruiser alive.

No one answered until John keyed his microphone. "This is Echo Bravo, roger, out."

John swallowed. They'd fired the first shot. Now it was time to see who paid for it.

"Echo Bravo, *Fletcher*, torpedo speed and tonals match a TEST 83 torpedo," Nancy Coleman reported.

"What?" John didn't realize the question was his until heads turned. Everyone except McNally stared at him blankly. "The TEST 83 is a French and Indian design. Did we just *sink* at an Indian *Kilo*?"

No one answered.

"Fuck." John didn't swear often. This was worth it.

He didn't doubt Nancy. Not Nancy, who memorized adversary capabilities and limitations for fun.

"Echo Bravo, *Kidd*, my SSES reports multiple Indian radars on the horizon!" the aft destroyer reported just as the formation turned right again, still locked in torpedo evasion maneuvers.

There wasn't much room to run in the strait; the SOM was less than ninety nautical miles wide here, and the traffic separation scheme's lanes averaged about two miles wide.

"Admiral, I recommend continuing right and leaving the lane," John, leaving the battle watch captain to acknowledge *Kidd's* report. "We have no room to maneuver here, but if we turn before Rupat Island, there's good water to the west."

McNally nodded choppily. "Okay," he whispered. "Was that sub Indian?"

"I think so, sir." John waited for McNally to give the order, but his white-face boss went silent again. John keyed his own microphone. "All ships, this is Echo Bravo. New formation base course two-two-five."

Every ship sounded relieved to acknowledge that order. Room to maneuver meant room to avoid the torpedo. A TEST 83 had about fourteen minutes of gas at its top speed. John looked at the clock. How had it only been three minutes since the *Kilo* fired?

Belleau Wood lagged behind *Enterprise* as they came around to the new formation course. Their once-straight formation was ragged, with *Fletcher* out on *Enterprise's* starboard bow instead of directly ahead of her. Astern, *John Finn* was slightly off *Belleau Wood's* port quarter, with *Kidd* astern of her. John would have to sort the formation out soon, but there was no use trying until the torpedo ran out of gas.

Chapter 21

The Storm Cometh

"This is ridiculous!" Fowler slammed his butt into a chair as soon as everyone reached the office, and Alex brought his team up to speed. Both security guys stood just inside the entrance, their body language tense and eyes scanning the tube outside for threats. "You're overreacting!"

"Maybe," Alex replied. "But what if I'm not?"

"We saw the same thing happening down at the Cameron." Bradshaw leaned against the wall, trying to look casual despite his drawn features. "A shit ton of French marines and a bunch of civilians who are Americans or our bestest friends."

Olson looked up from her phone. "My friend at the Hilton says they're there now."

"What?" Fowler's mouth hung open. "But—but..."

"This is clearly a pattern," Alex cut in. "What we need to know is why. Olson, does your friend have any idea why the French are pulling people out? And where's he from, anyway?"

The last thing he needed was for Olson to be distracted because her boyfriend was a hostage or exile or whatever.

"Madagascar. No one pays attention to him." Olson quirked a smile. "He says they're just using that same international agreement line."

"Which is horseshit." Admiral Hamilton's voice was stern. "You said something about a bridge-to-bridge radio, Commander?"

"Yes, ma'am." No one was in uniform, but Alex wasn't stupid enough to disrespect an admiral. Particularly *this* one. "But it won't work from down here."

"I didn't expect it would." Her glare was withering. "All right. The only question is if we all go topside or if some people stay here. Do you think they'll come looking in your office?"

Alex shrugged. "I'm not the most popular person here, so if Ledoux suddenly has a hard on for hating Americans, she won't forget us."

"What *did* you do to make her dislike you?" Hamilton asked.

"Someone told her I was *Kansas'* XO." Alex managed a cold smile, meeting Hamilton's eyes.

She knew *Kansas* hadn't shot a single damned torpedo. They both knew that was his fault. But the world blamed *Kansas*, and Ledoux's closest target was Alex. Hamilton pursed her lips, and then finally looked away.

Was that a victory? Sure didn't feel like one.

"Platform Three's elevator bank is just around the corner," Steph volunteered. "I can jet up there with Bradshaw and try to reach *Earhart*. If they answer, I'll call your cell."

"Sounds like a plan." Alex nodded, holding his breath to see if Hamilton would object.

Bradshaw got in first, starting off the wall, eyes wide. "Why me?"

"Because everyone owes you money." Steph's grin was all teeth. "That's got to be useful for more than making you rich."

"I'm not rich," Bradshaw muttered. But he didn't object when Steph grabbed him by one shoulder and the bridge-to-bridge radio in the other hand.

The two ducked out of the office as Jesse spoke up. "I can go take a look around and see what's happening. I know pretty much every wholesaler around here, and if they don't owe Bradshaw money, they like me."

Alex blinked. Jesse wasn't the type to volunteer for much; he was good at following orders, but not exactly high on what Alex would call initiative.

"I'll go with him," Maria Vasquez said from Hamilton's right. The admiral's head snapped around, and Maria shrugged.

"Unless there's someone else who can speak a language well enough to pretend they're from another country, I think I'm the logical choice. My grandparents were from Columbia."

Hamilton frowned. "Be careful. This kind of thing really isn't our game."

"Careful's not a problem, ma'am." Vasquez's grin was brief. "I want to get the hell out of here."

"Fine." Hamilton's nod was more of a glower, but she didn't argue. Fowler continued his rant-like conversation with his aide and ignored everyone else, going on about how this couldn't be happening, and it was all some giant mistake.

Maria and Jesse left, too, leaving Alex to manage an admiral, a politician, and a politician's bored-looking aide. *I hate this job.*

"Mon Capitaine." Camille touched Jules' shoulder before he even realized she was in Central.

Not reacting was hard, but Jules Rochambeau was the face of French military might. So, he remained relaxed in his chair at the center of Central, eyes alert but calm.

"Oui?" He tried to keep annoyance out of his voice. The marines had gathered almost half the American, British, and Australian tourists—they left the Canadians alone, because half of them were French speakers, and Canadians never meddled in this corner of the world, anyway. The plan was proceeding nicely.

"Admiral Bernard just sent word. The *Enterprise* Strike Group just sank an Indian *Kilo*-class submarine in the Strait of Malacca."

"*What?*" Jules hated jumping like a fool. "Has Admiral Khare said anything?"

"I sent his aide to wake him so he can confirm with his government."

Jules blinked. "How—how could such a thing happen?"

He had been so careful to prevent bloodshed. France's best interests lay in America retreating with her honor bruised but not bloodied. The ULP would be reasonable, removing American influence without violence. The war with China would consume America's resources, anyway; there was no need to start a second confrontation. French politicians spent liberal diplomatic capital convincing India of that after the fracas at Diego Garcia—and now *this*?

"Because they are uncultured swine who believe brute force can solve anything," Admiral Khare growled in English, striding into the room with his uniform blouse still unbuttoned. His hair was rumbled, but Khare's eyes blazed. "This changes everything."

"I take it your reluctance concerning our objectives is no more, Admiral?" Jules asked in the same language, smiling as he rose.

"Do not jest, Captain. More than fifty of *my* Navy's sailors are dead because of American arrogance."

"My condolences." Jules bowed his head, meaning it. "They are my brother and sister submariners. May they rest easy on eternal patrol."

His imagination was sufficient to conjure up what those last moments would be like: water rushing in before the sudden implosion, and then utter, utter blackness. Jules sometimes dreamt of meeting his end that way—and once, of the civilians on the Neyk he consigned to that same fate. *I may send many others to the bottom before this is done.* There was not time for regrets.

Camille quietly echoed his sentiments before turning to him. "Your orders, mon Capitaine?"

"Return to *Barracuda*. Brief the crew. Stand by for anything." Jules's mind whirled as he looked at Khare. "We must assume the Americans will fight back if we cannot present them with a fait accompli, non?"

"Undoubtedly." Khare bared his teeth. "But you need not worry about the *Enterprise* Strike Group. INS *Vishal* and her escorts are closing with them, now."

Jules' breath caught. *Vishal* was an aircraft carrier, although not a supercarrier like *Enterprise*. Still, if the Indians meant to make a fight of it...so much for the peaceful solution. "Then we shall do our part." He lifted his radio. "Commandant Moreau, accelerate your removal of our unwanted guests. Feel free to use the threat of deadly force, but do not harm civilians."

"Oui, mon Capitaine," Moreau replied, spinning on her heel and heading out.

Aida Ledoux, silent until now, stepped forward. "This was not part of our agreement!"

"Madame Ledoux, we must free your station of undesirables quickly, or we will not get the chance to do so."

"Mais..."

"Non. We are committed, Madame. American civilians—and their allies—will crumble at the threat of force." Jules' own orders were clear. Once the operation started, France could not afford to stop.

No more would his nation bear the reputation of a country of cowards. France would not run. France would *win*.

Steph and Bradshaw made it into the elevator before French marines got near their part of the station. Steph didn't know what to make of this, didn't know what to *think*, but she had a job to do, and she was damned well going to do it. She'd trained for something like this, or almost close enough, so the idea of armed enemies surrounding her wasn't going to make her cry in a corner.

The problem was that in training, she knew what the enemy wanted—and if they were the enemy at all.

"This is fucking insane," Bradshaw muttered after the elevator doors dinged shut.

"You can say that again." Steph wiped her sweaty palms on her jeans. She hadn't changed into uniform when Alex called, and now she was glad. There weren't a lot of people out on the TRANSPLAT at this hour—one in the morning wasn't exactly prime loading or unloading time, even for cruise ships—but wearing a Navy uniform was a fantastic way to get spotted.

And then what would happen? Steph wasn't going to test that theory today.

The elevator doors opened, and Bradshaw hesitated. "What's the plan, anyway, Ops? We just shout into the void and hope *Earhart* listens?"

"Pretty much." Steph looked both ways and then walked out of the elevator, into the humid night air, trying to pretend she belonged. The salty sea smell was a welcome change over Armistice Station's canned atmosphere, which always smelled a little metallic. "Come on."

Muttering obscenities, Bradshaw followed. "Never again volunteer yourself. I should've fucking listened to that."

"I saw your reenlistment request." Steph grinned as they headed out to the platform proper. "You can quit faking."

"I like my *job*." Bradshaw scowled. "This ain't my fucking job."

"Yeah, mine neither."

Steph was trained to drive and fight ships. Sometimes, surface officers ended up doing odd jobs—like anti-terrorism, which she'd trained in on her first ship—but stuff like this wasn't her core competency. Swallowing, Steph pushed those thoughts aside.

Passing a group of drunk Panamanian sailors, Steph stopped next to a towering silver and green yacht. The damn thing was gorgeous, with sleek lines and waterjet propulsion that made Steph burn to take her for a spin. *We don't get toys like that in the Navy*. They were in *Earhart's* old berth, across from the French frigate.

The frigate looked like any warship in the middle of the night, with a few watchstanders peppered around topside but otherwise quiet. There was a Norwegian Cruise Lines ship astern of her, sending lines to the pier. It was an odd hour for a cruise ship to tie up, wasn't it?

She lifted the bridge-to-bridge radio. "U.S. Navy Oiler Six, U.S. Navy Oiler 6, this is Naval Detachment Armistice Station calling you on channel one-six, over."

At least the international maritime hailing channel was quiet this time of night.

Too quiet. *Earhart* didn't answer.

Steph swore under her breath. She wished her phone would work, that she wasn't stuck using Armistice Station's proprietary network that the bastards could just turn the fuck off. Why hadn't the navy issued their detachment an iridium satellite phone? Then they could just call *Earhart's* external phone line.

"U.S. Navy Oiler Six, U.S. Navy Oiler 6, this is Naval Detachment Armistice Station calling you on channel one-six, over," she repeated.

Seconds passed; then static.

Finally, a voice replied: "Naval Detachment Armistice Station, this is Oiler Six, roger, over."

Steph sagged in relief. "Great to hear from you, Oiler Six. We need an immediate evac for some VIPs. How soon can you be here, over?"

There was a long pause; Bradshaw muttered. Steph knew *Earhart* couldn't be far. Bridge-to-bridge radio was VHF, which had a maximum range of around sixty miles on a really good day. Finally, the radio crackled.

"My max speed available is two-zero knots; I need sixty-seven minutes to reach your position, over."

"Roger, break, please make best speed, over," Steph said in her best professional voice. Why was she so nervous? She talked on bridge-to-bridge radios all the time as a surface warfare officer.

But it wasn't the radio making ants crawl up her spine. There was something else.

"Navy Oiler Six, roger, out."

Steph lowered the radio, glancing at the yacht again. Seas were calm, which would make a small boat transfer easier. And they'd have to use a boat. No way would Armistice Station allow *Earhart* to come alongside, even if they had pier space. Or maybe they would? They wanted Americans to leave.

"You know, we could just hop on whatever boat the locals want us to get on," Bradshaw said. "Wouldn't that be easier than all this skulking around?"

"Did you really just use the word 'skulking' unironically?"

Bradshaw glowered. "No fair playing grammar police, ma'am. Just answer the question."

"Can you imagine the optics of the U.S. Navy just going where French marines told us to?"

"They're not our enemies."

"Not yet." Steph snuck a look back at *Bretagne.* The frigate remained the perfect picture of a sleepy warship. *Would we be that sleepy if U.S. Marines were running around a station rounding people up?* Her skin crawled.

"C'mon, Ops, you can't believe that." Bradshaw rolled his eyes. "It's the twenty-first century, and the French have been our friends since—holy shit, there are a bunch of marines headed this way. They've got a group of civies with them, too. Looks like a couple hundred."

"Those rifles they're holding are really friendly, huh?" Steph's smile felt poisonous. She tried not to stare at the confused people following the group of marines. Staring got people noticed. Ignoring things was hard when a French marine shoved a civilian for walking too slow, though.

Bradshaw grabbed her arm. "Oh, shut up and let's walk casual-like to the fucking elevator. Ma'am."

"You speak any Spanish?" she asked as they headed down the platform towards the elevator bank.

"Huh? I know a couple swear words, I guess."

"They probably don't, either. Try to stick to *Si* or *No*, okay?" Steph shoved her hands in her pockets and started babbling in her parents' native language. She bet the French couldn't tell the difference between her Mexican Spanish and Castilian Spanish, and even if they could, no one said anything about kicking Mexicans off the station.

Bradshaw managed to look like a surly know-it-all even without understanding a word Steph said. He nodded along or argued, depending on her tone. That got them past the marines and into the elevator. One marine looked at them curiously, but a complaining civilian distracted her, and she didn't follow the pair.

"For the record, I *never* want to do that again." Bradshaw slumped against the back wall of the elevator the moment the doors closed.

"Copy that." Steph *almost* answered in Spanish.

"You gonna tell me what you said, or am I just gonna piss myself instead?" he asked.

"A long essay on you're the worst cook in creation and your culinary arts stink of elderberry."

"What? *Really?*"

"It was the best thing I could of on short notice, okay?" Steph refused to let herself relax. Not until they were on *Earhart* and outbound from Armistice Station.

Nancy almost ran to the bridge when the *Kilo* fired torpedoes, but now she was glad she hadn't. Modern battles had to be fought in the Combat Information Center. The bridge maneuvered the ship, but CIC detected and countered threats.

The evals she worked on earlier were somewhere on the floor; Nancy alternated between monitoring the tactical plot and watching Striker 964's FLIR video. The forward helicopter now ranged thirty miles out from the formation, trying to find the source of the Indian targeting radars.

Nancy wished Ying could be down here so she had someone to rant to. Was McNally *mad*? He fired on another nation's submarine in peacetime—and it turned out to belong to a *different* nation than expected!

Yeah, the Indians shot at U.S. destroyers near Diego Garcia, but only eighteen sailors died that day. *Only*. One torpedo just killed almost three times that many. With *China* shooting at them today, why borrow trouble with India?

The FLIR video jumped, and then went blank.

"ASTAC, TAO, check the Link connection with the helo, will you?" Lieutenant Commander Attar said over the net.

"Holy *shit—Vampire, vampire, vampire!*" *Fletcher's* air warfare coordinator's shout was loud enough that Nancy could hear it without her headset. "Multiple missile launches bearing zero-nine-six, range a hundred and ten nautical miles!"

Nancy wheeled back to the plot, watching the angry upside down "V" icons of hostile missiles blossom on the screen. She smashed the foot pedal down on her microphone for the tactical net.

"All ships, *Fletcher*, vampire, vampire, vampire! Inbound anti-ship missiles bearing zero-niner-six!" She swapped to her ship's internal net. "Bridge, Captain, all back full!"

Every destroyer captain knew their primary mission was to protect the carrier. To do that, *Fletcher* needed to be between *Enterprise* and the firing ships, and the best way to do that was slam on the brakes. The formation's ragged maneuvering meant *Fletcher* was the only ship that could get there in time—Nancy just hoped it wouldn't make her destroyer eat the torpedo still out there somewhere.

Nancy's hand left hand snaked down on its own, finding the Firing Interdict Switch, or FIS key. The FIS was a warship's last safety; once it turned to green, any computer-controlled weapon on the ship could be fired with the push of a button.

"FIS is green! TAO, you have batteries release. Activate doctrine and defend the carrier."

Chapter 22

Furball

"Comms are being jammed!" someone shouted right after *Fletcher's* vampire call rocketed across the command circuit. John paid it little mind; his eyes were on McNally, who was dangerously pale.

All McNally did was lick his lips, his eyes wide and glazed over.

"Admiral?" John whispered. No answer. "Sir?"

McNally finally turned to look at him. His hands shook. "What have I done?"

"There's no time for that." John's heart raced, his eyes flicking back to the flag plot. There were too many missiles headed their way; *Enterprise's* combat systems struggled to count them all. The command circuit was silent as the jamming cut off their communications right when they needed them most. And McNally didn't know what to do. The admiral's mouth was open; no words emerged.

"Change to alternate frequencies!" John ordered. Holy hell, what *were* those missiles? And why the hell had Striker 964 vanished? Racking his brain revealed one answer; the Indians owned the fastest reliable anti-ship cruise missile in the world. The BrahMos NG missile travelled at Mach 7, over 4500 knots. At this range, they had barely a minute—

What was *Fletcher* doing? *Enterprise*'s forward camera caught the destroyer backing down hard, water boiling at her stern.

"My God," John whispered as Nancy Coleman threw *Fletcher* between *Enterprise* and the incoming missiles.

Light flared in the night; SM-6 Block 1B standard missiles burst out of *Fletcher's* vertical launch system, racing towards the incoming firestorm.

"...*Belleau Wood*, birds away!" The alternate command circuit took over in his headset, just in time for John to hear the cruiser announce her missile launch.

Thank God Captain Rosario created air defense sectors as soon as the strike group got underway. No one expected to *need* them, but Navy tradition revolved around training. Now, that practice meant that the three destroyers and the cruiser used slightly overlapping fields of fire, so their standard missiles didn't commit fratricide or go after the same targets.

Meanwhile, *Enterprise* steamed quietly at the middle of the fray, slowing down to stop outrunning her escorts. The carrier was armed with short range ESSM and shorter ranged point defense RAM missiles; she wouldn't fire unless leakers made it through the shooters' defenses.

More light flashed on the video screen; *Fletcher's* second launch roared into the night. *Belleau Wood* and the other destroyers' launches came a split second later, but all John and his fellows on *Enterprise* could do was watch.

Commander Tyler Marshall of USS *John Finn* (DDG-113) was on the bridge when the Indians launched on the *Enterprise* Strike Group. The bridge was dark, illuminated only by radar and navigation screens covered by red plastic. Marshall sat quietly in the captain's chair in the forward starboard corner, staring into the night and wondering if another submarine would appear.

He heard the report of inbound missiles, but it didn't register for a few crucial seconds. The Indians were too far away for Marshall to see the missiles—that would change all too quickly—and he *wanted* to think this was all a mistake.

"TAO, Captain, say *again*?" he said over *John Finn's* internal tactical circuit.

"Incoming missiles, bearing one-zero-three!" the TAO replied. "Multiple incoming missiles, bearing one-zero-three!"

There was a tactical repeater above the captain's chair on *Finn's* bridge, so Marshall saw the V-shaped symbols representing hostile missiles appear over one hundred miles away. There were too many to count, too many to—

"Captain, TAO, do I have batteries release?"

The words echoed in his ears as Marshall stared at the display, *willing* the missiles away. This wasn't supposed to happen. The U.S. Navy never faced a modern Navy in combat. The U.S. Navy was the best in the world, unchallenged and supreme. *No one* dared fire on them. The Indians had to be insane!

"TAO, Air, all incoming missiles are BrahMos NG anti-ship missiles," his air warfare coordinator reported.

Dear God, the BrahMos travelled at Mach *Seven*. His hands were numb.

Marshall's destroyer had ninety-six cells in her vertical launch system. Thirty-two of those held Tomahawk Land Attack Missiles, useless against a surface or air threat. Another five held RIM-162 Evolved Sea Sparrow Missiles (with four ESSM per cell), which were fast enough to catch a BrahMos. And ten held SM-6 Block 1B missiles, the best anti-air missile in the American inventory. But the rest held SM-2 Block IV missiles.

The SM-2 was the bedrock of American air defense since the 1980s, incrementally improved until the introduction of the SM-6 in 2009. The SM-6 was faster, longer-ranged, and had a larger warhead, but the Navy's inventory still held a lot of SM-2s. As a result, *Arleigh Burke*-class destroyers like *John Finn* usually deployed with a mix of SM-2s and SM-6s. Bad luck gave *Finn* more of the former.

The SM-2 travelled at Mach 3.5, half the speed of the Indian's BrahMos. It couldn't match the speed of a BrahMos' tactical maneuvers, no matter what *Finn* did. And that storm of missiles contained a hell of a lot more than ten BrahMos missiles targeted at *Finn.*

Marshall never felt so cold in his life. His hands gripped his chair's armrests with white knuckles until the Officer of the Deck shook his shoulder.

"Captain, we need you," Lieutenant Aspen said.

Marshall blinked. "Right." He keyed the microphone for the tactical net. His mouth felt dry. "TAO, Captain, batteries release."

"TAO, aye! Air, TAO, kill tracks in our sector."

"Air, aye. Killing with birds, selecting SM-6 preference."

It wouldn't be enough. Marshall knew that. He knew he should race to CIC, but he'd never make it before the missiles hit. He would have to trust his Tactical Action Officer to fight the ship, would have to hope against hope that *Finn's* outdated missiles would somehow do the job.

VLS cells opened; missiles launched from *Finn's* VLS banks, their boosters burning brightly against the night sky. Marshall couldn't count how many, but there were more than ten.

And his hesitation cost *John Finn*; while *Fletcher*, *Belleau Wood*, and *Kidd* got off three launches—two standard missiles, one ESSM—*John Finn* only managed one. That launch contained all ten SM-6s and twenty SM-2s. Standard Navy tactics demanded at least two missiles be allocated to each incoming missile, and *Finn's* Aegis combat system detected nineteen missiles headed for her assigned sector.

Unfortunately, *Finn's* watchstanders neglected to activate doctrine, which allowed Aegis to defend the ship autonomously. Instead, human reflexes fought to overcome the incoming storm, and humans just weren't fast enough.

Fireworks filled the night sky as American missiles raced out to meet Indian. *Finn* was aft of *Belleau Wood* and *Enterprise*; a corner of Marshall's mind noted how *Fletcher* dropped back to be between the carrier and the threat bearing. *Belleau Wood*, just fifteen hundred yards ahead, launched dozens more missiles than *Finn* managed. The cruiser had one hundred and forty-four launch cells, and Captain Rosario somehow put forty missiles in the air to engage the threat.

It was almost enough to cover *Finn*. Like Nancy Coleman on *Fletcher*, Rosario activated her ship's doctrine, the computer-controlled self-defense plan sailors jokingly called "Armageddon mode." The Link connection between the cruiser and *John Finn* told *Belleau Wood's* combat system that *Finn* couldn't launch enough missiles. But *Belleau Wood* was too far back to engage missiles aimed directly towards *Finn*; she only had seconds to hit those missiles with crossing shots. Seconds were not enough.

"Brace for impact!" Marshall ordered at the last moment.

He clung to his chair as *Finn's* missiles did their damnedest to kill their faster enemies. Nine of the ten SM-6s killed a BrahMos; the last wasted itself on a target one of its sisters already destroyed. A surprising four SM-2s managed the same, but that left six missiles out of the nineteen in her assigned sector. *Belleau Wood* got two.

The remainder targeted *Finn*. One lost lock and slammed into the ocean a hundred yards shy of her port side. Two were sucked away by her TAO's last ditch launch of Nulka, a tactical decoy designed to distract missiles. The last two dodged bullets from her CIWS—close in weapons system—and slammed into *Finn's* port side, exploding right where the line usually formed on the mess decks.

The destroyer rocked right, shuddering from bow to stern. Her lights flickered once, twice, and then died. The impact threw Marshall out of his chair and into the bridge windshield, where his head broke the double-paned glass, leaving a spear of blood over a foot long.

Lieutenant Aspen slammed into the helm console, taking both helmswoman down with him in a heap; one broke her ankle and screamed. Other sailors fell like dominos, some catching themselves, others never rising again.

Below decks, the twin blasts carved a twenty-foot hole in *Finn's* port side, destroying everything in their path. The first missile broke through the hull into Main Engine Room Number Two, its shockwave ripping one main engine off its mounts and throwing fragments and debris into the main reduction gear.

Number Two Gas Turbine Generator tripped offline, and piping burst, causing a major fuel oil leak. Two watchstanders were killed immediately; the third made it to an escape trunk before the resulting fire caught her.

Radio, the Engineering Central Control Station, and six other spaces were left open to the sea. Electrical power failed, and with it any pumps capable of combating the flooding. Watchstanders evacuated, rushing up ladders as *Finn* listed to port. Other sailors raced to combat the damage, not knowing how big the hole was or where the danger lay. Some fell into chasms and never returned. Others groped for firefighting equipment in the darkness.

Then, one of the two missiles sucked away by *Finn's* Nulka decoys found a new target: *Enterprise*.

"Birds away!" *Fletcher's* air warfare coordinator announced as *Fletcher* surged forward again. The destroyer steamed less than six hundred yards off *Enterprise*'s starboard beam, right between her and the Indians.

"All stations, this is Striker 961," the second helicopter in the air reported over the command circuit. Nancy listened with half an ear, her eyes riveted on the missiles raining down on her ship. "I have visual on Striker 964's debris and a long-range look at the enemy. Looks like one carrier and at least six destroyers, over."

"*Belleau Wood*, roger, break are they launching aircraft, over?"

"Affirmative. They look like MiGs, over."

"Leaker, leaker, leaker, track 7089! Doctrine engaging," the Combat Systems Officer of the Watch said, and Nancy felt her destroyer shudder again. Another three SM-6s launched from *Fletcher's* forward VLS bank, and Nancy held her breath.

The BrahMos NG missile, called PJ-10 by NATO, was a ramjet supersonic anti-ship cruise missile. Based on a Russian design, the second generation BrahMos missiles had a range of over 120 nautical miles and topped Mach 7. Its 440 pound conventional armor-piercing warhead was enough to rip a destroyer's thin skin open—or punch irreparable holes in an aircraft carrier.

The days of World War II gun battles where ships hammered one another for hours with heavy shells were over. Modern ships couldn't take a lot of damage, not in missile combat. Their survival lay in air defense.

Fletcher shuddered again as her third launch of missiles erupted from her VLS cells; these were ESSM, or Evolved Sea Sparrow Missiles. Many NATO ships used ESSM as surface-to-surface missiles, but the United States used them for point defense. Nancy held her breath; an ESSM launch meant *Fletcher's* AEGIS weapons system was on its own, using pre-programed routines to shoot down missiles too fast for humans to track.

The distinctive *burp* of *Fletcher's* CIWS guns came next. The Phalanx Close In Weapons System was the marriage of a phased-array radar and a M61 twenty-millimeter Vulcan Gatling gun. Capable of firing up to 4,500 rounds per minute in full auto, *Fletcher's* CIWS was programed to fire in bursts of 100 rounds, each of which shot out at approximately 3,600 feet per *second*.

Nancy's sailors liked to call it the CIWS fart every time the system fired in exercises, but this was not training. Nancy braced herself. If CIWIS missed, *Fletcher* would be ripped apart—

The inevitable explosion never came.

"Tracks killed with CIWS," Lieutenant Commander Davud Attar reported, his shoulders slumping in relief.

"Very well." Appearing the unaffected and professional captain was impossible with her heart hammering so loudly. Nancy licked her lips, and then dared look at the rest of the strike group.

Enterprise matched *Fletcher's* course and speed, still off *Fletcher's* port side. *Belleau Wood* was right behind her, with *Kidd* and *John Finn* astern—but *John Finn* was dropping back, her speed decreasing rapidly.

"Train the OSS to *John Finn*!" Nancy ordered, punching in the code to place the view from the Optical Sight System onto the large screen display.

"Sweet Jesus," Attar whispered.

John Finn listed heavily to port, on fire, with black smoke billowing out of her superstructure. A gaping hole marred her port side, and she seemed locked into a starboard turn that brought her perilously close to *Kidd*.

Muzzle flashes lit up the night sky; the OSS operator swung the system to follow them as *Enterprise's* CIWS burped, tracer rounds arching out to meet an incoming missile. Nancy's heart clenched. The first few groups missed until a round finally got a piece of the missile, and it tumbled into the sea less than a yard short of *Enterprise's* starboard side.

"Where did that come from?" Nancy demanded.

"Captain, AIC, *Finn* launched a Nulka," one of her watchstanders reported. "Looks like the missile went for *Enterprise*."

"Fucking stupid," someone whispered.

Nancy gulped. Using Nulka was a great way to defend your ship, but when the decoy deflected missiles, there was no telling where those missiles might go. And in a tight formation like this one, Tyler Marshall's last ditch effort to save *Finn* almost killed the carrier.

Attar gasped. "Oh, God, *Finn's* going down."

The OSS swung back to *John Finn*, still burning. Her rudder was still stuck hard over, and as she continued turning starboard, the destroyer's bow dipped deeper and deeper into the water. Each time, *Finn's* bow rose a little less.

Nancy stared for a long moment, thinking of Tyler—a friend of over a decade—and his crew. Her chest felt impossibly tight. *Finn* and *Fletcher* were in the same destroyer squadron, trained together, fought together. White specks appeared on the video, hitting the water and exploding into bright orange life rafts. Human-sized shapes followed them, but not nearly enough.

The other destroyer deployed with 350 sailors, many of whom would not escape that fiery inferno.

"Focus, people." Nancy's voice sounded harsh, even to her own ears. She spoke into the tactical net: "Surface, Captain, range to the Indians?"

"One-zero-one miles, ma'am," her surface warfare coordinator replied.

"Still too far for Harpoons." Nancy hissed aloud. She wanted to hit the Indians back, but she needed her SM-6s to defend against those horribly fast BrahMos missiles, and supply snafus back home meant none of the ships deployed with Naval Strike Missiles except *John Finn*, who wasn't going to fire them anytime soon.

NSMs had a range of about 115 miles, which was more than thirty nautical miles *greater* than Nancy's Harpoons—but that knowledge did her zero good. Nancy scowled.

"You think those sub guys over on the carrier remember little things like Harpoon ranges?" Attar asked.

"We'll find out." Nancy shook her head, trying to clear it, then remembered the ASW helo her crew was ordered to launch a few minutes earlier. "Get the helo back in the barn. No one's sub hunting today."

"TAO, aye."

Armistice Station's internal network was still up, so Alex poked around on his computer while Secretary Fowler paced and Admiral Hamilton read a book. Little though he liked her, Alex was more impressed with the admiral than the politician; Hamilton appreciated the trouble they were in, but the woman had nerves of steel. Fowler was in denial.

Olson looked up from texting. "Sir, my friend at the Hilton says the French Marines are getting more threatening."

"Define more threatening." Alex's eyes narrowed.

"Like, they're actually pointing weapons at people." She walked over to show him a picture on her phone, which showed a French marine pointing a rifle at a clumped group of civilians.

They've pulled out rifles. Much more threatening than handguns. Alex's throat felt tight. "This is going downhill fast. Same thing's getting mentioned all over the internal boards as people wake up. They're hauling residents right out of their quarters."

"But why?"

"Hell if I know." Part of Alex demanded he *do* something, but what difference could they make? His team of five—even if you added in their four guests and their security duo—had no legal authority.

He clicked through another update on the station administrative chat group, and then froze before continuing to another page. *Was that...?*

"Holy shit, is that a list of the people they're rounding up?" Olson leaned close to look at the monitor.

Alex clicked the link. "Guess someone was stupid and forgot to turn my access off."

There weren't many perks to his job, but some decade-old agreement said that the OIC got administrator level access. That meant Alex could see documents and pictures shared with a small group, mainly the mayor and her regional managers. The list of authorized users was at the top, and Alex's name was above that of the group's newest member: *J.Rochambeau.*

The names on the left side of the list outnumbered the right. The two headers read: *Gathered: 757* and *Remaining: 501.* Alex licked his lips, his eyes scanning the list on the right.

Yep, there were nine names he recognized. Right at the top. His heart pounded in his ears.

Then the outer door slid open with a hiss, and Alex's head snapped around.

"Boss, *Earhart* will be here within the hour." Steph sailed past the security officers and into the office. "But things are getting dicey topside. The Frenchies brought a couple hundred civilians up to Platform Three. Not sure where they're going, but my money says it's a ship."

"You want to see if you can hack your way to finding that?" Alex asked, vacating his chair. "Try it with my access."

"I will try." Steph grinned as she threw their alma mater's motto at him, plopping down.

Alex turned to Bradshaw. "You see anything interesting?"

"Other than the empty ass Norwegian Cruise Lines ship pulling in?" Bradshaw snorted. "Looks like they're exiling people in luxury."

"You sure it was empty?"

"Sir, ain't no cruise ship going to come in with no one hanging off the balconies. At the very least, there'll be drunks awake, and someone's gonna be butt naked." He snickered. "Not that I'd know that from personal experience or anything."

"Noted." Alex took a deep breath. "All right, folks. We sit tight until *Earhart* is close enough, and then we go topside. She'll have to send a boat, so there won't be much room for luggage."

That sentence was mostly aimed at Fowler and his aide, both of whom were surrounded by suitcases. Fowler sniffed. "My belongings include critical State Department papers—"

"Then you'd better shred them," Hamilton interrupted, not even looking up from her book. "We can't have State secrets falling into the wrong hands."

Was that sarcastic? It was impossible to tell. Alex kept his mouth shut.

"Don't be ridiculous," Fowler said. "As I've said *before*, hiding here is the height of stupidity. Whatever methods the French are using to move civilians, they'll be more careful with a diplomatic delegation. They *have* to be. There are rules."

"Marines with rifles tend to make their own rules, sir," Alex said when Hamilton ignored Fowler.

Fowler rolled his eyes. "You military types all think force will solve anything, don't you?"

"No, I think it creates more problems than it solves, but in case you missed it, Mr. Secretary, we didn't start this dance," Alex replied. "We're just stuck with the music."

"How naive. Any diplomat will tell you—"

"Turn the lights off!" Olson hissed.

One of the security guys—the tall one with black hair—complied right away, plunging the office into darkness. Steph swore as the bright screen in front of her grew brighter, turning off the monitor, but Alex turned to Olson.

"What's up?" he whispered.

"Bunch of marines outside, heading this way. Better if they think we're all still stupid and in bed," Olson replied. She crept forward, peeking out the lone side window. Both security officers took cover so no one could see them through the windows in the doors, and Alex felt a strange chill roll down his spine.

A minute ticked by in slow motion, and then two. Even Fowler held his breath. Finally, Olson said: "They're gone. But we might want to keep the front lights off."

"Good idea."

"You people are paranoid." Fowler's laugh was as brittle as it was arrogant.

"It's their job, isn't it?" Gage asked.

Olson and Bradshaw shifted unhappily, but neither politician noticed. They continued disparaging the military, forgetting they shared the room with seven people who wore the uniform. But they did stay away from the windows.

One hour. Alex just had to put up with this bullshit for one more hour.

Chapter 23

No More Diplomacy

Khare hung up his phone and turned to Jules with a vicious smile, standing in the middle of Central like a conquering hero. "The *Vishal* Battle Group has damaged one destroyer and is closing with the Americans to destroy the rest of their ships."

"How fortunate for them." Jules glanced at the monitors to his right, which showed internal security cameras. Two platoons of marines herded several hundred civilians towards the Platform Three elevator bank. Resistance appeared light.

Khare hissed aloud. "They fired on *my* navy first. If the United States believes that India will roll over for them like a dog, they are very much mistaken. Is France prepared to do so?"

Jules bristled. "We will continue to round up the Americans. The objective here is to humiliate our former friends, not murder civilians."

"You are conveniently forgetting the *military* personnel on this station." Khare crossed his arms.

What to do with them? Jules' original orders said to force the Navy personnel off with the rest of the civilians—gently but firmly. But if those Americans learned of their carrier being shot at...

"I must call my superiors for instructions." Jules hated temporizing, but he was not authorized to kill anyone. Not yet.

"Of course, *Captain.*" Khare's smile grew sharp. "Do so. While you do, I will send people to search for American naval personnel."

"Non." Jules shook his head. "Those marines are under my command, mon ami. A moment."

Jules knew Khare's blood was up; if Jules did not manage things carefully, the semi-organized chaos on Armistice Station would become a bloodbath. Bloodbaths had their uses—as did terror and chaos—but Jules would not cause one by accident. Particularly not if it went against France's best interests.

Punching in the code to bypass Armistice Station's jamming, Jules dialed Admiral Bernard. It was just after twenty-two hundred back home, so he called the Admiral's personal cell phone.

Three rings later, a sleepy Jérémie Bernard answered the phone. "Capitane Rochambeau, this best be an emergency."

"Oui," Jules replied, wishing Khare did not speak French. Alas, the Indian admiral spoke twice as many languages as Jules. "Have you heard about the battle in the Strait of Malacca?"

"The *what*?" Something crashed in the background. "What has happened?"

"The Americans sank an Indian *Kilo*. Now the Indians have attacked the *Enterprise* Strike Group." Jules sighed. "We have not yet rounded up all of our targets, although we are on schedule."

"The Indians have *attacked* the Americans?" Bernard sounded stunned.

"Oui. They have damaged one destroyer. It may be worse by now. I need to know what to do with the military targets on Armistice Station."

"*Merde*."

Jules let his words sink in while a marine lieutenant approached, handing him a list of the American, British, and Australian residents and visitors already rounded up. *Total: 1658. Gathered: 757. Remaining: 501.*

"I must call the president," Bernard said after a moment.

"I understand. But do not take long. Our Indian allies grow...impatient," Jules replied. "And they will remind me of our agreement to support them, even with military action."

"I will call back," Bernard promised, and hung up.

Of course, he provided no guidance. That left responsibility on Jules' shoulders. Jules was not a stranger to accountability; he would not captain a submarine if he did not live for the thrill of independent command. However, he preferred to avoid responsibility for national policy.

"Well, Captain?" Khare crossed his arms.

"We will continue rounding up the undesirables," Jules said. "I see no reason to visit violence upon civilians who do not resist."

"And the *non*-civilians here?"

Jules shrugged. "I will await instructions."

"We are at war, Captain. They are enemy combatants."

"If a few shots started a war, the world would have many more wars." Jules waved a hand.

"And if your country's policy of humiliating America bore fruit, we would not be in this position," Khare said.

"Have you forgotten China, Admiral?" Jules wanted to shake him, but one did not do that to admirals, even ones from other navies. "If you spoke to your allies before—"

"It is too late for that. They sank our *submarine*!"

Jules walked away before he said something his country might regret. In theory, he was not against a war; it was his profession. But *accidentally* falling into one? Wars were instruments of diplomacy, a means to the end a country desired. His country needed unhindered access to resources in the Indian Ocean. America's meddling restricted that. If his nation desired war to clear the path to those resources, Jules would be happy to strike the first blow.

But his nation did not want war. Otherwise, they would not have chosen subterfuge, would not have acted when America was distracted elsewhere. Jules scowled. He did not like how rapidly things were changing.

"They will negotiate an end to hostilities," Khare followed him to say. "America no longer has the will for a long war."

"And how many *limited* wars has your country, fought, sir?" Jules spun. "France learned the folly of that tactic while you were still a British colony."

Khare turned an interesting shade of purple as Aida Ledoux walked in.

"My communications team detected a bridge-to-bridge radio transmission, mon Capitaine," she said to Jules, ignoring Khare. "The American naval detachment called *Amelia Earhart* to pick them up."

Jules froze. "I thought you jammed all incoming communications?"

"Not bridge-to-bridge. We still have ships to dock. Would you prefer I shut down the lifeblood of this station?" Ledoux glared, hands on her hips.

"No, of course not." Jules took a deep breath to calm his suddenly-racing heart. "Are the Americans still on one of the platforms?"

"Non. They disappeared back into the station."

Jules held up a hand before Khare spoke. "It seems we must be in agreement, Admiral. Allow me to call my marines and have them round up our friends from the United States Navy."

"I hope they won't be *too* gentle." Khare's grin turned vicious again.

"We shall act as circumstances dictate."

He would send Camille with the marines, Jules decided. Firstly, because Admiral Hamilton deserved a modicum of respect. She also knew Commander Coleman, which could help. The sooner they rounded up their new enemies, the better. Then Jules could return to sea where he belonged.

"Sir, *John Finn's* going down," Rubino said.

A long silence followed. No one knew what to say. Grief and fury swirled like fire in John's throat, warring with shocked numbness. The U.S. Navy hadn't lost a ship to enemy action since World War II. Yet here they were. *Kidd* launched a helicopter a few minutes earlier, and it hovered over the stricken destroyer, feeding FLIR video to the rest of the strike group. Every eye on the flag bridge watched the screen as *Finn* rolled left, going down bow first as sailors jumped overboard, swimming for life rafts. Water bubbled at her grave and then went still, leaving less than half of her crew behind.

"Send—send someone to pick up the survivors," McNally whispered, his eyes still the size of doorknobs.

"We can't afford to slow, sir." John's throat was bone dry. "We'll have to come back for them."

"We can't leave people in the water!" McNally came out of his chair, stabbing a finger at John as he towered over him. "Those sailors are my responsibility, and—"

"And the Indians will attack again if we don't give them a reason not to!" Should John yell at his admiral? The waiting was killing him. Every muscle in John's body tensed; why hadn't the Indians fired? Modern war was fast paced. Why were they waiting?

McNally went red. "Then shoot some goddamned Harpoons at them while we slow, for Christ's sake! Why the *hell* haven't those destroyers done so already?"

"We're outside Harpoon range, sir," Rubino answered for John.

"What? But—" McNally's mouth snapped shut. He was a submariner, like John. Submarines didn't fire Harpoon anti-ship missiles often, but they *could*, and McNally should've remembered that the maximum range for a Harpoon II + ER anti-ship missile was eighty-two nautical miles. "What about NSMs?"

John grimaced. "Only on *Finn*." Heading to the bottom, now, he didn't add.

The Indian formation slowed five minutes ago, keeping the range at an even one hundred nautical miles. *Enterprise* and her escorts could steam straight at the Indians and brave their fire for twenty nautical miles—an eternity if the Indians steamed *away* from them to keep the range open—or they could somehow change the odds.

"Sir, we need to launch an airstrike," John said.

"We can't launch in the traffic separation scheme," Rubino objected. "International law says we can only transit to our destination."

"I think that went out the window the moment the Indians started shooting," John replied. Silence hovered over the flag bridge like smoke; John could feel every eye on him. "Now, since the Indians are jamming our long-range communications, we either need to open the range until we can get instructions—or *talk* to the Indians—or we need to shoot back."

"The U.S. Navy doesn't run away," McNally snapped.

"Call it a tactical retreat if you want. But even if we do, we need to launch aircraft first, because we won't get a chance if they start shooting again."

McNally collapsed back into his chair. "Someone—someone get a satellite phone. I need to call this in."

"It might not work, sir," John said. "They've got airborne jammers up."

"I'm damned well going to try!"

Grabbing the phone from his aide, McNally beelined out of the flag bridge, leaving John sitting at the command console by himself.

"What do you think they're waiting for, sir?" Rubino asked.

"Instructions from home." John shrugged. "Same as us."

"What happens if they get them first?"

John looked back at the large screen tactical display. With *Finn* sunk, *Fletcher*, *Belleau Wood*, and *Kidd* grouped around *Enterprise* like guard dogs. But he heard the reports over the tactical net. The cruiser and both remaining destroyers used almost half their inventory of anti-air missiles in that first strike. *Enterprise* had two-thirds of her ESSMs left, but they wouldn't last long against the Indian battle group.

"Then we're in for a world of hurt," he said. No one answered. John took a deep breath. "Find me those jammers."

The French President called the Indian President, already awake thanks to the report of the *Kilo*-class submarine's sinking. News that there were no survivors from that attack accompanied the notification that the admiral on INS *Vishal* fired on the *Enterprise* Strike Group.

In another time, the Indian President would have called the White House and dealt with this via diplomatic means. But not after the second shooting incident this month, and not after the admiral on *Vishal* choose to engage Americans instead of talking to them.

This stuck the Indian President in a corner, one that would require apologies—and possible reparations—to exit. No one in India was willing to bow that far. Not now. So, he backed *Vishal's* admiral up to the hilt.

Parliament was not in session, which meant the French President's decrees had the force of law. He gathered the Prime Minister and the Council of Ministers, anyway, because such decisions could not be made alone. Within ten minutes, the Russian President joined the call, and the three conferred.

India's economic reasons to push American interests out were obvious. France also still owned significant territory in the region, along with multiple underwater stations around the French islands surrounding Madagascar. Russia's intentions were less organic, but Russia was a rising power.

The bad old days of the Cold War were back in one way: anything that decreased American influence increased Russian. France and India knew Russia would not help them out of the goodness of her government's heart, but for now, Russia was a friend. A friend with a larger Navy than Russia sported since the heyday of the USSR.

Their choices were simple. One, withdraw now and negotiate a settlement, blaming local commanders for the conflict. Two, continue the battle and destroy the *Enterprise* Strike Group. Claim Armistice Station by force and eject American influence from the region, risking war. Three, hold what they'd taken, and hope China remained a threat significant enough to keep the United States distracted.

They all knew the third choice was unlikely. A fresh day already dawned in China, with reports of a three-way civil war looming. Four separate governments claimed legitimacy in China, now, none of which looked ready to back down. At least two of them possessed nuclear weapons.

Whatever happened in China, odds were that the Americans would adopt the same wait-and-see attitude as the rest of the world. Facing off with a unified Communist China was one thing; civilized nations did not use nuclear weapons. Factions and rebels, on the other hand, might not be so discerning.

In the end, they reached an agreement.

"I'm into the security system," Steph said.

Alex walked over to where she still sat at his desk. "Good job." He patted her on the shoulder. "Keeping an eye on the, uh..."

"The enemy?" Steph twisted to look at him, her smile crooked. "We've got to call them something, sir."

"Yeah." He swallowed. "I guess."

"Looks there are two groups of French marines out there. They've cleared everything southwest of Habitat Nine and west of West Cook," she said. "It doesn't look like they've tried clearing Newell and its offshoots yet; I think they're still on the south side of Mattera."

"Sounds about right based on what I saw, earlier." Alex sipped his coffee. That meant the French hadn't gotten to the section of the station the Naval Detachment occupied but were moving in their direction. "They're concentrating on the hotels and the habitats before weeding out people like us."

"That fills me with confidence." Steph pointed at a camera view of a marine squad. "I'm not sure where this third group's going, though."

Alex squinted. "Is that Camille Dubois? Can you zoom in?"

"This isn't TV, sir. I can't remote zoom the cameras if you don't want them to know I'm doing it." Steph snorted. "I'm not sure these cameras *can* zoom, anyway. They're ancient technology. Not even 4k."

"Right. Sorry." Alex grimaced. "So, where are these guys?"

"By the Crowne Plaza. See that sign in the corner? It's for the TRANSPLAT Five elevator bank."

"A moment, Commander?" Hamilton cut in. Surprisingly, she put aside her book and moved to the far side of the conference room.

Chest tight, Alex rounded the table and came to her side. "Yes, ma'am?"

"I'd like to know your intentions." Her gaze was intent, but Alex couldn't tell what she was thinking.

"My priority is to get you, Secretary Fowler, and your aides off this station, ma'am. *Earhart* is the best way to do that." Too late, Alex realized he hadn't bothered asking permission—he'd just done what he thought was right. Admiral Hamilton was three or four lightyears senior to him; Alex was the station's officer-in-charge, but he should've run his plan by her.

She crossed her arms. "And then?"

"Then I want to get my people out. Preferably at the same time." He smiled without humor. "This station's going to hell in a hurry, and I don't think it's a fun time or place to be an American."

"And you're including yourself in your 'people,' Commander?"

Did that mean she wanted him to stay? Alex couldn't puzzle out her expression, so he went with the truth. "I can't imagine I'd do a damned bit of good staying, ma'am."

"Not unless you wanted to give the French a propaganda victory." Hamilton frowned. "And that's not happening. Understood?"

"Crystal clear, Admiral." Alex wanted to point out he wasn't an idiot, and he sure as hell wasn't some wannabe hero like Chris Kennedy, but Hamilton wasn't the kind of admiral you said that to.

Alex's experience with admirals was that they were better avoided. None of them wanted to waste energy on a non-due course officer, anyway. Even the one that kicked him off his chosen career path. So, he said nothing and counted the minutes until *Earhart* returned.

Chapter 24

Deadly Force

Lieutenant Commander Maria Vasquez and Lieutenant Jesse Lin hung a left out of Elkman tube and headed into the south end of Cook. Maria couldn't help staring at the underwater adventure park in the middle of the circular Cook tube; even looking at Cousteau's didn't make her believe it existed. Who in their right mind wanted to ride an underwater rollercoaster? There were even parts of it that went above the domed roof of the tube, encased in specialized protective glass casing.

Rumor said they planned to build a ski slope in one of the new hubs. If anyone could top the indoor ski slope in Dubai, it would be Armistice Station. She snuck more glances at the theme park as they headed towards the bottom of Cook. It really weirded her out.

Cook East was administrative, but Cook West was the wild side. There were bars, stores, and every tourist spot imaginable. Maybe this place would be great for vacation, but why anyone with a brain put an international conference *underwater* mystified Maria. As a submariner, she was more than comfortable underwater, but the impracticality drove her batty.

The loudspeaker to their right crackled. "Guests and residents of Armistice Station, please remain within your quarters. The station is experiencing technical and environmental difficulties. However, all hotels and habitats are safe, so please remain inside. We will notify you when the situation changes. Thank you."

The announcement repeated in multiple languages; Maria listened to the one in Spanish, picking out enough words to guess it meant the same thing. She wasn't fluent in Spanish, much to her aunts' chagrin. She could stumble through a conversation, but a rebellious, college-aged Maria took Latin instead. Much good it did her.

"It's too quiet," Jesse whispered.

"Yeah?" Maria saw a few people, mostly young. "It's after one A.M."

"Night life's crazy here." Jesse shook his head. "We're coming up on Fisher. Bradshaw calls it the Row of Sin. There's four bars, two strip clubs, a dance studio, three 'smoke' shops that'll sell you almost anything, and a place that *definitely* doesn't arrange escorts, if you know what I mean."

"Sounds fun." Maria grinned. "If, uh, not a magnificent idea while on active duty."

Jesse shook his head. "Tell that to Bradshaw."

"He sounds like he's a joy to lead." Maria knew LS2 Bradshaw's type . There'd been six of them in her department on her last boat. No matter how often the brass tried to manage them out, colorful sailors were the Navy's heart and soul.

"He's barrels of laughs." Jesse's smile vanished as two French marines came around the corner from Earle. "Crap."

"Keep it cool," Maria whispered. "We won't be Americans if they ask."

He shot her a sideways look. "There aren't a lot of other countries you and I can both be from. Sure, you can pick anywhere Latinix, but how many other places can you get someone who's half-Japanese and half-Irish American?"

"Um." Maria bit her lip, studying his face. Jesse looked like the Japanese side of his ancestry, just taller than average and with hair a few shades lighter. "Yeah, that's harder. Maybe we can call you Columbian if they squint?"

"I'm not sure even *our* marines are that dumb."

"I wish I disagreed." Maria glanced towards the French marines again, just as another group came around the corner from the Earle tube, leading a gaggle of surly-looking Americans. "Where are they coming from?"

"Habitats One through Five are down Earle," Jesse whispered.

"You live down there?" Those seemed to be the closest habitats to the naval detachment's offices.

Jesse laughed. "Nah, they stuck us out in the boonies. Me, Olson, and Steph are out in Habitat Nine. Commander Coleman and Bradshaw are up in Seven. Longer walk."

"That's crappy."

"Yeah, well, they didn't like the *Kansas* Incident much around here." He shrugged.

Maria pursed her lips. She knew too much about that; working for Admiral Hamilton gave her a ringside seat to the investigation four months ago. Maria wasn't sure who she agreed with. Commander Kennedy was on the fast track, a go-getter who seemed poised for great things.

But he also hit on her with the subtlety of an enraged bear, and anyone who lacked self-control around women wasn't someone she wanted to work for. Hamilton didn't like Kennedy, either, but Maria knew the boss reserved the bulk of her ire for Alex Coleman.

Hamilton didn't like people who worked outside the rules. She disapproved of *cowboys*. Hamilton completed two successful command tours without putting a foot wrong, and she demanded the same from everyone else. Maria was fine with that; she, too, was a perfectionist. But nothing about the *Kansas* Incident was simple, and just thinking about it left Maria uneasy.

"Hey! You!" A French marine shouted, and Maria froze. "Stop!"

Jesse grabbed her arm. "*Say* something!"

Maria swallowed, turning as innocent eyes on the Marine as she could manage and groping for the right words in Spanish. "Nos?"

"Oui." One marine strode up. He was young and fresh-faced, probably the junior guy who got the suckiest jobs. Maria tried not to glance at the rifle slung over his right shoulder. "You. You are American, non?"

"No." Maria shook her head. "Colombiana."

"Colombiana?" The marine frowned, and then turned to an officer and spoke in rapid-fire French. Finally, he turned back towards them. "You will come with us."

"Why?" She couldn't think of the Spanish word and asked in English.

"All Americans come with us."

Jesse tried speaking up: "But we aren't—"

"Ca n'a pas d'importance." The marine shook his head. "Come with me."

"We're Columbian!" Maria tried to hang back, but the Marine grabbed her by the arm and propelled her towards the crowd.

He said something in French, but the eyeroll was universal: *Sure you are.* The second marine gestured with his rifle, and Jesse followed her without protest. They found themselves in the front ranks of the American crowd, next to a pair of old ladies dressed to the nines.

"It was a good try, dear," one of them said with a smile. "Better than we managed when they pulled us out of the Stars and Shells Casino."

"I—I don't know what you mean." Maria tried to infuse a Spanish accent into her voice and failed.

"Of course, you don't." The second woman, dressed in red and black, patted her on the shoulder. "I'm Pam, and this is Cassie."

"Maria and Jesse." She wouldn't mention their ranks. The French seemed polite enough—if forceful—with civilians. How would they treat naval officers? Maria didn't want to find out.

Her chest was tight, tight enough that she worried her breathing would give away her nerves. Maria wiped her hands on her pants, wishing she dared take her phone out and send a text.

Pam tutted. "Aren't you two cute? Welcome to the horrific end of an otherwise lovely vacation."

"Thanks, I think." Maria glanced around, counting marines. *Twelve. That's a lot to watch twenty-six civilians.* Were they paranoid or just thorough? The marines walked on the edges of the crowd, their attention flicking between the civilians and the path ahead. *They're well trained...and obeying that training.*

"Where are you taking us?" Jesse asked the lead marine, the one who looked like an officer. Maria wasn't sure what three shoulder stripes meant for a French marine, but it was more than anyone else had.

"To a cruise liner." The officer's English was good; his sneer was, too. "You will be taken off-station in comfort."

"But to *where*?" Pam nudged forward, eyeing the marine like a recalcitrant grandchild. "I'm too old for a round-the-world cruise, young man. I hope you're not going to try to take us all the way back to the U.S. in some dingy ship."

"You'll go to Madagascar."

"*Madagascar*? Really?" Pam reared back as if slapped. "Couldn't you at least take us to the Seychelles? They have better casinos."

The marine ignored her. Maria continued looking for escape routes, but every time she drifted to the edge of the crowd, that same young marine was there to glare until she returned to the old ladies' side.

Did they realize what she was, or were they just paranoid?

McNally had been gone too long.

A ball of tension coiling in his spine, John grabbed an inter-ship radio and headed after the admiral. The Indians still hadn't followed up on their initial attack, which left John uneasy. Maybe not picking up *John Finn's* survivors was a mistake. Had the Indians realized what a monumental mistake they'd made? Sure, Indian MiGs continued to circle their carrier, but they hadn't headed towards *Enterprise* and her escorts...yet.

Twenty-five minutes felt like a lifetime. That was more than enough time for McNally to call someone important and get updated Rules of Engagement. Standard ROE said they could only fire if fired upon, but no one expected one major nation's carrier strike group to attack another's.

The U.S. had to be the responsible adults, a fact that burned in John's gut like acid. *Do we really have to stand by and let them sink an American destroyer and kill God knows how many sailors*? That outcome was likely if their luck continued. John hoped like hell McNally got another answer. Or that the Indians would back off and let the diplomats handle things.

He should *want* a diplomatic solution, right? Not revenge. Revenge was for movies; John lived in the real world, where war was a terrible thing.

Finding the admiral was easy. He hadn't gone out on the bridge wing; instead, McNally walked down two levels to stand near a chaff launcher two sailors were busy reloading. He held the satellite phone at waist level, staring out at the ocean with that same blank expression from earlier. John swallowed back a rising tide of dread.

"Sir?" John asked; McNally didn't twitch. "Admiral."

Finally, McNally turned. "John. How are things?"

"Quiet so far, but the Indians have launched aircraft. You get ahold of anyone, sir?" John wanted to shake sense into his boss, but he feared it wouldn't work.

"None of the numbers we have are answering." McNally looked back out to sea. His voice was tiny. "Even the strike group home contact went to voicemail."

John swallowed. "Radio should have a list of emergency contacts. Can't you just call the Seventh Fleet duty officer?"

Enterprise's homeported was Norfolk, Virginia, as part of Second Fleet. But their operational commander was Seventh Fleet; upon entering the Strait of Malacca, they CHOPed, or CHanged OPerational Command, from Fifth Fleet to Seventh Fleet. John had never operated in Seventh Fleet's area of operations, but he knew how this worked. He was an east coast sailor, spent a lot of time in the Arabian Gulf and the Atlantic, with the occasional Mediterranean Cruise thrown in to keep sailors happy.

McNally blinked. "I suppose I could—"

The roar of jet engines cut him off, and John whirled around to see a F-35 catapult off the deck. Flight deck personnel ran about with grim purpose, readying more aircraft. Before John could open his mouth, a second F-35 took off, with replacements already taxing towards the carrier's catapults.

"What the hell is Edwards *thinking*?" McNally went red again. "If he thinks he can launch without my permission, he's got another thing coming!"

"Come on!" John grabbed his admiral by the arm and dragged him to the ladder. Yeah, the carrier CO should've requested the admiral's permission before launching aircraft. Particularly in this damned powder keg! But Captain Edwards was no idiot. If he gave the order to launch, they were in trouble.

John shoved McNally up the ladder first, the deafening sounds of jet engines growing louder. They sprinted forward twenty feet, where John threw open another door so they could climb another ladder, this time inside the skin of the ship. The doors to the flag bridge were open, and they burst through.

"Indian aircraft inbound!" Rubino said. "Six-zero nautical miles and closing fast!"

John slammed into his chair and threw his headset on. The tactical plot showed at least a dozen aircraft inbound; *Enterprise* so far launched four in response. "How fast can we get more aircraft up?" he asked.

"We've only got four catapults, sir," Rubino replied. "It'll be a few."

"They changed formation course without permission," McNally muttered, shaking his head. "Why would they do that?"

"Echo Bravo, this is Echo Whiskey," Captain Rosario on *Belleau Wood* said over the tactical net. The callsign Echo Whiskey designated *Belleau Wood*—and her CO—as the air defense commander, which meant the cruiser had tactical control over the aircraft and the entire strike group's missile defense. "Request batteries release to engage incoming aircraft, over."

"Don't you dare!" McNally spun on Rubino when she opened her mouth to respond. "We can't fire on those aircraft unless they fire on us!"

John almost choked. "Admiral, their destroyers *already* fired on us!"

"It's not the same!"

"Echo Bravo this is Echo Whiskey, five minutes to enemy aircraft intercept, over,"

John started at the screen as the red icons representing Indian fighters drew closer and closer, swallowing back fear.

The Mikoyan MiG-29M was an old but reliable airframe. Designed for the Russian Navy in 1988, it ended up in India first. Operational since 2004, MiG-29 remained the mainstay of the Indian Navy, with twenty-four carried by each of India's four aircraft carriers.

Aircraft were not John's area of expertise—he knew more about helicopters than fighters, because helos hunted submarines and fighters were too fast to bother. But he knew MiG-29s carried the Russian-made Kh-29MP missile, nicknamed "Kedge" by NATO. That missile was slower than the BrahMos missiles the destroyers threw at them earlier, but the fighters would shoot from *much* closer.

"Sir?" Rubino gestured at the plot. Damn, those fighters moved fast.

McNally stared wide-eyed at the screen. "I still need to call..."

"Admiral, we've either got to shoot them or expect to be shot," John said.

The tactical net crackled. "Echo Bravo, Echo Whiskey, four minutes to intercept. Enemy range, five-zero miles. Warnings have been sent and ignored."

McNally said nothing.

"Admiral?" John tried one more time, silently counting to five. He didn't know what was wrong with McNally and didn't have time to care. Someone had to do something. He keyed his microphone. "Echo Whiskey, this is Echo Bravo, batteries release. Engage incoming aircraft, over."

"Echo Whiskey, roger, break *Kidd*, engage bandits, over!"

McNally whirled on him. "John, you—you—"

"I'd rather be damned for shooting than not, sir."

In the sky, four *Enterprise* F-35C Lightning fighters faced twelve Indian MiG-29Ms. The American aircraft were newer, faster, and better armed than their Indian counterparts, but they were severely outnumbered. Each Lightning carried six AIM-120 AMRAAM anti-air missiles. In contrast, the Indian MiG-29s carried two KH-29 anti-surface missiles and four Vympel NPO K-77PD anti-air missiles. The two sets of anti-air missiles were roughly equal in warhead power and speed.

Directed by *Belleau Wood* into sectors ahead of the *Enterprise* Strike Group, the American fighters fired first, each Lightning shooting salvos of two AMRAAMs. The missiles streaked out from under the aircrafts' wings, jets of light against a still-dark night sky. Each salvo targeted one Indian fighter, and the Lightnings kept firing.

The Lightnings knew their only chance to defeat the Indian fighters was to shoot them down before they could return the favor. But the MiGs started firing seconds after the Americans, twenty-four Vympel anti-air missiles arcing out from their aircraft. The Lightnings evaded, attempting to shoot the incoming missiles down. One fighter managed, another ate a missile and ejected, and then the Indians fired their second wave of Vympels. Three Indian fighters exploded before they could fire, but that still left nine MiGs and eighteen anti-air missiles in the air.

The three remaining American fighters went evasive, heading back towards the strike group for support. A second was shot down, and then the third, before *Kidd* started firing SM-2 missiles at the Indian fighters.

Kidd was a hairsbreadth too slow. All nine remaining MiGs fired their KH-29 anti-surface missiles at the strike group.

Chapter 25

Sour

"All stations, *Enterprise*, *Enterprise* is hit. I say again, *Enterprise* is hit."

Nancy's head whipped around as those words came over the tactical net. Her OSS operator heard them, too, and slewed the camera over to the fireball on *Enterprise's* flight deck.

"Oh, *fuck*," Nancy whispered, knowing what must have happened.

One missile made it past their defenses and slammed right into the most precious piece of real estate in the entire strike group. The impact was forward of *Enterprise's* first two catapults, burning fiercely. Though the OSS, Nancy could see sailors rushing out to fight the fires, but she couldn't afford distraction, and she couldn't help. Instead, she looked back down at her tactical plot.

At least *Kidd's* SM-2s downed the last MiGs. Only one Lightning remained in the air, and unless *Enterprise* got that fire under control, no others would launch. *That guy can't land, either.* The Indian strike group remained about one hundred miles south, with their shadow, *Porbandar*, twenty-five miles north. Nancy frowned.

Porbandar didn't shoot during the first engagement. Why not? Stopping BrahMos missiles from her would be a right bitch. She was too close for multiple counter missile launches.

"What the hell is *Porbandar* waiting for?" she asked.

Attar frowned. "Maybe they're not loaded with war shots? We're in the Indians' backyard. Maybe they don't carry live missiles for training any more than we do."

"I hope you're right." Nancy leaned back and stared at the display. *Porbandar* remained out of visual range. They had a good radar track on her, though. Nancy keyed her mic for the tactical net. "Echo Bravo, this is *Fletcher*. Request permission to engage shadowing Indian destroyer with bulldogs, over."

There was a lengthy pause.

"*Fletcher*, this is Echo Bravo. Negative, that unit has not fired upon us," the battle watch captain replied. Nancy thought she heard arguing in the background.

She scowled. "*Fletcher*, roger out."

Attar shrugged. "It was worth a—"

"Vampire, vampire, vampire!" her air warfare coordinator said over *Fletcher's* internal net. "New strike inbound bearing zero-eight-eight! Estimate forty, I say again, four-zero, missiles inbound!"

"Air, Captain, designate one bird per incoming missile." Nancy hated giving that order, but her destroyer had only twenty SM-6s left. She had thirty-six ESSMs, too, but those were short-ranged weapons. *Fletcher* needed to shoot down one third of the missiles aimed at the strike group; using one missile per threat on the first salvo meant she'd have missiles left for follow-on salvos. Plus, her ESSMs were for last-ditch defense.

Damn, she missed *Finn* right about now.

"Air, aye," her air warfare coordinator responded. "Birds away!"

Fletcher vibrated as thirteen SM-6 missiles erupted out of her forward and aft cells. Nancy swallowed and tried to appear calm. Yet again, the flight time was about a minute, and the Indians remained out of Harpoon range. They had to take the fire until they could fight back.

"Why the hell is Admiral McNally waiting so long to close the range?" Attar asked.

"I wish I knew." Nancy could ask, but the tactical net was for *tactics*, and McNally had a staff for that. John had to be all over this. He wasn't an idiot.

Still, Nancy was learning that combat made idiots out of a lot of people. She could only pray John Dalton wasn't one of them.

"All stations, *Enterprise*, am launching aircraft using midships catapults," Captain Edwards said over the tactical net. "Request you confirm positive ID before committing birds, over."

Nancy's jaw dropped; Attar acknowledged the message and then turned to her with wide eyes.

"That's ballsy, ma'am," Attar said.

"Captain Edwards can count, Davud." Nancy licked her lips. "He knows we'll run out of missiles before the Indians do. And they can keep us out of range, so the only way to hit back is to get Lightnings in the air."

What were the Lightnings armed with? Likely AMRAAMs. Could those hit a ship?

A bunch of American pilots were about to find out, assuming *Enterprise* could get them off deck. Nancy watched the battle through the OSS camera, holding her breath. She couldn't do anything to defend her destroyer aside from giving the orders she already had.

Modern technology made her crew mere bystanders as *Fletcher's* Aegis combat system selected targets and married missiles to them. Two fighters screamed off *Enterprise*'s deck between *Fletcher*, *Belleau Wood*, and *Kidd's* missile salvos, turning immediately into the safety corridor between the ships' launch zones. Another two fighters taxied to the catapults far quicker than they'd normally dare, deck crews sprinting around them to line each Lightning up for launch.

SM-6s roared out faster than *Kidd's* remaining SM-2s; their last *Arleigh Burke*-class destroyer spent all her more advanced missiles against the first wave. But there were *more* missiles in this wave than the one that killed *John Finn.* Nancy swallowed. Damn the Indians for exploiting known American tactics. *Kidd* put all twelve of her remaining SM-2s into the air, but they were far too slow. Only two intercepted the maneuvering BrahMos missiles, leaving the other ten for the strike group's second salvo.

Fletcher quivered again, launching another eight SM-6s. That left her with only seven anti-air missiles, but Nancy had no choice. Conserving ammunition only helped if the ship survived—as the two dozen missiles *John Finn* took to the bottom proved.

Belleau Wood launched another five SM-6s, and then all three ships' Aegis weapons systems shifted to Evolved Sea Sparrow missiles. *Kidd* launched eight ESSMs with the other ships' SM-6s, and then *Enterprise* joined the fray, launching four ESSMs of her own as the BrahMos missiles closed from fifty miles out to twenty in the blink of an eye. *Fletcher* launched another eight ESSMs, but *Belleau Wood* did not.

"Hang fire, hang fire, *Belleau Wood* deluging cells in forward VLS!" a panicked voice said over the tactical net; Nancy held her breath.

The cruiser was their most powerful unit, and her forward VLS bank had room for seventy-two missiles. How many of her remaining ESSMs were in the forward bank? They were loaded in packs of four, which meant the hang fire put at least three other ESSMs out of commission. A hang fire was a missile whose rocket booster ignited without the missile restraint bolts releasing; the immediate response was to deluge the eight-cell VLS module with water, which might drown as many as thirty-two ESSMs.

Nancy forced herself to watch the tactical display instead of worrying about *Belleau Wood.* Missiles met missiles; explosions peppered the night sky. A corner of Nancy's mind imagined the view from the bridge, but her place was in CIC.

"All targets destroyed," Attar reported.

Nancy nodded, lifted her chin. "We're getting better at this."

"All stations this is Echo Bravo, immediate execute, new formation course one-three-five," Captain Dalton's voice ordered. Someone in the back of CIC whooped; Nancy didn't turn to see who. "Formation speed three-one knots, over."

Nancy felt the tightness in her chest ease. The second two Lightnings launched, followed by two more. Nothing would make up for *John Finn's* loss, but the *Enterprise* Strike Group turned to close the enemy.

"Now we get our shot." Her eyes narrowed as the range decreased.

They were ninety-six miles away from the Indians. They needed fourteen nautical miles before Harpoons from *Fletcher, Belleau Wood,* and *Kidd* could reach out to touch someone.

Commander Camille Dubois' cell phone rang. "Oui, mon Capitaine?"

"I have received word from Admiral Bernard," Jules said without preamble. "He wishes the American admiral taken alive, and also their Under Secretary of State."

"The others?" Camille asked.

Jules chuckled. "We would prefer them alive. If reasonably practical. If not...use deadly force as required."

"I will capture the officers alive." Her smile hurt her face. The idea of Alex Coleman as a prisoner of war warmed her heart.

"The objective of this operation remains the humiliation of the American government. The more prisoners we take, the greater leverage we have. But do not take unnecessary risks and *do not* let the Indians find them first." She heard him snarl. "I will have *Bretagne* deal with *Amelia Earhart.*"

"Merci." Camille schooled her smile down. "Bonne chance."

"Merci." Jules hung up, leaving Camille with her twelve Marines. That was enough to capture five naval officers, two sailors, and four civilians, was it not? She turned to Lieutenant Travers, the senior marine.

"Lieutenant, you have my permission to shoot the two security officers if they do not surrender," she said.

Travers stopped cold. "Pardon?"

"We will ask them to surrender." Camille met Travers' eyes. "But we will not wait too long. Understood?"

Travers swallowed. "Oui."

"We will not let the Indians capture the Americans, Lieutenant," she continued. "The American admiral presents a unique intelligence opportunity that *France* will capitalize upon, not India."

"Are the Indians not our allies?"

"Oui. But alliances are temporary, non?"

Camille spent too much time in intelligence to think otherwise. India and Russia were today's friends. Tomorrow might be different. She still found the Indians' precipitous attack on the American carrier strike group difficult to stomach, if only because it was foolishly done. And the American attack on the *Kilo*-class submarine was just stupid. What kind of idiot attacked a submarine which had not shot at them?

One afraid of being sunk. Camille suppressed a smile. The Americans were afraid. That was a first.

"Come," she said. "Their office is not far."

Camille consulted her map of Armistice Station. The place was a maze growing outwards from the original hub of Cook Tube. She and her team were south of Cook now; they split off from the group clearing Habitat Ten and the Armistice Crowne Plaza. Those marines continued dragging enemy civilians out of the hotel while Camille led a dozen others north, towards the center of the station. Once they reached Cook, they would have to bypass Earle—which included Central, where Camille's captain remained in command—and then turn down Elkman, which ran parallel to Earle. From there, it was a quick walk to the American Naval Detachment office.

With that office at the end of Elkman, they would have nowhere to go.

This would be easy.

"Captain, DCO, forward fire is under control," *Enterprise's* Damage Control Officer reported over the radio. "Midships fire is out. Reflash watch set. Overhaul in progress. Fourteen wounded transported to medical. Three confirmed dead by Doc Holmes."

Captain Ernest Edwards couldn't sigh in relief and weep simultaneously, so he took refuge in professionalism. "Thanks, Wes," he replied, and then turned to his officer of the deck. "How're we holding up, Simon?"

Lieutenant Commander Simon Pickering was one of the few surface warfare officers assigned to *Enterprise*, but he was a hell of a ship driver. "We're holding thirty-one knots, but Cheng says the vibrations will get worse if we go faster." He grinned. "Apparently, a hole in the flight deck does wicked things to our structural integrity."

"Imagine that." Ernest didn't want to think of what that hole did to the innards of his beautiful carrier, aside from causing the two major fires his crew fought to a standstill. *Enterprise* would need a long time in the yards to fix that hole, but she could still launch aircraft. That was enough.

"Captain, CDC, we have four ESSMs remaining," his Tactical Action Officer reported over an internal net.

"Yeah, I noticed you covering *Kidd's* sector in the second salvo," he replied, chewing his lip. "Pass the word to Pri-Fly to arm the second squadron of Lightnings with LSRAM."

"LSRAM, aye. That'll delay launch a few minutes, Captain."

"I know." Ernest sighed.

The AGM-158C Long Range Anti-Ship Missile was the best anti-ship missile the Navy had—and most warships still didn't carry it. He wished to hell that some of the shooters had LSRAM in their VLS cells, but the best they had were late model Harpoons.

However, the LSRAM had a range of up to 200 nautical miles, which was enough to reach the Indians. It wasn't a quick missile, but the fighters could get it in close. *I need to stop thinking like a pilot defending the carrier and* start *thinking like a carrier CO using all available tools to survive*, he thought, and then asked:

"How's CIWS looking?"

"Plenty of rounds for all three mounts," the TAO said. "But—"

The roar of two fighters launching drowned out the rest of the response; Ernest bared his teeth. That made six more Lightnings in the air. If the Indians didn't hurry, he would lay down a world of hurt on them.

He just hoped the pilots from his three downed Lightnings could survive in the water until the strike group turned back for them. Two parachutes had been visible after the fighters went down, and Ernest prayed the other escaped. But there was no time to check, only time to keep charging at the enemy.

"TAO, Captain, say again. Lost you in the jet wash," he said, watching the next two fighters taxi to the catapults.

"Sir, we're getting weird rumblings from the flag bridge. Something's wrong up there."

"Define 'something.'" Ernest felt cold. He made the call to launch fighters—and change formation course to support that—without asking the admiral because it protected his ship, but he expected McNally's support on that front.

The TAO's pause spoke volumes. "I'm not sure, sir, but I recommend you give the admiral a call," she said.

"Captain, aye." Ernest put the internal net phone aside and picked up the inter-ship telephone, punching in the number for the admiral's station on the flag bridge.

It rang for far too long.

"Flag bridge, Dalton."

"John, it's Ernest." He pushed aside lurking worry. "Is the admiral available?"

"He's...otherwise occupied right now, sir. But if you send your traffic, I'll relay." Dalton's voice was *almost* normal.

"My TAO thinks there's some hijinks going on down there, but I'm trying to launch fighters with a hole the size of a semi in my flight deck. I don't have time for drama. Tell me the ground truth," Ernest said.

John hesitated. "The Admiral's okay, sir. We're focused on closing with the enemy and getting comms with the home guard."

"Right." Ernest didn't believe a word of it, but one didn't call your fellow captain a liar. Not without evidence. "Any luck getting through this jamming?"

"Nothing long range," John replied. "Short range comms are fine, but no one answered the numbers the admiral tried to call. I sent his aide to try again. We're looking for the jammer, but they're hiding pretty good up there."

Yeah, something was wrong if McNally was calling instead of engaged in the *combat* problem, but how could Ernest say that? He thanked John, hung up, and turned his attention back to his wounded carrier.

Eight fighters in the air.

Nine.

Then twelve more Indian MiGs dove out of the clouds just twenty miles from *Enterprise*.

Chapter 26

Shots Heard 'Round the World

Chest tight with nerves, Alex wandered over to talk to the security officers still standing near the doors. Both worked for the Diplomatic Security Service, which was the State Department's version of the Secret Service, just less famous. They seemed professional, but Alex hadn't even gotten their names—a choice which now felt very foolish.

"You guys need anything?" he asked, feeling Hamilton's eyes burning into the back of his head.

"We're good," the taller one said. "Though a way out of this underwater coffin wouldn't go amiss."

Alex grinned. "Give me ten minutes and I'll have something for you."

"Yeah?"

"Yeah. *Amelia Earhart* should be here then." Alex watched both guards relax. "But it's better if we keep our heads down until the last minute."

"We're all for that," the shorter one said. "Less trouble you guys find, the better. I'm all for a sedate walk up to a ship."

"It'll be a walk up to a boat to the ship, but we'll try to keep it quiet." Alex chuckled. "Just for you. You guys got names, by the way?"

"Eric Dixon," the tall one replied.

"Damien Montero."

"It's a pleasure to actually meet you both." Alex shook both hands. "Sorry we didn't—"

"Boss, I think they're coming this way."

Steph's words made Alex's head snap around. "The marines?"

"Yeah, plus that chick in a naval officer's uniform. The one you recognized." She leaned close to the computer screen. "Small group of them just reached the southern end of Cook."

"Shit." Alex walked back, needing to see for himself. His heart sank. This time, Camille Dubois stood much closer to a camera, and there was no mistaking the sneer on her face.

"On a shingle." Steph's grin was brief. "What's our move?"

Alex hesitated, looking at the monitor and then at the time. *Earhart* would probably need longer than ten minutes. Even if she *was* on time, putting a boat in the water took time, and if the locals were a mite touchy about it...

"Holy shit, someone got shot!"

It started with an argument. Two twenty-something year olds didn't agree with a French marine pushing them to take a left towards the bottom of Cook. They objected, a marine said something obnoxious, and next Maria knew, both youths were on the ground.

"Get off me, dude!" The blonde girl scrambled to her feet, shying back as one of the marines grabbed for her arm.

Her friend, a dark-skinned man, was a touch slower. Another marine grabbed him, gesturing with his rifle. "You both come. This is not optional."

"Leave us alone!" The girl stepped forward to push the marine away from her friend.

Crack.

"Beth?"

The marine stumbled back, his eyes wide. The friend surged forward. *"Beth!"*

The blonde swayed and dropped like a rock, red blossoming in her midsection as she collapsed to the ground. Maria stepped forward without thinking, only to find a rifle in her face. She froze.

"Stop," another marine hissed. This one was short and young. To Maria, he looked like a kid on his first deployment, in over his head and trying so hard to follow orders. But those orders didn't cover a girl being shot, and everything in Maria screamed to *do something.*

"I can help her." Maria tried a steadying deep breath, barely able to tear her eyes away from the bleeding young woman. *Beth.* "I know first aid."

"Non. You stay."

"Look, man, if you don't want dead civilians on your hands, you need to let us help." Jesse stepped up beside her. "That doesn't have to be fatal, not if we get her help fast. I'm sure one of you has a first aid kit, and—"

"You stay!" The rifle jerked for emphasis. Jesse stopped cold, holding his hands up.

"Don't be an idiot." Pam marched forward like a sassy and glittery fairy godmother, glaring at the marine and shoving his rifle aside. "Whatever your superiors want, it's not a bunch of dead tourists. So, pull your head out and step aside, young man."

"You step back!" The young marine's eyes were wide, and his rifle swung to point at Pam. He added something in French, something high-pitched and panicked. One of his compatriots knelt next to Beth, but another two turned their direction.

"Look, sonny, I'm not trying to argue with your big, bad gun," Pam said. "But that girl needs help, and these people seem ready to do just that. So just let them—"

"Tais-toi! Shut—shut *up!*" The marine surged forward instead of stepping back, and too late, Maria saw his finger tightening on the trigger—

"No!" Jesse shot forward. Maria grabbed for him and missed, a split second too late.

Crack!

Pam's eyes went wide, and she stumbled back. For a moment, Maria thought she was shot, but the old woman caught her balance as Jesse crumbled to the ground, blood spurting from his neck.

"Jesse!" Maria shoved the shocked marine aside, nearly earning herself a rifle butt to the head and never noticing. "Shit shit *shit*! Anyone got a cloth, scarf, *anything*?"

Jesse had been in motion, and nerves jerked the marine's rifle high. The bullet hit Jesse high in the left shoulder, shattering his collarbone and digging into a major artery. Maria fell to her knees at his side, desperately pressing her palms to the wound.

"Hang in there, Jesse," she whispered. He didn't seem to hear her, but blood bubbled up between her fingers, and—

"What the hell is *wrong* with you people?" Pam knelt at her side, handing her a sparkling blue scarf. "Here, dear."

The glitter couldn't help a wound, but an infection beat bleeding to death, so Maria pressed it against the wound with blood-covered hands. Jesse gurgled something, his brown eyes glassy—and then went silent.

"Jesse?" Maria shook him. *"Jesse?"*

Shouting in French came from above; Pam's hand squeezed her shoulder before someone jerked her away. Pam yelped, but Maria ignored her. Her right hand felt for a pulse as she held the scarf down left-handed, finding nothing, *nothing*, and—

Hands pulled her up. Maria fought blindly, trying to pull away, but two French marines pulled her along, shouting at the rest of the civilians to follow and shoving them when they did not.

"I am sorry, Madame," the French officer said, but Maria didn't hear it.

"Say again?" Shock forced the words out of Alex's mouth; he froze, still next to Steph.

Bradshaw gestured at the security feed on Steph's laptop, where he and Olson watched one set of marines and civilians while Steph spied on the other two. "Like, no shit, shots fired, and someone went the fuck down. Can I rewind this thing, Ops?"

"Not without them knowing." Steph sounded as numb as Alex felt.

"Someone like *who*?" Fowler demanded.

Even Hamilton looked up from her book, her brow furrowing. "A civilian?" she asked.

"Looks like, ma'am." Bradshaw swallowed. "Oh—*fuck*—that's Lieutenant Lin!"

"What?" Alex rushed over, but a crowd blocked the view of whoever was on the floor—lying in an ever-increasing puddle of blood. *Oh, God.* Alex's hands wanted to shake; bile rose in his throat. Could that be Jesse? Bradshaw would know.

"What the hell?" Hamilton was by his side, glaring wide-eyed at the same screen. No one answered. A French marine pulled a kicking woman away from the dead body.

"Jesus, that's Jesse." The whisper was ragged; Alex needed several moments to realize it was his.

"And Maria," Hamilton added. Her voice sounded hollow.

They watched in stunned silence as marines pulled Maria away. Two lifted Jesse's body by the legs and arms; another pair lifted the first victim. Was either alive? Alex didn't think marines carried *living* victims casually. They exited that camera view while Alex and the others stood motionless.

Jesse was dead.

Alex swallowed. "How the hell could—could..."

"I don't know, but there's going to be hell to pay." Hamilton met his eyes, and for the first time, they agreed on everything.

Silence roared around them. Jesse was dead. What was Alex going to say to his girlfriend? Samantha came out to the station just a month earlier, and Alex knew Jesse planned on popping the question next time he went home. She was a nice girl and so crazy about Jesse. *Jesse.* Damn it all. He was kind to a fault and yeah, sometimes slow on the uptake, but...

Alex shook himself. He couldn't focus on that, not now. First, they needed to get out of here. Then Admiral Hamilton could light the French on fire.

"Um, not to be that guy, but aren't those same assholes headed here?" Bradshaw asked. "Kinda seems a bit more, um, problematic, now."

"Yeah." Alex squared his shoulders. "Time to head upstairs, folks." His chest was tight, but his voice was surprisingly even. "Steph, bring your laptop and download everything you can. I think the government will want this footage when everything's over."

"Sir, we can't..." Olson trailed off, still staring at the screen. Steph unplugged it and closed the laptop, shoving it and the cord into a bag she shouldered.

"We've got to," Alex said around the lump in his throat. "We've got two guns between the eight of us and no authority. The best thing we can do is make sure the entire fucking world knows what happened here."

Steph glanced at Alex's computer again. "They're up to Earle and Cooke. Looks like another group is coming from the habitats further down Earle."

"Let's go. Leave anything you can't easily carry." He directed the last at Fowler and Gage, who seemed to think there would be room on a small boat for their rolling suitcases.

Both ignored him as Alex led the group out of the office and down the Elkman tube, dragging those stupid suitcases and glaring at the security officers when neither offered to help.

Both DSS officers had their guns out. Neither said a word about the shooting, but they didn't have to, did they?

"Where are we headed?" Dixon asked Alex. The taller security officer was one step behind Alex, and *his* hands weren't shaking.

"Just down this tube into the elevator up to Platform Three. That's where *Earhart* moored before and that's where she'll meet us."

"Are you sure using an elevator is wise, Commander? Couldn't they cut the power?" Hamilton asked from right behind him.

Alex resisted the urge to jump away from her. "Unless you really want to climb three hundred feet of stairs, it's our best chance."

"I see." He could hear her frown, but Alex glanced over his shoulder, anyway.

"Did you get ahold of Commander Vasquez?" he asked.

"No." A glower. "She's not answering her phone."

Alex bit back a swear as they reached the elevator bank. He punched the up button. "Keep trying."

Hamilton's glare was withering. "I'm so glad I have you to remind me of that, *Commander*."

"Ma'am, I..." The elevator dinging saved Alex from further response. "Let's go."

They piled into the elevator, bags and all. Alex had no time to grab anything from his quarters. But what was there that he cared about? Alex hadn't brought anything to Armistice Station he couldn't live without. Sixteen years as a submariner taught him not to haul much around. Yeah, he'd miss his scuba gear and the two custom suits he got at Fromo's, but they weren't that important.

The elevator ride seemed to take forever; no one spoke after the doors slammed shut. Steph hugged her bag to her chest, eyes a shade too wide but anger making her posture stiff. Bradshaw still looked stunned, too stunned to yelp when Gage dropped a suitcase on his foot. Olson, closest to the security guys, eyed their sidearms enviously, while Gage and Fowler watched the stupid suitcases.

"Good *God*," Hamilton's whisper sounded so out of character that Alex did a double take. Her face was white and her eyes wide, staring at the phone in her hands as the elevator rumbled upwards.

"Admiral?"

"Maria texted me," Hamilton replied. "She confirmed that Jesse—Lieutenant Lin—is dead."

Alex closed his eyes on tears he would not shed.

Ding.

The elevator doors opened as Hamilton extended her phone. Alex read the words numbly, staring at the screen. *Got caught up in a group the French rounded up. French shot civilian and Jesse Lin. Civilian wounded. Jesse dead.*

Olson shoved Alex out of the elevator, making him stumble. "C'mon, sir," Olson said. "Let's get out of here."

"Yeah." He made himself nod. "Steph, get on the radio to that oiler."

He led the group down the pier, glancing at the French frigate. Its quarterdeck was lit up, but shadows shrouded most of the warship. There didn't seem anything other than the normal night watch stationed, but you could hide a lot of sailors inside a ship.

Was that a radar rotating? Did surface ships do that in port? Subs didn't, but subs had a lot fewer radars.

"This doesn't make any sense," he whispered. Alex's muscles felt like compressed springs waiting to explode.

"Maria said they shot him by accident." Hamilton's shoulders slumped. "Just a stupid accident."

"But why shoot anyone at all?" Alex couldn't wrap his mind around it. "Why kill anyone? And bullets...bullets are a shit weapon inside an underwater station. What the hell do they think this will accomplish for them? The international community won't stand for this."

"I don't care." Hamilton's voice was hard. "I'm going to *bury* them."

"You?" Fowler sniffed. "You'll need *my* help with that, Admiral."

Hamilton spun to glare at Fowler. "Are you saying you won't?"

"Of course, I'm not." Fowler crossed his arms as Alex stopped the group near a ladder leading down from the platform. It was a good place for a boat to come alongside, although there was no way to get suitcases to the water fourteen feet down.

Oops.

"Navy Oiler Six, this is Naval Detachment Armistice Station calling you on channel one-six, over." Steph spoke into the radio, her voice clipped and quick. Alex glanced her way, noting her tight features and stiff shoulders in the bright lights of the pier.

"This is Oiler Six, roger, break, am one thousand yards out from Platform Three with my boat at the rail, over."

"Oiler Six, we're halfway down the pier and awaiting your boat." Steph lowered the radio and pointed. "I think that's them out there."

Alex squinted into the dark. Spotting one ship's lights against the horizon was hard in at night, worse when standing on a well-lit pier. He thought he could see a pair of masthead lights and a starboard running light, but there was no way to tell if they were *Navy* lights. "You sure?"

"Not positive, but—"

A sharp *ringing* filled the air, and Alex's head snapped around to find the sound. "What the hell is *Bretagne* doing?"

"Get down!" Steph dragged him with her as she dropped flat; Alex's right knee slammed into the pier, making him grunt. "Those are salvo warning alarms!"

Alex opened his mouth to ask what the hell those were when fire-like daylight blossomed, illuminating the frigate's stern like noon in Texas. He stared helplessly as two of *Bretagne's* VLS hatches snapped open and missiles roared into the air.

Chapter 27

Sucker Punch

As twelve MiGs burned towards the *Enterprise* Strike Group, Captain Rosario's still-cool voice came over the tactical net: "All stations, Echo Whiskey. Engage MiGs with ESSM only if they break through the fighter screen, over."

Lieutenant Commander Attar acknowledged the order with wide eyes.

Nancy swore under her breath. "If those fighters can't kill them, we're going to get sucker punched."

"Yes, ma'am, we are." Attar licked his lips, sweat starting to bead on his forehead.

"Well, we'll know one way or another in about three minutes." Nancy shrugged, and then she raised her voice. "Look alive, ladies and gentlemen. If we get leakers, we won't have much time to respond."

The MiGs came in high, diving down through the clouds to meet the nine F-35s. This time, however, they didn't wait to close the range and fire their anti-air missiles; the Indian fighters opened with Kh-29MP anti-ship missiles. Each MiG carried two, and four fired before the American pilots caught on and fired their AMRAAMs.

Eighteen AMRAAM missiles streaked into the air, and the F-35 pilots hit their afterburners to close the range before firing eighteen more. The MiGs went evasive, and the incoming threat distracted most of the pilots from attacking the strike group. Two, however, held course long enough to fire another two Kh-29MP anti-ship missiles each.

"Vampire, vampire, vampire! Ten Kludge missiles inbound on the strike group," *Fletcher's* air warfare coordinator reported.

"All units, Echo Whiskey. Active Linked Doctrine, over."

Nancy hit three keys on her weapons console...and waited.

The Kh-29MP was too fast for even Aegis to determine which ship the missiles were aimed at; from twenty nautical miles away, the missiles needed less than two minutes to reach the strike group. Two minutes was a long time in anti-air warfare, however, long enough for *Fletcher's* AN/SPY-6(V)1 phased-array radar track every incoming missile.

Fletcher's Link connection then fed that information to the strike group, complementing tracks from *Belleau Wood's* identical radar and *Kidd's* smaller AN/SPY-6(V)4. *Enterprise* had the less capable AN/SPY-3 radar, so *Fletcher's* Aegis system gave less weight to those tracks, although it synergized that track information into the Link, too. What resulted was a cohesive track picture using four different high-quality radars. All four ships knew where the enemy missiles were to within inches.

Unfortunately, the cruiser and four destroyers only had thirteen SM-6s and sixty ESSM between them. Those numbers sounded high until you remembered that any counter missile only got one shot at an incoming threat; the Kh-29MP would hit a ship before even an ESSM could turn to chase.

All ships activated doctrine, putting *Belleau Wood*'s Baseline 12.2 Aegis Weapons System in the driver's seat. The cruiser's super-fast brain understood their missile shortage and chose which ship to fire.

Linked Aegis doctrine had never been tested outside of software validation and training—it was that new—but they had no choice. The shooters didn't have enough missiles left to fight the conventional way; they would have to let *Belleau Wood's* Aegis system dole out missiles and hope it could destroy every threat.

Fletcher's computers responded to the remote command and put four ESSMs in the air. *Kidd* and *Enterprise* launched none; *Kidd* was down to only eight ESSMs, *Enterprise* four. *Belleau Wood* had twenty-two available after the misfired missile in her forward VLS bank, and her computer launched six of those, followed by two more when the first two missed their targets.

Fletcher leaned port as Ying Mai put her into a hard turn from the bridge, again closing the distance with *Enterprise* as the destroyer's CIWS mounts started firing. Nancy heard the extended fart down in Combat, although she couldn't hear *Enterprise's* CIWS join in. *Kidd* and *Belleau Wood's* CIWS targeted the missiles as well, tracer rounds lighting up the night sky. Then a trio of Kh-29MP missiles junked up and dodged the American missiles.

Kidd fired four ESSMs as her aft CIWS mount slewed wildly to engage the threat. Nancy cringed; doctrine didn't fire those missiles. A nervous watchstander overrode the system, and none of the missiles could intercept the two Kh-29s aimed at *Kidd*. Instead, they spiraled into the sky, looking for targets. The destroyer's CIWS got one; the other slammed into *Kidd's* aft missile deck. *Kidd* rocked with the blow, fire spewing out of her deck and filling the air with thick, black, smoke.

A third Kh-29 dove low to the deck, sprinted past *Kidd*, and struck *Enterprise* above the waterline three quarters of the way down her port side. A chorus of panicked voices announced those hits over the net as the last Kh-29 missiles died.

Meanwhile, three Lightnings went down, exchanged for six of the MiGs when air-to-air missiles crossed paths with one another in the sky. Chased by missiles, the remaining MiGs bugged out towards the Indian strike group, but *Belleau Wood* ordered the six Lightnings left to stay on Combat Air Patrol instead of hunting them down.

Nancy finally remembered to breathe, and then called the bridge. "XO, Captain, report damage."

Commander Ying Mai's smile was audible. "We've got a little debris forward, possibly a missile fragment. Bunch of shell casings from CIWS. Otherwise, nothing."

Nancy opened her mouth to respond, but a voice on the tactical net cut her off: "All stations, *Enterprise*, my max speed two-zero knots, over."

"*Enterprise*, Echo Bravo, roger, break, immediate execute, formation speed, twenty knots, over."

"*Fletcher*, roger, out," Nancy replied around the lump in her throat. Then picked up the still-active line to the bridge, whispering. "Shit. We'll never catch them at twenty knots."

"And we're still out of range for Harpoons," Ying replied. "You think *Enterprise* can launch more fighters at this speed?"

Nancy gritted her teeth. "Not enough wind over the deck."

"We can't take another attack like this, ma'am. We're down to what, eight SM-6s?"

"Seven." Nancy glanced at her display. "And twenty-two ESSM."

"*Belleau Wood's* got to be worse. And *Kidd* looks like trash," Ying said. "She's listing port and on fire aft. Nothing's coming out of her aft VLS. Probably never again."

"We've got more missiles left than the cruiser." Nancy swallowed. "More than anyone, now."

"On the bright side, the Indians have to be about out of missiles, right?" Ying didn't sound hopeful.

Nancy swallowed and said a silent prayer Ying was right.

"*Earhart* this is *Kansas* Actual. We are forty nautical miles out from you and closing," Kennedy said. "We will cover your retreat from Armistice Station, over."

Master Chief Casey tried to ignore his captain's pompous smile. Kennedy's fury over being rerouted towards Armistice Station wouldn't stop him from playing the hero, would it? Oh, no. Not this prick.

Kansas' attack center was quiet, and not because it was the middle of the night. None of the watch standers wanted to poke their irate captain; Kennedy spent the last twenty minutes pacing while he waited for someone to reach *Amelia Earhart* on a secure communications net. Finally, they found a satellite uplink that broke through the inexplicable jamming near Armistice Station, but Kennedy grumbled about how that required *Kansas* slowing to stream her communications wire.

He perked up a bit when *Earhart* told him she planned to evacuate the entire Armistice Station naval detachment. Kennedy leaned forward upon hearing that something was wrong on Armistice Station, but Casey wasn't holding his breath. Sure, something could be wrong on the station, but that shouldn't mean *Kansas* would do anything other than escort *Earhart* away from trouble.

"Holy shit, *Kansas*, we're—" Static filled the net as the transmission cut off without warning.

"What the hell?" Kennedy whirled to glare at the radio watch. "What the fuck happened to my transmission, Jin?"

Petty Officer Jin shrugged. "Circuit's still open, Captain. Something must've gone wrong on their end."

"That's not acceptable. Get them back."

"Aye, Captain." Jin turned to his station before rolling his eyes. Casey spotted it, but he wasn't saying nothing.

He stepped forward. "Captain, you want to come up to periscope depth and use the radio mast?"

"And slow even more? No." Kennedy crossed his arms. "Jin *said* the problem was on their end. I'm sure those civilians forget to maintain their gear all the time."

"Maybe." Casey shrugged, not believing a word. The civ-mars who ran the Navy's oilers were a professional bunch, not to mention better paid than the junior enlisted sailors who did maintenance on Navy ships and submarines. "Maybe we can see if there's anything on bridge-to-bridge using the wire?"

"That's an excellent idea, COB." Kennedy smiled. "Do it, Jin."

"Already on it, sir. Channel sixteen up."

More static, then:

"Mayday, mayday, mayday, this is USNS *Amelia Earhart*. We have been struck by two French missiles, and—"

The transmission cut off again.

This time, no further transmission followed.

Boosters ignited; two of *Bretagne's* missile hatches flipped open. The flight time for the pair of Exocet MM40 Block 3 missiles was less than 15 seconds. *Earhart* was so close that the Block 3 Exocets fired never reached their cruising speed of 600 knots, and the missiles barely transitioned to cruise. Instead, they arched up into the air and then came straight down, blazing towards the American supply ship.

Earhart was designed to sport two CIWS guns, but no one armed navy supply ships in peacetime. A Phalanx Block 1B CIWS cost $5.6 million per mount, and the brackets were empty. Paranoia made *Earhart's* navy security detachment man three of her fifty caliber machine gun mounts, but they were about as effective as spitballs against subsonic missiles. *Earhart's* master, on the bridge, scarcely had time to realize there were missiles in the air before they hit.

Both struck *Earhart's* flight deck. One failed to explode, ricocheting off the deck and into the port helo hanger, ripping the door off its hinges and burrowing into the SH-60 helicopter inside. The helicopter, fully fueled, burst into flames. But that wasn't the worst of it. The other missile's 364-pound warhead burned through the flight deck and exploded inside the enclosed fantail, fragments ripping through mooring equipment before its fireball melted three bulkheads forward and two below. The blast opened *Earhart's* starboard side to the sea, and she started to list.

Now she was easy to pick out against the night sky and lights around Armistice Station; Alex, still on one knee, turned to stare at the conflagration.

"Dear fucking God," he whispered.

Fowler whimpered something about this being impossible, telling Gage this couldn't happen, no one would dare. Hamilton's silence screamed disbelief. Steph, next to Alex, seemed frozen. Bradshaw and Olson, too. Everyone gaped as *Earhart* burned, flames growing bright against the night sky. This had to be a nightmare. French frigates didn't launch missiles by accident.

The bridge-to-bridge radio Steph dropped crackled. "Mayday, mayday, mayday, this is USNS *Amelia Earhart*. We have been struck by two missiles and are burning. My location is one thousand yards north east of Armistice Station Platform Three. Request immediate assistance!"

Earhart's boat was still in the water, a black silhouette against the orange-red flames of her mothership. It turned back towards the supply ship, racing to provide the only help it could.

"Mayday, mayday, mayday, this is USNS *Amelia Earhart*—"

A screaming alarm drowned out the mayday call, and Alex's head snapped around just in time to watch *Bretagne* launch two more missiles. These, too, shot into the night sky before coming back down for *Earhart*, and as much as Alex wanted to look away, he watched in terrified fascination while the two Exocets slammed down into *Earhart's* bow. Both exploded.

Earhart rocked in the water, rolling left and then right before listing still further to starboard. Small black figures ran around on her deck, some on fire and others jumping into the water. Smoke billowed around the ship, drifting towards the group on the pier just a thousand yards away. *Earhart's* boat darted into the inferno, dodging a white life raft canister. *Earhart* would sink. Alex didn't have to know much about surface ships to guess that—but *why*? Why would the French open fire?

"Les voilà!" The shout came from down the pier; when Alex turned, he saw Camille Dubois leading a group of marines. She pointed, and the marines surged forward.

Jesus. *They're coming for us.* Why no longer mattered. The tightness in his chest became a roar of terror.

"Let's go!" Alex dragged Steph to her feet, then reached out to do the same for Admiral Hamilton. She was already up, fury making her face white as she yanked Fowler off the ground. He yelped; no one cared. "Come on!"

Fowler pointed at the French marines, who were at the elevator bank. "But they're—they're—"

"This way!" Alex shoved anyone in reach towards the end of the pier—away from the marines.

"Someone help me!" Fowler struggled to pull his suitcase along until Bradshaw kicked it aside. The suitcase bounced off a bollard, almost tripping Gage as he hauled his own luggage forward.

"Forget the fucking suitcase, sir!"

"But—" A push from Bradshaw made Fowler cut off in a howl.

"Gun!" Montero shouted. "They're—"

Crack! Shots rang out, and three people went down.

Chapter 28

First Blood

"Struck by *what*?" Kennedy wheeled on Petty Officer Jin. "What the fuck did they just say?"

Faces in control were sheet white; Master Chief Casey felt cold seeping into his bones. No way. No fucking way had a longtime American ally just shot a U.S. Navy ship. Hell, their friendship with France went back to the goddamned Revolution. This was insane.

Kennedy snatched the bridge-to-bridge handset from Jin. "*Earhart*, this is Navy Warship Eight-Zero-Two. Say *again* your last, over.""

Static.

Kennedy repeated himself. Then again, louder.

Nothing.

"What the fucking fuck is this?" Kennedy twisted to glare at Casey. "Did they say *French* missiles?"

Casey shrugged. "Fuck if I know, sir. But it's got to be wrong. We're still friends with the French, right?"

"We were yesterday." Kennedy shook his head like a punch-drunk fighter. "Two missiles would tear the fuck out of an oiler. They don't have a lot of defenses."

"They don't have jack, you mean, sir. I did a tour on one," Casey replied. "They don't even have CIWS."

"Shit." Kennedy slumped; Casey did the math. A *Lewis and Clark*-class ship's crew was about the same size as *Kansas*'...and almost all civilians.

"Sir, if they shot at *Earhart*..."

"Then we fucking find whatever French ship did that and send them to the bottom." Kennedy turned to the chief of the watch. "Set battle stations, retrieve the wire, and make best speed for Armistice Station."

INS *Vishal* was down to eight MiG. Six of them were from the last strike and had to land to rearm and refuel before heading back towards the enemy. Two were survivors of the first attack. The Indian carrier turned into the wind to recover them, but four of her escorting destroyers—those with BrahMos missiles left—continued towards the American strike group at thirty-five knots.

So far, the Indian strike group shot seventy-six of their ninety-six BrahMos missiles at the Americans. Indian fighters added twenty-eight Kh-29MP missiles, in exchange for sinking USS *John Finn* and hitting *Enterprise* twice. Eighteen of *Vishal's* twenty-four fighters were shot down. But the Indian admiral knew they would face a lopsided hit-to-missile ratio in the first salvos. That was why four destroyers: *Ganga, Rana, Ranvir,* and *Mormugao* kept five missiles apiece. Now, they closed the distance to increase accuracy and decrease flight time.

Vishal would keep the eight MiGs in reserve. All the Indian destroyers' air defenses were intact, and their admiral knew that the Americans used the same missiles for air defense as they did to attack aircraft. One more missile attack would guarantee that the Americans had nothing left to shoot down the MiGs.

Encrypted communications flashed between the Indian carrier and her escorts—and INS *Porbandar*, still just thirty miles away from the Americans.

Bradshaw cried out; Olson lunged for him, dragging him behind an orange shipping container on the pier near the yacht. It hid them nicely; shipping containers were the size of train cars and made of durable steel. Alex grabbed Montero, the closer security officer, but by the time he pulled him to safety, the trail of blood behind him proved Alex was too late.

Montero took two shots to the throat and one to the head, which was half-severed, dangling by skin and bits of something unidentifiable. Bile rose in Alex's throat, and he almost puked. Meanwhile, Steph and Admiral Hamilton pulled Dixon behind the container. The second security officer had two holes in his chest, and his every breath gurgled.

Alex had attended first responder training at the Naval Diving and Salvage Training Center a lifetime ago. Bullet wounds weren't on the curriculum, but he didn't need a degree to tell Dixon's wounds were fatal.

Bullets ricocheted off the container, making a metallic ping-ping-ping noise as Alex cringed and ducked. Someone swore; he fought the urge to crawl beneath the nearest object and hide. This wasn't what he was trained for, wasn't *supposed* to happen! His head swirled and his breathing was short, a thousand times worse than it had been when he knew Chris Kennedy was about to kill a bunch of innocent civilians.

"Take my gun," Dixon panted. "There's two spare magazines in—in my jacket." He coughed up blood, spraying Steph right in the face. "Same for Montero."

Alex's shaking hands moved to pull two magazines out the inner pocket of Montero's jacket, trying to ignore the blood and the way Dixon's breath rattled. Steph did the same for Dixon, who tried to say something else, only for his eyes to roll back and his breathing to stop.

Montero's handgun felt heavy in Alex's palm. He had to pry it out of Montero's still warm fingers, swallowing back yet another urge to vomit. It wasn't the standard Navy nine-millimeter Beretta he shot two whole times a year, and Alex couldn't find the safety. Did it have one?

"Need some help here!" Olson said.

Alex turned to see Olson applying pressure on Bradshaw's upper left arm. Bradshaw's face was stark white, and he sweated in the cool night air, swearing at Olson through gritted teeth.

Everyone stared at one another with wide eyes, but footsteps were coming and Alex had to *do* something.

"Steph, watch the French!" Alex forced his wooden legs to work, crossing to Gage's suitcase. Fowler's aide dragged it behind the container like an idiot, but now it was useful. Throwing the suitcase open, Alex hunted for something that would work as a bandage.

"Hey! That's mine!" Gage started forward, only for another *ping-ping-ping* of bullets to hit the container. He dropped flat.

Crack. Steph leaned around the edge of the container to return fire. Gage and Fowler flinched away from the sound as Alex pulled three cotton shirts out of the suitcase.

"Here." He extended the pistol to Olson. She was a gunner's mate, presumably better trained for this than a guy who spent his career in submarines. "Help Ops."

"You got it, sir." Olson scurried over to Steph's side as Alex looked at Bradshaw's wound.

There was too much blood to tell if the bullet passed through or clipped Bradshaw's upper arm, so Alex just wrapped the arm in a shirt and tied it off as fast as he could. "You gonna pass out on me, Bradshaw?"

"You think it might scare the French off, sir?" Bradshaw's smile was tight.

"Come out with your hands up!" Camille Dubois shouted. Alex couldn't see her on the other side of the container, but her voice still sent a chill down his spine. "Come out and we will not shoot!"

Gage shuffled closer. "What are we waiting for? We have to listen, right? They have *guns.*"

"So do we." Olson twisted to glare at him. "And if those ass-clowns *opened* with shooting, what the ever-fucking *fuck* makes you think they'll stop?"

Gage's mouth dropped open, but no sound emerged.

Steph peeked around the edge of the container. "They're holding about fifty yards away." She didn't look back. "What's our move, boss?"

Alex glanced around. Only Bradshaw was hurt; Gage looked ready to faint and Fowler seemed offended by the whole business, but they were unharmed. Hamilton's expression was unreadable, but her brown eyes burned holes in Alex every time he glanced her way. Next to Alex, Bradshaw squirmed, hissing in pain.

"There's a hatch down the end of the pier." Bradshaw grimaced. "No elevators, but there's a bunch of storerooms that have stairs going down."

"Beats going towards the bastards," Olson said.

"We can't—" Gage started again, only for the sudden whirring of a machine gun to cut him off.

Light flashed from Alex's left. Was that—holy shit, it was. *Earhart's* boat roared back towards the pier, spraying the French marines with fire from their bow-mounted fifty caliber machine gun. Cries filled the air; someone screamed as the boat did a second pass.

"Come on!" Alex pulled Bradshaw up. "Everyone, let's move! Bradshaw, get to that hatch!"

Gage hesitated, until Hamilton shoved him forward. The admiral dragged Fowler along, ignoring his inarticulate protests. Alex lagged back, shouting for Steph and Olson to join them as the French started firing back at *Earhart's* boat. The boat danced away, out of easy range of the French marines' rifles—and then motion caught Alex's eye.

Still sprinting, he turned just in time to see *Bretagne's* 76-millimeter OTO Melara training to the frigate's port side. The OTO Melera was a tried-and-true weapon, used as an anti-air or anti-surface gun by over forty navies worldwide. *Bretagne's* advanced variant of the gun fired up to 120 rounds per minute. She only needed nine.

The first three rounds splashed into the water around *Earhart's* boat as the civilian coxswain firewalled the throttles and tried to run. The three navy personnel in the boat shouted for her to close the pier, but she didn't understand they wanted her to get inside the OTO Melera's *minimum* range.

Instead, she sent the boat skipping over the waves towards the open ocean, which allowed *Bretagne's* next three round burst to straddle the boat. The coxswain tried driving in a zigzag pattern, but the French frigate had their number. Two of the next three rounds exploded in the air right over *Earhart's* boat, shredding the five sailors inside and popping the boat's inflated sponsons.

Alex never saw what else happened to those sailors. Hamilton helped Bradshaw wrench open the hatch, shoving Fowler through first. Gage kicked down his damned suitcase before following, and then Bradshaw squirmed down the ladder one-armed. Alex was last through, yanking the heavy metal door down and dropping into a still-dark room.

Enterprise's best limping speed was twenty knots, which gave the Indian destroyers fifteen knots of overtake. Somehow, *Kidd* managed the same speed, despite the fires burning on her aft end. John had never been on an *Arleigh Burke*-class destroyer, but he imagined a lot of critical systems were in the stern—things like engines and steering. Could *Kidd* keep up the pace? And could he do anything to help her crew save the ship? He scowled.

"If they're chasing us, they've got some missiles left, Admiral," he said.

McNally wasn't much use during the battle, but it turned out they didn't need him. Captain Rosario on *Belleau Wood* commanded the strike group's air defense, and John knew she was the reason four ships remained afloat. John tried to follow the air battle with his limited knowledge, and from where he was sitting, they'd done okay. There'd be hell to pay for losing *Finn*, but the strike group started outnumbered, surprised, and with their communications jammed.

Even the U.S. Navy had bad days.

"We need to find the jammer," he said.

McNally turned to him. "It's got to be an aircraft." The admiral sighed. "With all the civilian air traffic up there, we don't dare shoot."

"Unless it's that destroyer that keeps shadowing us. They've got to be hanging out so close for a reason." John's eyes narrowed. "Admiral, we need to kill her."

McNally shook his head. "Absolutely not. This might be the work of one lunatic commander. If we shoot at a ship that hasn't shot at us, we're starting a war!"

"Sir, I think they already have," John whispered.

"Echo Bravo, this is Echo Whiskey," Captain Rosario's voice blared out of the speaker to John's left. "Recommend killing track 7065 with Bulldogs, over."

McNally's face went red. "What the hell are you two conspiring at?" He grabbed a headset before John could answer. "Echo Whiskey, Echo Bravo *Actual*, negative, do not kill track 7065. We will not shoot at a unit that has not opened fire. Over!"

John swallowed. He hadn't chatted the idea over to Captain Rosario on *Belleau Wood* on a secure computer. But he would've if the thought occurred to him.

McNally tore his headset off and twisted to glare at his staff. "The next person who tries to tell me to shoot that fucking destroyer gets to swim home! Is that *understood*?"

"Vampire, vampire, vampire!" The tactical net filled with Nancy Coleman's voice again. "Inbound missiles bearing one-zero-zero!"

"All stations, Echo Whiskey, estimate one-eight missiles inbound. Remain on active Link Doctrine. Out."

John felt his hands shake. He didn't know how Rosario kept her voice so calm. But he did know that eighteen inbound missiles were more than the entire strike group had standard missiles remaining. *Fletcher* had the most with seven SM-6s. *Belleau Wood* only had five. *Enterprise* was down to just four ESSM. Same for *Kidd. Fletcher* and

Belleau Wood still had thirty-six ESSMs between them, but ESSMs were short ranged. They only allowed for one shot at each incoming BrahMos missile.

Any Indian admiral with a brain would aim for *Enterprise*. She was the prize, and John was a helpless passenger. All he could do was watch and pray the shooters could intercept those missiles in time.

Chapter 29

Winchester

The hatch slammed shut, cutting off what little light came from the outside world—more than there should've been, with *Earhart* burning—and leaving them in musty darkness. The smell of water and plastic invaded Freddie's nostrils. Lovely.

"Someone might want to find a light switch before we fall down a hole," she said.

"I got it," Bradshaw said. Freddie tried to find him in the dark, but she couldn't even see shadows. She hadn't been able to see much before climbing down the ladder, either, just enough to know that the room was long and full of something.

Someone whispered; she couldn't catch the words. Freddie didn't like the way her breath rattled in her ears, growing louder and louder with each passing moment. She wasn't afraid of the dark, but being shut in a semi-submerged storeroom was a novel experience. She was a goddamned admiral. Admirals didn't get nervous.

"What the fuck did they think they were doing?" Steph asked, her voice echoing.

"Starting a war," Coleman's said.

"Not necessarily." Freddie's voice sounded harsh and alien to her own ears.

Sinking a ship owned by the U.S. Navy *should* guarantee that. But Freddie knew her history, knew that shots fired didn't always mean war. The seizure of USS *Pueblo* and the attack on USS *Liberty* disproved that theory. Maybe Freddie had been an admiral too long. She looked at things from too much of a distance. An American officer was killed minutes ago. Then an American ship ate four missiles in front of her face. What else did it take to get to war?

But *France?* They'd been friends with France from before there was a United States to be friendly!

The lights flickered on, illuminating a long and narrow room full of plastic-wrapped pallets in eerie yellow. To Freddie's right were cereal and potatoes; the left had coffee creamer, rice, and charcoal, followed by three pallets stacked high with cases of Jim Beam and Jack Daniels. She scowled. *Definitely a cruise ship's loadout.*

"Everyone okay?" Coleman asked. Freddie bit back the need to swear at him, to blame this troublemaker for everything. The knee-jerk instinct to vilify Alex Coleman died, however. The desire to strangle a politician did not.

"Where *are* we?" Fowler demanded.

"A cargo loading bay. Cranes pull these pallets out to load them on ships," Bradshaw said. "Sorry for the grunge. Was the best I had on short notice."

"We shouldn't be *hiding*," Fowler snapped. "I'm sure if I could just reason with those people, *someone* would set things right."

"By lifting *Earhart* off the ocean floor and bringing her dead crew back to life?" Coleman snorted. "Yeah. Let me know how that works out."

"You—you—"

"Enough," Freddie cut in, and then twisted to look at Coleman. "You have a plan, Commander?"

"These storerooms connect under the platform." He glanced around. "We should be able to take a ladder down, right, Bradshaw?"

"Yeah. I've done it before." Bradshaw's quick smile was ghostly in his drawn face.

"Better question," Steph said, pointing up. "Do those giant ass cargo doors open from the *inside* or the outside?"

Distant shouting in French came from above before Bradshaw shrugged, one-shouldered. "Dunno. Lieutenant Lin would've."

Everyone went silent; Freddie swallowed. She hadn't known Jesse Lin well nor paid him much mind. But now he was dead, a dead naval officer on a station in the middle of the Indian Ocean when the *French* suddenly started shooting. The world was upside down.

Was Maria okay? She'd never forgive herself if Maria got hurt. *I didn't think there might be danger when I let her go out there.* Regret threatened to make her dizzy.

"We'd better get out of here before we find out," Coleman said. "Bradshaw, find the down ladder."

"Looking now, sir," Bradshaw replied. Olson went to help him, and Freddie eyed the pistol in her hand. Was she a good choice to hold one of their two firearms? Freddie couldn't even remember her rate. Hopefully, Olson wasn't a knuckle-dragging boatswain's mate who'd forget to put the gun on safe.

"I still don't understand what's going on," Fowler said. "We need to negotiate and—"

"With all due respect, Mr. Secretary, that hole in Bradshaw's arm doesn't seem very fucking reasonable." Coleman's voice was harder than Freddie imagined it could be. "I can't stop you if you want to go up there and get your ass shot off, but do the rest of us the courtesy of waiting until we're gone."

Fowler went red. "I'm not going up there alone!"

"Then shut your face." Freddie earned herself a shocked glare. "This isn't the time for stupid arguments."

"There's no need to be insulting, Admiral." Fowler sneered, and she could see him making mental notes concerning her career prospects.

Screw him. Freddie turned away, looking for a hatch in the floor to match the one they'd climbed through. She crossed behind two pallets, stepping over a giant power cord that looked like it belonged to a ship's shore power configuration. Three pallets of fresh fruit and one of energy drinks blocked her path next. Zigzagging back towards the ladder they'd come down, she tripped over something in the shadows and fell to her knees.

"What the hell?" Freddie twisted, spotting the offending object. Damn, her ankle hurt. "You brought your *suitcase* down here?"

Gage wilted. "I—I thought—it has important papers in it!"

Someone pounded on the hatch, and Gage skittered back.

"Open the hatch now!" a female voice demanded. "Open or we will execute anyone we find!"

Execute. The word made Freddie freeze. Even if they were at war, that wasn't a legitimate course of action for the French.

The world wasn't supposed to work like this. Surrender wasn't an option—never had been—but where the hell were they going to hide? Freddie hated not knowing things.

"Block that hatch the best you can, Steph." Coleman's order broke through Freddie's fog. "Olson, watch the hatch with Ops. Bradshaw, help me break open this pallet of coffee creamer."

"Boss, I know you love your coffee, but this is weird, even for you." But Bradshaw tromped over to join Coleman as Freddie blinked.

"What *are* you doing, Commander?"

"Science." His grin was brief as Coleman upended Gage's suitcase and dumped clothes, papers, a tablet, and two plastic bottles out onto the floor. "This stuff's non-dairy."

She stared. "What the ever-loving hell does that have to do with anything?"

"Sodium aluminosilicate is flammable. I'm going to cook up a surprise for our friends." His smile vanished. "Just need a few ingredients and a little time."

The pounding on the hatch intensified as Gage snatched his tablet from the pile, gripping it in white-knuckled hands. Freddie frowned. "You think they'll give you that time?" she asked.

"Hatch is sealed from the inside," Steph said, twisting to look at them. "And I thought you liked your coffee black, sir."

Coleman chuckled, throwing can after can of the creamer into his backpack. "I do. But my wife loves this shit. Is there any charcoal around here?"

Freddie frowned. "Three pallets left of you."

She could have offered to grab some, but she still didn't know what this idiot would do with it. Freddie was a nuclear engineer, too, but nuc school was a long time ago. Besides, the instructors at prototype stressed *not* making things explode. Chemistry at the Academy was even further in her past. She liked facts and numbers, not whatever this was.

Coleman darted over to grab a bag of charcoal and then pulled the plastic bottles out of the mess of Gage's clothes, shoving them in his backpack, too. "Let's get out of here. I'll set the trap on the next level."

"Trap?" Freddie's eyes went wide. "Do you have *any* idea what you're doing?"

Coleman stopped to look her in the eye. "Ma'am, if you've got better ideas, I'm all for them. All I've got is this." He gestured with the Nalgene bottle. "We've got to run, and maybe this'll slow them down. Maybe it won't. It's your call. You're the ranking officer."

He was smart enough to dump this on her, wasn't he? But Freddie Hamilton never shrank away from responsibility. She wouldn't be the highest-ranking female submariner in U.S. Navy history if she did. Freddie scowled. "Do it."

"Let's go, folks," Coleman pointed at the hatch leading down. "Steph, take point."

"You got it, boss." Steph pulled the hatch open. "This is starting to feel like CQB training back at the Wick." She disappeared down the hatch, slithering down the ladder with athleticism Freddie envied. *I need to get to the gym more.* And what the hell was the Wick?

"Yeah, except this is a lot less fun." Coleman glanced at Bradshaw. "You good with ladders?"

"With execution as the alternative? You bet your ass I am, sir." Bradshaw reached out and grabbed Gage. "C'mon, buddo. You're with me. Leave the fucking suitcase this time."

Gage squeaked but didn't protest. Freddie gestured Fowler ahead of her, ignoring his dirty look. Did the idiot still think there was a diplomatic solution to this mess? If the United States' honor would survive it, she'd leave him behind, but she refused to give any enemy a goddamned Under Secretary of state. She followed Fowler, and her feet barely hit the ground in the next room down before a backpack dropped from above.

"You're insane!" Freddie shouted up at Coleman. "You almost dropped that on my head!"

"Sorry, Admiral." He sounded like he was grinning.

Freddie sighed.

"One minute," *Fletcher's* air warfare coordinator announced.

Nancy sat very still, her calm expression disguising the nervous tingle running up her spine. Her ship was still the first on the threat axis, with the best shot at keeping missiles from hitting *Enterprise.* Protecting the carrier was the purpose of an air defense destroyer, but training never mentioned how terrifying it was in real life.

Clearing her throat, Nancy keyed the mic for the bridge. "OOD, Captain, close with *Enterprise.*"

"Captain, OOD, current range is eight hundred yards."

"Make it four hundred."

"OOD, aye," the officer of the deck replied.

Nancy bit her lip. *Fletcher* withstood two missile attacks from the Indians already, escaping relatively unscathed. She should have every reason to believe her ship and crew could survive another—but terror coiled up in Nancy's stomach, dark and dangerous. A Hollywood captain would say something inspirational to her people, but Nancy refused to distract them.

"Captain, Surface, range is down to eight-two nautical miles!" her surface warfare coordinator said over the net.

Nancy's eyes snapped down to the display. She was so wrapped around the incoming missiles that she forgot that the Indians kept closing them—and so had everyone else.

She stomped down on the foot pedal microphone for the tactical net. "All stations, *Fletcher*, initiating Harpoon engagement, out!" Nancy swapped to her ship's internal net: "Surface, Captain, target the two lead destroyers with four bulldogs per track."

"Surface, aye!" Seconds ticked by; Nancy held her breath and watched the sixteen BrahMos missiles close.

"Birds away!" Air announced. "Seven birds away, doctrine swapping to ESSM."

"Bulldogs away!" Surface reported a hairsbreadth later. "Eight bulldogs transitioning to cruise on lead Indian destroyers."

Nancy bared her teeth, exchanging a vicious smile with her TAO. "Your turn, assholes."

"All stations, *Belleau Wood*, bulldogs away!" Rosario's voice came over the tactical net a moment later, followed by the same report from *Kidd*.

Twenty-four Harpoon Block II + ER missiles raced towards the Indian strike group, eight each from *Fletcher*, *Belleau Wood*, and *Kidd*. The two newer ships each launched half their loadout; *Kidd*, older and without the ability to fire Harpoons from her vertical launch system, fired all eight Harpoons stored in canisters on her stern.

Their Link connection ensured none of the ships chose the same targets, spreading the twenty-four anti-ship missiles out among the six destroyers accompanying the Indian aircraft carrier. Harpoons were slower than standard missiles—about half the speed—but they were fire-and-forget missiles. Those twenty-four Harpoons would find those Indian destroyers no matter what happened to the ships that fired them.

INS *Vishal* was a higher-value target, but its air wing was almost spent. Nancy and her fellow captains knew that. They'd save the carrier for their second Harpoon attack; *Fletcher* and *Belleau Wood* still had eight Harpoons each, enough to turn the carrier to toast.

Assuming they lived that long.

Meanwhile, *Fletcher's* Aegis Weapons System fought to defend the ship. *Belleau Wood* remained the brain of the strike group, with her Aegis deciding which SM-6 took out which incoming missile. The twelve SM-6s *Fletcher* and *Belleau Wood* launched took out eight incoming missiles, but that there were still too many. Ten

BrahMos made it past the outer ring of defenses, and there just weren't enough ESSM left.

Fletcher's missiles picked off two; so did *Belleau Wood*. *Kidd's* remaining four destroyed one, and every missile *Enterprise* launched missed.

"Winchester! I say again, *Kidd* is Winchester!" *Kidd's* captain, Commander Anka Walczak said over the tactical net. "Engaging with guns!"

"All stations, *Enterprise*, *Enterprise* is Winchester, over."

"Well, that's great news." Nancy grimaced.

Her TAO nodded choppily. "Looks like it's up to us and *Belleau Wood*, now."

"Yeah." Nancy kept her calm expression in place with an effort. Would *Fletcher* run out of missiles next? A ship out of missiles was a sitting duck.

Eight more ESSM launched at the last minute, a quartet each from *Fletcher* and *Belleau Wood*, blasting out of their launch cells when the BrahMos missiles were less than thirty seconds from impact.

That barely gave the missiles a chance to reach cruise altitude, but each missile still veered to intercept their assigned targets. *Fletcher* trembled as both of her CIWS mounts began firing in full auto mode, targeting the same five BrahMos missiles her ESSM were after.

Unfortunately, three of the five went for *Kidd*. Like Fletcher, *Kidd's* close in weapons systems were in full auto, round after round ripping out of their Phalanx guns. Both destroyers' CIWS held 1,500 rounds in their magazines, which only allowed about twenty-one seconds of fire at 4,500 rounds per minute. That would've been enough—until *Kidd's* aft CIWS jammed.

Two missiles homed in on *Kidd's* dual helicopter hangers, burst through the doors, and incinerated both MH-60R helicopters inside. One missile wasted itself against the helo hanger's forward bulkhead, but the other, just a few seconds behind its friend, blasted through the hole the first missile made and exploded against *Kidd's* aft bank of vertical launch cells.

Kidd had no missiles left to fuel secondary explosions, but the carnage was bad enough. The missile's 440 pound warhead ripped through the destroyer's sixty-four cell VLS module like paper. A shockwave continued forward, tearing into *Kidd's* innards. The resulting inferno killed three out of every four sailors stationed in the back half of the ship, including every watchstander in Main Engine Room Number 2, Auxiliary Machinery Room Number Two, Aft Steering, and Repair Three.

Meanwhile, *Fletcher's* proximity to *Enterprise* put her between the carrier and the last incoming missile. *Enterprise* carried short-ranged RIM-116 Rolling Airframe Missiles for point defense, stored in two twenty-one missile launchers. An earlier KH-29 hit took out the port side launcher, but the starboard launcher still had seven missiles left. It spat four out as the last BrahMos came in, each reaching Mach 2 in under ten seconds.

Then the BrahMos missile executed its terminal pop-up maneuver, and one of the RAM lost lock, instead zeroing in on *Fletcher's* aft CIWS mount. The Phalanx radar on mount recognized the missile's changed profile and adjusted its targeting to the incoming American missile, but RAM was too fast; the rounds sailed right past.

Fletcher rocked forward as *Enterprise's* missile detonated on top of her aft CIWS mount, blasting the mount and the sailors waiting to reload it into smithereens. Two lucky sailors went overboard more or less intact; the other six died instantly.

Seconds later, two of *Enterprise's* other missiles intercepted a BrahMos. The other one burst past them and slammed into *Enterprise's* port side one hundred feet aft of the previous hit.

PART 4: WISDOM

Chapter 30

Hide and Seek

"Mon Capitaine, they have somehow sealed the hatch and are hiding below the platform." Camille's annoyance was clear, as was the call; phones worked surprisingly well on the local network. Jules' encrypted radios were less reliable, which was why he called Camille's cell, instead. He sighed.

"They will not stay there. Not with the American oiler gone," he replied. Sinking *Earhart* was not an easy decision, but Admiral Bernard made France's position clear. The Indians already sank two American destroyers. France would stand with their friends and continue the fight. Better to sink *Earhart* before the Americans could use it to evacuate their people. "We cannot afford to lose them, Camille. Find them."

"Have my orders changed?" she asked.

"Non." Jules bit back the desire to shout. He could feel Admiral Khare's eyes burning into the back of his head; the Indians had their own team out in search of the Americans. *It's almost like they don't trust us.*

"Their security guards are dead," Camille said. "There was an...exchange of gunfire."

Jules scowled. "I saw the video." He did not bother saying he knew his people shot first. It no longer mattered, not after the shooting incident inside the station. France was committed. Letting these Americans escape would damage her reputation just when France needed to appear strong.

"The oiler broadcast a mayday call on bridge-to-bridge," Camille said.

"What?"

"It cut off, but..."

"Oui." The word was a growl. "Next time, we torpedo the enemy."

Missiles were wasteful and stupid. They caused fires, which gave quick-thinking people time to call for help. A good torpedo, however, broke a ship's keel and that was that. No one called for help until the ship was already sunk.

Jules missed *Barracuda*. This was not the type of warfare he trained for.

"We will find the Americans, mon Capitaine," she said. "We have almost broken through the hatch."

"I will send another team to assist." Jules crossed his arms and glared at the display of Armistice Station's schematics. Central was an excellent base of operations, but being chained to an information node chaffed. *Especially when I do not like the information it provides.* "Call if you need anything."

"Yes, Capitaine."

Jules hung up and turned to look at the still-scowling Khare. "Is there a problem, Admiral?"

"Your Marines killed civilians. That was *not* part of the plan."

"No, it was not." Jules heaved a sigh. "I am aware—"

"Our countries agreed to minimize casualties! Legitimate military targets are one thing, but I will *not* have my nation take the fall for your inability to control your personnel."

"One of those killed was a Navy lieutenant." Jules rolled his eyes. "And I will deal with the fools who opened fire. *Excusez moi.*"

He walked out of Central without looking back, trusting Ledoux to ignore Khare if he had another tantrum.

Steph crouched next to where Alex worked a dozen feet away from the ladder leading down from the storeroom above. "Sir, you might want to listen to this."

"Hm?" Alex asked, his voice muffled by the phone tucked under his chin. He'd turned the lights off, forcing everyone to use their phone flashlights. Luckily for him, the down ladder was near a wall and a power panel. Even better, the light switch was on the other side of the compartment.

"Secretary Fowler's saying he should be in charge." She groaned. "Loudly."

"Let 'em. Keeps him busy." Alex tried to force a smile, but it felt wooden. His hands wanted to shake, wanted to drop Gage's purple Nalgene bottle. Somehow, he poked a hole along its bottom edge with the multi-tool he carried since college. Pocketing the multi-tool, Alex gestured at his backpack. "Grab me some charcoal, will you?"

"What the hell are you doing, boss?" She grabbed a bag of charcoal out of the open bag and handed some over as he put the bottle down.

"Making a fireball." Alex dropped the phone and propped it against the wall. "Used to do this at the Wick for fun."

Steph laughed. "Okay, I guess that's not a surprise, but I still don't get it."

"All you need for an impressive fireball is black powder, a spark, and non-dairy coffee creamer. I made some that were fifty feet high back at Norwich." Alex's degree wasn't in chemistry, but he'd enjoyed the class, and Norwich cadets had a tradition of getting up to some really weird shit. "Almost got expelled for it my senior year."

"You people are crazy," Fowler shouted before Steph could respond. "This is *all* crazy! We can't go anywhere now that *Earhart* is gone! What use is running?"

"It beats surrender." Hamilton growled, twisting to look at Alex. "I presume your 'science' is something useful, Commander? Common sense does say we should put as much distance between ourselves and the enemy as possible."

Alex looked up from smashing up charcoal with the bottom of the Nalgene bottle. "Discouraging pursuit."

"What the hell is that supposed to mean?" Fowler asked.

Alex scooped smashed charcoal into the bottom of the bottle. He wished he had a better propellant, but cruise ships didn't exactly carry around black powder. Or quick fuses, for that matter. He' just have to make do. "It means I'm making something that'll explode and scare the shit out of the marines following us."

Fowler went white. "*Explode*?"

"We're at the waterline and heading downwards." Hamilton's eyes narrowed. "You think an explosion is *smart*?"

"Nope." Alex grinned. "But this is really just a big ass fireball. It'll burn you but won't do much else. Coffee creamer won't cut through bulkheads."

Hamilton crossed her arms; Alex used his multi-tool to cut a vague circle out of one of Gage's shirts. Gage squeaked but didn't object when Alex shoved the circle on top of the charcoal and then poured coffee creamer in, filling the Nalgene almost to the top. He left the lid off, lowering the Nalgene to the floor carefully.

Alex's heart pounded as he slid a wire from the power panel into the hole on the bottom of the bottle. This opportunity wouldn't present itself again; the ladder down to the next level was in the other room, and the light switch was on the right wall. Perfect storms didn't happen twice.

Banging floated down from the room above; metal screeched in protest. "Everyone head into the next compartment," he snapped. "Get down the ladder and keep heading down. Olson, take the lead."

"On it, sir." Olson bobbed her head and darted out, gun at the ready.

"You gonna wait and flip the switch?" Steph whispered.

Alex grimaced. "Yeah."

"Then I'll cover you."

"Steph—"

"Don't give me that look, boss." White teeth flashed in the dim light as she grinned. "You might be good at chemistry, but I grew up in backwoods Louisiana. My daddy took me hunting in a baby carrier. I can shoot a hell of a lot better than you, and I run faster, too."

"No question about that." Alex swallowed, his throat dry. He qualified bi-yearly with the nine millimeter when on sea duty, but that was it.

Hamilton paused in the doorway to look over her shoulder. "Don't linger too long, Commander. I'm not doing the paperwork that comes with you getting yourself shot."

Alex barked out a laugh. "I'm starting to think you like me, ma'am."

She glared, and then Hamilton disappeared down the hatch on Fowler's heels, with Gage and Bradshaw bringing up the rear. Alex let out a slow breath, listening.

Another crash. Someone yelped, and then metal gave with a high-pitched squeal. Alex grabbed Steph by the shoulder, guiding her to the far side of the compartment. His palm was sweaty when it hit the light switch.

"This better work," Steph whispered.

"Charcoal's a shit accelerant if you can't filter it properly, but I used enough that it's going to explode." Alex bared his teeth. "Just be ready to run."

Footsteps sounded on the metal ladder steps before Steph could answer; Alex pulled the door mostly shut and held his breath, peeking through the opening. Four marines led the way, with Camille

Dubois on their heels. They fanned out around the room, turning on rifle-mounted flashlights.

Camille said something in French; Alex didn't understand a word of it, but he bet she was looking for the light switch.

Steph nudged him.

Alex watched another marine come down the ladder, then another, with a third following like proper little ducks. Should he wait for more? There was no way to know how many *Earhart's* boat chased off or shot, and—

"Où sont-ils allés?" Camille sounded angry.

A fourth marine started down the ladder.

Screw it.

Pointing Steph towards the ladder leading down from their current compartment, Alex waited three heartbeats...and then he flicked the light switch.

The blinding flash of light reached him right before he slammed the door shut.

"Striker 961 reports good visual on the Indians from two-zero miles away," *Belleau Wood's* air controller reported. "FLIR video on LSD three."

Captain Julia Rosario sat back in her chair in *Belleau Wood's* combat information center. Much to her surprise, her hands had stopped shaking somewhere during the second missile attack. Now she waited for the first *American* missiles to strike their enemy, an excited shiver running down her spine. "Very well."

"Harpoon impact in ninety seconds," another watchstander said.

"We're in decent shape if you discount the lack of missiles," she said to her XO, Commander Mitchell Saldivar, needing to fill the silence. He stood to her left, short enough that she didn't have to look up much. They served together for the last eighteen months, eighteen months of training, port visits, liberty incidents, and inspections. Sometimes, Julia felt she knew him better than she did her own wife.

The last hour only welded them closer. Their cruiser remained afloat—albeit almost toothless. But she still had eight Harpoons, not to mention the eight sailing at the enemy.

"Thank God the Harpoon is fire-and-forget," Mitch said. "*Kidd's* definitely not going to give hers any mid-course corrections. "And *Enterprise* looks like shit. She's down to six knots."

Belleau Wood's OSS feed showed on the middle of four screens, displaying the carrier in all her bleeding glory. Julia thought it a testament to Newport News Naval Shipyard that *Enterprise* remained afloat, but her speed dropped as fires raged aft and amidships. She chewed her lip. "Captain Edwards says they've got a fire in one of their reactor compartments and he's had to take that reactor offline."

"Oh, goodie." Mitch said. "Today gets better and better, Captain."

"Yeah." She sighed. "I think we'll have to take her in tow."

He grimaced. Towing was one of every surface warfare officer's least favorite activities; it took forever to prepare for and handicapped the ship doing the towing. "Can we make *Fletcher* do it?"

"She just took a hit aft. And she's too small." Julia wished she could delegate that, but *Fletcher* was three thousand tons lighter than *Belleau Wood*. "*Enterprise* might accidentally run her over, and then where would we be?"

Mitch snorted. "Captain, don't make me laugh. It's hard to be the scary XO when I giggle like a schoolgirl."

"I don't think you need to scare discipline into anyone now, Mitch," she said quietly.

"No shit." He shook himself. "Okay. I'll go grab the First Lieutenant and get the towing party together. We'll have to strip one of the Repair Lockers to man the foc'sle, though."

"Do it." Julia grimaced. "There's not much likelihood of us needing repair parties if we get hit, anyway."

She'd watched *John Finn* and *Kidd* go from sleek warships to flaming messes in mere minutes. Modern missiles just didn't give you much room for survival. Mitch knew that, too, and he hurried out of CIC, heading forward to gather personnel.

"Harpoons on final approach, Captain," the TAO reported.

"If anyone wants to say a prayer, now's the time." Julia grinned towards her watchstanders. Most smiled back, gathering to watch the FLIR video from Striker 961. Julia knew she should order them back to their stations, but critical watches were manned, and damn it if her people didn't deserve to get some of their own back.

"Captain, Bridge, *Kidd's* abandoning ship," the officer of the deck reported.

Julia swallowed, squeezing her eyes shut. At least they were going slow enough to pick up survivors. This time. "Captain, aye."

"Your turn, fuckers," Senior Chief Brummelman whispered from her right.

Julia's eyes popped open. Twenty-four Harpoon II missiles roared in, and the Indians launched their Barak-8 anti-air missiles. The Barak-8 was roughly on par with the SM-2, but the Harpoon's slower speed meant the Indians might manage two defensive salvos. However, each Indian destroyer only carried sixteen Barrack missiles, and each of the four destroyers in the lead group had four Harpoons to contend with.

The first wave of Barak-8s took out ten Harpoons. Julia swallowed. "We should've concentrated our fire."

"Nothing we can change about it now, ma'am," Brummelman said.

Julia nodded numbly, counting numbers down in her head and watching the tactical plot instead of the video. *Belleau Wood's* SPY radar wasn't her best radar for tracking surface contacts, but Striker 961's radar fed the Indians' tracks into Link. SPY *could* detect the launch of each individual missile, however. The Indians' second counter missile launch came when the Harpoons were just fifteen miles out from their strike group, boring in on the American missiles—

"Those are hits!" Brummelman almost jumped out of his chair. "Fuck, yes!"

Several sailors cheered. Julia raised her voice: "Good job, people. Set up on the undamaged destroyers to do it again."

"Yes, ma'am!" Brummelman's grin was infectious; Julia returned it before looking back at the plot. She couldn't see details, but two of the Indian destroyers slowed down, dropping out of formation. That could only mean one thing.

"We only got two of them, Senior," she said in an undertone. "Don't get cocky."

"Not a chance, Captain. We'll get the others next time. It's *our* goddamned turn to fire on ships without fucking missiles left."

Julia almost opened her mouth to tell him not to give the Indians ideas, but they both knew the four closer destroyers were out of BrahMos missiles. *Thank God.* She took a breath, and then keyed the microphone for the tactical net. "*Enterprise* this is *Belleau Wood.* Stand by to be taken in tow, over."

Chapter 31

Unpleasant Truths

Jules Rochambeau snapped an order in French and the marines stopped cold. He strode up to the group of refugees huddled at the corner of Earle and Cook tubes, two armed sailors on his heels. Marines were better shots, but Jules trusted *Barracuda's* crew more than the marines sent to do the dirty work. The reason he left Central was a case in point.

This group's senior marine officer was Commandant Armand Moreau. The rank of commandant was not as impressive as it sounded; the equivalent of a British or American major, commandant was two ranks below Jules' own *Capitaine de vaisseau*. Two ranks and two *hundred* percent in brainpower. Jules wanted to slap Moreau. Instead, he settled for pulling the younger man to the side.

"What were your people *thinking*?" he hissed in French. "You've critically wounded a civilian and *shot* a naval officer. We are trying to do this without bloodshed, you fool!"

Moreau cringed and then gaped. "We didn't—a naval officer?"

"Yes, you imbecile!" Jules bit back a curse. Moreau wilted so fast that it burned out most of Jules' anger. He sighed. "Tell your marines there must be no further casualties. We cannot afford the political repercussions."

"Yes, sir," Moreau whispered.

Jules turned away in a huff, and his eye caught Maria Vasquez. He knew who she was—he researched Admiral Hamilton prior to the summit—but he couldn't guess how she and Lieutenant Lin ended up with this group. Their fellows continued to run Camille in circles, but these two were here. Why were they separated?

Vasquez wasn't shy about staring at him. Her brown eyes were dark with fury while she stood with two older women, her shirt and hands coated in dried blood.

Jules lifted a hand and swapped to English. "A moment, Commander?"

She ignored him until heads started turning. Then Vasquez's eyes widened with feigned innocence. "Me?"

"S'il vous plaît."

"We'll be right here, honey," one of the old women said, earning herself a wan smile as Vasquez walked over to Rochambeau. Her scowl returned when he led her away from the clump of confused Americans.

"What do you want?" Vasquez asked.

"I cannot change what has happened, and I will not insult you by offering an apology," he said. "But I can promise you that those responsible for this carnage—and Lieutenant Lin's death—will be punished to the full extent under French law."

"You knew." Her eyes narrowed. "Did your marine know when he shot Jesse?"

"Non. He did not." Jules made himself meet her angry gaze.

"I find that hard to believe."

"I am not concerned with what you believe." Jules stepped on his own temper. He had not wanted bloodshed with the civilians—all of whom now looked at him like they expected murder—but the consequences were his to deal with. "But I will reiterate: I regret what has happened and we will punish those responsible."

"Including yourself?" she snapped.

"My patience is *not* infinite, Madame." Jules gritted his teeth. "Do not test it."

Her brown eyes flashed. "Is that a threat?"

"Of course not." He could not make himself smile, though Jules knew he should. "You will be well cared for. You all will. We desire to hurt no one."

Jules raised his voice for the last sentence, eyes sweeping the crowd of refugees. Most looked wary, if not outright terrified, but the older women near the front glared. Jules turned away; what did he care if they hated him?

What mattered was sending an unambiguous message to the United States: their presence was neither wanted nor welcome in this part of the world, and it was time they focused on their own hemisphere.

All the better that he could commandeer a cruise ship from a company based in Miami to do it—Norwegian Cruise Lines was displeased with the purpose of this charter, but money was money. *Besides, their ships are all flagged in the Bahamas.* Jules always thought it foolish of the Americans to allow their companies to use flags of convenience instead of insisting they fly the American flag, but that was not his problem.

"Get them to the cruise ship," he told Moreau in French, gesturing for his sailors to follow. "*Without* further incident."

"Oui, mon Capitaine!"

Jules scowled and headed back towards Central, only for his phone to ring. "Oui?"

Coughing filled the airwaves for a moment. Then Camille's voice came through, high and sharp: "They are setting off explosives!"

"*What?*"

"We are"—more coughing—"under Platform Three. The Americans are threatening the entire platform!"

Jules heart wanted to jump into his throat. "Is there flooding?"

"Not yet." Camille kicked something. "But I think we were lucky. We must be above the waterline here."

"Bien." He tried to call up an image of what the area under the TRANSPLAT piers looked like, but Jules had never been there. He shook his head. "Find them before they destroy something vital."

Would the Americans be so suicidal? Camille's marines killed both security officers, which left Admiral Hamilton, Commander Coleman, and assorted followers without gun-toting protection. Hamilton and Coleman were submariners. Surely they'd not do something so stupid.

Unless they had nothing to lose.

Stopping, Jules turned to glance at Maria Vasquez's back. Two of the older women clumped close to her; the trio spoke softly. Would a hostage prove useful? The very idea was barbaric.

"They know the station better than we do," Camille snarled. "If they lose us—"

"Then do not let them." Jules started walking again, his long strides eating up the ground between himself and Central. "I will have Madame Ledoux determine what route they will take."

Another cough. "Fine. We will follow them once we get this damned door open." Camille swore at someone else; Jules only caught half the words.

"Hurry," he said before hanging up.

Jules hated this job.

"Let me know if the admiral comes back," John told Rubino. She nodded without looking optimistic, and John patted her on the shoulder. "I'll be outside."

John stepped outside the flag bridge to look at the damage and wished he hadn't. Black smoke filled the air, billowing out of the wounds on *Enterprise's* port side. Sailors raced around on the flight deck, dumping water and firefighting foam through the holes to reach the inferno below. They seemed to be winning—at least the fires weren't spreading—but John didn't want to know how many died already.

The black smoke looked particularly bad now that sunrise arrived. Now John could see sailors from *Kidd* swimming and clinging to life rafts, and he swallowed, thinking about *John Finn's* crew miles back in their wake. Could he send someone back to get them? Not with the Indian Strike Group still willing to attack *Enterprise*. The strike group looked respectable back when *Enterprise* had four escorts; now she was down to two, one damaged.

Belleau Wood maneuvered in front of *Enterprise*, shooting over a tow line. The cruiser looked amazingly intact compared to *Enterprise's* lamed state. To port, an oil streak, life rafts, and sailors in the water marked *Kidd's* grave. Meanwhile, *Fletcher* came around the carrier's stern to pick up as many sailors as she could. John could see the giant black scar where the destroyer's aft CIWS mount used to be, now a mess of bent and scorched metal. But *Fletcher* seemed operational despite the damage. She was more maneuverable than *Enterprise*, too, though that didn't take much.

Lieutenant Debbie Pitner, McNally's flag aide, approached. Her dark-skinned face was hard to see in the dark. "Sir, I've got Seventh Fleet on the line."

"Finally," John breathed. He handed off the satellite phone to Pitner before the last Indian attack, without hope that she'd get ahold of anyone. It was after working hours on America's east coast, and jamming kept them from contacting any of the usual chain of command out here. But Seventh Fleet was based in Japan, where it was just after seven in the morning.

"Hey, COS, the Harpoons nailed two Indian destroyers!" Rubino stuck her head outside the flag bridge to shout.

John grinned. "Good. Tell them to do it again."

"Captain Rosario's on it, sir." The door to the flag bridge clicked shut; John turned back to Pitner. She offered him the phone.

"Thanks for getting them, Debbie," he said, and then put the phone to his ear. "This is Captain Dalton, *Enterprise* Strike Group COS."

"I'm glad you could finally pick up the phone, Captain," a gravelly voice replied. "This is Admiral Kristensen."

John almost dropped the phone. Vice Admiral Jonas Kristensen was Commander, Seventh Fleet. He swallowed. "Admiral, I'm glad we got ahold of you. We're being jammed—"

"That lieutenant said something about an Indian Strike Group *firing* upon you," Kristensen said. "Please tell me she's freaking out for no reason."

"Um, no sir. We mistakenly identified and sank an Indian *Kilo*-class submarine in the SOM about an hour ago. INS *Vishal* and her escorts engaged us shortly thereafter. *John Finn* and *Kidd* are sunk. *Enterprise* took three hits and *Belleau Wood* has us under tow. *Fletcher* and *Belleau Wood* are almost out of missiles," John replied. "We just damaged two Indian destroyers with Harpoons, but they've hung out of range and taken pot shots at us 'till now."

A long silence came from the other end. "Son, you'd better give the phone to Admiral McNally."

"I wish I could, Admiral, but I'm not sure where he went."

"Say again?"

"He...freaked out a bit when *Kidd* went down, sir." John grimaced. He didn't like diming his boss out, but he wouldn't lie. "He should be back soon."

"Fine, give me your deputy commander," Kristensen growled.

"Sir, he's home on baby leave."

"Are you telling me you're the senior person at this disaster?"

John gulped. "Technically, no. Captain Edwards and Captain Rosario are both senior to me."

"Who the hell is Rosario?" Kristensen asked.

"CO *Belleau Wood*," John replied. "She's sharp, sir. Without her, we'd all be dead."

"Tell me everything."

"Let's take the fucking elevator," Bradshaw panted, skidding to a stop. Six flights of stairs would leave anyone winded, especially someone who'd been shot. Alex was surprised Bradshaw remained on his feet.

Olson got there first, jamming her thumb into the down button three times. The bank had eight elevators—four on each side—which ran from the top of the platform to the bottom.

"You sure this is a good idea?" Hamilton looked angry, but she'd kept up, which wasn't bad for an admiral. She was somewhere way north of forty, closer to fifty, and admirals weren't known for staying in shape. Predictably, her glare found Alex.

"Better than trucking all the way down the platform leg." Alex sucked in a deep breath, his heart still racing. "It gets narrower from here."

"Narrower?" Fowler's head whipped left and right like a pair of windshield wipers. "There's only one room on this level!"

"And there's only a leg after this." Bradshaw hissed as Steph examined the makeshift bandage on his arm. "Jus' the stairs and the elevators."

Hamilton glanced back warily. "What if they stop it somehow?"

"Ma'am, we can do that or tromp down another twenty-three stories." Alex's smile felt like a rictus. "They've probably figured out that my friendly little explosion didn't do a lot of damage. We *might* have enough time."

"Twenty-three *more* stories?" Gage looked ready to swoon.

Alex shot him a grin as the elevator doors opened. "You can swim if you want."

"Shut it, Commander," Hamilton snarled. "Let's move out."

They piled into the elevator, with Fowler and Gage bolting inside and everyone else following. Olson brought up the rear, her eyes scanning for threats.

Nothing.

Worry gnawed at Alex's innards. No fucking way was it going to be this easy.

"You think we lost them, boss?" Steph asked.

Alex shook his head. "Not unless our luck changes. You still got your tablet?"

"Yeah, why?"

"Any chance of you hacking in and fucking up the elevators?" Alex jerked his head at the elevator doors. "Would give us a hell of a head start if they have to use the stairs."

"Head start to *where*?" Hamilton asked. "In case you missed it, our ride is in flaming pieces." Those harsh words made even the admiral flinch, but Hamilton still met Alex's eyes.

"Can you, Steph?" Alex's mind whirled through options. Hamilton's glare deepened.

"Probably." Steph frowned. "The entire elevator bank's got just one control panel, so it's worth a shot."

"I didn't realize surface officers were hackers, Ms. Gomez." Hamilton's eyes narrowed.

Steph shrugged, but her eyes gleamed as she pulled her tablet out of her backpack. "It's a hobby, ma'am. Not one I'm given to practicing on government computers, though. I like my security clearance."

Hamilton chuckled before turning back to Alex with those same angry eyes. "My question remains, Commander."

"I've got a few ideas." No good ones, though. He chewed his lip, then was saved from answering by the elevator doors dinging open.

"Wait a sec," Olson said, ducking out of the elevator. Tense seconds passed as she looked around. "Clear!"

Alex led the others out, glancing around. A right or left would take them up or down Cook Tube, but Earle—and Central—was to the left. A lump filled his throat. *Jesse was murdered down there.* His heart wanted to thunder straight out of his throat. But his hands moved on their own, yanking Gage's second Nalgene bottle out of his backpack. Who bought an orange Nalgene bottle?

Coffee creamer. T-shirt. Charcoal. Smash the charcoal up, and all he needed was a fuse. It was funny how easy it was to jury rig something he'd agonized over in college, building bigger and better fireballs until he and his roommate were almost expelled. *If only Paul could see me now.*

Then again, having a Recon Marine around would be pretty fucking awesome right now. Grinning, Alex pounded the charcoal into dust as Steph darted over to the access panel on the far wall.

"Gimme a few minutes to wreck these elevators," she said.

"Are you sure we have time for that?" Fowler's eyes started the windshield wiper thing; he and Gage stood close together, fidgeting like erratic dancers. "I think I hear voices."

"That group of marines and civilians is still near Earle and Cook," Steph said, glancing at the camera feed on her tablet. "They're close."

Alex pinched the bridge of his nose, trying to stave off a growing headache. "Just when we ditch one group, huh? I think we need to—"

"Toi là!" a voice shouted in French before swapping to English. "Come out *immédiatement*!"

"Shit." He twisted to look at Steph. "Can you finish that thing?" She didn't reply; Alex resisted the urge to kick her. "Steph!"

"I need thirty seconds."

Olson peeked around the corner. "Frenchies about a hundred yards away. The assholes upstairs must've called them."

"Stay back!" The same French-accented voice seemed pointed away from them. Then it boomed in their direction: "Whoever you are, come out!"

Coffee creamer seeped through his fingers as Alex scooped it into the bottle. "Olson, take point! Go to the outertube station at Fieux!"

"Let's go!" Olson grabbed Gage; Bradshaw shoved Fowler. Hamilton paused to glare at Alex, whose eyes were on Steph.

Hamilton crossed her arms. "Time to go, Commander."

"Almost got it." Steph typed furiously on the tablet.

"Go ahead, ma'am. We'll be right behind you." Alex tucked the Nalgene under his arm and picked up the nine millimeter from the ground next to Steph.

"You know how to shoot that thing?"

Alex snorted. "I probably qualified more recently than you, Admiral." Not that his time on *Kansas* was recent. But when had Hamilton last been assigned to a submarine? Probably when Alex's daughters were toddlers.

"Being a smart ass will *not* help!"

"Shut up, I've got an idea." Alex dug in his backpack for another container of coffee creamer. Was he a good enough shot?

"Got it!" Steph jumped to her feet and snatched the gun in one fluid motion. "Let's go!"

"Come out!" the French marine shouted. "We will not ask again!" Footsteps shuffled forward. "We will open fire!"

"Can you shoot this?" Alex brandished the coffee creamer.

Steph paused. "From your hand? Sure, but you'll lose fingers."

Alex snorted. "Do I look that stupid?"

"You really want me to answer that, boss?"

"Probably not." Alex ignored Hamilton's gaze. Why the hell wouldn't she run with the others? "The fireball won't be as good as the one I made earlier, but it'll make them pause." He had ten more cans of the non-dairy coffee creamer in his bag; did Alex dare throw two of them?

"Sounds good to me." Steph bared her teeth. "Let 'er rip."

The threesome bolted around the corner together. Alex paused long enough to look right into the eyes of the French officer in the lead; he was young, blonde, and was that blood on his uniform tunic?

His mouth opened to shout, green eyes following the rolling can of coffee creamer as Alex let it go.

The French officer cocked his head, then jumped as the distinctive *crack-crack* split the air. Steph double-tapped the can, and a cloud of powder shot into the air—only to ignite a split second later.

A fireball filled Cook Tube as Alex, Steph, and Admiral Hamilton sprinted away.

Chapter 32

Jury-Rigged

Brilliant yellow and white light filled Cook Tube as the fireball exploded out of the can of coffee creamer. Jules Rochambeau could see it from a hundred meters away and ducked away as quickly as he could, plastering himself against the wall. A moment earlier, he'd paused at the intersection of Cook and Earle to call Camille again, learning that the Platform Three elevators were broken. He was sure the Americans were responsible, but the explosion stole his attention.

Jules sprinted back to the marines. They were in disarray, reeling back from the fireball, taking cover behind storefronts. Several coughed. The civilians with them fled even further back, clumping together on the edges of the tube and whispering frantically. Several hid inside SeaWise Cellular, where the marines had forced the doors open. The air reeked of...artificial sweetener? Strange.

Moreau was one of those hiding in SeaWise. Jules stalked in. "What happened, Commandant?"

"They used some sort of explosive, sir!" Moreau jackrabbited to his feet, speaking in rapid French. "I—I do not know what it was. But I fear leaks. What if—"

Jules looked back out into the tube, his practiced eyes sweeping across the overhead and the side walls. He couldn't see a leak—and, more importantly, his ears hadn't popped the way they would from a pressure change. "If there were a major leak, you would be drowning." He snorted. "Your indiscriminate use of *bullets* earlier caused more danger."

"I..." Moreau's mouth flopped open like a dead fish.

"Where did they go?" Jules demanded.

Moreau shook his head. "I—I do not know. We could not see them through the *bolide.*"

A snicker came from Jules' right; he turned to glare at Maria Vasquez, barely remembering to swap to English before asking: "Is there something you're not mentioning, Madame?"

"Nope. Nothing at all." She crossed her arms. "I don't know jack, but I'm enjoying the show."

"It's always nice to see the oppressors fuck up a bit," one of the older ladies added. The other one giggled before offering Jules a wide smile.

He turned away before he could say something regrettable. "Commandant, split off a team of marines to find the other Americans. *Immédiatement.* And then take these people to the cruise ship before someone gets hurt."

Moreau cringed. "Capitaine, the elevators do not work."

"*Merde.*" Jules had not thought of that. "Take them to Platform Four. I will have the cruise ship move." Its captain would complain, but what did he care? Better to take it away from where *Bretagne* sank the American supply ship, anyway. Lord only knew how the civilians reacted to *that.*

He would need to make sure *Earhart's* survivors were fished out of the water, too. *Must everything be my problem?*

"Oui, mon Capitaine!"

Whoever selected Moreau for this mission needed their head examined. Jules turned to Moreau's second-in-command, Lieutenant Juliette Davout. She was short, fierce, and dark haired. And Davout *wasn't* hiding in SeaWise. "Lieutenant Davout will chase the Americans. Pick a team and go, Lieutenant."

Moreau said nothing; Davout saluted. "Oui, mon Capitaine. I will find them."

"Allez!" Jules pointed down Cook, wishing he knew all the places those Americans might hide.

Again, he contemplated questioning Vasquez, but she was new to the station, too. She might know her admiral, but Vasquez would not share that information without methods Jules found reprehensible. No, he would have to trust the marines.

He watched Davout's back with narrow eyes as the lieutenant selected five marines and jogged away. His mission was not in danger as long as he caught the Americans. The grand sweep of history would not care how *hard* they made it, only that France won.

Moreau gathered the civilians and pushed them onwards, heading around the bottom of Cook towards the TRANSPLAT Four elevator bank. Surely the fool could escort a group of civilians there without supervision?

Mon Dieu, he missed his submarine.

Alex hated running on principle. Fool that he was, he signed himself up for plenty back in the day by attending a military college, but he made a point of avoiding the sport ever since. Still, swimming kept him in reasonable shape, which meant he reached the outertube station at Cooke and Fieux only a few steps behind Admiral Hamilton. Steph brought up the rear, hardly even panting.

"Next outertube in a minute thirty," Olson said, glancing at the readout next to the doors. They were big silver things, set slightly back from the tube proper in an alcove. There was a roped off area for the usual lines that formed, but the station was deserted.

Shouts trickled forward from back down Cooke; Alex tensed, expecting French marines coming around the corner at any moment.

"Can't you make it come faster?" Fowler took two steps towards Alex like he wanted to peek out of the station before retreating behind Olson.

Alex laughed, butterflies dancing in his throat. "Sure, let me just override the laws of physics for you."

"There's no need to be rude," Gage said. Fowler glared.

"We don't have time for this shit," Alex said. "They're right behind us."

Slinging his bag off his shoulder, Alex dug for the other Nalgene. He'd packed it tightly, so the charcoal hadn't mixed in much; he'd have to hope it created a big enough bang as-is. There was no time to fix it.

Gage sniffed. "We've *got* a minute seventeen, apparently."

"When did you put on your asshole pants?" Bradshaw asked.

Steph and Olson snickered; Hamilton opened her mouth, but Alex got in first. "Steph, wire this up to the light panel for a detonation thirty seconds after the outertube departs."

She snatched the Nalgene from him in exchange for her gun, sliding over to the nearest lighting panel. "You sure want it that far off, boss?"

Damn, she was right. Alex swallowed. "Don't shave it closer than ten."

The outertube's arrival and departure tolerance was thirty seconds off schedule, but thirty seconds was a damned long time when people with guns were chasing you. How long did the doors stay open? Alex couldn't remember.

More shouting. Bradshaw, cradling his injured arm, eased his head around the corner. "They're coming!"

Alex's hands were clammy on the pistol. Despite what he told Hamilton, he hadn't touched a gun since before *Kansas* left for deployment seven months earlier. God, had he really been on *Kansas* four months ago? That seemed like another life. He chewed his lower lip until he tasted blood, then shook himself and pulled another can of coffee creamer out of his bag.

"This is taking too long," Gage whispered, rocking back and forth. "This is taking too long."

"Be quiet, Mr. Gage," Hamilton snapped, glaring at the Time-To-Arrival display. *1:01.*

Olson trotted over to stand next to Alex. "Ready to shoot, boss?"

"No." He gasped out a laugh. "But I'll do it, anyway."

The shouting stopped. Was that a bad sign? Alex's heart pitter-pattered.

Bradshaw snuck another look. "They're—*fuck!*" He threw himself around the corner as gunshots cracked through the air.

Alex met Olson's eyes as Steph swore and pulled wires out of the panel to shove into the Nalgene. He held up the coffee creamer. "Can you shoot this?"

"I can try." Olson eyed the can like it was poisonous. "Is it gonna do anything?"

"Explode, if we're lucky. Ops managed it earlier."

"Then, roll 'em."

Crouching, Alex darted far enough around the corner to roll the coffee creamer towards the French. Bullets whizzed over his head, and he cringed. Yet the world slowed down as the can rolled forward; Alex's eyes picked out six of the enemy. All were armed with long rifles, whatever the French equivalent of the MP-4 or AK-47 was.

"*Attelons*!" one shouted, and the marines dove for cover.

Crack! Olson appeared at Alex's side, aiming for the coffee creamer. She missed with the first shot, and then the second. She aimed again and missed before Alex pulled her back around the corner.

"Sir, I can—"

"You can get your face shot, that's what," Alex cut her off. Had they bought enough time?

"Twenty seconds!" Hamilton said. Fowler stood next to her, bouncing up and down on his toes.

"Let's go." Alex shoved Olson towards the outertube. "Steph?"

She typed furiously on her tablet. "Set!"

The deck vibrated; the outertube chimed. Under normal circumstances, Alex found the sound annoyingly happy. Today it was the mocking chirp of an evil bird.

Voices in French; was that someone swearing? Alex remained precariously close to the corner. *Ding-ding*-dah-*ding!* The outertube arrived with a song; Alex twisted to watch through the thick windows as it settled into the docking cradle. The external set of double doors opened first, and then another chime announced a good seal. Finally, the inner doors *hissed* open.

Fowler and Gage bolted in, almost flattening Hamilton in their rush. The admiral paused to let Bradshaw go, then Steph darted in with Olson on her heels. Alex brought up the rear, jumping through the doors a split second before French marines boiled around the corner.

"Get down!"

Everyone dove away from the doors as weapons came up.

"Come out!" the French officer shouted. "You are cornered!"

"Close the fucking doors!" Hamilton hissed.

Gage slapped the door close button once, twice, five times. "It won't work!" he all but wailed.

Steph groaned. "It's a goddamned safety feature."

French marines crept closer. "This is your last warning!"

"We have to do something." Gage whimpered. He pushed the button again. Nothing happened. "We have to do something *fast*."

"Will someone shut him *up*?" Bradshaw asked from a back corner. His face was pale and his wound bled through the bandage; he looked terrible and Alex couldn't do a damned thing for him. "And who the *fuck* thinks guns are a great idea on an underwater station, anyway?"

Worry wanted to gnaw an acid hole in his stomach. Swallowing, Alex scooted forward on his knees towards the front of the outertube. Shoving the pistol into his waistband, he scrambled upright next to the small control console.

Outertubes were run by a computer in central, but international law required each to have emergency manual controls. Yanking the plastic cover back, Alex slammed his palm down on the red button labeled in six languages: *Emergency Release from Track*.

"*Décochez!*"

"Take cover!" Alex snapped. He didn't need to know French to guess what—

A shower of bullets slammed into the outertube as the inner doors slammed shut. Someone cried out; bullets *tinged* off the far side of the compartment, ricocheting. The outer doors, thicker and made of steel, followed a second later, accompanied by the same *Ding-ding*-dah-*ding*. Alex snuck a glance at the telltale panel, where green lights claimed the outertube's structural integrity was sound.

Then the outertube rocketed off the track, slamming Alex onto his ass.

John finished his call with Seventh Fleet and stood in stony silence, staring at the water. *Belleau Wood* finished preparing the tow while *Enterprise* lolled on the waves, making little way. The smoke was thicker, now, and the carrier had a distinct list to port. She'd eaten two missiles, enough to sink a smaller warship, but somehow, *Enterprise* remained afloat.

Inside the skin of the carrier, sailors raced to combat fires and plug holes. Unlike her older sisters, *Enterprise* had a water mist firefighting system installed in all her spaces, and that saved her. Although the explosions cracked some piping and vaporized others, there were enough working nozzles to put water on the flames. The fine mist quieted the raging inferno into a manageable fire, which *Enterprise's* sailors attacked with gusto.

John slumped against the lifelines railing the bridge wing and sighed. Seventh Fleet knew the truth. They couldn't do a damned thing—the *Enterprise* Strike Group was too far away to help—but at least John wasn't the senior person with a secret.

Scratch that. His *admiral* now wasn't left holding the bag. Hard to forget about McNally, who sucked down a cigarette not fifteen feet away.

"I guess a few ashes from that won't make a difference here." John wandered over. He was bone tired; every step felt heavier than the last, and he just wanted to sleep. When was the last time he got any shut eye? It was past six in the morning, local time, and he'd been up all night. Shifting time zones meant he hadn't *quite* been up for twenty-four hours, but it was close enough.

McNally stared at the horizon, his features slack. "Now what, John?"

"We shoot the rest of our Harpoons and go home, I guess." John shrugged. They didn't teach this shit at the submarine school's prospective commanding officers' course. Sub commanders shot the enemy and slipped back into hiding. Stealth was the name of their game, but how the hell did you hide an aircraft carrier who'd already taken two hits and could barely steam through the water?

McNally shook his head. "I just started a war. *Another* war." The last words were a ragged whisper.

"Here's hoping someone above our paygrade can figure out how to stop it before things get too ugly." John took a deep breath. "But for now, we need you, sir."

"For what?"

John gaped, struggling for words. "We need you to lead us." *To do your job*, he couldn't add.

He expected to be yelled at. Instead, McNally slumped. "You're right. Just...give me a moment."

The admiral looked back at the survivors in the water, now surrounding *Fletcher* as the destroyer's crew worked to pull as many of them on board as possible. *Fletcher* strung nets down on both sides and had a J-bar davit working on her foc'sle to lift any swimmers who lacked the strength to climb up to her deck. Meanwhile *Enterprise* drifted forward as *Belleau Wood* tested the tow. Were they sitting ducks out here?

John was too exhausted to be properly frightened.

"They *what*?" Jules could not believe his ears. He'd sent someone *competent* after the Americans, and now Moreau told him—

"They escaped into the outertube after exploding another bomb." Moreau spoke so fast he was hard to understand through the radio. Lieutenant Davout is injured and may lose fingers! I do not know—"

"*Tais-toi*!" Halfway to Central—would he *ever* make it there?—Jules saw red. Not going back to strangle Moreau took a herculean effort. "Take your captives to the cruise ship. *Immédiatement!*"

"Oui, mon Capitaine!" Moreau sounded terrified. Jules did not care.

Instead, he stalked through Armistice Station's passageways until he reached Central. Admiral Khare was present, alas, and he was regretfully unintimidated by an irate naval captain.

"Problems, Captain?" he asked in his hither-to-be-damned British-accented English. The man probably attended the Royal Naval Academy alongside all of Jules' pre-war friends and allies.

Friends no longer. He shot a poisonous glare at Khare, wondering when the Indians would become enemies. It would be nice to sink the egotistical admiral. He spoke through gritted teeth: "Oui." Lying would be counterproductive. "The Americans escaped into an outertube car. If you will excuse me, I would like to track it."

Khare's eyebrows met his hairline. "They escaped your marines?"

"Unfortunately." Jules twisted to Aida Ledoux. "Madame, if you will assist?"

"Of course." Swallowing, she pulled up the proper display. The station schematic took up most of one wall, color coded by area and habitat. The outertube track was blue, covered in flashing green dots. "This shows all of the outertube cars. There are fifty of them on the track, synched to maintain safe spacing."

"Can you track an individual car?"

"Oui. Do you have its number?" Jules glared; Ledoux wilted. "Pardon moi. Where did it—"

A flashing alarm cut her off, blaring and turning a section of the track yellow. Ledoux swore.

"They have ejected the car from the track, Capitaine." She pointed; Rochambeau stared at the icon accelerating away from the track circling—and sometimes splitting through—Armistice Station. Ledoux smiled. "But I have its beacon."

"*Très bien.*"

Finally, something went right.

Chapter 33

Rules of Engagement

Several moments passed before Alex picked himself up off the deck, muscles aching. "How the hell does something this small accelerate so fucking fast?" he asked no one in particular.

His hip hurt where it bounced off the bulkhead to his right. He'd have a pistol-shaped bruise there when this was over, but bruises beat being *dead*. Holy shit. They got away.

"Someone *shot* me." Gage sounded more offended than pained, but red blossomed near the waistline of his sky-blue dress shirt.

Fuck.

"Got it!" Olson scooted forward to put pressure on the wound; Gage squealed.

Then the sound of breaking glass made Alex turn, watching as Bradshaw grabbed the emergency medical kit from behind its locked window. The kit was stocked according to IMO lifeboat standards, which meant it contained morphine. Dragging it one handed, Bradshaw squatted next to Olson. "Lemme do pressure," he said. "You'll need two hands to give him a shot."

Olson nodded; Alex forced himself to look away. His subordinates could handle that; he needed to focus on the submarine he'd more-or-less inadvertently stolen. The outertube car's manual controls were minimal, with emergency programming designed to pilot the car to the surface. Once on the surface, a beacon would tell Central—and Rochambeau—exactly where they were.

Where to go? *Amelia Earhart* was gone. Did the oiler get word out? Was help coming? The entire U.S. Navy would crash down on Armistice Station like the wrath of a vengeful god after the French sank a Navy oiler, but that wouldn't matter to Alex's people if they didn't survive.

Like Jesse didn't. Alex pushed that thought aside. Turning the manual operation key, he used the touch screen to stop the flow of air to the car's ballast tanks. Three more commands leveled the car out at one hundred feet, and Alex drove it forward at nine knots.

The car rocked back and forth like a cheap civilian submarine; Alex's fingers danced over the controls, gently leveling it out. Quick math said he could stay at this speed for two hours before surfacing. Did they have enough air for that? He had no idea what kind of supply the outertube cars held. Half the speed only gave them twice as much range. What kind of idiot designed the crap battery in this thing?

"Fantabulous," he muttered.

"Problems driving, Commander?" Hamilton looked ready to pounce.

Alex scowled. "No, but we've only got a range of eighteen nautical miles at nine knots. Thirty-six at four knots. We're sure as shit not outrunning *Barracuda* like that."

"I take it *that* wasn't part of the plan."

"Ma'am, I'm making this up as we go. If I could've anticipated this disaster, I'd be a fucking witch."

The admiral snorted. "Anything within thirty-six nautical miles?"

"Jack shit and nada."

"You're saying we're *lost*?" Fowler slumped in a seat on one of the starboard side benches, leaning into the plush thing like it would save his life. He ignored Olson and Bradshaw working to stop Gage's bleeding, with Olson using a medical stapler to close the wound. Fowler looked almost as bad as his subordinate, pale and sweating—minus the blood. The wall behind him was decorated in pastels, complete with pictures of DaVinci's diving bell and other scenes out of diving history, clashing with Gage bleeding on the floor.

"Nah, I know where we are." Smiling was hard. Adrenaline seeped out of his system now that bullets stopped flying, replaced by icy fear. "The problem is where we're going."

"I *told* you we should surrender." Fowler sniffed and wiped sweaty hands on his trousers. "Now we're going to die in some little bottle, miles from—"

"If you're in a hurry to die, Mister Secretary, I can just open the goddamned doors," Alex snapped as Hamilton's phone chirped. "If you're not, kindly do me the favor of shutting the fuck up."

Fowler gaped. Alex turned back to the controls, studying the electronic chart and a schematic of Armistice Station. Their car—now a mini sub—rocketed off the track near the old center of the station. Cook Tube formed an oval, off which other tubes grew like spindly legs. Heading north would take them clear of Armistice Station within a mile, which the Three Minute Rule said would take about nine minutes. Getting away from the station in any other direction would take twice as long.

"I've disabled our homing beacon," Steph said from the maintenance panel in the stern. "But it won't take a genius sub hunter to figure out a search area using our maximum speed."

"And Rochambeau is a submariner," Alex finished for her.

Steph's smile went taut. "We can always hope French submariners are idiots."

"I wish. But his XO's no dummy. Vindictive and sneaky, sure, but not stupid." Alex scowled. Camille Dubois' neat little blame game left *Kansas* holding the bag for that Neyk's sinking, and it still burned.

"Maria texted me," Hamilton said. "They're taking our people to a cruise ship on Platform Four."

Alex blinked. "We could make that."

"To surrender?" Hamilton reared back as if he'd slapped her.

"I was thinking more like hitchhiking." A crooked smile creased his face. "Followed by hijacking."

"*Hijacking?*" Steph gaped.

"You're crazy." Hamilton spoke almost conversationally.

Alex shrugged, feeling strangely calm. "Crazy has the advantage of being unpredictable."

"Well, that describes *you* to a 'T.'" The admiral slumped against the outer bulkhead and shook her head.

"If we can get on board—while armed—I doubt the French will dare send a lot of armed guards," Alex said. "And then we convince the crew to change course."

"That's a gamble, boss," Steph said.

Alex shrugged. "So's swimming around out here. If the French want to hold Armistice Station, they can't afford to send half their marines off with a cruise ship. I think we've got a chance."

"Sir, I've got Seventh Fleet Actual on the phone." Captain Tenaglia's voice was a whisper, and her face stark white, but Rear Admiral Marco Rodriquez jumped up and headed to her console before he realized he was moving. A half-disassembled battle lantern sat forgotten in his wake, its casing bouncing off the deck. No one noticed.

Marco snatched the phone. "Rodriquez."

"Marco, it's Jonas Kristensen," the voice on the other end said. "*Enterprise* CSG is under fire at the entrance to the SOM. How fast can you get there?"

"Under—*fuck*." Marco swallowed his questions. "My amphibs are already making best speed at twenty-five knots, but I can cut the four hours to about two hours fifty if I shift my flag to a destroyer."

"Do it. We need shooters up there as fast as we can get them," Kristensen ordered.

"Call the bridge and tell them I need a helo to *Morton* yesterday," Marco said to Tanya. "You, me, our battle watch captains, and anyone else you can fit in two trips. Tell them to bring enough uniforms for god knows how long." He returned his attention to the phone while she sprinted away. "What the fuck happened, sir? I didn't think the Chinese had anyone in the SOM."

"They don't. An Indian *Kilo* spooked Jeff McNally and he sank it." Seventh Fleet's commander sighed, sounding a thousand years old. "Then an Indian SAG opened fire. Two destroyers sunk, *Enterprise* is damaged, and the other escorts are almost out of missiles. It's bad, Marco."

"The fucking *fuck*?" Marco felt like someone dumped a bucket of ice over his head. He *knew* Jeff. The man wasn't an idiot. "What the hell made Jeff sink a goddamned *Indian* submarine?"

"Jamming kept McNally from reaching out until about thirty minutes ago." Kristensen summarized the battle while Marco took frantic notes, writing on Tanya's console with a grease pencil. At the end, Kristensen added: "But now no one's answering the Iridium phone."

"Double fuck." Marco swallowed, looking around at his suddenly deserted flag bridge. "Admiral, I'll call you back once I'm on the destroyer and we're turning and burning north. Want I should send *Lionfish* ahead to sink any Indians she can?"

"Not yet. Hold her close until I can kick this upstairs. For now, fire only on ships you can positively ID as having fired on *Enterprise* and her escorts."

"With all due respect, sir, that's fucking stupid."

"It's a political decision, Marco," Kristensen said. "People back home are still waking up."

"Then wake 'em up faster. I need some goddamned rules of engagement before I get in strike range." Marco loved math, and math loved him back. If the Indians hit *Enterprise* right after she entered the Strait of Malacca, that was still 700 nautical miles short of the Sunda Strait, which Marco's ships would take to the SOM. How far in *Enterprise* got before getting hammered would determine how fast Marco could find the enemy.

Fuck, that was right on the edge of the F-35B's range, wasn't it? *Tripoli* was a helicopter carrier and only carried six SVTOL (Short Vertical Takeoff and Landing) Lightnings, but six fighters beat a pencil through the eye.

"I'll try to have something for you when you call," Kristensen said.

"I'm scrambling F-35s now," Marco replied. "I want friends in the air if this is turning into a shootout. At the very least, they can get a look at what the fuck is going on."

Kristensen hesitated. "I'm not sure that will help deescalate—"

"Is anything going 'deescalate' this after they've sunk *two* of our destroyers, Admiral?" The grease pencil snapped in Marco's hands. He threw it down and never watched it land.

Kristensen didn't have an answer, so Marco hung up and sprinted down to the flight deck to shift his flag to USS *Dudley W. Morton* (DDG-170). For once, the destroyer being named for one of the U.S. Navy's most legendary submariners didn't make him smile. He had work to do.

Alex surfaced the outertube car several hundred yards away from TRANSPLAT Four. A wave smacked the port bow, rolling the car like a dead hippo. Fowler, unprepared, upended out of his seat and fell to the deck. The politician squeaked and grumbled; everyone ignored him.

"You need me to take the wheel, sir?" Steph's grin looked almost normal. "Now that we're on the surface and all."

"Shut your face." Alex chuckled. "If this thing had a proper periscope, we wouldn't even need to be up here."

Up was a bit of a misnomer; not much of the craft showed above the surface. Wiggling forward, Alex craned his neck to see through the top window. He was just tall enough to make out the platform in the distance, but the big, white cruise ship was hard to miss, even in the pre-dawn darkness. It moved slower than a blind turtle as the ship shifted from Platform 3 to Platform 4. *Score one for Maria Vasquez.*

Steph slid up next to him. "Your crazy ass plan just might work, boss."

"Thanks for the vote of confidence." Alex tried not to let his voice crack. What the hell was he thinking? No way would this work. He *was* insane.

"Don't chicken out when we're already committed, Commander." Hamilton didn't quite sneer. Was she eavesdropping? Probably. The car wasn't what Alex considered spacious.

Alex twisted to glare at her. "The last time I tried to save a bunch of civilians, it didn't work out so well."

Hamilton blinked, but admirals weren't exactly known for apologizing. She scowled. "How long do you think you need to get this ungainly thing over to the pier?"

"Less time than they take to moor." Alex swallowed. Cruise ships had to be better at that than submarines, didn't they? Subs drove like drunk whales on the surface. But that big white monster sure was moving slow. Maybe having that much sail area made it harder. Besides, there were *ocean* currents out here, not measly tides like Alex was used to at naval bases. He didn't envy that cruise ship captain.

Particularly not if they succeeded in hijacking it.

Alex ignored another poisonous look from Hamilton. She'd hate him forever. Fine.

That stopped mattering two hours ago.

Chapter 34

Illumination

Forty tense minutes after their harpoons struck the Indian destroyers, *Belleau Wood* got the carrier under tow. Breathing felt easier; Nancy even sat back in her chair and contemplated making coffee. She and Captain Rosario already decided that shooting their last Harpoons off at the fleeing Indians was a bad idea; with their defenses terrifyingly thin, they needed to preserve an offensive punch to keep the Indians honest.

"Active illuminators bearing two-nine-two!" Chief Carlotta Tamayo's voice broke into *Fletcher's* internal net. Chief Tamayo was the senior watchstander in SSES, the top secret workspace dedicated to detecting enemy ship radar emissions and cracking their communications.

"Two-nine-two is *Porbandar*!" Attar's eyes widened. "That fucking Indian destroyer—"

"Kill it!" Nancy stamped on her foot pedal. "*Belleau Wood, Fletcher*, active illuminators from track 7065! Re-designating Bulldogs, over!"

"Surface, TAO, kill track 7065," Attar ordered internally before *Belleau Wood* could reply.

"Surface, aye! Kill track 7065." Three seconds passed; three too many. "Bulldogs away!"

Porbandar was less than thirty nautical miles away, and their Indian shadow still had a (presumably) full missile load out. Sinking the destroyers who already attacked them was nice, but not if someone closer could reach out and touch them.

Finally, Rosario's voice came back: "*Belleau Wood*, roger, break, *Belleau Wood* holding fire, out."

Fletcher's last eight Harpoons roared out of her forward VLS cells. Nancy's eyes flicked to the forward camera to watch them go, wincing as the *Kidd's* survivors dove to the deck on the foc'sle. Then her eyes returned to her screen to glare at *Porbandar*'s track. If Nancy's crew launched fast enough, they *might* hit *Porbandar* before the Indian destroyer could launch her BrahMos missiles—

"Shit," Attar whispered.

Red icons blossomed next to *Porbandar's* diamond-shaped track on the display. These were the upside-down Vs of hostile air tracks. They were too clumped together to count, but Nancy knew how many there would be. *Visakhapatnam*-class destroyers each carried sixteen BrahMos NG missiles.

That was more attack missiles than *Fletcher* had ESSMs left. She mashed the pedal down with her right foot again. "Vampire, vampire, vampire! Track 7065 launching BrahMos, over."

No one replied; no one needed to. Nancy sat tense in her seat, trying not to swallow. Now wasn't the time to ask how many ESSMs *Belleau Wood* had left; they all knew it wouldn't be enough. Sixteen supersonic missiles shot out of *Porbandar's* tubes and into the sky, roaring towards the maimed strike group, ripping through the air at Mach Seven.

The only question was which of the three remaining American ships *Porbandar* targeted.

"Link doctrine designating ESSMs," Attar said. Nancy turned to meet his eyes, and her TAO shrugged. "Flight time thirty seconds once they transition to cruise."

"Holy hell, that's close." Nancy swallowed and keyed her microphone for *Fletcher's* 1MC, or general announcing system. Her voice came out steadier than she expected: "Incoming missiles. Brace for impact. I say again, brace for impact."

There was nothing left to do besides close her eyes and pray.

"Civilians are done loading." Steph squeezed up near the windows in the outertube car so she could see Platform Four and the cruise ship, giving Alex's neck a break. "I don't see a ton of marines, either."

"Brow still out?" Alex asked.

"One of 'em, aft. Looks like it's got a couple guards."

"Are you certain you want to proceed with this insane plan of yours, Commander?" Hamilton's expression gave none of her thoughts away. Did she expect him to run away?

And where the hell would they run to?

Alex swallowed. "I don't think we've got a lot of other options, ma'am." He took a deep breath. "Either we board that cruise ship or scream for help and hope someone friendly finds us. Which doesn't feel really fucking likely."

Should one swear at admirals? Shit, what did he have to lose?

"There will be hell to pay if this fails," she muttered.

"You can always stay in the car and nap, ma'am."

Hamilton's narrow-eyed glare promised a slow death. "I'll forget you said that, Commander."

At least she had guts. That was better than the politician; Fowler sat and poked at the medical kit, his face ashen. Alex chewed his lip and glanced at Gage, who lay glassy-eyed between Olson and Bradshaw. Half-conscious, he still had more spirit than his boss, though neither was exactly a prize to write home about.

"I don't think we have a lot of time for other options, anyway, Admiral," he whispered. "Gage needs a doctor."

"You're not wrong about that." Hamilton sighed. "Very well. You have my permission, for what it's worth. Not that I think you were waiting for it."

Despite himself, Alex grinned. "I'll remember that, ma'am." He turned to his people. "All right, folks, let's do this thing. Steph, you stay up forward. You're my eyes—try to keep me from ramming the pier with this clumsy thing. Olson, you're on the top hatch. Crack it the moment we're close enough. Then get lines over as fast as you can."

"You got it, boss," Steph said.

"Aye, sir." Olson nodded, pulling down the ladder for the emergency hatch in the car's overhead.

"Admiral, would you watch the ballast tanks and ballast us up to pier level when we get there?"

"I think I can handle that," Hamilton said.

"Brilliant." Alex turned to the car's controls, nudging it forward. His choice to lurk fifty yards off the pier was fortuitous, now; the car crossed the distance in minutes. A berth across from the cruise ship was empty, so Alex drove the car there. But the stupid car still steered like a brain-damaged elephant, leaving Alex to wrestle with the touchscreen wheel—the worst way *ever* created to drive a submarine—and input most commands twice.

"Couple feet remaining," Steph finally said. "Bring the stern left. You're about twenty degrees off parallel."

"Aye." Alex twisted the outboard motor to starboard, then amidships as he backed down. The stern drifted in while the bow's travel towards the pier slowed. What he wouldn't give for a decent rate of turn indicator—

The car hit the pier with a thud, followed by an ominous *creak*. Fowler yelped while Hamilton ballasted up based on Steph's directions; Alex tuned them out. Throwing the outboard motor ninety degrees to port, he pinned the car against the pier.

"Hatch open!" Olson announced, scurrying up the ladder. Alex held his breath, realizing too late that he hadn't sent someone to help Olson with the lines. Bradshaw only had one arm, and Steph was needed up forward.

Hamilton darted up the ladder. Topside, he heard her talking to Olson, and two minutes crawled by before Hamilton's head appeared in the hatch.

"Lines secured. They're terribly done, but we don't really need long, do we?" she asked.

"No, ma'am." Alex's knees wanted to go weak with relief, but that was the height of stupid. He still had a cruise ship to hijack.

A flare on the horizon made John's head snap around. His motion beat *Enterprise's* three CIWS by a split second; then, the port and forward mounts started spitting fire on full auto. Their loud, never-ending burp made John grimace. He didn't know how surface officers ever got used to that sound. He'd hear it in his nightmares for *years*.

"What now?" McNally's whisper was raw.

"They shouldn't have anything left to—oh, *fuck*," John hissed. He knew what this had to be, knew that it had to be *Porbandar*, that McNally's decision not to shoot the shadowing Indian destroyer was about to bite them in the ass.

But there wasn't time to do anything but yank McNally down towards the deck, hoping like hell one of those BrahMos missiles didn't explode right in their faces. McNally cried out as John dragged him down; John hit his left knee hard on the metal grating of the deckplates, but he never noticed his coveralls ripping open.

Enterprise's CIWS mounts continued firing. *Fletcher's* one remaining mount opened up, too, as did *Belleau Wood*. But the cruiser was too far ahead of *Enterprise* for a good shot at the missiles aimed her way.

Her port side mount had a crossing shot at the incoming missiles, but CIWS' maximum range was only five nautical miles. The Brahmos missiles covered that distance in three-point-eight *seconds*. Even the CIWS max firing rate of 4,500 rounds per minute meant *Belleau Wood's* port mount fired just two hundred and eighty-five rounds at the missiles aimed toward *Enterprise*.

Fletcher, further aft, had an even worse crossing shot. The geometry just didn't work; she remained stationary, surrounded by survivors It was bad enough that Nancy Coleman didn't bother trying to intercept missiles aimed at *Enterprise* with her forward CIWS; she reserved that for anything aimed at her own destroyer. Her fourteen remaining Evolved Sea Sparrow Missiles shot out, reaching into the sky for last-ditch intercepts. *Belleau Wood* pumped six into the air, all they had left.

Enterprise trembled as John craned his neck, trying to catch a glimpse of what was happening. He didn't need a tactical plot to guess that most of the Indians' missiles were aimed at *Enterprise*; they'd sunk two destroyers, but an American aircraft carrier was the Holy Grail of warfare.

Missiles moved too fast for John to track, some exploding against the Indians' BrahMos, others streaking past them into the early-morning sky. The world around *Enterprise* turned orange, white, and then black with explosions. Time seemed to slow. *Enterprise's* port CIWS locked up, out of ammunition, and the bow one slewed wildly, trying to pick up a trio of missiles the port one missed. An ESSM from *Fletcher* picked off one, and the secondary explosion from the impact knocked another BrahMos into the sea. But the third made it through, slamming into the carrier's already-damaged port side.

Enterprise jumped, surging right and up before coming back on an even keel—and then she heeled hard to port, her stern going right as her bow went left. *Belleau Wood* shuddered as the tow line snapped tight under massive strain, but the cruiser's screws dug into the water and she took the load like a champ.

Sailors fled forward, taking shelter behind anything they could find, hiding from taut tow line as much as from the enemy missiles. That line could cut a sailor in half it if broke; it was a greater danger to the cruiser than the missiles aimed at the carrier. And all the missiles were aimed at the carrier. Watching *Belleau Wood* meant John missed seeing a missile home into *Enterprise's* superstructure, slamming into her bridge and ripping Captain Edwards and his bridge team into smithereens.

The shock wave raced out before the carrier's superstructure started to collapse and burn, slamming into John and Admiral McNally. It picked both up and flung them off the deck like children's toys. John grabbed for the liferail, missed by miles, and then cold water rushed up to hit him in the face and everything went black.

He never saw a third missile explode dead center on *Enterprise's* flight deck, causing her superstructure to topple port. It disappeared into a gaping hole with hundreds of sailors inside, including Admiral McNally's entire staff.

The fourth missile was almost superfluous, but it blasted into the carrier's stern near the waterline, ripping into her aft engine room and tearing three of *Enterprise's* four shafts apart. Her outboard starboard screw kept turning for a few seconds before the carrier's nuclear reactors went into emergency shutdown.

Lights flickered, battle lanterns powered on, and USS *Enterprise* went dark.

Chapter 35

Trust

Getting Gage up the ladder and out of the car was a production. Procedure assumed injured passengers would be lifted out by rescue ships, not at the pier. But Alex lacked a handy rescue ship, which meant he and Olson rigged a line to the pier and tied it around Gage's waist. When asked to help haul his subordinate in, Fowler wandered off, which left Steph to push from below while Alex and Olson supported as much of Gage's weight as they could. Gage wasn't *quite* unconscious, but he didn't provide a lot of help.

They were all out of breath by the time Gage sat on the pier, chest heaving harder than anyone else's. Hamilton half-dragged Fowler back to the group, and Alex only caught a whiff of their conversation.

"You will *certainly* get shot if you try finding a hole to hide in," Hamilton hissed, her hand tight on the politician's arm.

"You don't know that. I—"

"Sound like an American," she snapped. "Just like I do. And in case you missed it, they're *shooting* Americans down there."

Fowler whimpered. Hamilton sighed.

"Stick with me and keep your mouth shut, Mr. Secretary. It'll be fine," she said.

Chewing his lip, Alex ignored Fowler's limp-limbed pout. He wished he shared Hamilton's confidence; they still had to get on the cruise ship, a much more daunting task up close.

"You ever been on one of these?" Steph asked as they looked up at the giant wall of white metal.

And artwork. Couldn't forget the artwork; Norwegian Cruise Lines didn't ascribe to the subtle days of old. Colorful waves and buildings decorated the side of the ship, labeled *Norwegian Dawn*. Was that a good omen?

"Nope. My wife and I thought about it for our honeymoon, but we were poor ensigns and had a new kid. My mother-in-law's taken a couple of cruises, though."

"Me, neither."

"Looks like you're on point, Bradshaw." Alex glanced at the wounded enlisted sailor to his left. "What'cha got?"

"*Dawn's* an older ship, probably can carry about two thousand pax. You said they had about fifteen hundred to round up, right?" Bradshaw paused for Alex to nod. "They probably chartered her, so she's empty except the evacuees."

"What kind of security do they have?"

"Nothing that won't run screaming from a pair of handguns. They aren't armed." Bradshaw shrugged, and then winced. "The rest depends on how many French marines tag along."

"All right, then." Alex flashed his team a grin. "Let's do this thing. "Steph, Secretary Fowler, please help Mr. Gage."

Fowler's eyes widened, but much to Alex's surprise, he didn't argue. What *had* Hamilton said to him?

"I've got rear guard," Olson said, tucking her nine millimeter under her shirt.

Squaring his shoulders, Alex led their ragged group across the pier, his mind whirling with options. Be confident and try to bluff his way through? No, French marines wouldn't listen to an American, not today. That left the stereotypical clueless American.

Alex's heart pounded in his chest during the brief walk across the pier; all too soon, a French marine gestured with her rifle for them to stop.

"Who are you?" she asked in accented English.

"We're, uh, kind of lost." Alex swallowed, trying not to stare at the rifle. What the hell else should he say? Couldn't this marine—

"They told us they were taking us to the ship," Hamilton's fidget looked surprisingly genuine. "Is this the ship?"

The marine stared at Hamilton for a long moment and then relaxed. "Oui. Did you get separated from the group?"

"Yeah." Alex bobbed his head. "Two of us are hurt—do you have a doctor?"

"Of course we do!" The new voice sounded British; Alex's head snapped up. A ship's officer approached, scowling at the marines. "Come aboard, please. Tell me what happened."

"Someone shot me," Gage whispered as the officer led them up the brow.

No one dared smile when the French marines didn't follow. Alex just looked up, counting decks to the bridge.

Yeah. They could do this.

John never remembered hitting the water. Later, he realized how fortunate he was when the explosion toppling *Enterprise's* superstructure blew him outboard instead of towards the carrier's deck, but bobbing in water full of burning oil, screaming sailors, and metal fragments didn't make him feel lucky. His right shoulder didn't want to work right, and his steel-toed boots felt heavy enough to drag him down.

Splash! John flailed in surprise, twisting right as a large white canister hit the water. Another splashed into the water a few feet away, and then a third; turning to the ship, John watched one of *Enterprise's* sailors hitting the manual actuation on the starboard side life raft canisters, dumping them into the water as the ship burned around her.

Other figures raced to help as the first life raft inflated with an earsplitting *hiss.* The red raft erupted out of the white canister, automatically inflating. The covered raft was large enough to hold fifty people, and *Enterprise* carried 127 of them, enough for 120% of her crew.

One look at the burning carrier told John they wouldn't need that many. Gasping and spitting as a wave smacked him in the face, John started paddling towards the raft. Three strokes in, he almost ran into McNally.

"Oh God, oh God, oh God..." McNally looked intact but shocked, staring at *Enterprise* as she listed further to port. The hull creaked, and then a roaring series of explosions rocked the ship.

John tore his eyes away. "Come on, Admiral." Talking and treading water was hard; his right arm remained sluggish.

"God, what have I *done*?" McNally stared straight past him.

"Come *on*." John tugged the back of McNally's coveralls with his bum hand, pulling him towards the life raft. That made his shoulder throb in a funny way, but he needed the left arm for swimming. Luckily, McNally seemed to be a better swimmer than John, who didn't enjoy the pool on his best days.

McNally made it to the raft first, climbing in when John shoved him. Clambering in was tricky with boots full of water; John flopped in on his stomach and hissed when his shoulder popped. A burning flash of pain rewarded him rolling onto it, but it faded as John scooted away from the opening. Two more sailors crawled in, making the total in the raft nine. Wincing, John maneuvered towards the opening, peeking out.

Enterprise burned fiercely against the dawn, sailors peppering the water. Frantic figures raced around on *Belleau Wood's* stern, hacking at the massive towing hawser with axes to free it from the cruiser's stern capstans. John knew jack about towing and figured the line would snap before it dragged *Belleau Wood* down with *Enterprise*, but he couldn't blame Rosario for not wanting to find out.

Something burned forward on the cruiser, but the fire didn't look bad from John's angle. At least not sinking-kind-of-bad. He shivered. Then the tow line *cracked* and broke, sailors diving aside as it snaked viciously into the water. Someone screamed and never came up again.

Minutes or hours passed; *Enterprise* sank lower as more sailors abandoned her. John hoped like hell the rest of the staff got off, but he didn't see any familiar faces as the raft filled up. He stayed near the entry, pulling up anyone who needed help, while McNally slumped next to him, soaked and pale. John's shoulder hurt less. Was he in shock?

Red rafts dotted the landscape around the carrier, but John's was one of the closest and filled up fast. They were close enough to hear *Enterprise* groan again, steel shuddering and bending as the carrier rolled over on her port side, fires still burning as her bow rose into the air and her stern went down. John stared at *Enterprise's* red-painted bottom, bereft of words, watching as America's most famous ship slipped beneath the waves.

Someone swore. A few others wept; no one commented.

"What the hell is *Fletcher* doing?" one of the other sailors asked after several long minutes of silence. John turned to look at her; she was a chief petty officer, gray haired and wiry. "Ballsy."

John followed her gaze, leaning out the raft's opening. "Damn, Nancy," he whispered.

Seeing *Fletcher* was a relief, though. At least his actions—or his admiral's—hadn't killed his friend. The destroyer remained astern of *Enterprise*'s grave; she'd been back there to pick up *Kidd's* survivors, but now the destroyer crept forward into the waters around the survivors, tossing lines to the life rafts and towing them together. To his right, *Belleau Wood* turned to do the same, even as sailors fought that fire around her forward five inch gun.

Were there more enemies out there? Neither warship looked ready to run, but John could count. He knew their missile cells were dry. Did they dare stop to pick up survivors? Somewhere back along their track, *John Finn's* survivors remained in the water. Would that be John's fate?

McNally muttered something broken; John didn't ask him to repeat himself.

"*Porbander's* going down, Captain," Lieutenant Commander Attar reported. "And the jamming's stopped. Looks like it was her after all."

Nancy nodded. "Very well." She let out a slow breath, ice coating her spine. "I'm heading to the bridge."

She already watched *Enterprise*'s last moments from CIC. Could anything be worse? *Enterprise* was America's flagship—not officially, but in everyone's hearts, going all the way back to World War II. Nancy's feet carried her to the bridge without thought; she nodded mechanical greetings to sailors along the way without really seeing them. Two destroyers and a carrier. Forty percent of the strike group lost in less than three and a half hours.

And John. God, how was she going to explain this to Janet if he died? Or to *Alex*?

But she couldn't cry. There were sailors to rescue, and her ship remained in danger. Grief and worry would have to wait.

Bile rose in Nancy's throat; she pushed it down, opening the watertight door to the bridge and then dogging it down behind her. Commander Ying Mai turned to face her, worry creasing the shorter woman's face.

"Captain?" Ying asked.

"It's time to shift gears to search and rescue," Nancy shoved the cold feeling aside. Standing on the bridge meant she could see the sailors in the water, see the bright red life rafts peppering the sea. "Besides, it's not like we've got anything left to shoot, short of the five inch and CIWS."

"Yeah, and no one's in range for those." Ying's smile looked strained. "I don't know where we're going to put them all."

Enterprise was the third *Gerald R. Ford*-class carrier, which meant she carried a complement of fifteen hundred fewer sailors than the old *Nimitz*-class, but that was still four and a half *thousand* men and women. Nancy's destroyer sailed with barely three hundred. *Belleau Wood* was a touch bigger, but not by much. Would they even have enough deck space for everyone to stand?

Her throat grew tight. "That's assuming most of them survived." Counting the heads bobbing in the water was impossible, but it didn't seem enough. "I don't think that's going to be a problem."

"We'll still burst at the seams with *Kidd* and *Finn's* crew aboard, too. And that doesn't begin to figure how we'll *feed* them all."

"I know." Nancy stared at the horizon, searching for ideas. "But for now, we pick up everyone we can, starting with those not in life rafts."

"Aye, ma'am. We'll make it happen."

"Head down and supervise recovery ops," Nancy ordered. Was it cowardice or duty to stay on the bridge? "I'll take it up here."

Ying nodded and vanished, leaving Nancy with an exhausted bridge team. Had she really been thinking about potentially getting out of the Navy two days ago? Anything before the battle seemed out of another life.

No way was she leaving during a shooting war. Her sense of responsibility wouldn't let her.

Fletcher's bridge was unscathed. Somehow, Nancy's destroyer survived the fight with only slight damage aft and six casualties. Nancy's job was keep it that way.

"All right, ladies and gentlemen." She turned to face the watch team. "We've got fellow sailors in the water, so let's get to saving them."

"*Enterprise*, this is Strike Group Seven-Four, calling you on Surface Secure, over." Rear Admiral Marco Rodriquez was annoyed enough to make the call himself. His staff spent the last forty-five minutes trying to reach the *Enterprise* Strike Group while USS *Dudley W. Morton*—callsign "Mush"—cut holes in the water.

Rodriquez's new flagship strained and shivered as she worked her way past thirty-seven knots; it wasn't as fast as *Lionfish*, out in front by three miles, could manage, but it was the best *Morton* had. She was the second ship in the brand-new *Ernest E. Evans* class, commissioned just eighteen months ago and already on deployment.

Hell, her Combat Information Center even *smelled* new. Marco'd never been on a destroyer before, and he didn't know if they were *all* this cramped, but stuffing his staff into the space along with *Morton's* regular watch made even a submariner claustrophobic. Tanya looked right at home, but she'd commanded one of these things a few years ago.

Grace Hopper, *Morton's* slightly younger sister, steamed a thousand yards off her port side. Both destroyers carried more missiles than *O'Bannon*-class destroyers like *Fletcher*, not that it did Marco much good.

His navy was mean, and bigger than in decades—but that wasn't enough. The U.S. hadn't commenced such a naval buildup since the years leading up to World War II, but Marco didn't like that analogy. It invited too many fuckups. *As if what Jeff goddamned McNally pulled doesn't qualify*. He growled aloud, swore, and then cut off when the surface secure command circuit fizzed.

"Strike Group Seven-Four, this is *Belleau Wood*, over."

Marco sat up so fast he almost fell out of his chair. "Talk to me, *Belleau Wood*," he snapped. Marco knew proper comms discipline and didn't give a damn, even if it made *Morton's* TAO cringe.

"Seven-Four, *Belleau Wood* Actual. Update to last report to Seventh Fleet: *Enterprise* sunk. *Belleau Wood* and *Fletcher* recovering survivors. Can you relay, over?"

Marco jerked his foot off the pedal that keyed the microphone. "The fucking *fuck?*" He twisted to stare at Tanya. "They sunk *Enterprise*?"

"My God," she whispered, her face white.

"Seven-Four, did you copy my last, over?" *Belleau Wood's* captain said.

Marco stomped the pedal so hard his foot hurt. "Strike Group Seven-Four Actual copies and will relay." He swallowed. "*Belleau Wood*, I'm in route with two destroyers and six F-35s overhead. The F-35s will shoot at anything that shoots at you, over."

It was shitty ROE. Normal Rules of Engagement *shouldn't* apply; not after an Indian strike group just spanked—and sank!—multiple American warships. But no one wanted to stick his dick out, least of all Admiral Kristensen, Seventh Fleet's commander.

It was the middle of the night back home, which meant the decision makers were safe in bed while Marco reached for the short end of a very pointy stick. No one wanted to take responsibility for starting a war. Fuck, no one *wanted* another battle, Marco Rodriquez included. But that meant he—and his fighters—could only shoot at someone positively identified as having already shot at American ships.

"We'll be grateful for any help you can provide, Admiral." A pause. "We're going to need space for the survivors."

"We'll be there in about two hours, Captain," Marco promised. "Any other threats in the area? And how many missiles do you have left?"

"*Fletcher* sank the destroyer that took *Enterprise* out." The voice on the other end sounded grim; Marco didn't know jack about *Belleau Wood's* CO other than she was—obviously—a woman. "We're both Winchester on surface-to-air missiles. I've got eight bulldogs left."

"Roger." Marco licked his dry lips. "Hang in there, Captain. We're—"

"Strike Group Seven-Four, this is *Kansas*, over," another voice interjected.

"Tell me you have some good news for me, *Kansas*," Marco said, twisting to look at Tanya. "Weren't they up by Armistice Station?"

"Seven-Four, this is *Kansas*, negative," the male voice on the other end said. "French forces sank USNS *Amelia Earhart.* There appear to be no survivors, over."

Ice water dumped over his head would have been an ass-ton more pleasant. Silence reigned in *Morton's* CIC.

"Well, I will be dipped in horseshit," Marco said, not bothering to turn the microphone off. "Tell me you've reported that up to Seventh Fleet, son."

"Negative, Seven-Four. We just came up to comms depth, over."

Great. Marco got to share all the good news.

First, he sent *Kansas* deep again, telling Chris Kennedy to keep his godforsaken comms wire out and creep in close to Armistice Station. Whatever the fuck was going on over there, Marco couldn't do a goddamned thing, so *Kansas* would have to do the old sub thing: lurk and listen.

Marco just didn't have time to babysit *Kansas*. He'd have to trust Kennedy to do the right thing.

Chapter 36

Eye of the Storm

Cruise ships' medical centers weren't geared towards treating gunshot wounds, but Doctor Anjou swung into action, helping Gage to a table and kicking the rest of them out of the room.

The waiting area was small and covered in weird paintings, but Steph supposed paying passengers cared about that more than sailors going through the revolving door of the Navy's medical system did. She was used to bland, government-issue surroundings, but maybe paintings were nice? Cruise ships probably felt obligated to make things look expensive.

A red-headed nurse patched up Bradshaw's arm on an exam table to the right, leaving Steph, Alex, Olson, Fowler, and Admiral Hamilton at loose ends in the tiny waiting area. Bradshaw was surprisingly brave about it for a dude who complained about everything out of habit, but Steph figured today wasn't exactly normal. Maybe Bradshaw would go back to complaining tomorrow.

Suppressing her adrenaline was hard. Steph had enough energy to run a marathon, but she had to act normal. Scratch that; she was playing a scared civilian. They were lost little puppies, right? Tapping feet didn't fit with that image, but how could she stop herself when it felt like the gun tucked into her waistband got heavier with every moment?

Not like they dared speak of their plans. Not with the nurse and one of the ship's officers staring at them. But she still itched to get on with it, to storm the bridge with their whole two handguns.

God, this was such an awful plan. Too bad the safe one meant surrendering, which just wasn't in the Navy's DNA. Or Steph's. She'd rather wrestle a goddamned alligator, despite that kind of stupidity crippling one of her high school friends.

"Am I the only one tired enough to sleep for a week?" she asked after the silence wore on for far too long.

"Only you, Steph." Alex shook his head, smiling.

How the hell did the boss look so calm? Even Admiral Hamilton was twitchy and trying to hide it.

"We'll take good care of you. No need to worry," the officer said. "I'm Staff Captain Ricky Moreno, by the way. We'll get you rooms and fed. I can't help the barbaric way the French treated you, but it stops now that you're on board *Norwegian Dawn.*"

"Will those French Marines stay on the ship?" Hamilton asked, her eyes a touch too wide and her voice tight. *Damn, the admiral can act!* Steph thought. Hamilton was a bad ass.

"None, if we can help it." Moreno scowled. "We don't permit guns on board."

"That's...good to know." Hamilton's relief didn't seem feigned. Steph fought back a smile.

Then again, no guns was damned good news, wasn't it?

"Would you like me to show you to your rooms, now?" Moreno asked.

"I think we'd all prefer to hear Gage is all right, first," Alex said, barely hiding his disdain for the younger politician. Not that they didn't all despise the man. Except maybe Fowler. It was hard to tell with him doing his best impression of a lukewarm glass of milk.

Still, if the boss was a crap actor, he was still rock solid under pressure. Remembering her earlier opinions made Steph cringe. *Shame he's not a ship driver. I'd go to war with Alex any day.*

Were they at war? Steph didn't know. A French frigate sinking a U.S. Navy oiler was an indisputable act of war, not to mention the chaos here on Armistice Station and Jesse's death. *God*, she still hadn't processed that. She kept expecting Jesse to come around the corner with that same kind smile on his face, befuddled by Bradshaw and so eager to help.

Steph swallowed. Navy ships were attacked before—even captured—without the U.S. declaring war. Would this be another one of those times where the U.S. acted in the interests of the world and ignored dead sailors? Even combined with the deaths on *Earhart*, Jesse was just a statistic as far as governments were concerned.

"What do you think the politicians back home will make of this?" she asked without thinking. Hopefully, it was a safe question.

Olson snorted. "Make a hash out of things."

No one missed the glare Olson shot Fowler's way, but he just shrank into his chair and muttered under his breath.

"I think that's a question best left to history," Hamilton said. Was that a warning look?

Fortunately, Doctor Anjou emerged from the back room before Steph could shove her foot in her mouth. "Mr. Gage will be fine, but I do need to keep him under observation."

At least that'd keep Gage out of the line of fire.

"Thank you, Doctor," Alex said, then turned to Moreno. "I think we'll take those rooms now, Captain."

Smiling—was that reflex for these people, or what?—Moreno led them forward and into an elevator. Steph clutched her backpack and eyed the outlandish décor. She figured she could drive this beast if she had to, but her experience with cruise ships was all from the outside.

They lit up the night at sea like a freaking fireball, waltzing wherever they wanted and ignoring Navy ships. Did people really enjoy sailing on these things? Steph did envy the passengers their adult beverages, though. *Maybe I can have a drink before we hijack this thing. After would be a terrible idea.*

So would before, but hey, this was all crazy. At least the elevators seemed normal, if decorative. She figured she could hack them in two minutes flat, assuming they didn't have some super special software. Contemplating that served as an enjoyable distraction from how she'd left a bunch of belongings back on Armistice Station. No way would the French mail her clothes or her growing snow globe collection to Louisiana.

At least she had her laptop and tablet, but her best uniforms were back there, and the Navy wasn't in the habit of reimbursing officers for lost uniforms. Even if they hijacked the great white monstrosity instead of ending up as Prisoners of Not-War.

She turned to Alex. "You think the French will reimburse you for your scuba gear?"

"Not likely." He snorted. "My wife's going to murder me if I tell her I lost her anniversary present, too."

Steph laughed, hating the way it went high pitched. "What'd you get her?"

"A kickass necklace from Marinna's Diamonds."

"Ouch." Steph wasn't the biggest jewelry fan—what you could wear in uniform was limited, and she liked rings better than necklaces—but the stuff at Mariana's was nice. "Guess you comm—uh, *bosses*, make the big bucks, huh?"

"Not big enough to spend them twice." Alex's smile almost masked the way his eyes narrowed in warning.

Steph tried to shrug an apology as they exited the elevator on the tenth deck. Moreno led them forward again, producing room keys for three balcony rooms on the port side. These the staff captain handed over as they paired off, two to a room. Hamilton glowered as she accepted a key for herself and Fowler, but the admiral got to take that one for the team. No way did a lowly lieutenant commander have to room with a politician; she was happy to share with her boss. That left the two enlisted sailors together, which would keep the Navy from flipping out about fraternization.

Bradshaw seemed much more cheerful on painkillers, joking with Olson as they disappeared into their cabin. Alex thanked Captain Moreno, and then he shut their door, too.

"At least it'll be easy to tell when we get underway from a balcony?" Steph glanced around the room. It looked like a hotel room, just smaller, with two single beds, a couch, and a bunch of drawers. She expected bigger, what with the size of the ship. "Not sure these monsters announce underway like we do."

"Probably not." Alex stuffed his hands in his pockets, shoulders hunching for a moment. "Check to see if they locked us in, would you?"

Steph nodded. The door opened when she tried it, which made her grin. The hallway was empty except for a cruise ship employee with a vacuum. He waved. Steph smiled and waved back before closing the door. Being polite never hurt.

"Guess they bought it," she said.

"Yeah. Now all we have to do is wait." Alex snorted. "My favorite part."

She shrugged. "Better than getting shot at, I guess."

He laughed. "Barely!"

"The beacon is gone." Aida Ledoux's face screwed into a ferocious scowl. She punched three keys on Central's main control console, then hit two more so hard Jules feared they might break. "Even with a system restart, we cannot track it."

"What?" Jules snapped in French, again wishing Khare didn't speak his language. Or would just go away.

"You've lost the Americans. Well done." The Indian admiral smirked. "Meanwhile, *my* navy has sunk an American aircraft carrier."

"What?" Surprise tore the word out of him again; Jules spun to face Khare.

Khare's thousand watt smile could've powered the Eiffel Tower. "*Enterprise* went down a few minutes ago, joining their two destroyers. Our submarine is avenged."

"*Avenged*?" Jules' jaw wanted to dislocate. "You great fool, you may have started a war!"

"Says the man who ordered a U.S. Navy oiler sunk." Khare snorted. "And besides, they shot first."

"An aircraft carrier is not a lone ship, you *couillon*," Jules snarled, gritting his teeth. "Governments can—and have—negotiated settlements following single acts of madness. *Enterprise* is another story. I am a student of history. She is America's pride and joy."

Jules also enjoyed science fiction television and was not ignorant to how a certain segment of the population, one that cared little for the U.S. Navy in normal times, would hate the Indians for sinking *Enterprise*.

"Yes, and *my* nation sank her."

There was no reasoning with idiots. Sucking in a deep breath, Jules turned back to Ledoux. "Madame, please tell the cruise ship to depart. *Bretagne* will find the Americans when they run out of battery."

Putting Hamilton and Fowler on *Bretagne* also meant fewer explanations for the French, later—Jules figured his government could hold onto them for at least a few months, even if war didn't break out. But first he had to catch them, which was not supposed to be this hard.

"The car's batteries should die in two to four hours." Ledoux nodded. "I will signal *Norwegian Dawn*."

"Merci."

Jules ignored Ledoux using the bridge-to-bridge radio and called Camille on his phone. She picked up after two rings.

"The Americans uncoupled an outertube car. Their last bearing was three-two-seven at one nautical mile from Central. Get *Bretagne* underway and find them."

"What? How did they—"

"It does not matter," he cut in, struggling not to shout. "Find them."

Camille gulped. "Oui, mon Capitaine."

Jules slammed his phone down on the console.

Chapter 37

The Hunt

Bretagne took in all lines and was underway within fifteen minutes. Her crew, at battle stations since before the attack on *Amelia Earhart*, spun up the frigate's engines and engaged her controllable reversible pitch propellers within seconds of receiving the order. Commander Dubois and her team boarded *Bretagne*, with Camille stalking to the bridge while her marines formed a boarding party.

Commander Adrien Richard was a classmate from the École Navale, and like Jules and Camille, handpicked by Admiral Bernard. In fact, Camille recommended him; they were friends going back to their days at *La Baille*. Adrien understood what was at stake.

"The cruise ship is underway," he said as Camille came to his side. Adrien Richard was tall, lanky, and dark skinned, sitting easily in his chair on *Bretagne's* bridge. Camille could barely make his features out in the pre-dawn light, especially with *Norwegian Dawn's* bright lights blaring a few hundred yards away.

"Oui, I can see that." Camille glanced at the pier; *Bretagne* drifted away slowly, using her bow thruster instead of tugboats.

"She is between us and the Americans' last known bearing," Adrien said.

Camille scowled. "Can you get around her?" She knew the water was deep everywhere around the station. Depth would not constrain *Bretagne's* maneuvers.

"Not until I am clear of the platform."

"Very well." Camille had no authority here; Adrien was her equal in rank and she could only advise him. "Please hurry."

"Bien sûr."

John clambered up the net hanging from *Belleau Wood's* starboard side, favoring his numb right arm. He didn't think it was broken, but it still felt off; being waterlogged didn't help. At least it wasn't cold. Even at night, the water in the Strait was around eighty degrees Fahrenheit. That could cause hypothermia over days, but *Enterprise* went down less than an hour earlier.

Belleau Wood cast off the life raft after the survivors climbed aboard, leaving it in the water for those who bobbed in life vests or clung to floating debris. The cruiser moved silently through the water as she turned towards the next life raft. How many were there? John's eyes were too tired to count.

"Admiral?" He turned to the man at his side.

McNally stood hunched over, arms crossed and expression blank. His wet brown hair pasted to his forehead while he stared out to sea, away from the swarm of survivors.

John elbowed him gently. "Admiral?"

McNally only swallowed.

"Admiral McNally!" The lieutenant in charge of the recovery effort must've heard John, and she bounded over, her youthful eyes old. The nametape on her uniform read 'Hunt,' and her enthusiasm was exhausting. "Welcome aboard. I'll call the captain and let her know you're here. We can get you set up in CIC right away."

Slowly, McNally turned to face Lieutenant Hunt, his eyes still dull. The silence stretched on until John cleared his throat.

"I think the admiral might need somewhere quiet to think," John said. "You mind sending us up to the wardroom or something?"

"I'll take you to the captain's in port cabin, sir." Hunt's eyes flicked between them; was that contempt directed at McNally? "I'll let the captain know you're there."

John and McNally followed Hunt inside the skin of the ship, squeezing through passageways crowded with soaked sailors. *Belleau Wood's* crew guided the newcomers to every space available; if the cruiser's decks were full, the interior was far worse. Officers from *Kidd* and *Enterprise* spilled out of the wardroom, most as shell-shocked as John felt.

Finally, Hunt opened the door to the captain's in port cabin. The *Bull Run*-class cruisers, of which *Belleau Wood* was the second built, kept the traditional in port and at sea cabins. But most cruiser

COs left the second cabin empty, unless an embarked flag officer occupied it.

John watched his boss sink onto the bed, staring at a painting of the Battle of Belleau Wood. Part of him wanted to shake McNally, but what was the use? All *John* wanted was a good, long sleep, but there were sailors in the water and enemies out there. Did they have anything left to shoot? Captain Rosario would know.

"You want me to take care of things, Admiral?" he asked.

McNally didn't answer. Sighing, John ducked back out into the passageway and ran right into Captain Julia Rosario.

She looked less composed than he remembered. Half Julia's red hair escaped her braid, and the circles under her green eyes said she'd been up as long as John had. But those same eyes were still sharp, despite the obvious fatigue.

"I'm sorry about *Enterprise*," she said. "Did Ernest get off?" she added, referring to Captain Edwards.

"I wish I knew." John swallowed. "The admiral and I were blown overboard when that last missile hit."

"Missil*es*." Julia grimaced. "We didn't have enough left to stop them. I'm sorry."

"It's not your fault. I'm not sure who to blame, other than the Indians—and maybe us, shooting that *Kilo*—but it's sure as hell not yours." Words rarely failed John, but his tired brain didn't like the truth. "Speaking of blame...the admiral's out of it. You're in command, unless Ernest shows up."

Captains Rosario and Edwards were both senior to John, and it made more sense to put a surface warfare officer in command now that they didn't have a carrier.

Julia didn't smile. "I'm not sure I want command of this shit show," she half-whispered.

"You've already done all the hard parts. At least now you'll get credit." Saying anything more was tantamount to insulting his boss, which John couldn't quite do. Even if McNally was out of his depth from the start.

"For now, let's concentrate on getting the survivors out of the water," she said. "I need someone to coordinate that—can you help?"

"Bet your ass I can." John smiled. "You just tell me what you need."

"My little sister's on *Belleau Wood*, Lieutenant Commander Hunt said. The XO stood next to Master Chief Casey on the far side of the attack center, away from where Kennedy paced like a rabid bear.

"At least she's still afloat." Casey cringed. "Sorry, ma'am. That came out wrong."

"Beats being on one of the destroyers. Or *Enterprise*."

That news shocked everyone on board *Kansas*. The last time the U.S. lost an aircraft carrier at sea was the Second World War. That kind of thing just didn't *happen* to the best Navy in the world. Sure, the last two decades hadn't been the Navy's finest, and other nations' navies crept upwards in both skill and number of platforms, but the U.S. Navy was still the best.

"Fuck," Casey whispered. "This has been a shit day for the skimmers."

"Yeah. No way is *Earhart* plus the Indian attack on *Enterprise* CSG a coincidence." Hunt shook her head. "And what does Armistice Station dropping offline before *any* of this have to do with things?"

"Good question, XO." Pity the captain wasn't interested in the answer.

"Talk to me, sonar," Kennedy commanded, stopping pacing.

"Got a couple of ships moving, sir," Senior Chief Salli replied. "One sounds like a cruise ship, moving on azipods. Other has traditional screws with a high RPM, might be a warship. System's still chewing on IDs."

Kennedy scowled. "Range to Armistice Station?"

"Nine thousand yards from station center," Sue replied. "About seven thousand from the end of the nearest platform."

Kennedy wheeled to glare at his hated navigator. "I wasn't asking for *our* range, Nav. I can read a plot." He sneered. "I wanted *their* range from the station. Sonar?"

"Cruise ship, tentatively ID'd as *Dawn* class bears three-five-five from the station at about three thousand yards and opening. Possible military contact bears zero-four-seven, range about one thousand and moving from right to left," Salli replied after a moment. "Tentative ID *Aquitaine*-class FREMM frigate, probably D650, *Bretagne*."

"Thank you, sonar." Kennedy paused to shoot a glare at Sue, who didn't wilt. Good on her. Then Kennedy turned to Hunt. "You think we've found our shooter, XO? French frigate, out near where *Earhart* got hit..."

"Could be, sir," Hunt replied. "We're mighty thin on evidence, though."

"*Earhart* reported being struck by French missiles. You see anyone else who could do the shooting around here?"

"The Block 2 Exocet has a range of almost forty nautical miles." Hunt chewed her lip. "Have anything else in that range, sonar?"

"Bunch of merchants avoiding Armistice Station like the plague," Salli replied. "Nothing moving that sounds military."

Casey frowned. Sitting doggo was still the best way to hide from sonar; subs couldn't hear things that didn't make waves. "Could be a sub, sir. Better deniability if no one saw who shot *Earhart*."

"Sure, but why use a sub if your frigate is already here?" Kennedy asked. "No, I think *Bretagne* is our target."

"Target, sir?" Casey asked as Hunt jumped. The poor XO just didn't know the captain the way he did. Casey expected this from the moment Salli identified that damned frigate.

"We can't let the French get away with sinking a Navy oiler and killing Americans." Kennedy crossed his arms. "We know what happened. We have to strike back."

Hunt's jaw dropped. "Captain, Admiral Rodriquez's orders were—"

"My orders from Admiral Rodriquez tell me to use my best judgment," Kennedy said, almost mildly. "I didn't take you for a coward, XO."

Fuck. Casey watched Hunt's back straighten, watched her face go red. Everyone else in the attack center turned away, remembering the last time their captain and XO disagreed on something. Kennedy *wanted* to shoot that Neyk; the fact that *Kansas'* old XO hadn't let him saved his career.

Not that it mattered in the grand scheme of things—the Neyk got sunk, civilians died, and now *Kansas* didn't have an XO who would stand up to the boss.

Casey's heart sank as Hunt shot back: "I'm no coward, Captain."

"Captain, I recommend caution." Casey stepped forward. "There's a lot of ways a torpedo shot can go wrong around here—if one hits the station, we could kill thousands. Or worse."

No way could he talk Kennedy out of avenging *Earhart*; five minutes under the captain taught Casey that. But maybe he could insert enough common sense that the idiot didn't make this worse.

God help us if we put two fish into the biggest underwater station in the world. Casey shivered. His short-lived liberty on Armistice Station had been full of people: merchants, sailors, drunks, vacationers. The idea of shooting holes in those thousands made his stomach heave.

"Good point, COB." Kennedy's smile turned blazing. "Nav, put us between the frigate and the station."

"Nav, aye." Sue shot Casey an unhappy look, but what could they do?

"There is nothing here." Commander Adrien Richard wore a scowl that matched Camille's as *Bretagne* crept ahead, searchlights scanning the water. They stood together on the frigate's starboard bridge wing, eyes straining into the dark. "No mini-sub—or, what did you call it?"

"Outertube car." Camille scowled. "Their beacon indicated they were on this bearing before *someone* disabled it."

Bad enough that Alex Coleman outfoxed her back on *Kansas*. Camille might forgive that, assuming she could capture him—and his annoying companions. She was certain her country would give them back after America was suitably embarrassed, but U.S. Navy captives would enhance that humiliation. So far, France (and India, alas) captured Armistice Station and exiled the troublesome Americans and their allies. Sinking the supply ship was necessary to stop Coleman and the others from escaping—but now they could not even find them!

"They must have doubled back." Adrien shrugged. "Or submerged. Sonar conditions are far from ideal when I cannot deploy CAPTAS."

"Yes, I am aware." Camille glowered. She understood that surface ships' sonar capability suffered from being *on* the ocean rather than in it. *Bretagne's* CAPTAS-4 Variable Depth Sonar dual-tow array was a NATO system, designed to survey 360 degrees out to over 70 nautical miles. Exercises against ships equipped with that VDS were a nightmare for French submarines.

But *Bretagne* was too close to Armistice Station to stream CAPTAS. The chance of the array getting caught on a platform was too high; moving further from the station nixed their chance of finding the Americans.

"Perhaps conditions will improve once the cruise ship departs," Adrien offered.

Camille hissed out a swear. "Perhaps."

"Excusez-moi." Adrien went back inside the bridge, doubtless to avoid from the storm clouds gathering in Camille's heart. She wanted to scream. How could a handful of Americans outsmart them like this? Where had they *gone*?

She transferred her glare to where *Norwegian Dawn* crossed *Bretagne's* bow at a range of one nautical mile. At least *those* Americans were out of play. Her country would transport them to Madagascar, a three-day journey away. The diplomatic corps would handle the rest.

If not...there would be war.

Camille bared her teeth. It was time the French proved themselves a world power again.

Chapter 38

Shell Shock

Destroyers didn't have a lot of outside phone lines, and when you tooled around in a carrier's wake, the CVN took up most of the satellite bandwidth, limiting them still further.

Not now.

"We've got to go back for *Finn's* people," Commander Nancy Coleman said more than an hour after *Enterprise* sank. She finally left the bridge for her stateroom, staring at the bed while she rubbed her eyes. It was 8:45 A.M., local time. *Enterprise* Strike Group entered the SOM almost ten hours earlier, but it felt like a lifetime.

Nancy hadn't slept in twenty-six hours, and her eyes burned like someone poured acid in them. Downing an energy drink just made her jumpy, but there was no time to sleep.

"I know," Julia Rosario replied, her voice scratchy. "At least *Tripoli's* fighters scared the Indians off."

The shooting was over. Nancy's feelings on that were uncertain; part of her wanted those fighters to sink the goddamned Indian carrier. To hell with de-escalation. Those bastards killed Americans, and she wanted their blood.

But the Indians had plenty of SAMs left, and they retreated when threatened. *Tripoli's* fighters didn't have enough gas to linger, and the five left from *Enterprise*'s air wing had nowhere to land. Since they weren't Vertical Take Off and Landing capable and lacked the fuel to get to land, those fighters had to ditch in the water, which they'd done thirty minutes ago. *Fletcher's* small boats rescued the pilots, and now *Fletcher* and *Belleau Wood* were underway again, bursting at the seams with survivors.

"Yeah. I'll take what we can get." Nancy shot another look at her bed, wondering if she'd sleep that night. The longest she ever stayed up was thirty-seven hours, back in her division officer days. Captains weren't supposed to break those records.

"Same." Julia's sigh was audible. "We've got one hour until *Morton* and *Grace Hopper* show up. Can your crew hold it together until then?"

"You bet we can, ma'am." A smile tugged at Nancy's lips. "We've taken the worst they can throw at us and we're still here."

"Dancing right on the ragged edge." Julia laughed, but Nancy could hear her exhaustion. *If* I'm *tired, she's got to feel run over by a two-ton rhinoceros.* Even an idiot could tell McNally froze up and left the fight in Julia's hands. Thank God she'd been up to it.

"Did you recover the admiral?" she asked, not sure if she wanted McNally alive to face the music or dead from his own mistakes.

"Yeah. Captain Dalton, too."

Nancy could breathe again. Blinking back tears, she sucked in a ragged breath before she realized how ominous the silence on the other end of the phone was. "Is there something I need to know?"

"The admiral's out of it, Nancy. Glazed over and useless as a dead fish." Julia groaned. "Dalton's not a bad egg for a sub guy; I've got him organizing and counting survivors."

"I know him. He's a good guy, not in the same league as Admiral McMicromanager."

Julia's cough sounded suspiciously like a laugh. "Remind me not to call him that to his face."

"I'm sure you're more diplomatic than that."

"Not right now, I'm not!" Julia's humor crackled out with a burst of static. "Not enough sleep and too much anger."

"Fucking A." Nancy usually tried not to swear at senior officers, but a captain wasn't *that* much more senior to a commander, particularly after surviving that battle together.

"Frankly, I'm ready to turn this shitshow over to someone more senior, but not someone who might get the rest of us killed, if you know what I mean."

"I'll back you to the hilt, ma'am," Nancy promised. "Anyone with sense will. John included."

"Here's hoping the Navy has an outbreak of common sense, then."

"We're underway." Maria Vasquez left the balcony, returning to the suite—no, *Garden Villa*—she shared with Pam and Cassie, the two older women she'd accidentally befriended.

The suite's opulence—complete with a grand *piano!*—drove her to incandescent rage. If this was the French way of apologizing for Jesse's death, Maria preferred to shoot the fools herself. Pam needed fifteen minutes to convince Maria to wash Jesse's blood off her hands; that done, she *would've* taken a shower if she had a change of clothes. But she didn't, because her dumb self volunteered to walk around the station with nothing but the clothes on her back.

Her clothes were back in the Hilton, and the bag containing her personal phone, tablet, and whatever else she'd packed in the dark was probably back in the Naval Detachment office. Thinking of that made her think of her admiral, and of the others. Would she ever know what happened to them? Maria swallowed.

"Hopefully *without* those French bastards," Pam said, seated at the piano. She didn't play it, just glared at the music.

"If our luck changes, sure." Maria sighed.

"You hear anything from your boss, sweetie?" Cassie asked.

Normally, Maria would bite the head off anyone who called her that, but she liked Cassie. Neither gaudily dressed old woman was the sort Maria would usually befriend ...but they kept her sane. And safe.

"No." She didn't want to say how much that worried her. "We'll be out of range of Armistice Station's cell service, soon, anyway."

"So, call her, silly."

"Aides don't call their admirals just because they're nervous." Maria tried not to swallow, not to admit she was terrified Admiral Hamilton was dead...or worse.

Pam arched an eyebrow. "Are you saying there's *anything* normal about this situation?"

"No."

"Then I think the old rules go out the window. Call the woman, sweetheart. It'll be okay."

Maria swallowed, then nodded. Call or text? Texting might not get noticed if the admiral was in trouble, so she opted for that, typing out a quick *Cruise ship underway. All okay on your end?*

The answer came lightning fast: *In a stateroom on deck 10. Port side.* A pause as Maria gaped. *10630.*

"What the...?" she whispered.

"Everything okay?" Cassie asked. Maria ignored her as Hamilton continued:

Come down to chat? Seems quiet.

"I...I need to go down to deck 10." Maria typed *okay* then slid her phone into her pocket. "Do you think the elevators work?"

"They offered us champagne earlier. I think they're trying to treat this like a normal cruise." Pam snickered. "Bet the crew won't stop you. Tell 'em your boyfriend's down there."

Cassie grinned. "Or girlfriend."

"I don't know what normal cruises look like." Maria shrugged. "My underways were all underwater, in a metal tube full of seamen."

Both women laughed. "Then grab a drink on your way down," Pam said. "No one will pay you mind."

Swallowing, Maria left the room—and then followed their advice when she passed a bar on deck 13 and the bartender offered her champagne. Unsure whether she should drink it or not, Maria clutched the plastic champagne glass until she reached room 10630. She knocked.

Admiral Hamilton opened the door, with circles under her eyes and her hair a mess. Yet she grinned and ushered Maria into a stateroom much smaller than the suite on deck 14. Secretary Fowler sat off to one side, watching a muted television. Hamilton gestured for Maria to follow her out onto the balcony. Was that a splatter of blood on her clothes?

"Are you all right?" Hamilton eyed the blood on Maria's shirt, too. *Jesse's blood.* She gulped.

"Yeah. I mean, yes, ma'am. I'm okay. This isn't mine."

"I think we can waive the formality a bit, Maria." The ever-by-the-book admiral sighed. "Today's been a day."

"Tell me about it." Maria glanced around, finding a table to put the champagne down on. No way was she drinking in front of her admiral. "How...how did you end up here, ma'am?"

Asking if Hamilton and the others got rounded up just wasn't diplomatic, but Hamilton got the hint. She snorted.

"Commander Coleman's *bright* idea." She rolled her eyes. "We'll see how that works out."

"Do I want to know?"

"You probably need to," Hamilton said. "We're going to...well, *borrow* the ship."

"*What?*"

Hamilton explained.

"Range?" Kennedy demanded.

"Twenty-four hundred yards to the frigate, still moving from left to right, sir," Salli replied. "Real slow, though. Barely making way. Looks like they're hunting for something."

"Very well." The way Kennedy stood in the middle of control, hands on his hips and eyes gleaming made Master Chief Casey's chest tight. He'd seen this before, seen the heroic pose and the glaring overconfidence. He wanted to smack that smirk right off his captain's face. "Battle stations."

Fuck, it was real. Sailors raced to take their stations as the bonging of the general alarm filled the hull—there was no silent call to battle stations, not with Kennedy's dander up. Worse, he couldn't be sure Kennedy was *wrong*. If those French bastards shot up *Earhart*, they sure as shit deserved to eat a fish or two. Anyway, tactics weren't a master chief's job, and strategy sure as hell wasn't, either. But he could still do his best to mitigate the clusterfuck.

"If that frigate's listening with even half an ear, Captain, they're gonna hear us," Casey said.

Kennedy twisted to glare at him, and then blinked. "They probably aren't paying attention, but that's no reason to be sloppy. Excellent point, COB." He grinned and leaned into the intercom. "Maneuvering, Captain, rig for silent running."

"Rig for silent running, Maneuvering, aye," the Engineering Officer's disembodied voice replied.

"Firing point procedures, tubes one and two, sierra—*track* 1098." Kennedy's grin gave way to a scowl. For once, Casey agreed with him; they were all still getting used to that blasted combat systems upgrade. It was nice and dandy to do things more efficiently, but did the stupid thing have to change the way they labeled contacts?

"Solutions set," Weps replied a moment later.

"Solutions checked!" Hunt sounded almost as gung-ho as Kennedy. Lord, what did she have to prove?

"Very well." Kennedy struck that damned pose again; Casey hid his scowl by glancing at the combination of helmsman and planesman they called a pilot. *What an old codger I am, missing the* Los Angeles-*class boats.*

Was his dislike for Kennedy clouding his judgment?

"Captain, if we sink a French warship, they'll consider it an act of war," Sue said.

"One *they* committed when they sank *Earhart*," Kennedy snapped.

"Sir, we don't know for certain that *Bretagne*—"

"We don't have to." Kennedy rolled his eyes without even looking up from the plot. "France took the first shot. What happens next is their fault."

Sue swallowed. "Captain, I strongly recommend reaching out to Admiral Rodriquez for orders."

"Your recommendation is noted." Finally, Kennedy turned his glare on Sue, who flinched but stood her ground. "You have your orders, Nav. Can you follow them, or do I have to relieve you?"

Silence fell like a cold curtain. Kennedy's knuckles were white, his fingers clutching the firing key like a grenade pin. No way would anyone hide it this time.

"I'll do my job, sir." Sue's glare put a kiss of death on her career; Casey was sure she didn't care.

"That's damned good to know." Kennedy leaned over the plot, eyes gleaming. "Make tubes one and two ready in all respects, including opening the outer doors."

Striding over to the weapons corner, Commander Kennedy inserted the firing key.

"Key is green."

Chapter 39

Integrity

The room had a coffee maker, which meant *some*thing was right in the world.

"Can you get online?" he asked Steph, sipping at a chocolate-something flavored blend. Chocolate coffee wasn't Alex's thing, but now that the adrenaline wore off, his body screamed for caffeine.

"Not without a credit card." She scowled. "Stupid thing asks for our room number, then tells me we have to set up an onboard account."

"Well, that's one way to keep the news from getting out." Alex sighed. "Smart, when you get down to it. Give the evacuees all the food and alcohol they want, but don't let them get online. Phones won't work in the middle of the ocean, so *bam!* Your secret is safe."

"Don't start sounding admiring now, boss."

"Admiring their tactics doesn't mean I agree with their motives." Alex opened the glass door leading to the balcony, mainly to hide the way his hands wanted to shake. He stared out into the lightening sky. "We're underway."

"Fucking finally." Steph came out to stand next to him. "Bang on zero-five-hundred, too. These cruise line guys know how to keep time."

"Sooner's better than later. That frigate's still searching for us." Alex jerked his chin towards *Bretagne*. The French frigate was further from Armistice Station, about two miles off *Dawn's* starboard side, opening the range with the station so she could use sonar. Like most underwater stations, Armistice Station frowned on anyone using active sonar—even the low-frequency rig the FREMMs carried. It scared off fish and gave people headaches.

"You think they'll catch on?"

"Maybe." Would it matter? Alex couldn't say. Steph clearly didn't want to speculate, so he kept his mouth shut. Knowing what they were about to do was nerve-racking enough. "I'm fucking crazy," he whispered.

Steph laughed. "What, for deciding to hijack this great white shark?"

"The list is admittedly long, but that *does* come to mind," he replied, his heart hammering in his throat.

"Best of a bunch of bad options." Steph shrugged. "Wish I'd thought of it."

A knock on the door made Alex jump, but he squared his shoulders, slipped past Steph, and strode over to open it. Admiral Hamilton stood there, scowling, with Maria Vasquez and Petty Officer Olson at her back. Vasquez held a plastic champagne flute, twisting it between her fingers.

Blinking, Alex stood back to let them in, shutting the door behind the trio.

"Where's Bradshaw?" he asked.

"Politician-sitting." Hamilton's frown deepened.

Olson, however, grinned. "He's high as a goddamned kite. Pity they're not sharing those meds, sir."

"Behave yourself." Alex shook his head when she laughed, gesturing the newcomers to sit down wherever they could. The two single beds plus the couch were spacious, and the smell of the sea drifting in from the open balcony was almost comforting. "I'm glad to see you're all right," he said to Maria.

"I'm sorry about Jesse," she whispered. "I couldn't..."

"It's not your fault." Alex didn't mention that it wouldn't matter if it *was*. They were in this together, and another friendly—and competent—face was welcome.

"All right, Commander," Hamilton said after a pregnant moment of silence. "This is your crazy plan. When do you want to move?"

"Depends on how far we get from that frigate," Alex replied, gesturing towards the still-open balcony door. "Last thing we want is the crew calling for help."

Hamilton's eyes narrowed. "Then can do that no matter how far away we are."

"Yeah, but so can we," Alex replied. "Look, whatever else is true, they wanted Americans—and our friends—gone from Armistice

Station. But they don't want us dead. If they did, no one would be here—we'd be in body bags. No way will they start a shooting war over a cruise ship full of civilians. All we need is to be close enough to some U.S. Navy warship that it calls their bluff."

"I think you're—"

Suddenly, the deck under their feet rolled right, and *Dawn* quivered as she picked up speed.

"What the hell?"

"Low-frequency sonar contact! Submerged contact bearing two-five-two, range one nautical mile!" *Bretagne's* tactical officer's voice rose over the speaker from the combat information center.

Camille's head snapped around, her jaw dropping as she stared at the bridge speaker. That was—

"Ahead flank!" Commander Richard snapped. "Right thirty degrees rudder!"

Bretagne's helmsman threw the wheel over, and the frigate shook as her screws bit into the water. However, her maximum speed using her electric motors was only eighteen knots. Faster than that required clutching in her gas turbine engines, and even a nuclear-trained submariner knew starting those would take too long.

"What kind of submarine?" she asked.

"Tentative identification American *Virginia*-class!" the tactical officer replied. "I have—I have transients! Torpedo in the water! Two torpedoes bearing two-four-three!"

"Action stations!" Richard ordered. "Notify the cruise ship!"

Camille froze. She could do nothing. She was a passenger on a ship she did not know—her knowledge was intelligence and submarines, and not in that order. "Why are they shooting?"

"Probably because we sank *their* ship." Richards twisted to glare at her. He turned away before Camille could respond, ordering: "Shift your rudder!"

One mile. One mile was not far enough. Usually it was Camille on the submarine targeting the surface ship, and as challenging as the *Aquitaine*-class frigates were, they were never a match for *Barracuda*. An American *Virginia*-class was louder and slower, but their Mark 48 CBASS torpedoes were still faster than *Bretagne*.

And they would crack the frigate open like an egg.

Throat tight, Camille stumbled a step closer to the door leading to the bridge wing. It was open; *Bretagne's* crew, still rushing to action stations, paid it no mind. She should close it.

"Range to torpedo?" Richards asked. His round face was pale and eyes wide; he could do the math, too.

Bretagne's speed reached eighteen knots. Below decks, her engineers raced to start and clutch in her gas turbine engines, but they needed another two minutes.

"Less than half a mile!"

Richard's brown eyes met Camille's green.

"Brace for impact!" Richard said; a sailor repeated it over *Bretagne's* general announcing system. Camille shook her head, searching for words, stepping closer to that open door.

The bridge speaker crackled. "Captain, Sonar, American submarine identified as *Kansas*."

"*Kansas*?" Camille spat, her jaw dropping. "Are you *kidding* me?"

The explosion rattled the glass of the balcony door, shuddering across *Dawn* like a tidal wave. Maria Vasquez dropped her champagne glass; Hamilton jumped to her feet and stared.

Alex, closest to the balcony, watched as a giant waterspout engulfed FNS *Bretagne*'s starboard side. The frigate's midsection leapt out of the water, arcing like a knuckle bent the wrong way. Then *Bretagne* slammed back down, keel broken, bow and stern each pointing to the sky.

"Holy fuck, someone just ate a torpedo," Steph said.

"The question is *whose*." Hamilton's voice was iron, her eyes cold.

"Who cares?" Alex shrugged when everyone turned to glare at him. "The problem frigate's gone. Let's move."

"And ignore the shooting war that might've just started?" Hamilton crossed her arms.

Alex met her furious gaze. "You think you can do anything about that right now, Admiral?"

She didn't answer; Alex resisted the stupid urge to say more. One last glance at *Bretagne* showed both bow and stern sinking rapidly. Steph was right—nothing but a torpedo shot would do that. Alex remembered a SINKEX back in his early days on *Kansas*, where one CBASS torpedo broke a decommissioned *Ticonderoga*-class cruiser right in half. *Bretagne*, though newer, fared no better.

They were too far away to see sailors jumping into the water, but Alex knew they would be. Swallowing, he forced himself to turn away. SINKEX targets were empty. Frigates like *Bretagne* carried crews of around 150. How many were already dead?

Should he not care because their friends shot at *him* and his people recently? The chaotic mix of emotions left Alex dizzy; he shook his head to clear it.

"Come on. Everyone else on this ship will be staring, too. No time like the present to take the bridge."

No one argued. Alex almost wished they would.

"One good hit, Captain." Senior Chief Salli's shoulders slumped; Casey understood how she felt.

Lacking something better to do, he walked over to the sonar consoles, grabbed a spare headset, and took a listen. Sure enough, the sounds of implosions, hull popping, and onrushing water greeted his ears. He remembered the latter two from the cruiser *Kansas* sunk in SINKEX 2036. But her watertight doors had been open to ease the flow of water—*Bretagne's* weren't. That caused the implosions, bulkheads giving way to water pressure and pulverizing everyone inside.

"Fuck me," he whispered.

Salli nodded, her eyes flicking to Kennedy. Their captain still stood in the middle of control like some goddamned action star, glowing with pride.

"She's going down." Casey straightened. There was nothing left to say.

"Good job, everyone." Kennedy beamed. "Now, maybe we can reach our people on Armistice Station. I'm sure Admiral Hamilton will be glad to hear from friends."

"Not once she fucking hears about this," Salli muttered.

Casey cleared his throat, heading over to stand next to Kennedy. "Captain, I think we should probably also report into Admiral Rodriquez." Lord only knew how the bombastic admiral would take this news. Hell, maybe he'd cheer.

Maybe he'd fire this glory-hungry son of a bitch before he killed anyone else.

"Obviously." Kennedy turned to Sue, still smiling. "Open the range to the station by another four thousand yards and stream the comms wire."

"Officer of the Deck, aye," she replied, and then hesitated. "Sir, should we help with search and rescue?"

Kennedy waved a hand. "I think Armistice Station can handle that. They've got more resources."

"You want to go up for a look-see and make sure, sir?" Casey suggested.

"Good call, COB. We'll snap some old-fashioned periscope pictures while we're at it." Kennedy grinned. "OOD, periscope depth."

"OOD, aye." Sue's grimace spoke volumes, but she conned *Kansas* up to the ideal depth without objection. Casey wanted to let the beleaguered navigator know she wasn't alone in thinking Kennedy was fucking crazy, but he was the goddamned Chief of the Boat. COBs didn't breach discipline, and Kennedy wasn't entirely wrong. The asshat just wasn't really right, either.

Casey watched with numb horror as *Kansas'* Modular Panoramic Photonics Mast breached the surface. Calling it "periscope depth" was a nod to the rest of the submarine force. The *Virginias* were the most numerous class of attack submarine in the USN, and their always-up mast replaced the traditional periscope.

However, even the newest version of the MPPM liked to break if you drove too fast, so Sue reduced speed to five knots before nudging *Kansas* up those last few feet.

The image of a dying frigate filled the viewscreen. Casey managed not to comment as Kennedy used the touchscreen to snap a slew of pictures like he was Mush goddamned Morton.

Then *Kansas* returned to the deep and streamed her comms wire, securing from battle stations while Kennedy got on the radio to check in.

Only then did Sue turn the watch over to her relief and join Casey in the corner. "This is crazy, COB," she whispered.

"You fucking think?"

She bit her lip. "Did we just start a war?"

"Fuck if I know, ma'am." Casey shrugged. "Wonder if it's too late to drop my papers and fucking retire?"

Dawn's bridge was on deck eleven. No one stopped them from stepping off the elevator on that deck—hell, there were cabins there! Alex hadn't expected that. He led his fellows forward as fast as he dared, seeing no security other than a locked door.

It had a keypad. Damn. The door looked thick, too, like the bulletproof ones they used on airplanes.

"I got it, boss." Steph grinned, gesturing with her tablet and handing over her gun. Alex took it before Maria or Hamilton could volunteer; Olson already had the door covered with her nine-millimeter, but handing any admiral a weapon still gave him the heebie-jeebies.

Minutes ticked by; Hamilton's glare burned into his back while Maria fidgeted. Alex fought the urge to pace, wishing for something to chew on while his heart pounded in his chest. He twisted to look at the admiral, who narrowed her eyes.

"You want to move a bit further back, ma'am?" he asked. "I don't think these guys are armed, but Navy'll have my ass if something happens to you."

She snorted. "That occurs to you *now*? I'll be fine, thanks."

So much for that. Alex shrugged and glanced at Steph. She answered his wordless plea with a groan.

"Yeah, I'm just about there. My program should—got it! Bam." Steph grinned as a *click* came from the lock. "Let's do it."

She grabbed the gun and shoved her tablet into his hands. Alex's jaw dropped as he fumbled it, but there was no time to argue. "Olson, you're up."

Olson was the only one qualified for this boarding team type horseshit. She opened the door with one hand, gun already up, bursting into the bridge with Steph on her heels. Alex followed them, his eyes sweeping left and right. Floor-to-ceiling windows encased the bridge, with a pair of seats dead center and navigation tables in the back. It was wider than *Kansas*' full beam, dwarfing the attack centers he conned submarines from. But the number of people on watch was far smaller—one helmsman, an officer of the watch, and someone in the back by the chart table.

All three froze when they barged onto the bridge.

"Sorry to interrupt your regularly scheduled programming," Alex said. "But we're going to need to borrow your ship."

"What?" The officer of the watch gaped. The shoulders of his uniform bore two stripes. In the Navy, that would make him a lieutenant—old enough to know better, but not senior enough to be in charge.

Alex shrugged, gesturing to Steph and Olson, both of whom had their guns trained on *Dawn's* bridge team. "We're not keen on going to Madagascar, so we need a change in destination."

"I—we've been—I mean, we're *charted* to take you there," the lieutenant said.

"Yeah, let's not get into how your 'passengers' boarded this ship." Alex rolled his eyes. "You want to complain afterward, feel free to whine to the U.S. Navy. But for now, two weapons to zero says we win."

"There's no need for threats," another voice said.

Alex turned to face a short woman with dark hair and four stripes on her shoulder boards. She came out from behind a bookshelf by the navigation station, her hands raised.

"We're happy to cooperate with the U.S. Navy," she said. "There's no need for guns."

Alex glanced at Steph and Olson, nodding. Both lowered their weapons but didn't tuck them away; without holsters, drawing them in a hurry would be hard, and Alex wasn't confident this situation wouldn't still go straight to hell.

"Thank you, Captain...?"

"Captain Lori Lawrence." She walked forward more confidently now that the guns were lowered, offering a hand. Her accent was familiar—Australian, maybe? Something not quite British. "You are?"

"Commander Alex Coleman, ma'am." It didn't hurt to be polite; Alex was fine with making nice if it got them the hell away from the French. He gestured at his companions. "This is Admiral Hamilton, Lieutenant Commander Vasquez, Lieutenant Commander Gomez, and GM1 Olson."

Lawrence's eyebrows rose. "All Navy? I guess you didn't get rounded up."

Alex chuckled. "Not exactly."

"I imagine it's quite a story," she said. "But one for later. So, Commander, where would you like to go?"

"Let's start by heading east, and we'll figure out the rest after the admiral makes a few calls."

Civilians often forgot that cell phones wouldn't work in the middle of the ocean, and even Steph couldn't hack a sim card into becoming a satellite phone. However, *Dawn* had satellite access aplenty, which meant Hamilton could call anywhere—provided *Dawn's* crew cooperated.

Captain Lawrence led Admiral Hamilton to the back of the bridge while Alex worked out a watch schedule with Steph, Maria, and

Olson. Trusting *Dawn's* crew was ludicrous, even if he wanted to. One of them would stay on the bridge at all times. Not the Admiral, though. Admirals didn't stand watch.

Chapter 40

The Bad News Bear

Periscope pictures of a *sinking* French frigate arrived via secure chat like goddamned lightning striking him in the face. Marco, still seated in *Morton's* Combat Information Center as she approached *Belleau Wood* and *Fletcher*, almost came out of his chair.

"What the fucking *fuck*?" He would've sworn more had a voice not blared out from the speaker to his left.

"Strike Group Seven-Four, this is *Kansas*, over."

Marco almost broke the foot pedal from stomping so hard. "Seven-Four, *go*." He stopped himself from railing at Chris Kennedy. Surely the idiot had an excellent reason for sinking a *French* warship when they were just about at fucking war with the Indians.

Shit. Did he know that? A chill ripped down Marco's spine. No one knew. *He* hadn't known until *Belleau Wood* told him, and *Kansas* came to that comms party late—

"Seven-Four, *Kansas* reports sinking one French FFG, same as sunk *Earhart*, over."

"Tell me she fucking shot at you, *Kansas*," Marco growled. "Or that you recovered survivors to prove it, over."

Tanya's gasp from his right made Marco's head turn. Her face was ashen. "God, it'll be the *Kansas* Incident all over again if they can't prove it."

"With the same fucking submarine." Marco wanted to reach through the radio waves and strangle Chris Kennedy. What kind of flaming *moron* put himself in a position to do the same thing he was accused of doing six months ago?

"Negative, Seven-Four. There appear to be no *Earhart* survivors, over," Kennedy replied.

"Roger." Marco took a deep breath to stop himself from swearing. "Make best speed to rendezvous with *Morton*, over." He needed this idiot somewhere controllable.

"*Kansas*, roger, out."

Marco ripped off his headset. "Fuck-fuck-fuckity-*fuck*. We are goddamned *screwed* if this turns into a three-way war. Or, better yet, two way, with France and India against us."

"Don't forget China," Tanya said, chewing her lip. "We thought we'd be shooting at *them* today, not India and France."

Marco closed his eyes, willing those periscope photos to disappear. Christ, that French frigate was trashed. Half her crew was probably dead, along with all of *Earhart's*. "Don't fucking remind me."

"Admiral, we've reached survivors in the water," Commander Anthony Tillman, *Morton's* CO called down from the bridge.

"Pick 'em up." Marco's eyes snapped open. "I'll be on deck in a sec."

No fucking way was he going to leave *Morton's* crew to pick American sailors up alone. He wouldn't be very useful, but Marco Rodriquez was damned well going to be there to help.

He was two steps from the door when Tanya called: "Admiral, we've got a call on the POTS line for you. Caller says she's Admiral Hamilton."

"Come again *what*?"

Shrugging, Tanya held out the phone.

Marco stomped back over and grabbed it. "Freddie, what the fuck? Aren't you down on Armistice—*ohhh.*"

"Oh isn't the half of it, Marco," his old friend replied.

Freddie and Marco served together back on their first boat, starting as frenemies who grew closer. Back when women were first allowed on submarines, the young officers in the first wave endured everyone's unease, along with a shit ton of resistance from the good old boys' club. Their fellow junior officers didn't like Freddie—she was too assertive, too focused, too damned *good* at her job—and Marco became her friend almost by default when he treated her like a human fucking being.

"You gonna make me wait, woman?" he growled.

"Well, we just hijacked a cruise ship," she said. "And Seventh Fleet bounced me to you. I'm on Norwegian *Dawn* with about fifteen hundred other Americans, Brits, Canadians, and Aussies. The French rounded everyone up and kicked us off Armistice Station."

It wasn't often something stunned Marco into silence. He shook his head like a punch-drunk fighter. "And you *hijacked* it?"

"Technically, it wasn't my idea." She sighed. "Never mind that. Seventh Fleet said you might need room for survivors."

"Damn straight I do. How fast can your cruise ship go?"

"About twenty-five knots. We're already headed towards you."

Marco grinned. "Now you're talking."

John was on *Belleau Wood's* deck when *Dudley W. Morton* and *Grace Hopper* arrived, too absorbed in recovery operations to notice them until *Morton* slid to a stop two hundred yards off the cruiser's port beam.

Immediately, both destroyers dropped their boats in the water and threw lines to nearby life rafts. *Belleau Wood* and *Fletcher* already recovered all the swimmers, but there were still close to a hundred life rafts in the water—and that didn't count *John Finn's* survivors, already on board *Morton* and *Hopper.*

Helicopters crisscrossed in the air over their ragged formation, guarding against a resurgent Indian threat. John tried to ignore that, focusing on rescuing survivors. The new destroyers could handle the inevitable shootout. At least they had missiles to shoot.

The attack never came. The sun started sinking below the horizon as the last survivors from *Kidd* climbed the net onto *Belleau Wood,* exhausted, hungry, and grateful. John took their names, Lieutenant Hunt handed them sandwiches and bottled water, and then a petty officer led them down to the mess decks.

The destroyer was full to bursting. Nearly two-thirds of *Enterprise's* crew of 5,000 survived, plus 367 off *Kidd* and *John Finn* combined. Scattering 3,724 survivors across a cruiser and three destroyers—each of which was designed to carry a maximum crew of 350—meant people in every rack, corner, and chair.

Everywhere except Admiral McNally's cabin, where John didn't care to return to. Instead, he ate a sandwich sitting on a bollard on the aft missile deck, staring at the sunset. Sipping a soda, John wondered if he could convince Captain Rosario to crack open *Belleau Wood's* liquor locker. A drink might loosen everyone up—and who cared about rules at this point? He ignored the announcement over the cruiser's 1MC:

"Expeditionary Strike Group Seven-Four, arriving."

Not tonight, but tomorrow, a beer or two might take the edge off for folks feeling claustrophobic and mourning friends. Giving people too much might cause fights, but with an extra nine hundred plus on each ship, they needed—

"You look like dogshit run over by a tricycle, Captain."

John's head snapped up, taking in a short Hispanic man wearing coveralls. His arms were crossed, but they didn't hide the double row of scrambled eggs on his *Tripoli* ballcap or the stars on his uniform collar. Or his name, thankfully. John was too tired to recognize admirals other than his own.

"Admiral Rodriquez." Blinking, John staggered to his feet. "When...oh. You came with *Morton* and *Hopper*."

Rodriquez's grin was tired. "Right in one. When's the last time you slept, son?"

"Sometime two days ago?" John shrugged. "Depending on what day it is."

"Still fourteen April, at least this side of the dateline."

"I guess that's something." That meant they entered the SOM about eighteen hours ago; John couldn't wrap his mind around how much happened since then. The rest of McNally's staff was dead. Ernest Edwards was dead. Two *thousand* American sailors were dead. God knew how many Indians followed them to the grave, mostly on his orders. "Are we...at war, sir?"

"Fuck if I know. That's above my paygrade. The politicians are awake, and we've stopped shooting, so your guess is as good as mine." Rodriquez sighed. "Now let's talk about the great goddamned pink elephant in the room: your boss."

John swallowed. "I'm...not sure that's my place."

"Captain, Jeff McNally is senior to me, but unless you say he's fit to command this goatrope, I'm what you've got. Captain Rosario tells me he checked the fuck out a few hours ago and left the two of you holding the bag. That true?"

"Yes, sir." John wouldn't lie.

"Seventh Fleet implied that he didn't do jack during the battle, either. Aside from shooting that fucking *Kilo* and kicking the entire shebang off."

"That's...accurate." John grimaced. "Captain Rosario handled the air battle. I did the rest. But not, uh, well enough."

John never denied ambition. The son of a retired admiral and air force general, he wanted to earn more stars than his parents combined. Not like this, though. He didn't know if he could've done better; there hadn't been time to think, to plan. He wasn't trained for missile combat, and while he'd done okay, John knew he'd dream of two thousand dead sailors for the rest of his life. He shivered.

"Shit, son, from what Rosario says, you're half the reason these two ships are still floating. Don't sell yourself short—there'll be plenty of numbnuts who do that for you." Rodriquez barked a laugh. "McNally fucking freeze?"

"Yeah."

"You gonna bitch if I take over?"

"No, sir!" Words didn't exist to describe how good it felt to have someone other than McNally as senior officer. John couldn't bet on his boss *staying* quiet, and he didn't have the energy to keep coddling Admiral McNally.

"Good. 'Cause Captain Rosario looked damned happy about it, and I'd hate to disappoint a lady." Rodriquez's grin was infectious; tired or not, John smiled back. "Besides, I've got a big damned cruise ship rolling this way to relieve the crowding."

John stared. "A cruise ship?"

"It pays to have friends in weird places, son."

Commander Camille Dubois was waterlogged and furious. Jules, standing on *Barracuda's* aft deck instead of conning his submarine, offered her a hand as she scrambled out of the water.

"It was *Kansas*." She wrung her sleeves out, flinging water everywhere. "We must go after them."

"They're long gone, mon amie." Jules grimaced. "Probably with Admiral Hamilton and friends."

"And Coleman," Camille spat. "Damn him!"

"Oui. Come below and change." He arched an eyebrow when she snarled obscenities, and Camille subsided. They threaded their way through the submarine. Crew members watched Camille warily; their XO had a temper, and everyone knew it. Jules disliked her petulant displays at the best of times, but she was good at her job.

He waited in his stateroom—next door to hers, as was customary on attack submarines—until Camille replaced her cold and wet clothing. Meanwhile, his crew continued fishing *Bretagne's* survivors out of the water. There were few. Torpedo strikes did that.

Camille slipped into the captain's stateroom without knocking. "What are our orders, mon Capitaine?"

"We remain near Armistice Station. The marines are leaving now that our...opponents are gone, but we remain to ensure the Americans do not get feisty." He grinned. "It appears they have their hands full with our Indian friends, anyway. The battle was not as *one*-sided as Admiral Khare believed."

Camille snorted. "My heart weeps for him."

"Moi aussi."

"We are supposed to let them get away?" Camille's green eyes narrowed. "Can we not pursue *Kansas*? Sink them before—

"*Non*. We follow orders, and we will fight another day." Jules would mind exacting revenge for *Bretagne*, but *Kansas* was not a target to get worked up over. He outfoxed Commander Kennedy and his crew once; doing so a second time would be simple.

Perhaps someday they would give Commander Coleman a submarine. *That* was a contest Jules could look forward to.

"I'm not sure how I feel about this, Commander." Captain Lawrence pursed her lips, staring out at the sea as *Dawn* steamed at twenty-six knots.

Dawn's captain and Alex stood on the cruise ship's bridge wing. Alex had a nine-millimeter he didn't need tucked into his waistband; *Dawn's* crew grew more cooperative by the moment, particularly after they heard about the Indian attack on *Enterprise*. "At least you're getting paid?"

"That's corporate's concern, not mine." She grimaced. "I don't like bringing my ship into a war zone. Your...refugees may not be my normal paying passengers, but they're still civilians."

"And so's your crew."

"Exactly."

Alex smiled crookedly. "We're not at war. Technically."

"You keep saying that." Lawrence sighed. "You been watching the news?"

"What this time?" Alex almost didn't want to know. Steph plugged into the internet, downing news like a junkie, but he spent the time he wasn't on *Dawn's* bridge catching up on sleep. That, and explaining the insanity of the last two days to his wife.

Almost forty-eight hours passed since *Dawn's* so-called hijacking. Admiral Hamilton's quick thinking led the United States to outbid the French charter for the cruise ship, a deed helped along by Norwegian Cruise Lines Miami, Florida headquarters. No one really thought *Dawn's* captain or crew would betray them to the French, but Alex and his people still kept watch on the bridge, just in case.

"China threatened to nuke Taiwan this morning."

Alex's heart threatened to jump out his mouth. "*What*?"

Lawrence extended out a tablet. "That's just the tip of the iceberg. Watch."

Swallowing, Alex hit *play* on the queued CNN video. The reporter was young and blonde, standing outside the U.N. headquarters in New York.

"The U.N. Security Council remains in an emergency meeting. An estimated two hundred thousand people have died already in the growing Chinese Civil War. While Taiwan has requested U.S. and U.N. assistance, India, Malaysia, and seven other nations have declared the Strait of Malacca closed to *all* American allied shipping, not just naval vessels. Just this morning, an Australian frigate was fired upon by Indian destroyers in the Java Sea."

She touched her ear bug. "This just in—France has proposed a U.N. resolution condemning the United States for sinking an Indian *Kilo*-class submarine just two days ago. Russia has seconded the motion and demanded the United States pay reparations to the dead crew's families. The U.S. has vetoed.

"Tensions continue to rise in the Indian Ocean. Just an hour ago, crew members of the cargo ships M/V *Jupiter* and M/V *Rose* were pulled from the sea by an Australian-flagged tanker. Their surviving crews report both ships were sunk by an Indian submarine in the approaches to the Strait of Malacca, and over half of the sailors from each ship are dead. Americans, waking up to this news, are furious, and the president has scheduled a press conference for this afternoon."

The video ended, leaving Alex winded, chest tight. "This is getting out of control."

"You see why I don't want to go anywhere near there?" Lawrence said. "Even with my Panamanian flag flying as high as I can manage."

"No one in their right mind will sink a cruise ship," Alex said.

"Or two cargo ships?" She gestured at the tablet again. "There are already protests outside the Indian embassy in D.C."

"Shit." Alex scrubbed a hand over his face. He needed a shave.

"In a word, yes." Her smile was strained. "I'm just glad we're charted to head to Australia after this."

"The escort won't hurt, I'm sure." Alex nodded towards the cruiser and three destroyers just cresting the horizon. From here, they couldn't see the battle scars on the ships; they were small gray blobs, roaring in at thirty knots.

The moment they arrived, his job would be done. Alex would become one of many naval officers on *Dawn*, and not even the second most senior. Then he could be...normal.

"You okay, boss?" Alex turned as Steph approached, her eyes also on the incoming ships.

"Yeah. It's weird knowing this is just about over."

"Weird, like, holy shit your crazy plan worked and you saved a couple thousand people?" She grinned.

"I...wouldn't put it that way." Alex swallowed. "We just did what needed doing. And it wasn't just me."

Steph laughed. "Keep telling yourself that, sir. I'm pretty sure Navy'll stick some medal on your or another for this."

Alex shook his head. "Don't make me out to be some hero, Steph. I was scared shitless. Taking over a cooperative cruise ship isn't heroic. It's *practical*."

Practical was a label Alex Coleman could live with. Hero was one he didn't want.

Epilogue: War

Watching the personnel transfer got boring very quickly. No one on the cruise ship needed Alex to organize anything, and his little "hijacking" was quickly deemed fiction once the U.S. government chartered *Dawn*. Avoiding Admiral Hamilton remained in his best interest, so it took longer than it should have for Alex to learn one of the battle-scarred destroyers was USS *Fletcher*.

Fortunately, free phone calls were part of *Dawn's* new contract, so Alex punched up the external phone line that he knew led to the CO's cabin on board *Fletcher*, his heart in his throat.

How didn't I think of it? He wanted to smash his head into something. *I* knew *Nancy's ship was going through the SOM. How did I fail to make the connection?*

One ring. Two. Four and then six. The Navy wasn't a big believe in voicemail, so Alex let it ring another two times, swallowing back the need to swear.

Finally, a groggy voice answered: "Captain."

"Nancy? Shit, babe, it's good to hear your voice."

He could hear blankets rustling as she sat up. "Alex, what the hell? Where are you? I saw some worrisome messages about Armistice Station—"

"About a thousand yards dead ahead of you. Long story, I'm on *Dawn*."

"*What?*"

"I could ask you the same thing. I hear it got pretty fucking busy there." Alex couldn't find words to voice his relief. The survivors on board *Dawn*—a mix of crew from *Enterprise, John Finn,* and *Kidd*—told hazy stories about a submarine sunk, an all-out missile battle, and a carrier and two destroyers now on the bottom.

"That's one way to put it," Nancy replied. "Another is that if I ever work for another sub admiral again, it's too fucking soon."

Alex blinked. "I'm *definitely* missing something here."

"We shot first, Alex," she whispered. "We sank an Indian submarine without properly identifying it. All because Admiral McNumbnuts couldn't fight his way out of a paper bag. We lost *three* ships and almost two *thousand* sailors, and for what?"

"I wish I knew what to say, Nance."

"Me, too." She sighed. "I don't know what's going to happen."

"Me, neither."

15 April 2038 – 1100R, Washington, D.C.

"Ladies and gentlemen, the President of the United States."

The Speaker of the House sat as the President walked to the podium, old-fashioned, printed notes in hand. There wasn't time to put this speech on the Teleprompter, not with the crowds gathered outside the Capitol.

The House galleries were full for the first time in recent memory, and protestors still shouted outside the Indian Embassy. News of Armistice Station's capture—no one called it anything else, not in the U.S.—further inflamed public opinion.

Then, for the first time since World War II, enemy fire sank American navy ships. Civilians were dead, both on the cargo ships and on Armistice Station. No one cared that Admiral McNally took the first shot. Not in the U.S.

The president cleared his throat, and then looked into the cameras. He had no idea his tie was crooked, and this appearance was scheduled so quickly none of his aides remembered to check.

No one cared.

"My fellow Americans, I come before you today with a grave duty. Nineteen hundred American sailors lie dead in the Strait of Malacca, slain by Indian naval forces without declaration of war. Thirty additional Americans are dead in the Indian Ocean, sunk by an Indian submarine without warning. One hundred and forty more naval personnel died when attacked by the French Navy, and then two more American civilians were slain by French marines on Armistice Station.

"That's two thousand, ninety-six American lives. Snuffed out by those we thought friends, all in the last forty-eight hours. Two thousand, ninety-six.

"This must be stopped. France and India have declared the Strait of Malacca closed to American shipping. They have ejected all American, British, Canadian, and Australian citizens from Armistice Station, the largest underwater habitat in the world. And they have killed our people. But the United States of America has never stood idle while acts of aggression are unanswered. The United States of America *fights* for our people—and if we must, to avenge them."

No one spoke. No one could believe it. Not in the modern world. First world countries did not make war upon one another. *Nuclear* countries—of which both France and India were—did not come to blows with other nuclear-armed nations.

But America only knew one way to answer violence.

"Ladies and gentlemen of Congress, I hereby request that Congress pass an act of war against the Republic of France and the Republic of India."

2330D, the Indian Ocean

FNS *Barracuda* received the news via old-fashioned naval message. Captain Jules Rochambeau read it, handed the tablet to his second-in-command, and headed for control. Within minutes, his attack submarine turned around and came up in speed.

"You were right," Camille said, joining him.

"I usually am." Jules smiled, a strange feeling sneaking over him.

He should be angry. War meant a failure of his operation. Yet, war also represented a glittering future in which France could regain lost glory. Not since the days of Napoleon had the French been so strong. Soon, the world would fear French naval might once more—with Jules Rochambeau at the forefront.

Camille licked her lips. "We will have much work ahead of us."

Jules leaned against the chart table, his mind whirling. "We will start near Diego Garcia. The American prepositioning ships are there, and underdefended."

"There is a destroyer or two with them, is there not?"

"Oui, more targets. C'est bon."

Dawn recovered her last lifeboat and the impromptu flotilla got underway an hour before midnight, *Belleau Wood* in the lead. *Grace Hopper* and *Morton,* both with full missile onloads, steamed a thousand yards off the cruise ship's port and starboard beams, while *Fletcher* brought up the rear.

Admirals Rodriquez and Hamilton—the later was slightly senior, but not about to piss in her friend's rice bowl—contemplated heading towards Diego Garcia, the closest friendly port. But that meant steaming closer to India, so they turned southeast, making best speed for Perth, Australia. Within hours, two Australian frigates left port to meet them.

Kansas caught up during the personnel transfer and was sent ahead to make sure no unfriendly submarines targeted the flotilla. Admiral Rodriquez didn't trust Commander Kennedy's judgment, but relieving the man when the world was on fire might be a bit much. He'd kick that one up to Seventh Fleet. *Tripoli* and *Harrisburg* (LPD-30) would meet his new task force halfway there, providing air cover and more missiles to match any incoming threat.

Most everyone finally felt safe enough to go to sleep. Alex, however, stood on *Dawn's* main deck, watching the dim shape of *Fletcher* back aft.

"Brooding, Commander?" Admiral Hamilton asked., walking up from behind him

Alex blinked. "Just thinking, ma'am."

"I take it you heard." Her narrow face held no amusement, but how was that new? Alex knew they'd never like each other, but as a terminal O-5, what did that matter? He was just marking time until retirement.

"Heard what?" Worry bubbled in Alex's stomach. "Unless you mean the Indian sub sinking those two cargo ships." He grimaced. "Or *Kansas* and the French frigate."

Leave it to Chris Kennedy to sink a ship when they weren't at war. Alex felt sorry for the crew...and for Kennedy's new XO.

"Congress passed a declaration of war," Hamilton said. "There were only twelve dissenting votes."

"*What?*"

"We're at war for the first time since World War II," the admiral said. "France and India returned the declaration within the hour... and so did Russia."

Alex's jaw dropped. "Russia?"

"Looks like they signed mutual defense treaties with France and India." Hamilton grimaced. "We knew they were selling technology to the Indians...but this is unexpected."

"Jesus Christ," Alex whispered, shivering. "Did we—?"

She shook her head. "We were the icing on the cake. It was already out of control."

Alex didn't know what to say. His eyes swiveled back to *Dudley W. Morton*, the destroyer named for America's most legendary submariner. "Mush" Morton changed the way U.S. submarines brought the war to the enemy back in World War II, redefining submarine warfare forever, but losing his life in the process.

How many more would die in *this* war?

"War changes a great many things in the service," Hamilton said. "I will never like you, and I disapprove of your methods. I'm not sure if it was cowardice or courage that made you refuse to shoot on *Kansas*. But you showed courage on Armistice Station, and we'll need people like you in the days to come."

"Me?" Alex spun back to face her.

"Name your reward. I'll pin a medal on you—one good enough to ensure you'll make captain—and find you a staff job. Or you can have your own submarine." She met his eyes. "Which will it be?"

Alex didn't have to think about that. There was only one thing he wanted, and it wasn't some shiny medal. He spent an entire career burning for a submarine of his own, and with his nation on the brink of war, he knew what to do.

"I'll take the boat, ma'am."

"Very well." Hamilton extended a hand. "Good luck, Commander."

"Thank you, ma'am."

Like this book? Witness World War III in all its blood and glory—and follow Alex Coleman into his first command—in *The War No One Wanted*!

Want more? Join my mailing list for a free copy *Pedal to the Medal*, an action-packed glimpse into the submarine warfare of World War III.

Also By the Author

War of the Submarine

Before the Storm

Cardinal Virtues

The War No One Wanted

Fire When Ready

Clean Sweep

I Will Try

Fortune Favors the Bold

War of the Submarine Shorts

Never Take a Recon Marine to a Casino Robbery (subscriber exclusive)

Pedal to the Medal

Age the Legacy

Shade
Shadow (Coming Soon!)

Night Rider
Before the Dawn (Coming Soon!)

Legacy Shorts

Prelude to Conquest (subscriber exclusive)
The First Ride (Exclusive on Ream!)
City of Light (Exclusive on Ream!)

Alternate History

Against the Wind

Caesar's Command

Other Works

Agent of Change (Portal Sci-Fi with an Alternate History Twist)

Fido (Cozy Fantasy Serial, high on humor)
Once Upon a Dragon (Exclusive on Ream!)

About R.G. Roberts

R.G. Roberts is a veteran of the U.S. Navy, currently living in Connecticut and working as a Manufacturing Manager for a major medical device manufacturer. While an officer in the Navy, R.G. Roberts served on three ships, taught at the Surface Warfare Officer's School, and graduated from the U.S. Naval War College with a masters degree in Strategic Studies & National Security, with a concentration in leadership.

She is a multi-genre author, and has published in military thrillers, science fiction, epic fantasy, and alternate history. She rode horses until she joined the Navy (ships aren't very compatible with high-strung jumpers) and fenced (with swords!) in college. Add in the military experience and history degree, and you get A+ anatomy for a fantasy author. However, since she also enjoyed her time in the Navy and loves history, you'll find her in those genres as well.

You can find R.G. Roberts' website at www.rgrobertswriter.com or find all her links at linktr.ee/rgroberts. From there, you can join her newsletter! Joining the newsletter will get you a free novella or short story, set in either the War of the Submarine or Age of the Legacy universes (or both, if you like both genres). Newsletters are a twice-a-month affair, so there won't be a ton of spam in your inbox, but you'll be the first to hear about sales, get sneak peeks of new writing, and get to read free short stories from time to time, too!

R.G. Roberts is also one of the authors trying the new-fangled site known as "Ream." It's like Pateron, but made for authors and readers – and especially for superfans! There you will have access to exclusive first looks at all of her works, including early access to chapters of novels, short stories, and more! You can find her Ream at www.reamstories.com/rgrobertswriter.

War of the Submarine

World War I was the war of the battleship. World War II was the war of the aircraft carrier. World War III will be the war of the submarine.

Undersea technology has changed the world, and every nation wants territory. No one wants war—or plans for it—but a series of unrelated incidents, mix-ups, and greedy grabs for ocean-floor real estate escalate straight into a shooting war that no one knows how to stop...one that engulfs the Indian Ocean and threatens to spill out towards the rest of the world.

Old alliances are overturned and new ones form, with the Grand Alliance of the U.S., U.K., and Australia facing off against Russia, India, and France. Caught in a three-way civil war, China is on the outside looking in, but minor nations are forced to pick sides in the war no one expected to come—and no one knows how to win.

For his part, Commander Alex Coleman is pretty sure that heroes don't explode coffee creamer fireballs and hijack cruise ships—but let's not talk about that where the admirals can here; one already hates him and that's quite enough. He's also certain they don't end up with a boat old enough to drink and his crew a few beers short of a six pack. No one expects him to make a difference...until the enemy gets a vote.

Conventional submariners rarely make history.

Submarines that make history rarely survive.

This is an ongoing series! Although your author isn't an outliner (the fancy term is "discovery writer," but I prefer "pantser"), there's a vague plan for 8-9 books. This could grow, as my original plan for book 2 became books 2, 3, and 4 – sometimes, the story just gets keeps rolling! So, expect a good-sized series. No promises on exact size, but there's definitely more to come.

If you're interested in joining my mailing list, doing so will get you a free copy of the short story *Pedal to the Medal*, set in the WOS universe.

Printed in Great Britain
by Amazon